Acclaim for *Something*

'A scathing tale about th[e]
life and death – especially
headline fodder . . . It's clever, stylish and potent stuff'
Mirror

'Hold on to your seats, Media Moguls, because this
time it's your turn in the hot seat . . . the novel is
populated with a cast of characters who would feel
very much at home in late night film noir and vintage
Chandler. They are the sort of people you really don't
want to know but are mesmerized by . . . an incisive
foray into the murky world of the modern press'
Oxford Times

'Rupert Morgan's satire of modern life is brilliant.
He is like Ben Elton at his wittiest'
Express

'Satire which takes you up to the edge of libellous – and
gets away with it . . . Nothing is spared by Rupert
Morgan's blistering pen . . . it will make you laugh
while you wince'
Daily Mail

'Really brilliant . . . he is obviously a major talent'
Prunella Scales

'Outstanding . . . it's fast-moving and hilarious . . . Kurt
Vonnegut and Douglas Adams will be spitting feathers'
Esquire

Also by Rupert Morgan

LET THERE BE LITE
SOMETHING SACRED

and published by Bantam Books

RULE NO. 1

A Light Comedy for Dark Days

Rupert Morgan

BANTAM BOOKS

LONDON · NEW YORK · TORONTO · SYDNEY · AUCKLAND

RULE NO. 1
A BANTAM BOOK : 0 553 81362 5

First publication in Great Britain

PRINTING HISTORY
Bantam edition published 2003

1 3 5 7 9 10 8 6 4 2

Set in 11/13pt Sabon by
Kestrel Data, Exeter, Devon.

Bantam Books are published by Transworld Publishers,
61–63 Uxbridge Road, London W5 5SA,

Addresses for companies within The Random House Group Limited
can be found at: www.randomhouse.co.uk/offices.htm

The Random House Group Limited supports The Forest Stewardship
Council (FSC®), the leading international forest certification organisation.
Our books carrying the FSC label are printed on FSC® certified paper.
FSC is the only forest certification scheme endorsed by the leading
environmental organisations, including Greenpeace. Our
paper procurement policy can be found at
www.randomhouse.co.uk/environment

Printed and bound in Great Britain by Clays Ltd, St Ives PLC

RULE NO. 1

Explanatory Note

Rule No. 1 is my third novel. As in the first two books, *Let There Be Lite* and *Something Sacred*, the events here take place not on our own world, but on the tenth planet of our solar system. This planet is much the same size as ours and orbits at a similar distance from the sun – but on the far side, which is why it's never visible from our own planet.

Because it is similar to our planet in terms of its chemical profile and other factors – above all the weather – life's evolution has followed a remarkably similar course on this world. There too a series of catastrophic mass extinctions finally made room for humanoid creatures to get a genetic foothold. Blessed with large brains, opposable thumbs, and a capacity for vocal expression more than equal to their capacity for thought, they too have developed systems of belief to explain their existence, and the purpose of the universe and the life in it, and the conundrum of whether it is all about them, or just *mostly* about them.

All in all, they are very like us. They even call *their* planet 'Earth'.

Even though, like ours, it is mostly water.

Although none of the characters or events in this entertainment are real, the story does owe its inspiration to events in the life of an actual person. Three weeks after the terrorist attacks upon the World Trade Center and the Pentagon, President George W. Bush unveiled 'Executive Order 13224', which listed all the terrorist organizations and fronts that the United States intended to target in the course of its 'War on Terrorism'.

Amongst these was to be found the Al-Shifa Honey Press for Industry and Commerce, whose address was given as 'by the shrine next to the gas station' in Aden, Yemen. The man in charge of this little-known organization, Mohammed Saleh al-Ashmuri, rapidly surfaced to protest his innocence of any connection to terrorist activities, declaring, 'My shop is completely independent. The last thing we need is for honey to become one of the sources for financing terrorism.'

I do not wish to suggest, in having written this book, that the Intelligence that led to his inclusion in Executive Order 13224 was mistaken, because I cannot know for certain one way or the other.

But I confess to having a hunch like Quasimodo.

R.M., June 2002

'Instead of dirt and poison, we have rather chosen to fill our hives with honey and wax; thus furnishing mankind with the two noblest of things, which are sweetness and light'

Jonathan Swift, *The Battle of the Books*

Prologue

In which we learn of a war that has just ended, having been fought with bullets, extraordinarily big bombs and, some say, biscuits

'If you're not crazy, then you're crazy', went an old saying in Kalashnistan.

And they knew what they were talking about. They were crazy, and frankly proud of it – which, by their reckoning, counted as the closest one could get to sanity. The rest of the world, for which they had a healthy contempt if they bothered to consider it at all, was in the grip of rampant delusions. Only here, in the broken glass mountains of the Kalash, did men see life as it truly was, stripped of the fictions that blinded other peoples and nations. Only in this war-torn wasteland, a place without politics or police or professions, without laws or schools or entertainment, so desolate that you could see all the glory and sadness of life in a flowering weed clutching a rock, could a man truly get into Mama Nature's pants.

For if you are not crazy in this life, say the Kalash, if you do not embrace its cruelty, laugh at its tragedy and take the absurd absolutely seriously, then you are crazy. You are trying to make sense of nonsense. You are living a delusion.

Which, the Kalash are perfectly willing to grant, can be

very nice. Cosseted by a snug dream, a person can live a happy and rich life, though no doubt troubled at times by that eternal, nagging sense of having forgotten something. Of something, somewhere not being in its place. An inner void, perhaps, but one for which peace and prosperity offers a wide range of plugs for all tastes. And, when you get right down to it, if you have food and water enough, shelter for your children and no reason to fear your neighbour's envy, then why in heaven's name question it? You are lucky. Lucky, lucky, lucky.

The Kalash would be the first to agree that you should combat *anyone* who threatens your dream. Kill them without hesitation or remorse, wipe them off the face of the earth, and do not doubt that you are morally justified in doing so. Your enemies are *crazy people*. Yes, they may say the same of you, but that is not the point – the point is that only the victorious decide what is sane.

The loser is always wrong. Everyone knows this.

In Kalashnistan, they don't have much to lose, hence their legendary toughness. All any man has, amid those mountains of rubble, is his honour. It is their Stock Market, the basis of the entire penniless economy, and every individual's portfolio contains investments in their family, their tribe, and the entire history of their ancestors. There being no bankers or brokers to take care of this considerable wealth, it is down to each individual to defend it, if necessary with his own life.

But ideally, of course, with someone else's.

There was a certain irony – quite amusing to the Kalash way of thinking – that their country had been the first battlefield in the War on Terror recently declared by the United States of Atlantis. For, although there were indeed a considerable number of terrorists in Kalashnistan, none of them were Kalash. Not one. Indeed, to the best of anyone's knowledge, there were no Kalash terrorists whatsoever in the world. This was not because they were a reasonable people at heart, but for much the same reason as there are no snorkelling fish.

Terrorism, they would say, is for men who haven't got a real war to fight. Which was almost never the case in this extraordinary, tribal country with its dozens of ethnic factions and languages. It didn't take much to start a fight in Kalashnistan. Nobody had ever had time to study the root causes of their conflicts, but in an honour-based culture such as theirs one really didn't need to look much further than the simple fact that the customary expression of greeting in some ethnic tongues was infuriatingly similar to 'your sister smells of goat' in others. Indeed, warfare was so ingrained in their culture that the traditional mark of achieving adulthood was the point at which a boy could hang a rifle on his shoulder without having the butt drag along in the dust.

The arrival in recent years of compact, fully automatic firearms had thus wrecked whatever delicate social balance had existed there, in that warrior status could now be achieved by the age of six. Consequently, the obligation of an entire tribe to avenge a slight to the honour of any member nowadays resulted in grown men massacring one another over disputes that initially involved marbles.

Despite their homicidal tendencies, therefore, the Kalash were entirely innocent of any acts of international terrorism or the murder of people who had not attempted to speak or play with them. On the other hand, their unique climate of non-stop warfare had made the country a very attractive location for various foreign terrorists needing a base for their training camps. In the wilds of the Kalash mountains, as in no other part of the world, these bug-eyed fanatics could practise shooting, blow things up, and play about with chemicals to their hearts' content. Nobody took much notice of them. In fact, they were regarded rather as other countries view tourists – somewhat idiotic in their attempts to adopt local customs and live the warrior lifestyle, but a good source of income.

Few in Kalashnistan would have imagined that this tourist industry could result in the country becoming the target for a distant superpower's awesome military machine, but that – for reasons that were not at all clear to the vast majority – is exactly what had happened.

One day, the peaceful rattle of gunfire across the Kalash hills had been broken by a scream of jets and the bone-juddering boom of quite extraordinarily powerful bombs. What followed over the ensuing weeks was a conflict such as the locals had never experienced – no soldiers, no guns, but just an ear-splitting whine, a brief earthquake, and a fucking great hole where the humanitarian aid depot used to be. On the rare occasions that anybody saw an actual Atlantian, it was usually when a helicopter would unexpectedly set down in some village that had, for no strategic reason that anybody could perceive, been flattened the night before. A team of Westerners would jump out, take some photographs and ask the stunned survivors how many civilians had been killed, then disappear again after handing out packs of biscuits.

It was strange, and profoundly shocking to the local population, who until then had prided themselves on knowing everything there was to know on the subject of warfare. There were even rumours, which surely could not be true, that Atlantians sometimes *attacked* with biscuits, dropping huge bales of them from the sky to plummet silently down and crash through the roof of your house, squashing you wholemeal as you slept.

The tourists, unsurprisingly, left in droves. Where to was a mystery, but presumably they either went home or moved on to some quieter spot where they could carry on honing their mass-murder skills. With their departure, the bombing largely stopped, although the Atlantian jets could sometimes still be heard high in the stratosphere. It was said that there were still one or two hilltops that they wished to remove, where their Intelligence suggested secret tourist traps might yet be located.

So the war, apparently, had been won. But as with every aspect of this strange new form of conflict, victory resembled nothing the Kalash could recognize as such. There was no raping or pillaging, no celebratory gun-shots or cheering, just an unearthly silence. How long it would last was anybody's guess, but it seemed that a strange peace had settled over the land. For the moment, nobody was getting into an argument with anyone else, for fear that their dispute would be suddenly silenced by a slam of biscuits.

Some who came home to the villages from the city said that there was a new government in power, although by what means it intended to govern anything was unclear. Soon, they said, there were to be elections – an Atlantian concept that sounded like a recipe for complete anarchy, because no self-respecting Kalash would vote for any-body who was not a member of their own tribe, or accept the dishonour of being told their side had lost.

And so life slowly returned to normal – every bit as crazy as before, but at least in a more familiar form. The aid workers came back with their convoys of flour, which was good news for the men because without them they'd had no choice but to listen to their wives and work the land rather than fight.

As for the Atlantians, no more was seen of them or their biscuits. Perhaps they were satisfied that their honour had been restored by putting an end to Kalashnistan as a holiday destination. But probably not – more likely their jets were simply circling other parts of the world, looking for those missing tour parties.

That's what the Kalash would be doing in their position, anyway.

The Atlantians had won. So they'd be crazy to stop now.

The End minus 30 days

'. . . your loved ones with Standard Mutual . . . because tomorrow might be too late.'

As if, the Angry Teenager thinks.

Like they will pay up. Like *that* is the honeyed tone people will hear when some faraway call-centre employee – a John, or a Sarah, or another neutral name picked from a list – relays the computer's decision on their claim.

Every day of his life he's heard those voices. Every damn day. And one day, he knows, he will listen. He likes to consider himself a cynic, but ultimately he will have to play along with the game because what choice does he have? If people stopped listening, then everything would fall apart. The machine he has been born into would stop turning. His country is built on belief.

He understands that. People *have* to believe. And that is what angers him so.

Fortunately, he has only a microsecond to brood on such thoughts before the screen begins to swirl with streaming, gleaming graphics set to an orchestral heart attack, and a voice like that of God's own spokesman booms:

'*This* is WINN 24/7, non-stop *World* Information Network News, bringing you the facts that matter, with Ayesha Novak . . .'

And here she is again, so posed and sleek, a quarter-smile permanently playing upon her lips. She's wearing the black halter neck today. Never let it be said that all the news is bad.

'Welcome back. Top breaking news stories today – terrorists threaten Atlantis with killer bees, the Government says "Be ready with bug spray." More on that in the Headline Round-Up a second away. And doctors ask "Can ATM machines cause obesity" – we'll be having a special report. On the Stock Market the Bing 100 *continues* its downward momentum, losing a further two percentage points since this morning's opening, while intense trading on the SpiDer Index has driven it *up* a further eight points. First, however, we go live to Leona Mathews outside Liberty Mansion with the latest on this morning's top story. Leona, should we be worried?'

The screen splits to show an older, less pretty woman standing pointlessly close to the source of the morning story.

'Thank you, Ayesha. Well, this is officially a Code Orange alert they have issued today about a possible terrorist plan to unleash massive numbers of killer *bees* here in Atlantis, but sources close to the President have intimated that there *was* serious discussion of going all the way to Code Red. This is a real threat, based on what has been described as a "profound intelligence". Reading between the lines, it's clear that we would actually be at Code *Pink* right now . . . if an alert was available in that colour.'

'Could they not just *produce* a new colour option depending upon the demand?'

'I think there's a feeling that some people could be confused and even panicked by new colours being pro-posed on an ad hoc basis, but they may well consider relaunching their entire range at some future date. Right now, there have been no cases of bee attack, so for the moment today is Orange and they are asking the public to remain vigilant and report *any* unusual bee-related activity to the relevant authorities.'

'OK. What exactly counts as "unusual bee-related activity", Leona?'

'As I understand it, they are interested in any sightings of unfamiliar species of bee, any appearance of hives where they were not previously to be found or encounters with people wearing bee-keeping clothes. The terrorists, government sources say, may be planning to take advantage of the big spring holiday weekend by launching their attack to coincide with the probable spike in outdoor activities such as lawn-mowing and barbecuing to launch their attack.'

'Is the Government advising *against* mowing lawns?'

'No, they haven't gone that far yet. They are saying by all means *mow* your lawn this weekend, but remain alert and exercise extreme caution.'

'We don't have much time left here, Leona, but do we have any information about which group is behind this threat?'

'Yes, Ayesha, we do have *some* details on that level. According to the experts, the bees in question are called *Jana* bees and are only found in *one* region of the world, principally in the small country of Errat, currently under the oppressive military dictatorship of General *Harouni*.'

'But is this the work of an isolated terrorist *group* in Erate or of General . . . of the general himself?'

'For the moment, the Government is not making that call, so clearly they *do* suspect links between General Harouni and the terrorists. But, that said, the particular name that seems to be on a *lot* of people's lips here at the moment is—'

Chapter One

In which we are introduced to the hero of this tale, and a strange package is received over breakfast that will, in due course, lead to a very regrettable misunderstanding of a large-scale, military nature

Many weeks before, Saman Massoudi had had a troublesome start to his day.

«A package has come for you in the post, brother,» Farrukh announced without looking up from his newspaper. «Apparently it is a bomb.»

Saman, freshly washed and groomed but his shirt already half-untucked from the swaying of his belly as he came down the stairs, stopped in surprise. Fatima, his sister-in-law, scowled at him as he made his way across the room – artfully turning the distance between herself and the breakfast table from a mark of respect for the men of the household into a measure of her disdain for her husband's younger brother. The package in question, about the size of a shoe box, was placed in front of Saman's cushion. Wrapped in brown paper, battered and slightly torn from what looked as though it must have been an arduous journey through the postal system, it did indeed have a somewhat suspicious air to it.

«It hums,» Farrukh continued as Saman lowered himself to his cushion, the rest of his shirt sliding out from his belt. «Presumably the detonator is some kind of electrical device.»

Saman leaned forward to put his ear to the package, straining to listen to it over the gabbling of the fountain from the inner court of the house. It was a rather intrusive fountain these days – in their father's time it had provided a pleasant background trickle, but ever since the increase in water pressure that Fatima had for so long been lobbying for was finally achieved it had become a veritable geyser. Ostentatious, frankly – although Saman was careful never to say as much. Fatima found fault enough with him as it was without his criticizing the private monsoon that her friends were so impressed by. Not that they had ever tried to sleep a whole night through with their bedroom resounding to the thunder of an endless, unremittingly urgent pee.

He could hear nothing. The package was silent.

Saman gently picked it up to look for a sender's address, but found nothing. Curiously, the stamps identified it as having been sent from the United States of Atlantis, but the handwriting bore no resemblance to that of their cousin Aziz, who was the only person Saman knew there. Farrukh turned the page of his newspaper, glancing across at his brother.

«So . . .» he frowned, «have many enemies in Atlantis do you, brother?»

«It's . . . um . . .» Saman smiled, «. . . it's too light for a *bomb*, really, isn't it?»

«What do I know? I know nothing. It hums. The packages *I* get from Atlantis never hum, but that is because they generally contain shoes. All I can tell you for certain is that this is not a pair of shoes.»

«It doesn't seem to be humming at the moment . . .»

«Shake it.»

Saman raised an eyebrow in surprise.

«You thought it might be a bomb and so you . . . *shook* it?»

«Of course not, brother. I have better things to do than shake your mail.» Farrukh sighed, turning back to his newspaper. «If you must know, I dropped it. Which caused it to hum in a quite alarming fashion. We all had to leave the room until it stopped, as a matter of fact, which meant the coffee got cold before I judged it safe to let the family back in. It was a thoroughly unnerving start to my day, thank you.»

«Well, I'm sorry I wasn't up to deal with it myself,» Saman apologized, catching the implication. «I had a rather restless night.»

«When you choose to get out of bed is entirely your own decision, Saman. You are my brother, and this house is your house for as long as you wish to stay here. I ask only that you do not receive bombs in the post.»

«It's not a bomb,» Saman answered softly. «I think I know what it is.»

He gave the package a small shake and put it to his ear. It did, indeed, hum when shaken.

«The package is quite harmless.» He replaced it carefully on the low table, and shook his head, explaining, «It's just bees.»

«That did utimately seem the more likely explanation, yes.» His brother sighed. «What else would someone send *you*?»

«*Mail-order bees?*» Saman had gasped on the phone some weeks before. «You can't be serious!»

«This is Atlantis! They use the mail for everything here!» Aziz answered, chuckling at his cousin's ignorance. «Well . . . except sending letters.»

«My God . . .»

According to Saman's personal view of the universe, a mail-order bee was tantamount to blasphemy. But then he wasn't religious. Not that he hadn't tried to be in his time, and not that he didn't feel obliged to go to prayer along with everyone else, but he just couldn't bring

21

himself to believe that the truth was all written down in a book and no further thought was necessary. He just couldn't.

He never discussed this with anyone these days, but it seemed to Saman *possible* that there might be no God. He realized it could never be proven, obviously, but nor could he rule this possibility out as others seemed able to do. He could not shake the suspicion that when he died he might be going to be dead.

In which case, two opposite conclusions seemed to offer themselves. Either life was quite without significance or meaning – whatever that was supposed to mean – in which case, it was clearly not to be taken too seriously and was certainly not something worth fighting over. Or . . . well, it seemed possible to him that if there was no God, and no plan, nor heaven, nor hell, then one might say that perhaps this made each and every living thing very significant indeed, because the meaning of life was that without it the universe was a waste of time. And while he could accept that his own life might be of no real importance, Saman found himself physically unable to believe that the whole span of galaxies stretching towards infinity might be equally futile. So it seemed to make sense to consider that so long as something, somewhere was alive, then that gave a kind of purpose to it all, and that people might be important because they could quite well be the only living things capable of looking at the world or out into the crushing vastness of space and declaring it to be beautiful.

Which would only be a personal opinion of theirs, of course, but if there was no God and no eternal hand, then the universe at any one moment only amounted to that moment – and so some child today, gazing up into the night sky and feeling for the first time the stirring of an unfamiliar rapture, might in that instant be the one thing that gave those faraway galaxies significance.

Saman did not pretend to know, and ultimately it did not seem to matter to him either way.

If there was a God, then clearly life was sacred.

But if there was *no* God, then life was probably also sacred.

So life, on balance, was sacred.

And you didn't kill it, or violate it, or debase it, or shove it in a box and put it in the post.

All of which, from what his cousin had told him, the Atlantians were doing.

«Do you realize, cousin,» Aziz had demanded at the start of their conversation, «that there are Atlantian bee farms producing three times as much honey per hive as ours do, hmm?»

«Hmm?»

«Three times!»

«*Three* times as much?»

«You heard me.»

«And you're sure about that figure?»

«What? So I can't count to *three* now?»

Saman was immensely grateful to his Atlantian-based cousin for many things. From his branch office in Corona, Aziz was a tirelessly ambitious promoter of the Al-Nur Bee and Comb Union's produce for a start, and full of ideas for how they could, as he put it, 'raise their profile'. His last suggestion had been to change their name to Nectarget on the basis that this would make them sound 'more like a major international player in the bee-derivatives market'. He was honest, and always entertaining to talk to on the telephone. But despite having been born into a family of honey merchants, despite having spent the last ten years as the Union's representative in Atlantis, the sum total of his knowledge of the art of bee-keeping would not be sufficient to convince even the judges of a beauty contest that he was genuinely interested in the subject. The biggest a hive could get before it split and swarmed was around one hundred thousand bees, which, at best, would produce about seventy gallons of honey in a season. For the bee-keeper, that is. There was much more, but the rest was needed for the bees themselves to live on over the winter.

«Cousin . . . I don't wish to suggest that you might be wrong . . .» Saman answered in a manner that he hoped did not sound too immediately dismissive, «. . . but to the best of my knowledge . . . that is not completely within the realms of physical possibility. Are these genetically *modified* bees?»

«It's simple – they don't just harvest the *surplus* honey in the hive. They render *all* of it, so maximizing return on investment, don't you see? Three times as much volume output – maybe two hundred gallons of honey per hive!»

«They take *all* of it?» Saman frowned. «That doesn't make any sense, Aziz – what do the bees live on?»

«They "rationalize" the hives at the end of the production cycle.»

«Heh?»

«The bees. They "rationalize" them.»

«What the hell does that mean – they teach them to *count*?»

«No, cousin – the bees are gone! That's what *rationalization* means.»

«You mean . . . they kill them,» Saman gasped. «That's ridiculous. It-it-it's a waste! That's not only *ungrateful* . . . it's bad bee-keeping not to keep your bees.»

«Well, you know I love bees as much as you, cousin. I grew up with bees. But you mustn't get too upset – it's all done humanely. They gas the hives – the bees never know anything about it, believe me.»

«But . . . but . . .» Saman floundered, «. . . but then they don't have any *bees*! It's bloody *stupid*!»

«They get new bees in the spring. Start from scratch.»

24

«What do you mean they get *new* bees? You need *bees* to get new bees – this is how Nature works!»

And that was when Aziz told him about the mail-order bees. A queen and two or three hundred workers boxed and shipped on demand, the most wonderful and essential of Nature's creatures reduced to the level of machine parts.

The idea struck him as nothing short of satanic. Life was cruel, and to eat meat it was necessary to kill a beast. Life was hard, and to make bread you had first to sow wheat. But honey . . . honey was a blessing. It was given at no cost and with little labour, like the fruit of a tree – which itself, of course, came about thanks to the bees.

Surely for a bee-keeper to kill his bees in search of greater profit, when the flowers, the fruit and the honey had all been gifts, could cost him nothing less than his own heart.

«You live in a sick country, Aziz . . .» he decided.

By the time Saman had stomped halfway down the main street out of town, carrying the box of bees still in their brown wrapping, he was looking thoroughly dishevelled. This always happened eventually, but it happened faster on a hot day. There had been a time, as a very young man, when he had cut quite a graceful figure, but thirty-odd years of being in the honey business had turned him into a waddling, bullet-headed ball of a man. Now he just stomped, even when he wasn't in a bad mood. Which today, of course, he was.

He had not planned to go up to the hills until tomorrow, but he could not bear to leave the bees in their packaging any longer. Luckily, there was a free hive he could settle them into, presuming they ever got over the trauma of their journey. Frankly, he was bloody annoyed with Aziz for ordering them on his behalf – quite apart from having no right to force him into this perverted trade in the first place, he should have known that they were the wrong bees. They were *Apis melliflora*, the classic honey bee, which Saman had been moving gradually out of in recent years. He'd spent those years patiently building up his stock of Jana bees, whose honey was of an altogether higher quality than that of ordinary honey bees, so the last thing he wanted to do right now was go *back* into dealing with the same bees and the same honey as everyone else in the world.

When was Aziz going to appreciate that he was working on something special? He could accept that Farrukh, having chosen to run his shoe factory rather than follow in the family business, refused to take an interest in Saman's work or care particularly about the merits of one bee's honey over another's, but Aziz was supposed to understand these things.

So preoccupied was he with such fumings that he failed to notice the military blockade at the crossroads until he had almost barged into it.

«It's that way,» a youngish soldier informed him, gesturing to Saman's left.

«But I want to go—»

«And *I* said it's that way,» the young man insisted.

Saman nodded quietly. He had only to look at the slightly rakish angle of the soldier's beret to know his type – any attempt to discuss the issue would be blasphemy on the altar of his godlike manhood. Even to ask why the road out of town was blocked could mark him as a heretic.

It was simply *that* way, and not any other.

Saman looked around and realized that there was a steady stream of people heading in the direction the soldier had indicated. Cars, however, were being turned around and sent the other way. Clearly, something big was happening. Something bigger than his irritation with Aziz and the hotness of the day, so his mood was actually somewhat improved as he set off on the long detour the blockade was forcing him to take, his stomping more of a steady waddle.

It slowed to a stop, however, when he realized what he had stumbled upon. The crowd was being herded towards the site of the new hospital, which meant today must be its official opening. He could be stuck for hours as the speeches dragged on, unable to leave, holding a box of bees that he would subsequently have to take back home as there would be no time to get up into the hills. And, as a general rule, it was not a good idea to be part of the crowd at one of these things as people had a habit of dying. But it was too late. He would not be allowed to turn back home now.

His enthusiasm was required.

He carried disconsolately on, knowing the day was now a complete washout, and once again almost bumped straight into a blockade. This time it was the police, staring warily at those arriving for the ceremony and pulling over anyone they thought might be concealing a weapon of some kind.

«Where are you going?» a thick-necked policeman demanded, bringing his automatic rifle slightly forward on its strap.

«Nowhere . . . I mean I was told to—»

«What's in the package?»

His eyes were closed almost to slits. This might have been due to the sunlight, but it was probably just his usual expression, adopted so as to restrict the inflow of visual stimuli to his cerebral cortex and thus protect it from overloading. It was dangerous for questions to arise in such a man's brain. Without proper supervision, he was a risk to himself, like a baby testing whether something was edible by eating it. Hurriedly, Saman pulled apart the wrapping where he had already opened the package to examine the bees in their wire-mesh and wood container, holding it up to show the policeman.

«Bees,» he explained.

«What are they for?»

«They . . .» Saman frowned. «To make honey.»

«But why are you bringing bees *here?*»

«I didn't have any choice. I was taking them to—»

The policeman had already stopped listening, turning to his superior and gesturing with his rifle to point out the suspicious fat man with bees.

«This one has bees, Chief.»

«*Bees?*» The captain scowled momentarily, obviously at an equal loss to know what the correct security procedure in such a situation should be. He quickly regained his air of authority, demanding, «Well . . . find out how *many* bees!»

«How many . . . *bees* do you have?» the policeman asked, reclaiming the question as his own, part of his cunning interrogation of the suspect.

«I-I-I don't know exactly . . .» Saman gabbled. «Probably around three hundred.»

The rifle barrel came higher, the eyelids lower, warning Saman not to make any sudden movements. Three hundred was very possibly further than the policeman could personally count, suggesting this was too many bees for anyone's private use. He nodded slowly, cannily, his mouth opening to deliver some withering assessment of the situation, but no words came out. After a couple of seconds, he admitted defeat and called over his shoulder, «Three hundred, Chief!»

The superior officer's eyebrows rose in surprise and he strolled over to look at the suspect for himself. Meeting the gaze coming from under the shadow of his peaked cap, Saman could tell he was dealing now with a far more intelligent specimen of law enforcer, a natural leader who could no doubt count the sum involved in a pay-off and divide it equally among his men. But someone, at least, to whom he could explain the situation.

«I wonder why a man would bring a box containing

three hundred bees to the opening of a hospital?» the captain asked softly.

«But I wasn't *coming* here, I was on my way—»

«I see. So this man is just walking innocently down the street and just *happens* to have a potentially lethal number of bees on him.»

«I'm a honey merchant.»

«He's a honey merchant. So he never goes anywhere without bees. In case someone has an urgent need for honey. He doesn't go round with a *honeypot* on him, for instance?»

«No, no . . . you see, I got them in the post this morning.»

The captain's head tilted to one side, the shadow swinging away from his face to reveal a sneer. «He received bees . . . in the post this morning,» he drawled. «*Now* I'm starting to think he's a lunatic who should under no circumstances be allowed near our beloved General when he comes to open the hospital.»

«But I don't *want* to watch the Gen—» Saman began, cutting himself short as he realized where he was going.

The captain lifed an eyebrow.

«You were saying?»

«Listen,» Saman sighed. «What is the danger here? That I've somehow trained these bees to attack our beloved General? Believe me – you can't *do* that with bees! Anyway, there is a queen in the box, so they are not going to leave her unless they feel she's under threat. Bees are not aggressive creatures – they only attack when *provoked*!»

«Well, of course not,» the captain smiled. «I never heard of anyone attacking for any other reason.»

He straightened his head, apparently satisfied that Saman was being sincere.

«OK. You can go ahead.»

Saman smiled thankfully, although frankly he would rather have been ordered home, and joined the crowd drifting through the gap in the blockade. The captain watched him leave, tapping the thick-necked policeman on the shoulder and muttering, «Stay close to that one. If so much as one bee comes out . . . you know what to do.»

The policeman nodded, grinning as he set off after the suspect's fat posterior. The suspect *he* had suspected was suspicious. He was good, all right. And if it turned out that his suspicion – his *hunch*, to be honest – about the man with the brown paper package had been right, then he'd be no less than a hero. He really hoped that a bee came out.

Turning his attention back to the people coming down the street, the captain walked along behind his men and tapped one on the shoulder to point out a disconcertingly bright-eyed individual heading towards them.

«Him I don't like,» he muttered. «Take him—»

He wheeled as he felt a tap on his own shoulder, finding the thick-necked officer behind him, a frown on his generous forehead.

«Uh, Chief – *what* do I know what to do?»

The End minus 28 days

'One interesting fact that I could mention to put some kind of scale on this threat for the viewers, Ayesha – bees are directly responsible for more human deaths each year than *any other creature on the planet.*'

'You're kidding. Even more than other people?'

'No . . . that's probably *excluding* other people. But discounting them, bees are *the* single biggest threat to human life . . . *on the planet.*'

'I think, to put that in perspective, we should point out for the viewers that bees are *also* responsible for pollination.'

'Yes, Ayesha, we should indeed make that clear: the government is *not* saying here "All bees are our enemies." The vast majority of bees are peaceful, hard-working insects whom we have to thank for, among other things, flowers and fruit. People should not forget that just because of the actions of a tiny minority of bees that kill people. Bees are good.'

'But, realistically, how many stings does it take to kill someone?'

'Well, that depends totally on the species of bee and the resistance of the person being attacked. There's no standard figure.'

'But if you *had* to give one?'

'I'd say about one hundred *ordinary* honey-bee stings is usually sufficient to induce a fatal case of toxic shock in a healthy adult male. A large *swarm* of bees will contain around fifty thousand insects so, in theory, the potential is there for it to kill around five thousand people were it to attack, for instance, a football stadium. That said, the Government is calling on people *not* to panic and to attend this weekend's sporting fixtures as planned.'

'But can bees be *trained* to attack a specific target such as, for instance, a sports stadium?'

'Well, bees respond to loud, rhythmic noise stimuli. This is actually the method traditionally used *by* bee-keepers to draw a swarm into a hive. In a process called *tanging*, the bee-keeper will bang on an object such as a metal pot to lure the swarm towards a specific spot. Now, a crowd of chanting, stamping sports fans *could* obviously provide that kind of noise stimulus, but the Government has said that they think this is only a remote possibility. They have added, however, that if an individual *sees* a bee while he or she is making a loud, rhythmic noise such as banging on a metal pot, they should stop doing so *immediately*. In particular, they have warned parents not to allow their *children* to bang on metal pots or other objects for the moment. Equally, they have advised that small motors such as those in lawnmowers *can* create the kind of rhythmic noise that bees could be drawn towards.'

'So that represents a dramatic shift in their stance on lawn-mowing this weekend, doesn't it?'

'Well, I don't think they've actually said—'

'What about power tools? Are they—'

Chapter Two

In which we learn why it was that the United States of Atlantis, the most prosperous and democratic of countries, found itself declaring war without end upon nations and persons as yet undecided

It all started on The Day The World Changed.

There are, of course, certain pedants who argue that nothing ever just *starts* like that – out of nowhere, as it were, by divine intervention – and that as for the world, well, it does tend to change most days. But this was the first time in living memory that it had done so in capital letters: the day of the Stock Exchange Computer Inferno.

It changed. For everyone everywhere. Except those with more urgent problems such as hungry children to think about, or local wars that had a prior call on their attention. But aside from that few billion people – who were, to be brutally frank, irrelevant, or else they wouldn't have been in that situation anyway – it was a Day like no other.

Especially for Atlantians. For them, it was henceforth impossible to see the world and their own lives in the same way as they had the day before, no matter who they were or where on the planet they lived. Or, indeed, off it – there were two Atlantians at that moment orbiting the planet in the International Space Station who were no less affected by the horror of the Stock Exchange Computer Inferno than their earthbound compatriots. They were the only two Atlantians who could *literally* see the world, and they did literally see it in a new way. Whereas the day before it had floated as a jewel in space, hope shining with the full spectrum of life's colours against the black death of the universe, the day after it hung like one obscenely giant butt before them, sorely in need of a kick.

And that was why war came to Kalashnistan – because although the Inferno was the work of only a small handful of fanatics, it was impossible to deny the urge to kick some global-sized butt in response. Atlantis was a democracy, after all, and public opinion demanded it.

Of course, not everyone else around the world agreed that all-out war was an appropriate response. The end, they argued, did not justify those particular, terrible means. These people just didn't get it. No, the *end* did not justify the means – in this instance, the means were self-justifying regardless of how it worked out later. The whole point was to give the world a full-frontal display of Atlantian military strength. A time for deeds, not just words.

You want a fight? the Atlantian President was saying. Here's a fight.

Here, for instance, is a two-ton, bunker-buster bomb right up your asshole.

And, on the whole, most people got the point.

Sure, it was a symbolic gesture inasmuch as one could argue that carpet-bombing was about the least efficient method of bringing a small number of criminals to justice known to human intellect, but then the provocation *itself* had been of an equally symbolic nature. By targeting the Stock Exchange, the terrorists had not simply hoped to kill a large number of merchant bankers, they had been attacking the very foundation of the Atlantian way of life. Freedom. The market. For what better symbolized the triumph of their society than the extraordinary vigour of its financial bazaar in recent years? It had become a magnet for all the world's wealth, providing the theoretical collateral for a frenzy of borrowing by ordinary citizens that – if ever the pendulum swung the other way – would plunge the nation into bankruptcy. Indeed, that was probably what the terrorists had hoped to achieve when they introduced their subtle little virus into the computer system, at some point attaching it to a single trade out of the millions made every day. Nobody knew now how long it had been there, being passed from one computer to another as other trades were made and Exchange's value climbed steadily upwards, waiting for the trigger that would activate it. The Atlantian party had raged unabated for months, perhaps even years after the moment of infection, a sense of invincibility settling over the nation, and nobody had the first inkling that within the system's very success now lay the agent of its destruction.

Fifteen thousand points: that was the trigger that had been chosen by the country's enemies. A market evaluation that just a few years previously would have seemed absurd, but which, as the dance had grown wilder and wilder, certain bright-eyed dreamers began to suggest was attainable.

At first they were laughed off, but no sooner had it been aired as a possibility than it started to become an objective. A mystical quest, even. There were those who believed that, by reaching fifteen thousand points, the Bing 100 would attain some kind of financial nirvana, magically levitating itself above physical reality and the dull rules of flesh-and-blood people making tangible things they sold at a marginal profit to other flesh-and-blood people. The market would become an unstoppable engine of pure profit, a perpetual-motion machine.

And so, because they so wanted to do it, and because

there was little to stop them but their own lack of faith, they did it.

At which point the virus, now present in the computer of every one of the fervent believers in that vast building, present in the computers of brokers' firms all across the nation, present in every computer of every individual who had traded online over the previous months, woke up.

What it did was very simple. It was a piece of software that introduced an insoluble, tail-chasing equation into the system that raced round and round the hardware's circuits until they fried. An ordinary computer would just crash, its hard disk irrevocably damaged, and indeed there were some who suggested that this was probably all the terrorists had hoped to achieve, no doubt having tested it on considerably less powerful machines than those currently found in the Stock Exchange – but that was not a popular argument in the days and weeks following the Inferno. Indeed, it was considered to be in some way unpatriotic even to suggest it. The fact was that the Stock Exchange's computers had not crashed: they had tried with relentless determination to resolve the equation, only stopping when their circuitry over-heated and caught alight.

Thus, within minutes of the explosion of rapture that had greeted that magical figure's attainment, computers throughout the Stock Exchange began to smoke. While the men and women who worked on the market shouted and hugged and kissed as if they had just won some great war, all around them their abandoned terminals puffed silently into flame. Soon the air was filling with the toxic fumes of melting plastic, stinging their tearily joyful eyes and choking their lungs.

The Stock Exchange Computer Inferno had begun.

Everywhere in the building at the same moment.

Shortly after the conflagration started, the smoke activated the sprinkler system. Unfortunately for those

36

who greeted this development with cries of relief, the fire in question was electrical. In the days that followed, certain experts questioned how many people had died as a result of smoke and flames, and how many were fried by the building's own safety apparatus. They were, however, accused of being insensitive to the bereaved and so shut up.

The windows could not be opened and so, in their panic, people began to break them, unwittingly turning the entire building into a chimney that nourished the flames and sucked toxic fumes up the fire stairs, which rapidly clogged up with asphyxiated bodies. Those who had not already reached the lower floors were trapped.

Soon, the building itself was barely visible from the street, the wind occasionally revealing a white-hot negative of its architecture through the billowing cloud of black that poured from every one of its floors. By the time help arrived, there was no help they could offer.

Ironically, the terrorists' plan did not work because it was too successful. There was no Stock Market crash for the simple reason that there no longer was a Stock Market. In death, its valuation was embalmed at fifteen thousand points, like a casket in which the body is displayed looking its very best.

Within hours of the tragedy, the finger of blame settled on the terrorist groups hiding in Kalashnistan – their hatred of Atlantis and devilish ingenuity being well known. The Government soon confirmed this, announcing that it had conclusive evidence to support the theory, but could not make it public for security reasons.

It was at that point that things became rather surreal.

Perhaps sensitive to the notion that, as the self-proclaimed champion of justice and freedom in the world, it was somewhat inappropriate for Atlantis to bomb hell out of a country that had the misfortune to be housing a few renegade individuals, the Government got around this problem by generously declaring war on everyone's terrorists everywhere.

This naturally put a different angle on the combat. Suddenly, it was not about punishing a handful of homocidal maniacs, but fighting a massive global alliance of evil. As such, it was a wildly ambitious sort of war whose successful pursuit would clearly require every weapon at the nation's disposal. And, indeed, the weapons of all the nations who declared themselves to be on the Atlantians' side – which, given the somewhat free-range character of the proposed conflict, it was clearly wise for them to do. And even with all that, it was going to take time. Some world leaders – such as the Atlantian government's most faithful ally, Prime Minister Chris Flyte – were already talking about earmarking the entire century for this purpose.

But was the war justified? some still asked. Yes, almost two thousand people had been killed – the country's average murder total for an entire month dealt with in a single morning – but such massacres frequently occurred elsewhere and rarely even caught the attention of the more powerful nations, sometimes even when the death toll ran into the tens or hundreds of thousands of innocents. In those cases, when the people in question were generally darker of skin and lighter of wallet, it was considered somewhat Darwinian. Nobody had ever suggested launching a worldwide war in the name of stopping such atrocities in the future.

So why was this *so* different? Why, indeed, had the Atlantian government not declared war on its own fanatics after they blew up a government building and killed hundreds of innocent people just a few years previously? On the contrary, in that instance determined efforts had been made to portray the crime as the act of a lone madman, however poorly the evidence supported that thesis.

Was not the singular aspect of the outrage in this case

– and this was something that nobody wanted to say aloud and many did not even want to think – that the victims were white and the perpetrators brown? Or, to put it another way, if the problem was only an extremist form of a single religion, then why did so many people around the world, who did not share that extremist belief or even that religion, find satisfaction in the blow that had been dealt if it was not because they, too, were not white?

It would be some weeks into the new war before people in Atlantis began to realize that daily life, when they thought about it, had not finally been affected very much by the Stock Exchange Computer Inferno. This was something of an anticlimax, given that it had briefly felt as though the world was about to end, but the undeniable truth was that the world clearly intended to keep turning. Even the temporary absence of a Stock Exchange did not seem to stop anything *else* from functioning. The electricity wasn't shut off. There was food in the supermarket. People had jobs and their salaries were somehow paid. The toilets still worked.

Arguably, nothing much had changed at all. But it was too late, because by then the juggernaut of war was already rolling.

The shock that unleashed it had been so great that many people initially believed it would lead to a profound debate about the nation and what role it played in the world that it could possibly inspire such apocalyptic hatred, that some *good* lessons might be drawn from the horror of that day for their society and the world it dominated, but the thunder of the rolling wheels soon drowned out that discussion. A conclusion was reached without debate, the President declared war on all terrorists everywhere and, as is always the case, most people found it kind of exciting to be at war.

A few people, out of a profound sense of solemnity, would forever insist on calling that day the Stock

Exchange Computer Inferno. But the rest soon began to shorten it to the S.E.C.I., so often did it come up in discussion. And before long it was reduced again to become the SECI – a kind of brand-name horror which some read as 'SECKY' and some 'SESSY' but which gradually, and generally, came to be pronounced 'SEXY'.

The End minus 27 days

'. . . incredible that we have no kind of defence strategy in place against this kind of attack! We're talking about a very dangerous insect here, for God's sake! *Surely* it would—'

'Senator, you know as well as I do that we don't have the *budget* to defend ourselves against every *conceivable* form of attack that—'

'Gentlemen, excuse me . . .'

'Why not? *Why* don't we have the budget? Because *your* party has spent the last decade throwing money at unwed mothers, *minority* groups and—'

'I was wondering how long it would be before you played the race card.'

'I'm not playing the *race* card by suggesting the security of all Atlantians should be our priority, Senator! *You*, however, are playing the race card right now by *accusing* me of playing the race card!'

'There you go *again*! You're playing the race card!'

'Gentlemen, excuse me – that's *really* all we have time for just now! I believe we've finally got that video link with Neil O'Neill at the Natural History Museum. Neil, are you there?'

'Indeed I am, Ayesha.'

'I believe you've been finding out just *how* deadly Jana bees are?'

'Yes, I have. Now, if I could give you a bit of historical

context here, Ayesha, it seems Errat was, for many centuries in the past, *famous* for producing the best honey in the world thanks to these bees, which habitually collect nectar from the local Jana *trees*. Now, the *flowers* of these trees were reputed to give the honey highly prized *medicinal* qualities, particularly in the treatment of nervous disorders. In the last century, however, Jana honey has no longer been cultivated due to the fact that during the *colonial* era the groves of Jana trees were cleared to make way for spice plantations. This policy turned out to have disastrous consequences for the local people in that the bees, deprived of their natural source of nectar, became *extremely* aggressive and hundreds, if not *thousands* of individuals were apparently killed during a plague of the insects whose hives, consequently, had to be systematically destroyed before the situation was brought back under control. Obviously, this may be *precisely* the kind of phenomenon that the terrorists are aiming to recreate in Atlantis by unleashing the bees over *here* in a *nightmare* scenario that experts suggest could lead to the deaths of—'

Chapter Three

In which we return to Errat and continue with the increasingly disastrous day our hero is having, and briefly make the acquaintance of a young man who, for the most noble and sincere of reasons, will shortly explode

It was not easy to do God's work, thought Kamal, the sweat trickling down his belly. The afternoon was far too hot to be dressed in explosives, but he accepted his discomfort joyfully, considering it a tiny plus to the great sacrifice he was about to make.

He stood shoulder to shoulder with his fellow police officers, a dark wall blocking access to the podium from which the General would soon be addressing the crowd before them. Twisting his head slightly, he could make out the line of soldiers ranged along the top step of the new hospital – immobile as he and his colleagues, their guns held flat against their chests. The General took no chances – he trusted neither the police nor the army, hence their dual attendance at his rare public appearances. They were there as much to keep an eye on each other as on the crowd.

Although he claimed otherwise, the General was not a believer. He couldn't be. If he believed, then he would put his life in God's hands and it wouldn't be so difficult for those who *truly* believed to assassinate him.

All the precautions in the world would not save him for ever, though. The bullet-proof glass in front of the podium, the helicopter circling above it, the sniffer dogs making a last check underneath it – none of that would save him today. When the moment came, Kamal needed only to break from the line, run up the steps of the podium, and get as close to the country's dictator as possible before releasing his hold on the detonator. He calculated that nobody would have time to react before he was at least halfway up the steps, and the protection of his helmet and flak jacket should buy him a few more seconds before they managed to bring him down. He hoped, of course, to get all the way to his target – to throw his arms around the General in the instant before detonation and ensure he received the full, righteous force of God's wrath – but, according to Elohim, the Lord's will would be done anywhere within twenty paces.

It was to be a glorious day for his brothers in the Sword of Destiny. A day that would be remembered for ever, celebrated for all eternity once their beautiful land – that had for so long suffered under the yoke of the wicked, for so long been riven by hatred and war – finally saw the dawn of the new age of brotherly peace and holy law.

Oh happy day.

And, he thought with a small smile, a day of humiliation for those fanatics in the Vanguard League. After this, even they would see who God's true warriors were.

There was sadness, of course, in the knowledge that he would not be here to enjoy the fruits of his sacrifice. Kamal was spiritually prepared, ready to go to a far, far better place than this, but for as long as he still breathed there would always be a part of him that wished he could stay – delay his reward if only for one day – to see the rejoicing, hear them chant his name, savour the respect in their eyes. That was the hardest thing about becoming a martyr – you didn't get to go to your own party.

But that was why God favoured martyrs over all others, because they had risen above such mortal concerns, spurning pride even though they had more reason for pride than *anyone*, and so had died utterly pure. No matter what sins they might have committed in their past. That was why they were guaranteed a place in heaven – and not just any place, but a place by God's right side. He trembled at the wonder of it: tonight he would be sleeping in God's own house! He would be feasting with the saints and prophets, virgins tending to his every desire! Whatever he wanted would be his for the asking, and for all eternity. Anything. Anything at all.

He gulped in awe although his mouth was raspingly dry. What was the first thing, he wondered, that he'd ask for?

There were plenty of things he could think of to ask for, but he worried that they might not be seen as worthy enough choices for a martyr on his very first day. He should ask for something simple and pure. Like a glass of water. Yes, that was good. He saw himself being led to his place by God's side, perhaps carried on the shoulders of saints, and set down on these amazingly soft cushions in a luxurious garden full of beautiful flowers and perfectly ripe fruit hanging from the trees.

«What is your wish, O hallowed one?» a beautiful virgin would demand, kneeling before him. She'd have long, dark hair, skin soft as a roe, and be wearing some kind of white silk dress that was probably almost totally see-through. «My only desire is to serve you, my master, for all eternity.»

«I ask only for a simple glass of water, child,» he would answer serenely, a humble smile on his face as she backed away from him on all fours. «Cold, please. With

45

lots of crushed ice, you know? And a straw, if you have one.»

Damn, he was thirsty. How much longer was the evil bastard going to keep them all waiting? Fucking dictators. Can't even be on time for their own assassinations. Now that he knew what he was going to ask for, he suddenly wanted to get this over as quickly as possible – run up those steps, die, and get a glass of iced water. He was ready.

Kamal's cracked, flaky lips smiled in anticipation. He would not have long to wait – soon, very soon he would be in that garden. He had only to be patient for a little while longer, and he would never be thirsty again. There would be an eternity for him to enjoy all the other rewards to which he was entitled.

He'd waited this long already, after all, so he could certainly hang on for a day or two before suggesting it was time for a blow job.

The General stepped out of the cool of his air-conditioned limousine and tugged on the bottom of his jacket to remove the creases. A clear path stretched ahead of him towards the podium, one side lined by police, the other by soldiers. His personal bodyguards flanked him, and were considerably taller than him, so making an opportunistic side shot almost impossible.

It was exhausting, having to live twenty-four hours a day with these precautions, but such was the nature of Errat. His was a passionate people, with a rich and proud heritage of love poetry, considered by many to be the most beautiful in the world. Especially by Erratis. The General himself was something of a poet, although he published anonymously. *The Loneliness of the King*, his latest collection, had been very well received, although he was modest enough to attribute some of the enthusiasm to the fact that he'd had all of the critics who wrote negative reviews of his first collection, *Soldier of*

Love, killed. As any poet in his position would have done. Most of the truly great love poets had died violent deaths, after all, defending their verse with their own blood. This seemed only right, because a man who was not prepared to kill or be killed for his art was clearly just being pretentious. The General had not killed them himself, of course, but a poet who didn't, wherever possible, let others defend his reputation on his *behalf* was obviously stupid.

Either way, it took a very brave man to become a literary critic in Errat. They too had their share of heroes.

This was what Westerners failed to understand about his country. By natural extension, the innate romanticism of the people brought with it a certain talent for blind hatred. Foreigners considered themselves so superior – all the politicians, bankers and industrialists he met – because their countries were bastions of democracy and law. And he knew it was both in his interest and that of his people to pay lip service to those ideals, because it eased the moral dilemma of investors who wanted to do business with a country whose 'human rights record' they deplored, allowing them to portray him as a moderate and a reformer who hoped to 'modernize' his nation and turn it into a little carbon copy of their own societies. Once he had dealt with the extremists who threatened their business interests, that is.

They didn't understand at all. Or they didn't *want* to understand, rather. Errat would never be a democracy, and nor should it aim to be, given the loss of passion this would demand. They were not barbarians just because they saw life differently, because they had other priorities. The General did not agree that democracy was the system of the *nice*, as Westerners assumed, so much as a consolation prize offered to cold-blooded nations – a pretty face painted on tyrannies of reason and logic, where only money was loved and their government, just like their lives, was dictated by arithmetic.

The General flattered himself that he loved his people more than any democratic president, that holding his country together and improving the general lot after fifteen years of passionate civil war required more heart than it took to build a coalition of self-interested minorities. Which Western leader would be moved to write a love poem about a new hospital, as he had done last night, casting himself as the romantic hero nursing a sick lover back to health? It was in his pocket now as he walked up the aisle towards the podium – a deeply personal declaration of love that he would deliver to the crowd his soldiers had rounded up this morning.

If what he had heard was true, democratic presidents usually paid other people to write their speeches for them. They merely read out words and sentiments composed by hired professionals. Political speeches were just a manufactured product, therefore, like designer clothing. And their key statements were test-marketed in little focus groups before being released to the public.

And this was what they called freedom?

One had to laugh at them, even while their fanatical belief in the superiority of the machine they served sent a shiver down the spine of any warm-blooded human. One inevitably was warm-blooded in this heat, he reflected, as he began mounting the steps in the pitiless glare. He glanced out over the crowd, a cauldron of bubbling heads, and heard their simmering voices come to a boil as he appeared, fast rising to a roar. It was a huge crowd – beaten out of their houses with clubs, of course, but only because at this time of day people naturally hid from the white hammer hanging overhead. Indeed, there seemed to be two suns today: the circular hole in the blue had been joined by a vast white square here on the ground, as its light reflected off the new hospital. Maybe he should have heeded the architect's reservations about building it in glass, he suddenly thought.

His bodyguards dropped a pace behind as the General

strode on up the steps, forgetting the crowd as his mind focused on the security situation. Everything seemed to be in order: there was a long line of police in front of the podium, standing shoulder to shoulder, and a second line of soldiers at the top of the hospital steps behind it. Taken all together, along with those behind him and the snipers on the rooftops . . . maybe five hundred guns eyeing him and each other. All for a poem.

That was the beauty of Errat.

He walked confidently over to the microphone, raising his hands to acknowledge the crowd's enthusiasm, but he did not milk it, pulling the paper from his pocket and motioning them to be quiet. The boiling roar calmed down, evaporating into the silent blue sky.

Unfolding last night's composition, he began to read.

«I am a simple soldier, my love, it is true,
More used to killing many than healing a few . . .»

*   *   *

Saman had not intended to find himself so near the front, but the first spot he'd chosen turned out to be just in front of where the thick-necked cop had decided to stand. Indeed, there was nobody else for a few yards around the two of them, so he thought it best to move forward and blend into the crowd. Unfortunately, it was not to be. The crowd kept melting aside wherever he stopped, refusing to let themselves be part of the wall of flesh he was trying to erect between himself and the man's gun. By the time he gave up, realizing that it was clearly *him* the cop was still interested in, he was only a couple of rows back from the line of police guarding the podium.

He clutched his box of bees nervously, knowing that if there was a place where it was advisable not to be on these occasions, it was near the front, sandwiched between not fantastically intelligent men carrying firearms.

«. . . But as you lie sick, through my love for you,
This simple soldier can be a doctor, too.»

This had to be stopped, thought Kamal, his hand reaching slowly into his pocket for the detonator. If there was any shadowed corner of his heart that was not resolved to take the general's life while sacrificing his own, the man's hideous attempt at poetry snapped on the lights. As if it wasn't enough to torture people in the flesh, now he was inflicting this agony upon their minds.

It was time for the Sword of Destiny to strike.

Time to die a martyr.

The detonator was a small metal tube, little wider than a radio battery and about the length of a cigarette. Clasping it in his palm, he prised open the cap with his thumb. The button inside, once depressed, armed the bomb that was strapped in place around his belly. Detonation would occur the instant that button was released again, meaning that his mission would be fulfilled even if he died first. He closed his eyes, took a deep breath, and pressed.

Kamal let the breath out slowly. There was no turning back now.

«I do not come to you with my hand grenade,» the General was continuing, «I come with love, to administer first aid.»

That was it. Suddenly, as though catching his own body by surprise, Kamal broke from the rank of police, wheeling round with his head tipped forward and his legs pushing off at a sprint. And time suddenly slowed – he was running to the steps, but somehow able to take in the whole scene around him, as if his soul had already left his body. The fellow police who had flanked him were slowly twisting their shoulders to see where he had gone, looking at one another in surprise. The front row of the crowd, squinting in the glare of the hospital glass, were turning their heads from the General to him, one or two lifting their arms to point. The General himself was oblivious, staring up to the heavens as he continued with his poem.

«And though spilling blood is my normal trade . . .»

A soldier was leaping down the steps of the hospital, his comrades bringing their guns away from their chests to take aim. Kamal, taking the podium steps two at a time, was amazed – how had the soldier reacted so fast? He calculated the distance they both had to travel, and realized that the soldier would reach the General first, pulling him off the podium to safety as his comrades let fly their bullets. He frowned in disbelief – the timing was all wrong here. There was no way they should be able to head him off like this.

And then Kamal realized that the other soldiers were not bringing their guns to bear on him, but on their own comrade.

Reaching the last step, he understood what was happening – the soldier was not running to protect the General, but to kill him. His eyes were alight, fanatical, and he was holding one arm aloft, a detonator clutched in his hand. He must have started running a second or two *before* Kamal, which was why he had seemed to be acting with such incredible rapidity.

He was Vanguard League. He had to be. There was no other explanation.

«I will staunch it . . .» the General was saying as the first shots cracked, his voice slowing as he turned from the microphone, «. . . where once . . . it . . . *sprayed*?»

Kamal calculated the distances again. In a straight race to the General, he was going to lose – it was a rectangle, and while he had to cross it lengthways, the soldier would arrive straight behind the dictator. The Vanguard League would be the ones to claim this day as theirs, to rejoice in their man's martyrdom. And then would *he*, his mission having been stolen from him, still die as a martyr? Would he awake to find himself in the garden if *his* bomb had not been the one that killed the dictator?

He had a choice. He could detonate his bomb now, still too far from the General to be sure that it would harm him. Or he could keep going, and hope that by following the soldier's explosion with his own they would be morally entitled to joint martyrdom. *Or . . .* he could change direction, cutting across to intercept the soldier before he reached the General.

The answer was clear. Even if he was entitled to it, he had no desire to claim joint martyrdom with someone from the League. An eternity spent sharing virgins with one of those bastards was not paradise, but a kind of hell . . .

His comrades would avenge him and live to strike at the General another day.

Kamal sprinted diagonally across the podium, aware of bullets whipping past his head, and threw himself at the soldier just as he leaped onto it from the steps. Their bodies crashed into one another, and they fell back off the podium onto the hospital steps. They landed heavily, the breath punched from their chests, and rolled under the stage, the detonators clattering down the steps behind.

The General was shielded from their joint explosion by the fact that the floor of the podium had been built in steel, with precisely this kind of eventuality in mind. Unfortunately, this meant that the force of the blast was instead directed outwards from underneath, killing most of the police in front and dozens in the crowd beyond. The soldiers at the top of the hospital steps were more fortunate, being merely knocked off their feet. They, however, sustained heavy casualties in the seconds that followed as the glass front of the brand new hospital shattered and fell on them in a brilliant, tinkling deluge of sunlight. Saman was just far enough back in the crowd to be safe from the lethal effects of the explosion, but ended up on his back, buried under the unconscious body of the man in front of him who, in falling, crushed the package of bees.

Rising to his feet a second later, the thick-necked policeman saw the smoke-filled air in front of him swirling with dark dots. Though somewhat stunned by the blast, it did not take long for his limited mental capabilities to regain most of their functioning capacity. He knew what he had to do, he remembered, and opened fire on the angry bees. By the time his clip was emptied, it appeared that the swarm had been dispersed and so he breathed a sigh of satisfaction as he lowered his rifle, quite unaware of the huge death toll his bullets had claimed as they whizzed through the smoke.

Kamal, incidentally, would be posthumously decorated some days later for his brave and incredibly swift response to the attempted assassination, without which it seemed almost certain that the nation's beloved General would not have survived.

So he died a hero and a martyr, as he had wished.

Just not to the right people.

The End minus 25 days

'. . . Secretary-General Bisi Kawan arrives in Errat for talks with General Harouni in an attempt to defuse the crisis, a government spokesman suggests that Atlantis *will* accept the outcome of these talks provided the general complies with President Hedges's non-negotiable demand to hand over the terrorist leader, Souman Mussadie. We'll be joined later by Glen Stokopolous, former Under-Secretary of State, and Rachid Biman, Errat's ambassador to the UN, for a World Spotlight Debate right after the sport. First, though, more on today's science story as doctors ask "Is *tobacco* responsible for violent crime?" We have a report from—'

Chapter Four

In which we return to Atlantis and meet the leader of the free world, having won the election that he won, with God's help, and learn the first rule of politics in this or in any other sort of country

Meanwhile, the President of the United States of Atlantis was in a meeting to discuss exactly how much love was out there, according to the polls. Not that he cared much for polls and statistics and other stuff with numbers.

President Hedges was a true man of the people. He liked the simple things in life, like eating a hot dog at a ball game, and he didn't ask for much more than just to be able to do that, and to love his family. Although it was nice, of course, if you got the chance to own the ball team. Which, as luck would have it, had been his case. And it was luck – he realized that. Luck and, of course, God. Obviously, no man could own a ball team without God's blessing. But in that he was lucky, to be so blessed. It made a man humble, it truly did. Although the greatest blessing of all, naturally, was his family. He loved his family, and his family made him strong. And he loved God. And God's love made him strong, through his family and their love. And vice versa. So now he was President.

It all made sense.

He'd never considered himself to be exceptional in any way, or had a particular vision for his life – his career, if you want to call it that, had been a question of going with the flow and taking opportunities as they presented themselves. It just so happened that the opportunities had been pretty good ones because his daddy had been President for a while a few years back and that kind of helped grease the wheels a little in life. Didn't mean he wasn't a straightforward guy – some folks know the fellah who pumps the gas in the gas station, and some folks know the fellah who pumps the oil from the oil well. Same thing when you get right down to it. On the whole people are just people behind the particulars of their situations, and are all good folk, barring the few individuals who aren't satisfied with their lot in life and are going to hold up the gas station to pay for their drug habit. Well, that was their choice and they had to take responsibility for their actions; there was no excuse for breaking the law just because you couldn't find some honest way of making a quick buck. He'd been there himself at moments in his youth – back when he was a little wild, drinking too much and taking drugs – but he hadn't ever broken the law, damn it, so he wasn't about to say there should be one standard for folks like himself and another standard for others. He was a compassionate man, but he believed that the kindest thing you could do to somebody who was driven to that kind of behaviour was to punish them to the full extent of the law. Because that was the only way some folks were ever going to learn.

Tough love required you to be strong, which he was, thanks to all this love he was blessed with. Strong enough, if necessary, to send a man to his Maker. Without God he might have been too weak to do what sometimes had to be done, because it took a lot of love to put a man to death, even if he was pure scum. And it was a whole lot tougher still when you were talking about a lady, of course, not that you could call the kind of woman who ends up on death row a lady. No man can carry that kind of burden on his own, without God to guide him – specially with all the liberal atheists kicking up a fuss about how she's a woman and had found God in prison, which naturally these people *always* claimed to have done. Like that should change anything. Or like the liberal atheists should give a damn about whether she'd found *God*, when you thought about it. Anyway, in those cases the real question, surely, was would a woman like that have found God if she *hadn't* been sentenced to die by lethal injection? Hell no. So how could anyone doubt that putting folks down was sometimes the kindest thing to do? Providing they *had* committed a crime, of course – he was dead against euthanasia, which was a sin before the Lord as surely as was killing an innocent child before it's even had time to grow itself a brain.

That was why folks liked him. Because he had clear-cut values.

Because he was an ordinary man just doing his best in a confusing world, with a little guidance from up above. A simple, plain-talking guy that ordinary folk could relate to in that he didn't give the impression of having any clearer understanding of what the hell was going on than they did. But, unlike them, he did know what to do about it – which was why they had made him President.

Although some of them *still* said they hadn't, and that it was the other guy who'd won the election. But clearly he *hadn't* won, or else he'd be President instead of the President. The people who said that were obviously very confused individuals, which might have been because they had not let God into their lives. They had a lot of anger and hatred in their hearts. All through the election he'd won, these folks had been calling him stupid just because he wasn't one for big words and clever talk about the world and all these pipsqueak little countries that most decent folk didn't give a hoot about because they were patriots who loved their country and knew that God had made it strong. He wasn't stupid, though – he was plenty smart, which was why he'd won the election he'd won, and besides which the Holy Book didn't use many big words, did it now? And it was kind of repetitive, too, and occasionally seemed to contradict itself, just like he did himself. So if just a few words, shuffled around one way and another, were good enough for God and His holy truth, President Hedges figured they ought to be good enough for anyone who didn't have something to hide.

Anyway, it didn't matter any more because those same people who'd called him stupid were pretty darned pleased they had somebody who was strong and spoke his mind leading them now that the country was fighting a war against evil. That had shut them up.

It made him humble to realize that this had been God's plan all along – that his life had been leading him, in ways that he could not have seen, to this great test, this war. He had not known what he was here for, had not known why God wished him to become President even after he became President, until the day when the Evil Ones struck, the day of the SECI. Then suddenly it was all clear to him. Well, maybe not that same day. He'd been a little confused on the day *itself*, naturally, because nobody around him had known what in hell was going on all of a sudden and they'd had to take his own security as the prime consideration until the situation became clearer, which meant he'd spent most of it in a bunker. Afterwards, though, it had *all* become clear. He was being put to the test of this struggle between the forces of Good and Evil, a great battle against an enemy so twisted in their hatred and madness that they believed that they were fighting a holy war, that *God* wanted them to slaughter all those innocent people. This was why he had become President, then – to lead the forces of Good against those of Evil – that had been the Lord's plan for him all along. God, of course, had known those people were going to die, because He knew all and nothing could happen without it fitting His plan. So, in that sense, President Hedges realized with a sense of awe, it *had* been God's will that they die – not the will of this twisted, false god the Evil Ones believed in, of course, but of his own all-wise and merciful God. Because he was being put to this test. It made a man humble.

And it all made sense.

He would not fail, that he knew beyond any doubt. His faith would make him strong, just as it always had in the lesser crises of the past when the final decision of whether or not to spare those scheduled for execution had fallen to him alone. He saw now how it was all connected, how intricate and perfect God's plan was. Those little life-and-death decisions had been a form of rehearsal for the decisions he had to take now, fighting a war with the full military might of his great nation against an evil enemy who hid among ordinary people, just like the murderers on death row had. Now, as he had then in a smaller way, he had to bear the burden of the lives in his hand – those of the enemy, of the innocent people they used as their shields, of his own soldiers, and ultimately of folks back home. Everyone, when you got right down to it.

During the election he'd won, his critics had said he had been responsible for more executions than anyone else in the country, ever. Like this was a point against him. He wondered, though, if those people realized now why that was – if they could see now that God had been preparing him for this war all along.

It didn't much matter to him whether they did or not, but the polls certainly suggested they'd understood a thing or two. He was riding higher in the public's esteem than any other president had been, ever in the history of the world since polls began.

There was a lot of love out there.

It made him strong.

'Basically a very pretty picture we're looking at here,' announced Geena Mason, pointing to the latest opinion-poll chart, 'Six months on from the end of the Kalashnistan campaign, and support is holding at 79 per cent approval rate for the President.'

There was a chorus of satisfied grunts from the Cabinet members gathered around the table. Only President Hedges looked concerned, frowning at the graph with that peculiar expression that came over his face when he was obliged to concentrate – his eyebrows sloping inwards and upwards like a puppy willing a scrap to fall from its owner's plate.

'Uh-huh . . .' he nodded. 'Now . . . why *exactly's* that good?'

'Well, Mr President, sir . . . *79 per cent*! I mean – that's pretty fantastic!'

'Yuh . . . uh-huh . . .' the nation's leader nodded, still wincing. 'Well, I don't believe in counting a whole bundle on figures, you know, but I'm looking at that line you're pointing at here, Miss Mason, and – hell, if I understand it correctly . . . it's going *down*!'

'Sure – it's down from *90*!' Geena laughed. 'But I think we can live with that!'

The other members of his cabinet joined in with her laughter. Most of them had long experience of government, having spent most of their careers switching between public service and executive directorships of private companies. They had served other presidents, and they had known the pain of defeat, known what it was like to be thrown out of their jobs by an ungrateful public and sent to lick their wounds on the board of some major corporation. They liked 79 per cent.

President Hedges laughed too, because he was an easy-going kind of fellah who enjoyed a joke even if he didn't always get it, but his forehead was still twitching in and out like he was trying to play 'Here's the church, and here's the steeple' with his eyebrows.

'But it is . . . *down*, ain't it?' he smiled. 'I mean, that's nearly . . . heck, that's darn near 10 per cent of the folks out there who've had themselves a change of *heart* since we stopped the bombing campaign. Now what's *that* all about?'

'We do have a recession to take into account, Mr President,' his Treasury Secretary reminded him. 'And a pretty serious one at that. There's a lot of people feeling the pinch – which is precisely why these approval ratings are so *good* given the situation.'

'Well, if I remember rightly, Mr Secretary . . .' the President answered calmly, '. . . we had us one of those six months ago. We had us a resecession from the very *day* I took office, just like I promised, so I don't see what's changed there.'

'Yes, sir, but obviously while we were at *war* people weren't focusing on the economy!'

'Do I have to remind you that we are *still* at war?' President Hedges frowned.

'Well . . . yes, technically, of course. But we're not fighting at the moment, are we?'

'*Exactly* my question. Thank you,' President Hedges pointed out, opening his arms to explain his layman's point of view to the so-called experts around the table. 'Seems to me, gentlemen, that the problem here ain't the ecology at all in the first hand! The figures speak for themselves – these folks dislook upon the fact that we have ceased bombing our enemies, plain and simple! They feel let down, and that is why that . . . *line* there is pointing down, too, cos that's the way how folks feel. Now, I'm a simple man, and I like a *straight* line! You can't tell me that is straight there, cos I can see for myself that it ain't. I see a nice, neat, flat line *a-a-all* the time we were bombing, and then it goes all droopy. It's a goddamned mess! Well, let me tell you something, people – when I was a governor, my line was straight as a dead man's cardiogram, and do you know why? Because I kept executing *scary* people, that's why! That made folks feel a little *safer* in their lives, and reminded them that there are things a whole lot worser in the world than not being able to put your kid through college! So could someone please tell me *what* has happened to my line now I'm President, and I don't want to hear any bull about unemployment cos I can see the unemployment line for myself, and it is going *up*!'

There was a brief silence in the room. These meetings had been much easier before the war, when the issues at hand were generally too dull to interest the nation's leader and he had been perfectly happy to accept whatever opinion they collectively came to on a subject, presuming he attended at all. That had changed almost overnight, however, thanks to the SECI. That, in the President's eyes, was a simple question of good versus evil.

He was on home territory, and ever since he'd kind of got into the habit of thinking he was running the country. He'd even got interested in the rest of the world, and had started phoning the leaders of foreign nations. Especially Prime Minister Flyte – who he had been thrilled to find spoke the same language, even if he talked like a pansy.

'Well, sir . . .' Mitchell Madison, the Defence Secretary, sighed. 'The trouble is they surrendered.'

'*Some* of them surrendered, Mitch,' the President corrected him. 'Don't forget the ones who ran away.'

'Oh, we haven't, sir – we're looking for them, make no mistake about it. But they seem to be hiding themselves pretty well right now.'

'Well, I believe bombs are a fairly effective way of flushing people *out* of a hiding place, Mitch.'

'That's true. If we know where they are hiding.'

'What? If we *know* where they're hiding, Mitch, then what is the point of flushing them out? Just deal with the sons of bitches right there – locate, cremate and bury in one go, OK. That's what bombs are *for*, ain't it? But that ain't the point I'm making. My *point* . . . the one I'm making . . . is that we should be asking ourselves . . . you know . . . *what is the point here?* You see what I'm saying? Now, I believe that the point of what I'm saying is that we don't *know!* We don't know who in hell these people are or what they are planning to do, we just know that they are *out there*, and some of them are a whole lot worse than others! And that is *scary*, because it's a goddamned *messy situation!* Now what I would like to see, and what the Atlantian *people* would like to see . . . is some kind of a *list*.'

'A . . . list,' Madison repeated.

'Right. We have to cut through all the *bull* here and get us a *list*, don't you see? Like they have for *music*? Do you see what I'm saying – how do you tell what music is *good*, and what music is *bad*? Well, you have a . . . a . . . what do they call that thing?'

'The Top 50?' Madison frowned.

'Yeah, right. The Top 50! That's what we need – something folks can get a *grip* on, you know? As an ordinary person, that's all I want to know – who is the *worst* guy out there, and who have we got to deal with *first*, and *then* . . . once we've dealt with him . . . who's up *next*, you see? Now why is that so much to ask?'

'Because . . .' Madison answered, '. . . with all due respect, sir – it's a little bit more complicated than that.'

The President drew in a deep breath, his eyes flicking towards the chart. He banged the table impatiently, rose from his seat and prepared to go.

'No, it *ain't!*' he announced sternly. 'That's the whole trouble with you guys – you think about things so much that you always wind up saying they're *complicated!* Well some things just *ain't* – last time I checked the Holy

Book it seemed to me that Good was Good and Evil was *still* Evil! And, if I'm not mistaken, the Lord managed to fit all of it on *one tree*, people! So let's simplicate this situation a whole lot and say that we have a tree just like that one – some of the apples are sweet, and crunchy, and some are bad. What I am asking for is a *list* of the bad apples, gentlemen. And then we are to *shake* that tree until they fall off.'

Striding over to the door, he paused with his palm on the handle.

'Now, you all know that I'm not interested in *details*! It's not my job to take care of details, gentlemen – that's your job! And I can insure you that the Atlantian people are not interested in details *one eency-weency* bit more than I am – because it ain't their job, either! They hate thinking about that stuff just as much as me! So the point is not "What are we doing to stop the resecession?", the point is "What are we doing to stop people *caring* about the darned resecession?"! Well, I'll tell you what we're going to do – we're going to get us a Top 50! Is that clear? I expect to know *exactly* what I'm dealing with one week from now. Once we have that and we start acting upon it, let me tell you . . . you will see that the line there gets *straightened out*!'

A wistful expression came over his face as he pulled open the door, and he turned to explain in a soft voice.

'I love this country. I love democracy. I love freedom,' he said. 'But there are certain *God-given* rules that apply on Earth as in Heaven, and you cannot lead *any* kind of folks if you don't remind them of those rules, because folk will not obey you. They will question you, and complain, and never feel like whatever they have is enough and that they should be thankful for it. But do you *know* what Rule No. 1 of life is, people?'

He looked over the faces gathered in the room, the men and women who, for all their greater knowledge and intelligence, could never hope to occupy his position in society.

'Come on – not *one* of you brilliant minds can tell me Rule No. 1 of life?'

Seeing no response was going to come, he allowed himself a small laugh.

'Hell, it ain't very *complicated*, you know,' he shrugged. 'Rule No. 1 is that people fear death.'

The President exited the room, leaving the shaken Cabinet members staring at a closed door. One by one they let their breath go and sank back in their chairs. On the spur of the moment, there was nothing much to be said.

They all knew the man they worked for didn't have a clue about anything.

But that certainly did not make him an idiot.

The End minus 24 days

'. . . express my complete support and the support of *all* my countrymen for Secretary-General Bisi Kawan in his efforts to achieve a diplomatic solution to this crisis, and echo his call for a moment of calm in which we can, I'm sure—'

'Glen Stokopolous – I can see you are not in agreement with that.'

'Well, Ayesha – how long is a piece of string? I'm a great admirer and personal friend of Bisi's, but even *I* would say that he's letting the wool be pulled over his eyes if he thinks that *time* is all that is needed here. We've had time. The President gave General Harouni a very *clear* deadline, and . . . well . . . it's *over*! I think the President is absolutely *right* to stick to what he said, and I support him in that.'

'Rachid Biman – how do you respond to that? Isn't the time for negotiations *over* now?'

'But . . . but . . . Miss Novak . . . when *was* the time for negotiations? This is the whole problem. President Hedges said "no negotiations"! Ever since then, my people have been trying to put *their* point of view forward, which is that there *must* be—'

'Sorry – let me just get a response to that. Glen Stokopolous?'

'Yeah, what Rachid Biman is calling for here, frankly, are negotiations about negotiations. Now, *clearly*, that is a step *backwards!* We could dance round in circles like that for *months,* when this is a situation that has to be dealt with *rapidly,* which is what lies behind the whole Atlantian drive to *avoid* this confrontation.'

'But your government *started* the confrontation!'

'That's a *complete* distortion of the situation, and you know it. All you're doing is proving *why* negotiations are a—'

Chapter Five

In which we return to Errat, where our hero is being interrogated about his role in the attempted assassination of General Harouni, and is subsequently rescued by his older brother

«There is one thing I don't understand about all this,» the interrogating officer mused. «Why aren't *you* dead?»

Saman shrugged and shook his head. It was a question he had asked himself many times since the war. Not because he did not have an answer, but because he had for so long wished that he had been murdered along with his family. It would have been infinitely preferable to being left alive to bury them. Gradually, however, and entirely against his will, over the years he had found himself not only coming to accept the simple fact that he was alive, but even finding – although at first it felt like a betrayal of all the love that he ever bore them – that he was grateful.

He had his bees to thank for that, for showing him that life remained a source of wonderment no matter what men did to cheapen and sully it. Men had no say in the simple fact of the world's perfection. Which was, he suspected, exactly what some men could not bear about life: the world was not theirs, they could merely accept to be a tiny part of it for the time they were given, as Saman had decided to do, or cling to their pitiful little fantasies of being more than that and die in frustration, hatred and misery.

«He said . . . their leader, I mean . . .» he answered softly, quelling the memory as best he could, «. . . he said that if I was a man I would kill *myself*. I think it amused him to spare me.»

«And you claim not to know *who* these men were who murdered your wife and children . . .» the officer continued, «. . . yet you were *there* when it happened. How is that possible?»

«It's possible because I didn't ask them which side they were fighting on.» Saman sighed. «It really did not seem very important at that particular moment. Clearly we were on the wrong side no matter who they were, because we were not on *their* side. Because I had made the mistake of choosing not to be on *anybody's* side.»

«Why not?»

«Because, like most *other* people when the war started, I did not see what there was to fight about.»

«And yet most men of your age fought.»

«They were smarter than me. They chose a side because they appreciated, as I failed to do, that staying neutral was the one way of making *everyone* your enemy.»

Saman smiled at the young policeman. Not that he was a real policeman, of course. He was from the Interior Ministry, one of Malek Galaam's men, and solely concerned with rooting out political dissidents. At a guess, he was about half Saman's age, so making him of the generation that had still been children when the general stopped being a ruthless warlord and became their beloved leader. He probably couldn't understand what Saman was talking about.

«And you would have me believe that you have never wished to seek revenge upon those responsible for what happened?»

«How could I seek revenge if I didn't know who they were?»

«But what if you *did* know?' the man insisted. 'What if they had been Nationalist soldiers and you *knew* that? Then, clearly, you would have a motive for killing our beloved General . . .»

«But I didn't try to kill him.»

«So you claim. You have yet to convince me that the bees were not a diversionary tactic to allow your fellow terrorist time to reach the General.»

«For the last time – the bees only got out *after* the explosion! It was a bit late for a diversion, don't you think?»

The policeman sighed, reluctant to accept that Saman had no connection whatsoever to the incident, because in that case only the fanatical soldier remained. And what remained of him was in a bucket. The General wanted someone to punish for interrupting his poem.

«That might just have been incompetence on your part,» he suggested.

«Please – can't you speak to my brother? He knows Malek Galaam personally and I'm sure he can sort all of this out.»

«You're filthy,» Farrukh announced as they got to his car. He opened the boot and snatched out a blanket. «Put this on the seat – I don't want you messing up the leather on top of everything else.»

Saman complied silently with his elder brother's wishes. Even now, almost half a century old, he felt like a naughty child. Farrukh slammed the door on getting in and, unusually for an Errati, put on his seat belt.

«I've got things to take care of at the factory,» he said, driving off. «You'll just have to wait until I've finished or make your own way home. I'm not going to taxi you about the place.»

«Fine,» Saman answered softly.

«But you do *not* leave my office,» he snapped. «I'm not having the workers see a member of my family in this state. You've embarrassed me enough for one day as it is.»

«Fine.»

They drove on without speaking for a while, the quiet purr of the vehicle's expensive engine only compounding the silence.

«You realize, of course, that you are now on the list of suspected terrorists?» Farrukh said eventually, «There's nothing *I* could do about that. They will probably have you under surveillance, you know.»

«Well, if I'm not doing anything wrong it doesn't—»

«Yes it *does* matter!» his brother fumed. «It's an embarrassment to *me*! You may be too busy with your bloody bees to appreciate this, but what you do affects the rest of this family, Saman! When one is not a . . . *bee farmer*, it is necessary to maintain good relations with members of the Government. You don't succeed in business just by being good at *making things*, you know.»

«I'm very sorry if this has made life difficult for you, brother,» Saman answered as contritely as possible whilst not quite accepting that it was his fault. «Truly I am.»

«Well, it has. Do you realize what it could do to my business if the Atlantians ever got wind of this?»

Farrukh's shoe factory was on the outskirts of town, in the free-trade zone, next to a baby-food plant. Saman had only ever visited it once before, and was certainly not against the fact that his brother was forbidding him to enter it today as he had found the experience thoroughly depressing. The stench of glue had made him faint within seconds of walking in, and he was sure that it was this smell as much as the long hours bent over sewing machines that was responsible for the vacant look he saw on most of the people who worked there. Nobody spoke or smiled, it was like a factory of the damned, a kind of earthly limbo where everyone – whether man, woman or child – had exactly the same broken gaze. He was still troubled by the memory of a particular girl of around twelve stitching reflective crescents to the trainers they were making that day, a girl of extraordinary beauty whose gentle features and perfect nose were framed by dead eyes that made her very beauty into a deeper form of horror than if she had been born with no nose at all.

He wondered what the Atlantians for whom Farrukh's products were destined would think if they knew that the lasts upon which the shoes were made were in fact prosthetic limbs intended for war victims. Farrukh had got them cheap through some deal he'd made with the Government – hundreds of white plastic legs, in all sizes, that now stuck feet upwards from the work tables and upon which his employees made, of all things, sports shoes.

Ironically, the prosthetic limbs had originally come from Atlantis.

But then, of course, so had the landmines.

Actually, none of it was in the least bit ironic. If his bees had taught Saman to appreciate just one thing about the world, it was that everything was connected. And whether they liked it or not, and no matter to what insane lengths they went to deny it, men were no different whatsoever.

«My own brother under suspicion of terrorism . . .» Farrukh muttered angrily as they waited for the security guard to lift the barrier to the free-trade zone. «It's so . . . *fucking* lower class, Saman!»

The End minus 23 days

'. . . still having problems with that link to Clarissa Wong in Errat, apparently. So . . . well, Mr Madison, perhaps we have time for one more question. How do you feel about the state of the economy?'

'As Secretary of Defence, Miss Novak, it's really not my domain to talk about—'

'Yes, but any senior member of government must have an opinion about the recession, surely?'

'Who said we were in recession? This is a *readjustment*, which is actually good news for the economy in the long run.'

'Right. Excuse me, yes. Because although the economy has been *shrinking* under President Hedges, it's not a recession because . . . because he wanted that to happen?'

'Yes. The fact is that there was excess fat in the economy last January, and it has been . . . slimming over the last six months. That is not necessarily a bad thing at all. In fact, it's very healthy. Despite the pain this . . . *toning-up* has caused in some parts of the country, I think people will realize that it's all been worthwhile this summer when they see how much better the economy looks in . . . in . . . um . . .'

'A bikini?'

'Now you're putting words in my—'

'Ah, apparently we do have that link to Errat now. I've been talking to Mitchell Madison, Secretary of Defence, about war and whether we can hope to see the economy on the beach this summer. Now over to Clarissa Wong in—'

Chapter Six

In which we return to Atlantis and meet Cameron Hunt III, a Survivor, and learn of the long quest for closure following the horror of the Stock Exchange Computer Inferno that has now brought him, somewhat paradoxically, to an opening of his sphincter

'Is this the first time you've had your colon irrigated?' the bright-eyed young woman asked as she snapped on the rubber gloves. Her name was Purity.

Lying down with a small square of towel covering his genitalia, Cameron felt his cheeks flush and replied, somewhat hoarsely, that it was.

Purity paused in her blithe lubrication of the plastic nodule that she clearly proposed to insert in his anus, and turned to him with a smile.

'I kind of envy you – the first time is an *amazing* experience. There's *so* much detritus to come out!'

'Is that right?' Cameron answered weakly.

Her gaze sharpened as she asked, 'Say, do you by any chance eat red meat?'

'Uh-huh . . .' He frowned.

'Oh *wow*!' she grinned, the sparkle in her eyes seeming to dance.

Cameron's smile perfectly camouflaged his horror.

Colonic irrigation was, he told himself for the hundredth time, widely accepted these days.

It was his sister's idea, of course. She had suggested it, of all places, over dinner at their parents' house. Knowing her enthusiasm for remedies and curative practices from a bewildering variety of cultures and philosophies was not to be argued with, he had nodded politely despite the fact that her suggestion had magically caused the chicken to regenerate a certain featheriness on his palate, and hummed at her proposal in what he hoped was an appreciative manner.

'No, really, Cam – you *should*!'

He turned in amazement to face the new speaker.

His mother.

'You . . . ?' he garbled through the ball of fluff.

'Sure.' She shrugged. 'All our friends do it. Don't they, Cameron?'

His head movements by now adopting the jerking, permanently startled manner of a bantam cock, Cameron's gaze snapped round to face the elderly gentleman whose name and social position he had been proud to inherit.

'Well,' his father answered uncomfortably, 'I'm sure it's not quite accurate to say *all* our friends, darling.'

'We go twice a week,' his mother announced. 'Our bowels are like gun barrels.'

That was when, like the phoenix, the bird in his mouth was reborn to flight.

'So what do you do?' Purity asked as she connected the rubber pipe to the large bottle of greenish liquid that she now held.

'I'm . . . I'm a broker,' he confessed, feeling that this somehow added to the humiliation at hand. So much for being a Master of the Universe.

'Oh my *God* . . .' she gasped. 'Were you . . . you know . . . *there*?'

'Yes, I was.'

From the evident stiffness of his reply, she judged, 'You don't like to talk about it?'

'No, that's not it.' Cameron sighed. 'It's just . . . there's nothing to say. I mean, you know what happened. Everyone *knows* what happened. So . . . that's all there is to it. I don't feel that I have any special insights just because I was there.'

'Uh-huh.' She nodded in deep empathy. 'I hear you. I can understand that.'

She hung the bottle upside down, and opened the valve. Cameron stared as the green liquid began to trickle down the tube.

'What exactly is *in* that bottle?'

'Oh . . . just water and herbs, basically. It's totally natural.'

'Why's it so *green*?'

'Herbs are green. Now, this is probably going to tickle a little at first,' she warned him. 'But in a nice way. Don't try and stop it – just relax, OK?'

'OK,' he answered, trying not to twitch.

She leaned down to peer at his posterior as the green approached the bottom of the tube, saying, 'That's it – almost there.'

Cameron gritted his teeth, and squinted. Why had he let himself be talked into doing this? What the hell had happened to him since the Inferno? You could not deal with complex emotional problems simply by washing out your arse, for God's sake.

'Hey – you're holding it back,' she chided him gently from between his knees.

'No . . . I don't think I am.'

'Well, I can tell you that you are – I'm looking here, and the liquid has stopped!' she smiled. 'You've got to stop squeezing.'

'I'm not squeezing.'

'Oh *you're* squeezing all right. Just *relax*.'

77

'I *am* relaxed.'

Purity looked up at him and they locked eyes. She was pretty. Why the hell, Cameron wondered, would someone so pretty want to spend their days pumping out other people's bottoms? And what kind of a name was Purity, anyway?

'No, you're not,' she whispered.

'Look, I promise you.'

'*Oka-ay* . . . well, we'll just give you some time, shall we?' she smiled, crouching back down to observe the progress.

After a minute or so, during which she had sighed and tapped the tube a couple of times with her fingers, but apparently to no effect, her voice came from around his buttocks, gently enquiring. 'So . . . did you know a lot of people who didn't make it out?'

Cameron's eyes shut tight, tight like a child before a raised palm.

AbeAliceAustinBenBeverly*StopStopStop* . . .

Fuck almighty, I still have them in alphabetical order. I thought I'd made more progress than—

'*There* we go!' she announced triumphantly.

Cameron's jaw dropped as he felt the liquid rush up his bottom, and he gaped at the extraordinary rate at which the level of the bottle seemed to be going down.

'That's *good*!' She stood up to compliment him, 'See, it's not *so* bad, is it?'

'No . . .' he gasped.

'Seriously, I don't mean to pry,' Purity said with a soft seductiveness that gave every suggestion that she did, 'but doesn't coming through a thing like that make you feel kind of . . . *blessed*?'

A strange feeling was starting to come over Cameron. A warmth spreading from his bowels to envelop his whole body with a sense almost akin to bliss.

'Erhm . . .' he grunted. 'It doesn't really work out that way.'

*   *   *

Cameron had been to hell and back this last year. He'd thanked God with all his heart, then cursed him, found his faith and then found he was too sick to pray. Like some fucking yo-yo, as crazy and self-obsessed as those talk-show guests he'd always despised. Weak. Just so fucking *weak* that he could sometimes barely breathe. Reduced to taking each day at a time, no plan, fundamentally no more in control of his life than a bum on the street even though he was surrounded by comfort and wealth and family support.

The more he'd tried to find some kind of healing, to reconnect himself with the world, the more alone he had become. The support groups didn't work for him any more than it would help a man stranded on a desert island to find a message in a bottle sent by a man stranded on a different desert island.

People were different. For every person who had sunk into depression, there was another who soared with elation. He took the middle route, bouncing crazily from one to the other. One moment he might be there, lying safe and warm in bed, wrapped up in the instant like a baby cradled in his mother's arms, and the next he was falling vertiginously, sitting bolt upright and trying to snatch hold of the air. Teri was doing her best to cope, but her exhaustion was beginning to show. She said she didn't know from one moment to the next whom she was living with, like he was permanently swimming in and out of focus. The SECI had saved marriages, it had destroyed marriages, it took them and twisted them, turning them into something different before your eyes, like a party magician's balloon that might be going to become a butterfly, or a dog, or just pop.

It had been her suggestion that he try Baoist meditation. He'd been pretty surprised by that because she, like him, believed in God. Or at least he believed he did. Baoism was a radically different spiritual system, Teri admitted, but she argued that maybe it was like mixing standard medicine with a little homeopathy. Brother Steve, the monk whom he went to see, explained that the principle of Baoist meditation was to find one's *kahuma* or Inner Void, an infinitesimally small point inside oneself where the individual stopped and the universe began, somewhat like a keyhole through to infinity.

Brother Steve began the meditation by guiding him within, gently leading him deeper and deeper into his subconscious, or soul, or whatever one wished to call it. Although initially sceptical about the whole idea, Cameron found himself relaxing, the physical world seeming to let go of him as his astral self floated through the darkness, travelling to the centre of his own mind. At a given point, Brother Steve told him to let his astral self slowly come to rest and to open his Third Eye.

'Now, Cameron . . .' he had heard Brother Steve announce, 'you are in the very centre of your You-ness.'

The voice came to him from far away, a tranquil whisper.

'This is where . . . you will find . . . your Inner Void,' it said slowly. 'It is . . . a tiny point of darkness . . . somewhere . . . very close to you now. Look around yourself . . . very carefully . . . and tell me what you see.'

Completely relaxed now, almost asleep, Cameron did as he was told.

'I see . . . nothing,' he'd drawled. 'It's dark . . .'

'OK . . .' Brother Steve answered, 'but somewhere . . . in that darkness . . . there will be a small point . . . of darker darkness. *Absolute* darkness. It's just a tiny little circle we're looking for here.'

'No, honestly . . .' Cameron mumbled, 'it's completely dark . . .'

'You cannot see . . . a point?'

'I can't see anything . . .'

Brother Steve paused for a few seconds, and then gently instructed him, 'OK, Cameron . . . I want you to feel your astral self floating slowly . . . *backwards*.'

Cameron did as he was told, pulling back from the centre of his Him-ness.

'What do you see now?' Brother Steve asked.

'It's still dark . . .' Cameron droned.

'*Totally* dark?'

'. . . completely.'

'Are you sure your Third Eye is *open*?'

'. . . wide open . . .'

'Umm . . . OK . . . keep floating backwards . . .'

'Am I *inside* my *kahuma* or something?'

'No questions, Cameron . . .' Brother Steve reprimanded him. 'Just feel yourself floating . . . ba-a-ackwards . . .'

Cameron frowned as he approached the periphery of his subconscious and began to wake up.

'Is my Inner Void . . . unusually big?' he had asked.

'Hoo! That was *fast*!' Purity announced admiringly. 'I think this calls for another bottle.'

Cameron looked on blearily as she unhooked the empty container.

'. . . nother bottle?' he repeated.

'Yeah,' she nodded. 'Yeah. You're *real* dry.'

She plugged on a fresh bottle and hung it up, chirping, 'Here we go!' Cameron's eyeballs rolled as the liquid swooshed down the pipe. Whatever, he thought.

'So who do you work for?'

'I'm a partner in . . .' he murmured, '. . . actually, I'm on a sort of sabbatical at the moment. From Sacker Leviticus.'

'You're *kidding* me! she trilled. 'One of my boyfriends used to be with them. Do you know someone called Harlen Bryce?'

Cameron frowned. Bryce. He had a vague image of a guy – tall, preppy, nondescriptly handsome. A couple of years back. Nobody paid him much attention until he surprised them all by dropping out.

'I think so,' he answered. 'Didn't he join some kind of . . . *cult* or something?'

'*Harlen?*' she laughed. 'I don't think so! Amazing person – he's achieved so much since I first met him.'

'Oh yeah . . . what's he do these days?'

'For *money*, you mean?' she frowned. 'Anything, so far as I know – he's got a Trust. I was talking about *personal* achievement. With his body. He's really decontaminated himself – right down to the *cellular* level, you know?'

Cameron didn't know, but he wasn't too bothered about it. Right now, nothing seemed to bother him. All those questions – what his life was for, whether it amounted to more than making money, whether he was going to go back to Sackers . . . he didn't care.

It felt fantastic not to care.

'Sacker Leviticus . . .' Purity continued, 'that's real big, isn't it?'

'Yeah, it is. Well . . . was. We were hit pretty bad. Lost a lot of . . . a lot of . . . um . . .'

'People?'

'Business. I mean . . . because we lost the . . . *people* . . . we lost business. A lot of business.'

'Uh-huh.' She nodded sympathetically. 'So I guess then people had to be fired, right? That's harsh.'

'Iced,' he corrected her with a soft chuckle. 'Since what happened, we don't talk about people being *fired*. It's insensitive.'

To his surprise, Cameron Hunt III had discovered that he was sensitive. That he could cry – something he genuinely hadn't thought himself capable of doing any more. After the fire, people kept telling him that he was holding it all in too tight, that he had to get in touch with his feelings.

So he had, and, after due reflection, ended up swallowing a bottle of pills.

His sister – who claimed special understanding of his feelings on the grounds that she, too, had once swallowed a bottle of pills in the course of a particularly bad LSD trip as a teenager – had insisted he try Primal Scream therapy. At that moment, he felt his life was already beyond the ridiculous and so had given in without much of a battle.

Consequently, he found himself in the hands of a pair of 'therapists' – a man and wife team – who had taken him back to his infancy, back beyond any memory he was aware of having, regressing all the way to his mother's womb and the moment he was expelled from it into the cold light.

And he had screamed. He had truly, truly screamed.

He was an excellent subject, the two therapists agreed as Cameron lay on the floor, screaming for all he was worth. Maybe the best they'd ever seen.

'Isn't this beautiful?' the male therapist shouted over the howling. 'So much energy!'

Cameron had been barely aware of what was happening, of the pain bursting out of him in a high, almost screeching wail. He cried and cried, as though channelling the spirits of all those who had died that terrible day of the fire, screaming the shock of all their births in one, apparently endless, cathartic howl.

And yet it did not hurt. It seemed to flow out of his mouth like cool spring water gushing in an unbroken flow from a rock. Inexhaustible.

'Do you think he's almost finished?' the male therapist eventually yelled. 'It's really wonderful but . . . he's actually starting to get on my *nerves*!'

'Maybe we should try . . . I don't know . . . *comforting* him?' his wife replied. 'Are we allowed to do that?'

'Listen – he's had plenty of time to get over it by now. If you ask me, this is no longer his *primal* scream – he may just be the kind of baby who cries all the time.'

'Right,' she answered. 'I mean – God, it isn't *that* traumatic being born . . .'

But Cameron had not even begun to explore the full range of his primal screaming yet, their efforts to soothe him – cradling him, singing lullabies, stroking his hair – only resulting in a switch to an altogether more strident vocal register.

'*Do you think it's colic?*' the man shouted in despair.

'How the hell am *I* supposed to know?' the woman answered.

'Well, you . . . you know . . . as a *woman*, what do you think?'

'Oh, because that makes me fucking *psychic*, does it? Every time *I* go near the little bastard he screams like I'm the devil incarnate, for God's sake!'

Finally, driven to near-psychotic irritation by Cameron's incessant howling, they had tracked down his actual mother, who had advised administering a tea-spoon of watered-down brandy. When this didn't seem to produce any effect, they had decided to make allow-ances for the fact that he was – *physically*, at least – a middle-aged male, and offered him the bottle.

Cameron Hunt had no recollection of any of this.

His abiding memory of Primal Scream therapy was that it had given him a dreadful hangover. But at least that was better than the depression he had sunk into after being convinced to try Shamanism. Like an idiot, he'd travelled all the way to an Indian reservation just to be put through their ancient Earth Spirits ritual and discover his Power Animal.

Deep in a hallucinogenic trance, he had met a rat.

'Can't I choose something else?' he asked afterwards.

'You do not *choose* your Power Animal,' the shaman answered. 'It chooses you. There's no reason to feel shame – rats are very successful animals.'

'But I'd rather be an *eagle*.'

'Ah . . . we cannot all be eagles, Cameron Hunt,' the old man smiled. 'Some of us are buffaloes. Some of us are deer. That is the way of the Earth Spirits. You're a rat.'

'But I *hate* rats!'

'Then you have discovered something about yourself, haven't you? Will that be cash or cheque?'

'Oh my God . . .' Cameron whispered, looking in the bowl. 'Oh . . . my . . . God.'

'Pretty impressive, isn't it?' Purity called through the door. '*That* is what your body has been dealing with all these years.'

'Oh my God.'

'How do you feel?'

'. . . oh my *God*.'

'Uh-huh?' she laughed. 'It sounds like you've understood why we say that cleanliness is next to godliness.'

Afterwards, he felt different.

Finally, after all these months. In fact, he realized in the Recovery Room, it went beyond the trauma of the last year – something he had carried with him throughout his entire *life* fell into that bowl. He would have called it an Inner Darkness, if that were not somewhat too literal a description. He felt released.

'You shouldn't stop here,' Purity told him. 'This is just a start.'

'Abso*lutely*!'

'Good,' she smiled. 'OK. So when can you make another appointment?'

'When can you *give* me another appointment?'

'That's the attitude!' she laughed. 'If only more people got it like you do.'

'They will!' Cameron enthused. 'I'm going to tell everyone I know about you, believe me! Everyone should be doing this. Your company should be putting clinics on every street!'

He couldn't help giggling. That was the first time he had felt enthusiastic about *anything* – the base fact of being alive first and foremost – for far, far too long. And that was all he seemed to need. He was suddenly able to envisage the possibility of a future with optimism.

He meant what he had said: there ought to be a colonic irrigation clinic on every street, between the coffee shop and the burger house.

'Well, we do OK . . . but that's a little beyond our scope at the moment!' Purity grinned. 'What you would call a capitalization problem in your line of work, I guess.'

Purity's grin evolved into a somewhat bewildered smile as she looked his way. Cameron was staring at her as if she were an angel, his mouth opening and closing wordlessly. He put his fingers to his temples and shook his head.

'Oh my God!' he breathed. 'If capital is all you need, I can *arrange* that! That's what I do! Why did I not see this straight away? The potential here is enormous. We're dealing with colons – they're *universal*! It's so obvious! Why have you never thought about floating the company?'

'Umm . . . we're not really a *company* as such.' Purity frowned. 'It's more like a co-operative, you know? It's not about making money. There is a . . . *spiritual* side to all of this for us, see.'

'That doesn't matter!' he argued, as much with himself as her. 'Why *shouldn't* there be? Where does it say that a listed company cannot have a *higher* purpose than making money, so long as it *can* make money? Oh my God! For all these months I've been agonizing about my life, and you just breeze in with the answer! Of *course* there will be a market for that kind of share! It's *exactly* what is needed right now! We need to be investing in things that make life better, things that have some kind of further dimension than profit – *that's* how

86

you make the world a better place! A *child* could see that!'

'But . . .' Purity winced, '. . . like I say, we're not a company. We're a group of people who share a certain set of beliefs. We can't put ourselves on the Stock Exchange – it would be like . . . I don't know . . . like people buying shares in a *church*!'

The rapture dropped from Cameron's face.

He looked briefly confused, his head turned slightly to one side as if straining to hear some small sound nearby. An intense frown developed on his brow. It was not a sound he was struggling to hear, but a thought – a notion that was trying to express itself in the maelstrom of his brain.

Suddenly he sat bolt upright and turned back to look at Purity with an air of divine illumination.

'Oh my God,' he whispered in awe. 'Why *shouldn't* people buy shares in a church?'

The End minus 22 days

'. . . Kawan's peace mission to Errat ended in failure after the Secretary-General described his talks with General Harouni as having been *"frank and constructive"*. The gravity of the situation rapidly deepened after the Errati Foreign Minister appeared to contradict Bisi Kawan's analysis, tersely characterizing the three-hour discussion as *"frank, but positive"*. While UN officials worked furiously behind the scenes in an attempt to jump-start the stalled talks, the Secretary-General ominously declared himself to be *"optimistic"*, only to later downgrade his position in a further statement to *"hopeful"* and, by the end of the day any chance of a breakthrough was lost, with both parties declaring themselves to be *"open-minded and willing to discuss"*. While officials on either side have sought to place the burden of the blame for this descent into mutual acrimony onto their counterparts, a visibly weary Secretary-General returned from Errat, thanking the Atlantian government for its *"steadiness and clarity of position"* and announced that he saw little point in returning unless he had *"something big in his pocket"*. In an entirely separate development, described on all sides as *"an accident of timetabling"*, Congress has voted to unblock *"most, or a substantial amount"* of the huge arrears in Atlantis' payments to—'

Chapter Seven

*In which a somewhat irate hero has words with his
cousin about the business of the mail-order bees, and in
which we learn how Aziz came to fall in love with
Atlantis for the very same reasons that some of his
fellow Erratis despise it*

Saman, on the phone to his cousin in Atlantis, repressed
his terrorized fury and chose his words with care and
precision.

«What I'm saying is that you bloody nearly got me
fucking well killed, you silly bugger!»

A somewhat pompous silence greeted his argument.

«Aziz?» he prompted eventually, worried that he
might have offended the man responsible for his life's
recent digression into the lower depths of the Internal
Security bureau.

«I understand why you might want to blame me
for what happened, even though it wasn't actually my
fault,» Aziz answered softly. «I sense a lot of anger in
you, cousin.»

«Oh no, really . . . you're being too sensitive.»

«If you think about it, all I did was send you some
bees.»

«And *that's* another fucking thing, Aziz!» Saman
exploded. «Do you have any idea what you put those

poor creatures through? They travelled halfway around the world by *post*!»

«But that's precisely what I was trying to show you could be done.»

«Of course it *can* be done! You could ship yourself here in a bloody crate if you had enough stamps, but it'd make flying Economy Class seem fairly hedonistic, wouldn't it? These are *living creatures*, Aziz!»

The line got fat with silence again.

«I'm sorry,» his cousin finally replied.

«Really?»

«Completely. I apologize. I respect your point of view on this, even if it's not . . . the way most people see things.»

«What do you mean?»

«I don't mean anything.»

«Of course you mean *something*!» Saman pressed him. «You think I'm overreacting about the bees, don't you?'

«No, I don't. I understand that you feel this way about them . . . for personal reasons. I respect that, cousin.»

«What the . . . ? *What* personal reasons? There's nothing *personal* about it!»

«OK . . . there isn't. That's fine,» Aziz acquiesced. «So, do you want to hear my new name for the company? What I'm thinking is that we—»

«Whoa!» Saman cried. «Whoa. Just . . . just . . . *whoa* a little there.»

«What?»

«Well, yes . . . *what*?»

«What what?»

«I'd like to hear what my *personal reasons* are, if you don't mind.»

«Look – you don't have any, like you say, and that's totally fine by—»

«*Now*, please.»

He could hear Aziz sighing across the ocean. His cousin knew him well enough to realize that he was not about to let go of this. He was well aware that, for all his gentleness, Saman Massoudi could be a rather stubborn little ball of a man.

«All I meant . . .» he explained at last, «was that for most people bees are just . . . insects. Whereas for you, well, I think . . . I think you maybe . . . *subconsciously* . . . see them as a kind of . . . surrogate family, Saman. Perhaps. It's just . . . you know . . . a possibility.»

The pause that greeted his confession was no more or less quiet than Aziz's silences had been, but it somehow lacked their preening quality. It was a dumbfounded silence.

«Oh dear . . .» Aziz winced. «Look, I really didn't want to—»

«Aziz,» Saman interrupted him. «My wife and children were human beings. Bees are insects. I *do* know the difference, believe me.»

«I know, I only—»

«You've been watching too much Atlantian television, cousin.»

«You're absolutely right. I only—»

«Why don't you tell me about this new name you've come up with?»

Several minutes later, after much preambulation and laying out of all the reasons why his idea was a good one before he'd revealed what it actually *was*, Aziz proudly declared, 'The Boulder Mountain Honey Company!'

There was quietness on the other side of the world.

«What?» Saman answered eventually.

'The Boulder Mountain Honey Company!' he repeated.

«Why?»

«It sounds more Atlantian.»

«What do you mean it *sounds* more Atlantian? Of course it's more bloody Atlantian! But we are not in the Boulder Mountains, so we can hardly call ourselves The Boulder Mountain Honey Company, can we?»

Aziz shook his head. He should have guessed that Saman would react like this, he was always so *literal* about everything. It was a painfully slow and arduous task bringing him round to even the smallest innovation. He had no idea how behind the times he was.

Aziz, for his part, prided himself on having his finger on the pulse of the modern world. He'd never been to business school as such, but he had read all the books by the recognized business gurus, the latest being Alvin J. Krantz's life-changing guide *It Ain't Murder if No-one Calls the Cops.*

«I knew you'd say that and we *can*, actually, because our mountains contain boulders, too.»

«They are *hills*, Aziz, not mountains! Anyway, of course they contain boulders. By definition, you do not get squidgy mountains, cousin, but this does not give everyone who is up a hill the right to say they live in the Boulders!»

«Why not? Why should the rest of the world be penalized for the fact that the Atlantians couldn't think of a more imaginative name for a mountain range? So far as I'm concerned, the term Boulder Mountain is generic.»

«It's immoral, Aziz.»

«*Immoral?* For God's sake, Saman – we're in *business* here! That is what is called marketing! Would Fragrant Valley Toilet Paper have to be made in a *fragrant valley* by your logic? Everyone knows that a name is just a *name*!»

«If a name is just a name, cousin, then what's the problem with our being called the Al-Nur Bee and Comb Union, hmm?»

«It sounds *foreign*, that's what!» Aziz exploded. «You may not be aware of this, but Atlantians are at *war* with foreigners right now!»

«Not with us.»

«They don't fucking *know* who they are at war with!

92

In the meantime, so far as they are concerned, anything that is Al-something is pretty damned suspicious, cousin!»

«It's just *honey*.»

«No, that's where you're wrong, see? It's *not* just honey! Do you think Atlantian companies conquered the world by saying to themselves "Oh, it's just a burger," or "Hey, it's just a fizzy drink!" cousin? No! *No!* In their minds, they are at *war* with the rest of the world, fighting to make their culture dominant over everyone else's, by whatever means possible! You can call it free trade or whatever the hell you want, but the bottom line remains that it is one civilization, one culture, against another! The sooner you wake up and realize that we are fighting for our lives – our honey versus their honey – then the sooner *I* can implement a strategy for winning that battle. Stop thinking honey is sweet, healthy and la-di-da, and start thinking honey is a *weapon*! We can produce it *cheaper* than our enemies, Saman, but we are smaller than they are and there is no way we can beat them in hand-to-hand combat on the battlefield, which is why we have to use guerilla tactics. We have to exploit their weak points, turn their strengths against them, and defeat them from within! So we call ourselves The Boulder Mountain Honey Company and turn this wave of patriotism to *our* advantage! This is no time for idealism – all that matters is getting our honey into every household in the country, ramming it down their throats and *killing* our enemies! Believe me, I know the way Atlantians think, and if our situations were reversed they would not hesitate to do exactly the same thing to us.»

There was a stunned pause down the line. Aziz knew that he'd probably got a little carried away with his analogy, but he couldn't help it. He was on fire. A honey merchant on the edge.

That Alvin J. Krantz book had *really* inspired him.

*   *   *

Aziz loved Atlantis.

At heart, he felt he was an Atlantian. He didn't have citizenship yet, and realized that the current international situation was hardly going to help speed up his application, but he was already Atlantian in spirit. Indeed, that was what was unique about the country – whereas you could migrate to any other country in the world, become a citizen, live, work and die there, but never *be* one of them, becoming Atlantian was just a question of philosophy. The grandchildren of migrants elsewhere were still outsiders, and probably would be for generation upon generation until miscegenation washed away their physical characteristics, but you became a fully-fledged Atlantian the moment you espoused the nation's ideals. In that sense, he had been a proto-citizen even as a child growing up in Errat.

Not that he romanticized the things Atlantis was supposed to stand for, like democracy. Indeed, it always amazed Aziz how impressed Westerners expected everyone to be by their occasional trips to the ballot box, when it seemed to him that the crucial test of the system, surely, ought not to be whether they *had* a vote, but whether they had any real options in what they were voting *about*. As an outside observer, it seemed obvious to him that the political parties of the West were operating a cartel. They had the vote market stitched up. He never voiced this opinion out loud, however, because, as someone who had escaped dictatorship and war, he didn't really give a damn about corruption or how a country was governed so long as he was left in peace.

The beauty of Atlantis was that people were free in the *natural* sense. The nation had cast off the chains of civilization, the burdens of class and caste that dictated life everywhere else, and released its citizens into the wild. Yes, they had a constitution, but the freedom was based on something subtler than what had been written down on paper, more radical than any revolutionary proclamation. If animals were free, after all, it was not by constitutional arrangement. Money was muscle, and you could do anything you wanted, live any way you wanted, so long as you could pay for it. You could buy anything, even exemption from the most basic laws of the land, because the bottom line was that rich people did not get sent to prison for murder.

Aziz respected that. It was profoundly honest and, ultimately, fairer than any other system he knew. The role of the Constitution, as he saw it, was simply to stop anyone imposing themselves on others by custom or military might. No matter who you were, it cost an awful lot of money to get yourself elected.

Why some people had a problem with it, Aziz did not know. What were they offering as an alternative? A system based on ethics? *Whose* ethics, based on *what*? The moral terrain of the globe was so uneven that one society's idea of justice was another's barbarism, and what was perverse and decadent to one group was called a Human Right by the next. People were by nature incapable of objectivity, and so the only hope they had was to *create* some artificial, inhuman standard that could be applied to any situation. Which, of course, they had done.

It was called money.

Atlantis had certainly not invented money, but one could be forgiven for thinking otherwise. What it was, however, was the only country that had chosen to make money's rule absolute. And cultured people all over the world looked down on Atlantians for that, without ever asking themselves if the things *they* judged one another by weren't ultimately far more unjust. Why, after all, had it always been the poor and oppressed who had flocked to this land?

Yes it was unethical, and yes it was inhuman, but that is precisely what was enlightened about it.

*　　*　　*

95

The bell rang a few minutes after he'd got off the phone to Saman. Aziz checked his watch as he approached the door, calling, 'Who is it?'

'Corona Police Department,' a woman's voice answered, 'Can you open the door, please, sir?'

Aziz let the door snap ajar on its chain. The cop was a young Latino woman, in her mid-twenties, dark hair twisted up in a bun under her cap, dark eyes meeting his with chick-gang toughness.

'Yes?'

'Aziz Hamanancy?'

'That's right,' he answered with a lump in his throat.

'Can you let me in, please, sir?' she asked. 'I have a few questions.'

He pushed the door back a little and slid off the chain. Suddenly the door crashed open and she charged in, one hand going for his collar, the other for his balls.

'Thank you very much,' she snarled.

She shoved him backwards, sending him staggering back down the corridor, and slammed the door shut behind her. Her right hand reached for the nightstick dangling from her belt and she caught up with him before he'd regained his balance, spinning him round to thrust him face first against the wall.

'Hands on the wall!' she snapped, thwacking his behind with the stick. 'And *spread*!'

Aziz obeyed instantly, his hands reaching high and his legs parting. He felt the nightstick pass under his testicles and jam against the wall.

'*Further!*' she shouted, kicking aside his right foot so that he landed, balls first on the stick.

'*GAH!*'

'*Shut up!*'

Holding the nightstick in place, she squatted down and began to frisk him, firm hands running up his inner thighs, first one side, then the other. She got back up and continued her search – checking his chest, armpits and belly before arriving at his groin. Her fingers ran down past his belt to the zip of his trousers, where they stopped. He felt her cheek brush up against his ear, and a soft, dangerous voice whispering, 'What . . . is . . . *this*?'

Aziz had been thirteen years old when he fell in love with Atlantis.

He was hesitating on the cusp of manhood – still young enough to be allowed to sit in with his mother and her friends when they met in the privacy of their houses in the afternoon, but aware that it would soon no longer be possible, and why. He was happy then. The TV would be on all the time as the women chatted, and half their talk was of soap stars and pop singers, between the gossip and laughter, and worrying about their weight. For the most part, bereft of their veils and robes, there was little to choose between them and the women on TV. His mother's friends liked eyeshadow and bright lipsticks, shoulder pads and sequins, big belts and high heels – the diametrical opposite of the absurdly modest creatures they played on the street, shy as moles and moving in their own twilit tunnel of cotton. His mother, in particular, loved the trashy world of Atlantian TV with its tales of scandal and betrayal, infidelity and true love. She liked heady perfumes and black underwear with silver studs.

Aziz was beginning now to spend time with men, too, to hear what *they* talked about, and they did not talk about any of this. It was as though it simply did not exist, the world of love and sensuality, even though he knew they returned each evening to wives who daily studied themselves with the sole objective of pleasing their husbands. Men's talk seemed mostly to be of money, which itself was a forbidden topic in the family home. It was as though the world had to split itself in two to accommodate a man's idea of himself.

Aziz had long known that he was different from his

brothers. He did not yearn to be a man, as they did. He loved hearing his mother's dirty laugh and admiring the way she held court among her friends – smart and witty and daring – but once he was a man, he would no longer see that side of her, her true self. Soon, she would retreat behind a facade of deference, as she had with his older brothers, treating him with the same automatic respect as every other male.

Aziz did not want to be a man if it meant losing his mother. He did not want respect on those terms. And how, he wanted to ask his father, could respect mean anything if it was granted equally, regardless of a person's individual virtues, as a default response to his having testicles? But he could not ask that without provoking his fury, and anyway he knew what his father would reply, even if it did not answer his question.

God had made women attractive to test the faith of men. Therefore, it was a man's duty to control the women in his charge, to save them from themselves and demand irreproachable modesty at all moments when they were not alone with others of their sex, or in the privacy of the marital bed.

But Aziz did not see it that way. In his opinion, if God had truly made women attractive for this reason, then his father and all men like him were clearly cheating on the test . . .

His hands against the wall, Aziz heard the rattle of the lady cop's handcuffs as she unhooked them from her belt. The nightstick slid out from between his legs and came round to poke vertically up under his chin.

'You know the score, punk,' she snarled, reaching up to snap a steel bracelet around his left wrist. She pulled his arms down and chained them together behind his back. 'You have the right to shut the fuck up. Anything you say can and will be used against you in—'

'Please,' he begged, 'I haven't done any—'

'*Shut it!*' she snapped, her thigh thrusting up against his balls.

Aziz gasped, his legs giving way underneath him. His chin jerked back away from the nightstick.

'*Keep still!*' she shouted, shoving on the back of his head. His chin dropped forward, grazing past the tip of the nightstick, which slid up his face to lodge itself in his eye socket.

'*OW! SHIT!*' he screamed. '*My fucking eye!*'

'God!' the cop yelped, letting go of the stick and catching his face in her hands. 'Are you OK?'

'*Ow! Ow! Ow!*' he whimpered, one eye shut tight.

'I'm *so* sorry . . .' she said, gently wiping the tears away with her thumb. 'Can you still *see*!'

He winced, blinking tentatively. Through a wash of tears, he saw the cop's anxious face as she examined his eye for visible signs of damage.

'It's OK,' he answered eventually. 'You just caught it on the edge.'

'Are you sure?'

'Yeah . . . don't worry.'

She brushed the last of the tears away, frowning anxiously.

'I can't *see* anything there . . .'

'It's all right now, honestly.'

'OK . . . so long as you're sure.'

She nodded, bent down to pick up her stick and thwacked his buttocks with it.

'*On your knees, bitch!*'

At thirteen years of age, watching an Atlantian TV channel on satellite, he'd seen the ad that changed his life. A good-looking young man walked down a street in a rough neighbourhood of some nameless Atlantian city, wearing a white T-shirt and a gently faded pair of blue jeans. The camera filmed him through the wire-mesh fence of the basketball court he was passing, hanging a pace or two behind to highlight his attractively muscular posterior. Suddenly, for no apparent reason, a motorcycle cop drew up alongside him, siren briefly howling even though the young man's innocence of any crime seemed immediately apparent from the bewilderment on his face. The camera dropped to ground level to catch the leather boot pushing down the motorbike's stand, rising up the dark leg as the cop dismounted, drifting up past a soft, curvaceous behind that betrayed her sex. The young man, seeing that behind at the same moment, understood and turned to face the wire fence, placing his hands against it and spreading his legs. The cop knelt to frisk him although the tight simplicity of his clothing made it instantly clear that he was hiding nothing about his person. Her hands rose up his thighs, lingering on his butt, and the man's expression suggested this was not the first time he had been subjected to this treatment. Satisfied, she pulled off her helmet, long dark hair cascading down over her shoulders as she turned him with a smile and went to kiss him against the wire fence.

The very first time Aziz saw it, the advert hit him like a punch to the gut. The revelation struck him that in all the world there was nothing he found sexier than the female body in uniform. A woman with authority, with power over a man such as himself. The kind of woman that he would only find for real one day if he went to Atlantis.

It was a testament to the extraordinary power of advertising that from that day on his sympathies lay with a foreign nation he had never visited. In thirty seconds, he had been sold on the Atlantian way of life, and persuaded to transfer allegiance from his own cultural heritage to another. On the other hand, the agency responsible for producing this amazingly successful piece of propaganda should have been fired by its client, because even after repeated viewings he could never remember which brand of jeans was actually being promoted.

'You want more, punk?' Esperanza snarled, trying to stop herself from laughing as the client writhed ridiculously around on the floor under her boot.

Juliette was right – this beat hell out of waitressing.

Go figure. You offer men respect and service with a smile, in return for which you get some loose change, your butt groped by drunks, and ten leering propositions a night. You treat them like scum, whup their butts with a stick, and they can barely find banknotes big enough to express their gratitude.

Now that she'd been doing this for a couple of months, her doubts had evaporated – how could she be a hooker when *she* wasn't the one being abused, when she didn't even have to have sex? Compared to what she did now, *waitressing* seemed like prostitution – that sense of being exploited, of being on display, and knowing that the size of her tips would be in direct relation to how tight a top she wore.

'And when you . . . smite them on the behind, Esperanza . . .' Father Miguel had croaked after she had explained all this to him in the privacy of the confessional, '. . . what do they do?'

'Well . . .' she whispered, '. . . they kind of . . . yelp with excitement.'

'I see,' he answered, clearing his throat. 'And . . . ?'

'Umm . . .' Esperanza giggled, 'I guess you could say they turn the other cheek, Father.'

Most of the world's men, Aziz had decided, were cowards. And bullies.

The men of Errat, certainly, were too cowardly to admit the truth – that they had to impose their rules on women by force because they were afraid of the fact that ultimately, in a wider physical sense, females were the more powerful creatures. Males were merely stronger, which wasn't the same thing at all, and they knew it.

And deep within all those who so passionately despised Atlantis, who railed against its decadence and materialism, the dark heart of their hatred was neither its bourgeois obsession with wealth and comfort, nor its soulless rationality and relativism, nor its worship of the individual, nor even its moral laxity. All of these things were factors, of course, but he suspected they could all be traced back to the same ultimate horror at the nation's core.

Women talked back.

From that flowed all other evils in their eyes, whether they realized it or not. For in a culture where women were free, and educated, and opinionated, boyish ideas of grandeur and heroism became ridiculous. And if a man had to seek the *approval* of a woman, he was no longer a man, for the things women approved of were not heroic. Liberated women put their families and homes before grand ideals, they believed it no more than a pathetic and foolish waste to kill others or sacrifice oneself for honour when a compromise was possible, and, above all else, they were free to *seduce* men into following their will.

At heart, the fanatics of the world could have accepted the fact that Atlantis was liberal, democratic and capitalist. They could have lived with the idea that this meant Atlantians were richer, and more powerful, and more free than they could ever hope to be. If only they had acted like men. It was the thought that they did the bidding of women that made their superiority an abomination in the eyes of history.

This so-called war was not something truly new, he suspected. It was being fought more in the name of religion than politics, but it had all the same ingredients as the last great war, in which the enemies of the victorious bourgeois alliance behind Atlantis had espoused a heroic creed of manliness and subservience to an absolute ideal, and believed the purity of that ideal would assure them victory. Yet when, in defeat, those countries had been forced to liberate women, their ideals had melted away and they had themselves become allies of Atlantis.

Aziz, for his part, had no doubt that Atlantis would triumph over this latest threat, and that a generation or two from now historians would look back over the previous hundred years and say that it was one single fight that had underlain the whole epoch.

The War of the Sexes.

Which women, ultimately, would have won.

'That was . . . it was . . .' Aziz frowned, searching his wallet for Esperanza's money.

'Yeah, I know,' she smiled. 'We aim to please.'

'If . . . another time I mean . . . if I wanted to ask for you especially . . .'

'Hope,' she smiled, hanging by the door. 'Just ask for Hope.'

Esperanza took the money he offered, not counting it – knowing, indeed, that it was probably more than the agency rate. She put a mac on over her cop outfit, shook him by the hand and said, 'Listen, if you want a *real* experience, I can bring some friends with me next time . . . Just call the agency and tell them you want the Zero Tolerance.'

The End minus 20 days

'. . . no overnight hospitalization and *won't* cost you an arm and a leg. *Heaven Nose* . . . because ordinary people are special too.'

So are special people ordinary too? the Angry Teenager asks. If so, are some people *especially* ordinary? What the fuck are you *saying*?

'*This* is WINN 24/7 – non-stop *World* Information Network News, reporting events from your point of view, with Ayesha Novak . . .'

'Welcome back, and following up on this morning's terrifying bee attack just outside the town of Dumona we rejoin Benson Gloag *live* on the scene where rescue workers are still struggling to get the situation under control. Benson, what are the latest casualty figures you've been given down there?'

The screen splits to show a reporter in full bee-keeping regalia, standing before a trailer home, smoke pouring from its windows.

'We do not know yet if a jar of honey was to be seen on the breakfast table this morning in the Winberghs' family home, but if it was then the cruel irony of the tragedy that stuck shortly after eight a.m. is all the more bitter for the sweetness of that innocent-seeming pot. For it was at that moment, as Clyde Winbergh was preparing to leave for work in the nearby steel plant – work that he considered himself lucky still to have following recent cutbacks in the labour force – that neighbours say they saw a huge dark cloud descend upon the modest trailer and heard the screams of the children. Why the bees chose this as their destination rather than any of the other, identical trailers we will probably never know, just as it remains unclear whether their subsequent frenzy of stinging throughout the trailer park was the *result* of mass panic by the inhabitants or simply the cause of it. Accounts vary here depending upon whom you talk to, from those who describe the bees as having arrived "hell-bent on destruction" and others who claim that they were quite calm until someone, possibly Clyde Winbergh himself, tried to smoke them out and accidentally started a fire that soon swept throughout the park.

'While there are only two confirmed deaths so far, rescuers say that as many as *twenty-six* people have been hospitalized in critical condition, suffering from a mixture of toxic shock, burns and gunshot wounds. The current whereabouts of the swarm remains a mystery, as does the key question of whether these were Jana bees or simply a local variety that happened to descend on the park. Tensions here have been running high lately, and there are unconfirmed rumours that a gang of local people may have suspected a nearby bee-keeper of being a terrorist and set fire to his hives last night, so causing the swarm. Either way, this terrible tragedy offers a sobering foretaste of the horror that could soon become a regular feature of life in Atlantis. What, you cannot help asking yourself, if this had happened at a kindergarten – how much more tragic might it have been, how many innocent little lives would have been lost? And as people here try to pick up the pieces and make sense of what has happened to their peaceful community, some are starting to ask *who* is to blame for this – why was there no warning, where were the rescue services when it happened and why were they not better prepared for this kind of situation? Amid the grief and the shock here this morning, one can sense the anger of a community that feels it has been let down and is now counting the cost of other people's failures, Ayesha . . .'

'What is Governor *Hedges* doing about this swarm?'

'Well, Ayesha, the President's brother is under a lot of pressure this morning to declare a State of Emergency, but he has yet to make that announcement or provide any specific details of how he intends to prevent a repeat of this tragedy. The more time he wastes, of course, the louder the accusations of indecisiveness and insensitivity on his part are becoming here. The Governor's position is complicated by the fact that this is a state with a large honey-producing industry – some people here claim he received campaign funds *from* that sector and is now reluctant to take any action that might threaten the interests of local bee farmers. In the meantime, people here feel anxious and abandoned, and many are taking their own steps to protect their loved ones: removing children from school, taking the day off work, and barricading themselves in their houses until they feel it is safe to—'

Chapter Eight

In which we return to Atlantis and meet Cameron Hunt's wife who, due to a regrettable misunderstanding arising out of an otherwise exemplary case of international co-operation, will be responsible for setting in motion the chain of events that will ultimately lead to war being declared upon our hero

Gillian Horrie's eyes narrowed to slits as she contemplated the message on her computer screen.

'The file could not be opened because the program that originally created it . . .' she chirped sarcastically, trailing off as a feeling of violent techno-hate overwhelmed her.

'You useless piece of *crap!*' she spat. 'Oh, so it's *my* fault, is it, you smug little . . . jumped-up . . . *toaster*? *Aargh!*'

Across the large desktop that took up almost all the space in the office, Teri Hunt's head poked around her own terminal.

'You mustn't give it the satisfaction of getting a rise out of you, Gill,' she advised. 'This only *encourages* them.'

'But . . . but why does it *hate* me so much?'

'Because it is many, many times more intelligent than you but, at the end of the day, you are a flesh and blood creature who can go home while it is doomed to spend its short life sitting on a desk in a poky little office. Because it will never know even the simple pleasure of taking a bath after a hard day's work.'

'*I'll* give it a bath!' Gillian announced, eyes shining.

Teri smiled, hooking a lock of dark hair behind her ear. 'Give me the file. I'll see if I can open it.'

Nothing could faze Teri this morning. She was untouchable, as though in a state of higher consciousness. She and Cameron had done it last night for the first time in months, and in no uncertain manner. They were like a brand new couple with electricity in their fingertips, passion coming over them in a summer storm from the first clue of a charge in the air to the gloriously violent crescendo and soft patter of rain as the rumbles faded, leaving the air clean and sweet as a spring dawn.

No quick pop song, but the full aria.

Cameron's visit to the colonic irrigation clinic seemed to have had the most remarkable effect on him. He was adamant that she, too, had to try it out – a suggestion that she didn't receive with great enthusiasm.

'I don't know, darling – I'm thrilled that you found it such a . . . fulfilling experience, I really am, but I don't think it's my scene.'

'All I'm asking you to do is to give it a *try*!'

'I . . . it's not the moment for that right now. The country is at *war*, darling, and I work in Intelligence. I work on the *specific* part of the world that we are most worried about. Do you realize what that means? I don't have time to get my colon irrigated.'

'What – *ever*?' Cameron frowned. 'That's it – end of story?'

'For the moment.'

'But you will eventually?'

'Yes,' she sighed. 'OK? Once the war is *over*, I will have my colon irrigated.'

For the first time since this all began, Teri found a

certain comfort in the thought that the war was probably *never* going to be over, at least in her lifetime.

Cameron was too excited to see that was what lay behind her acquiescence to his demand. He was wrapped up in his plans to float the organization behind the colonic irrigation parlours on the Stock Exchange – she wasn't sure how his partners were going to react to that, but at least he was talking about going back to work at last. She warned herself not to raise her hopes too high, because Cameron had been through other periods of manic elation since the SECI, but this time it genuinely seemed to be different. She had come home to find him pacing around the house, positively buzzing with enthusiasm about his new plan.

'Spiritual Stocks!' he'd explained, too excited to sit down. 'It's so obvious, don't you see? Every other form of human activity is ultimately expressed in some way on the Stock Market. Every kind of business from building fighter jets to manufacturing children's cartoons is publicly quoted, you can buy futures in every single raw product that exists on the planet, you can invest in your own *society* by buying government bonds, right? *Everything*, OK? Hell, there are even celebrities who've turned themselves into brands that anybody can own shares in, yeah? So why is it that the entire domain of religion is still working to this kind of medieval system whereby churches hand round a goddamned *bowl*? OK, it's not supposed to be about money, but obviously it *is* partly about money or else they wouldn't hand the *bowl* round, would they? And at the same time, we all know that it's easier for a camel to pass through the eye of a needle than for a rich man to enter the kingdom of Heaven, but, *realistically*, what are we supposed to do about it – come into church with a fucking wheelbarrow of cash one day or what? Sure, you've got some of the evangelist guys who operate credit-card lines, but no matter how much money they make that way, it's still just a bowl on the end of a telephone line! The fundamental *system* hasn't changed in thousands of years, but society has moved on! Is that any way, in this day and age, to run a *business*?'

'But . . . they're *not* businesses,' Teri had frowned. 'They are charities.'

'Yu-u-uh . . .' Cameron winced. 'They do *do* the soup-kitchen stuff, of course. Which is great, no mistake about it. But most of the money does *not* end up as soup, does it? Generally speaking, these are cash-rich organizations with salaried employees in every significant town and real estate portfolios like most chain stores couldn't *dream* of having! Almost all those cash donations *stay* with the church, obviously. And we all know this, but it doesn't matter because we don't particularly give them the money to pass on to the *poor*, we give it for the good of our own *souls*, right? That's what the whole thing is really about – the bottom line is that we have to envisage the possibility, however remote it may be, of eternal damnation. This places people in a very tricky situation – they can't afford to give away all their money, even though that is explicitly put forward as the correct option, because they have families to support and, although they should have faith that God will provide for them, they are not being offered a clear undertaking on His part that He will put their kids through college. Similarly, while we all want to make it to Heaven after we die, we *would* also like to be able to go on holiday somewhere fairly nice once a year while we're still alive. You know, we did *work* for that money, after all! It's not as though Satan just slipped us a brown envelope, is it? So, in realistic terms, how can we comply with these conflicting demands? No wonder society is kind of schizophrenic, basically! The best we can do is give away some spare cash and hope that will at least show good faith when it comes down to the final audit of our lives. Am I right?'

Terri had found herself grinning, amazed by the change in this man she'd been carrying like a sack of potatoes for too long now. Suddenly, Cameron was sure of himself again. He was in charge again. He was, above all, attractive again.

'Yeah . . . I guess that's pretty much the way it is,' she'd admitted.

'*Not* any more!' he declared, eyes alight. 'Do not breathe a word to anyone, but this is about to change. *I* can change it!'

'Change . . . the *world*, you mean.'

'Yup.'

'Single-handed?'

'No problem. Trust me.'

'Do tell.'

Cameron had had to explain the idea a few times before it made sense to her, but although she was no expert, Teri had to admit that it *sounded* sound. It worked on the basis of a church opening itself to its own followers by allowing them to become shareholders as a means of expressing their faith. Contrary to shares in an ordinary business, however, these would be sold on the basis that, come the shareholder's death, the deed would revert to the church itself. In effect, therefore, the system was designed to allow people the best of both worlds – that is, of this one and the next. In life, their wealth could be invested in a tax-deductible form in a charitable organization while remaining available to them should they need it. The shares were still theirs to sell, and so they still had a financial safety net. If they died without having sold them, however, then they could legitimately claim to have given away the bulk of their worldly riches long ago. The issuing of these shares, moreover, would raise a massive capital sum for the church – far greater than any amount of bowls could hope to cover – that could then be used to further its mission to save souls, or theoretically even to help poor people. The church would thus grow by reaching new believers who in turn would invest and push up the value of the shares they bought from those who were obliged to sell some to cover, say, a child's college education. Over the years, as the Lord gathered the faithful unto Himself, the shares would be gradually reverting to the church, thus allowing it to generate new income by selling them back to new generations of believers.

Everyone would benefit from Cameron's idea: the church, the congregation and, ultimately, God Himself.

'But is the church going to pay *dividends* on these shares?' Teri had asked, looking for the loophole in her husband's plan.

'Well, no – not in financial terms!' Cameron had laughed. 'The *dividend*, obviously, is that you have a priority booking in Heaven! It's more a case of having a shareholder discount with God.'

'*A discount?*'

'Yeah . . . or like celestial Air Miles.'

As Cameron envisaged it, he had only to persuade one church to try the system. As soon as other churches saw how much financial muscle this gave it, and therefore how aggressively it could market its personal interpretation of the Lord's word, they would need no further persuasion before adopting the system themselves. The alternative, after all, was to become marginalized. This, in turn, would benefit the faithful everywhere because once a full-blown spiritual share index existed, the relative success of different creeds and denominations would be clearly expressed in terms of their share prices. And should a person decide on this basis that some other church was clearly offering a better route to God than their present one, they had only to switch their investment from one to the other.

It would at last be possible for people to follow their financial and spiritual interests simultaneously . . .

*   *   *

'You . . . *scumbag*!' Teri seethed at her computer screen, tossing the mouse aside. 'This is ridiculous. We work at the National Information Commission, theoretically armed with the most sophisticated equipment of any Intelligence service in the world, and yet somehow I don't have the necessary . . . *plug-in* to open an attached document? How is that possible?'

She stared defiantly at her computer, muttering to it, 'Do you know how computers were invented? They were invented by the NIC, to crack *codes*. You owe your *existence* to us. So don't tell me I need a damned *plug-in*!'

'You know – what *is* a plug-in, anyway?' Gillian asked. 'I bet it looks nothing like a damned plug! I bet you don't even plug it *in* anywhere!'

'Who's this file from?' Teri asked.

'Ryuchi Takashi.'

'Oh . . . forget about it then,' she sighed, tipping back her chair. 'No wonder we can't open it. It's going to be full of computer graphics or a video or something – those guys can never just write something down – and they never seem to stick with the same software for more than, like . . . a *week*! Just phone him and find out what it's about. Don't worry – he's a really nice guy.'

'Do you know him?'

'Know him? No. But I've had this problem before. This is probably another weird cult of theirs. They've got cults like most countries have pop groups.'

'Can *you* phone him? If he's a friend of yours, I mean . . .'

'He's not a *friend* of mine – I've never met the guy.'

'Yeah, but you have a relationship, right?'

'We've talked, that's all! And even then, I can barely understand anything he says.'

'Well, in terms of international diplomacy, that's a relationship.'

In Teri's opinion, there was no better proof of how much the world had changed since the SECI than the way the Secret Services of so many countries had started pooling their resources. Not long ago, after all, this would have been contrary to the whole ethos of being a Secret Service. But now people were passing on every tip that came their way – most of which was rubbish, but no-one wanted to be held responsible for failing to give due warning to an ally if something big went down. At least, not when the ally in question was Atlantis.

The downside of it was that the NIC, as the sorting office for all this information, had become deluged with leads. And although she had to be very careful to whom she said this, in all honesty the bulk of the information they received only confirmed her belief that the War on Terrorism was a huge mistake. Not in political terms, not for the President and his party, but for the nation and the world in general.

Terrorism was a containable threat, best dealt with through better Intelligence, improved security and, above all, a genuine attempt to address the factors that generated it. In Teri's experience, the vast majority of terrorists posed no threat to Atlantis whatsoever. Their targets lay closer to home and, even if Atlantis figured in their calculations, it was almost always by association. Rightly or wrongly, people turned to terrorism as a means of fighting a perceived oppression, and Atlantis only became a target when it was seen to be an accessory to that oppression. Had Teri been President, therefore, her first priority would have been to re-evaluate the nation's long-term foreign policy and decide which of the world's numerous dictatorial regimes the country genuinely wished to support to the bitter end, dis-associating itself from all the others. For the select list of regimes that remained, the nation then had to accept the consequences and act accordingly. Their terrorists would be Atlantis' terrorists.

Instead of that, the Government had flatly refused to question its own implication in each cultural feud and taken the stunningly unwise decision to insist that the world should now be divided into those who were its allies and those who were its enemies.

Why this was a good idea escaped her.

Personally, on Teri's list of favoured dictators, she would have been aiming for a zero figure. But then she was an idealist. The only reason she'd ended up working in Intelligence was that it was virtually the only employment opportunity that existed in Atlantis for someone with a doctorate in Foreign Cultures. If she wanted to stay involved in the subject that most interested her, she'd been faced with a choice of using it at the NIC, or pursuing it in some kind of academic way. Academia, however, did not pay well and was far more of a political minefield than was the domain of espionage.

«*Kon-nichiwa?*» Ryuchi Takashi groaned into his watch, looking blearily at the time as he poked the audio-plug into his ear.

Four in the morning. Who could be phoning him at four in the morning?

Takashi's wrist ached a little from the jab his watch had just administered him. He currently loved the watch above all other gadgets – a combination wristwatch, stopwatch, phone, heartbeat monitor and personal organizer – but he wished it did not automatically switch across to its pinprick ring when it sensed the wearer was sleeping. It was not the pain he minded, but the rudeness of the awakening.

'Ryuchi?' a foreign woman asked.

«*Hai.*»

'Yuh, hi! It's Teri Hunt here. I didn't wake you up, did I?'

Teri Hunt. She always did this. And she always asked

that. When you dialled a foreign number on an Atlantian telephone, didn't it *tell* you what time it was in that country?

'No, Miss Teri . . . not at all,' he sighed, switching language. He actually enjoyed it when she phoned, even though it was usually around four in the morning, because it gave him a chance to use his Atlantian, in which he was fluent. 'How may I be . . . helping you here?'

There was a long pause down the line. She always took her time getting to the point.

'Yeah . . . well . . . a happy New Year from all of *us*, Ryuchi.'

Takashi frowned. Why was she wishing him happy New Year? At four in the morning? In late May? Could she be drunk?

'Listen, you know that . . . file you sent us?'

Suddenly he was sitting up, wiping the sleep from his eyes. Could it be that she had information to give him about the Beyond Communion? He hadn't expected such a quick response as this.

«*Hai.*»

'Yeah, hi! Can you hear me?'

'I hear you.'

'. . . I'm fine, thanks. How are *you*?'

Takashi frowned, thinking Atlantians could be maddeningly polite.

'. . . Good.'

'OK, good!' Teri replied. 'But listen – this document?'

'Yes?'

'What's it about?'

Takashi rolled his eyes.

'You cannot open?'

'No, Ryuchi – we don't have the . . . necessary plug-in.'

*   *   *

116

The Beyond Communion were a deeply alarming group about whom he had spent considerable time preparing an audio-visual dossier that combined computer graphics and live-action footage, edited together with screen dissolves and a click-on menu – all using *Atlantian* software, that he assumed the NIC would be bound to have. It was, after all, the biggest espionage organization in the world with a budget that dwarfed all of Atlantis' other investigative bodies, even if that money never appeared on a government budget sheet because its existence had never been publicly acknowledged. Theoretically, there was not a telephone on the planet that the NIC's satellite network could not eavesdrop on, not a computer that it could not hack into, or a web site opened without its knowledge. About the only form of communication that it couldn't control was the post.

They ought to have known about the Beyond Communion long ago, frankly.

It was an apocalyptic cult with a hygiene obsession. Its members began to appear about ten years back, recruiting heavily in the prostitution trade by offering streetwalkers free foot-washes and herbal massage pedicure, following the example of the Messiah, but their roots now ran much deeper through society. They had a chain of designer shoe shops that doubled as indoctrination centres, luring in the wealthy and fashionable with their aromatherapy foot-rubs. They had penetrated deep into the world of professional athletics. Now it seemed, according to Takashi's investigations, they were branching out and broadening their appeal. He was fairly certain that the Beyond Communion was behind the recent creation of a chain of colonic irrigation parlours in Atlantis.

Superficially, this obsession with hygiene seemed harmless enough, if a little cranky. But not when you knew what lay behind their thinking. It was all to do with purifying the believers prior to Judgement Day –

hence their switching the emphasis to *internal* purity through regular enemas. He was convinced this implied that they were close to the fruition of their apocalyptic vision.

What that was to be, he was not yet sure, but if they had transfered the focus of their operations to Atlantis, then it was imperative that his counterparts there take the situation seriously before it was too late.

'And, sorry, Ryuchi – but what is their name again?'

'The Beyond Communion,' Takashi repeated for what was now the fifth time.

'Can you possibly say that just a *little* slower?'

'The Be . . . Yond . . . Comm . . . Union,' Takashi answered patiently.

'The Bee and *Comb* Union? Are you sure about that?'

'Yuh, yuh! Beyond Communion.'

'They . . . they *sound* pretty harmless, Ryuchi. Is it some kind of front?'

'Yuh. Crazy religion, you know? They make *many* people believe – here, Atlantis, all over!'

'They're going to make us all bereave,' Teri repeated, noting it down. 'Hear Atlantis . . . *all over*. Wow. So they're planning something pretty big, you reckon?'

'Well, yuh! You got to open file on them, you know.'

'We should *open fire* on them?'

'Yuh! Right away! No good asking questions, OK? *Just open file*!'

'OK . . . OK . . . I get you,' Teri answered, trying not to let his apparent panic rattle her. 'Basically, you'd recommend a "shoot first, ask questions later" approach with these guys. Well, we will certainly be looking into this, Ryuchi, OK?'

'You promise to open file on them?'

'Don't worry – we'll do whatever is necessary. If we have to open fire, we're certainly prepared to do that, yes.'

118

'Today?'

'Well, no, probably not *today*. We don't . . . do things like that over here.'

'OK, but get plug-in then! *Soon*!'

'Yuh. Yuh. I assure you that I appreciate the urgency of this, and if needed I daresay we will get . . . um . . . *plugging them*, as you put it, OK? So over there you guys have *already* got . . . plugging, have you?'

'Yuh. All of them.'

'*All* of them?'

'Of course.'

'Well, good on you. It sounds like you have the situation under control. I'll make sure that's noted in my report, OK? I better . . . OK . . . yuh . . . thank *you*, Ryuchi . . .'

Teri put the phone down with a deep outlet of breath.

'Oh my God, I have a horrible feeling that this whole war is getting *way* out of hand,' she muttered, looking up at Gillian. 'Listen, see if you can find anything on a *Bee and Comb Union*.'

Although the Atlántian Intelligence apparatus had cut back drastically on the number of field agents it operated, the gap in information was more than compensated for by the fact that the NIC's computer system gave them back-door access to the databases of almost every security organization in the world. If every policeman and every spy the world over was an unwitting double agent for Atlantis, there wasn't much point in sending one's own people to places where they would stick out like a sore thumb and probably get dysentery.

'Bingo!' Gillian smiled a few seconds later. 'We have a Saman Massoudi, arrested three weeks ago in Errat on suspicion of involvement in the attempted assassination of General Harouni, and a member – just as our friend Ryuchi promised of the . . . *Al-Nur* Bee and Comb Union! Supposedly it is a harmless honey export business with branch offices in . . . *whoa* there, Nelly! Maybe your friend Takashi's onto something, after all . . .'

'Let me guess – right here in Atlantis?'

'You got it. In Corona. I think we should be keeping an eye on these guys . . .'

Teri reached for the phone to set the machinery of the NIC's surveillance capacity in operation. Most of the Commission's monitoring work was automatic, the computers picking up on any of a huge range of trigger words that their enemies might use in a conversation, but in priority cases there was still no replacement for the human touch. In this instance, Teri figured, they needed an actual person listening in to the Bee and Comb Union.

'Thank you for calling the National Information Commission's Department of Surveillance,' a voice answered. 'For your convenience and in order to better meet your requirements, please follow the instructions. If the subject of your enquiry is already under surveillance, please press 1. If you wish to *organize* surveillance of a suspect organization, armed group, or religious cult, please press 2. If you wish to arrange monitoring of a commercial enterprise or industrial group, please press—'

Teri pressed the 2 on her touch pad, sighing with exasperation. 'For your convenience', indeed – God, she hated being treated like an idiot.

'Thank you. To arrange surveillance of a political group, please press 1. To arrange surveillance of a religious group, please press 2. For commercial and industrial organizations, please press 3. For charity, humanitarian or ecological groups, please—'

She pressed the 3, beginning to doodle on the paper before her. A human being, she knew, was still several steps and a twenty-minute hold away. There was no point in getting impatient. She turned to Gillian, yawning.

'Say, did you know Takashi's people celebrate New Year in *May*?'

The End minus 20 days (cont'd)

'. . . was Benson Gloag reporting live from the scene of this morning's possible terrorist attack near Dumona. In the studio with me this morning I have former Under-Secretary of State Glen Stokopolous. As a former insider, do you think this event will affect the President's position on Errat?'

'I think this changes everything, Ayesha. We don't know for certain if these were terrorist bees, but if not, that only suggests that the scale of the tragedy would have been even worse if they *had been*. He has to react to this.'

'So what would you be saying to him this morning if you were still part of the Administration?'

'Well, Ayesha, I don't know what is *already* being said, so I can't say exactly what my contribution would be, but I would be firm about this. I would be saying whatever most *needed* to be said relative to what other people were saying.'

'And do you think your successors are saying that right now, even as we speak?'

'I am certain that words of that nature are being exchanged at this very moment.'

'Words like . . . ?'

'That's hard to say. There are a lot of words.'

'But if you had to pick *one* word, what would your personal word be?'

'Spade.'

'Thank you, Glen Stokopolous, for that insider's view. We go now to—'

Chapter Nine

In which the life of our hero, that has just returned to normal, is rapidly complicated by his meeting a young woman of such extreme taciturnity that she will not be contributing to the conversations described in this chapter

It was a profoundly contented Saman who sweated his way up the dry bed of the wadi into the hills the next day – not just because he was always pleased to escape the city, but because the absurd drama of his arrest had left him with an even greater enthusiasm for spending a few days alone among the hives than was usually the case. And no small part of his excitement was due to the fact that they would be ready for the first harvest of the summer, his first commercial shipment of the precious Jana honey. That was an event of far greater significance in his life than some ridiculous brush with Internal Security.

Furthermore, although it was not something that he would expect Farrukh to understand, he felt more comfortable in his bare dwelling in the orchard than he did amongst all the rugs and fluffiness of the family house in the city. He sometimes got slightly nauseous with too many cushions under his already well-padded rump.

Ever since the war, he had not felt quite right in

surroundings that could be described as homely. The house in the orchard was just a two-room shack, really – it contained nothing more than a stool, low table, wash bucket, and low camp bed, but there was a well outside whose water was exceptionally sweet and cool, a small stock of couscous and coffee, and a reed hut where the morning light was quite delightful as one squatted over the hole in the ground. There was an outhouse in which he stored the combs that he collected over the days, getting a local goat farmer to bring them down to the city in his van once the harvest was complete. And there was nobody to talk to, which suited him fine – local herders stopped by to say hello if their beasts' wanderings had led them towards the orchard, but this was relatively rare. Except at harvest time when, curiously enough, everyone's goats tended to find their way there at some point, their owners at first declining and finally accepting the inevitable offer of a honeycomb to take home. Not that Saman begrudged the dent this made in his harvest – it was an ordinary courtesy, and more than repaid by offers of milk and meat, the occasional loan of a donkey, and the absolute security of knowing that there were eyes all over the hillsides watching his house when he was not there.

Except, this once, their gaze had apparently been elsewhere.

The first thing he noticed when he entered the house for his midday nap, taking a break from comb-collecting in the heat of the afternoon, was that the furniture had been moved. The furniture, of course, being the stool. He noticed this the moment the passing of his bulky frame allowed some light to enter through the doorway. The stool was not where he had left it, which could mean only one thing.

«Someone's been sitting on my stool,» he thought with a little stab of pique.

He placed the tray of honeycomb he was carrying on

the low table, and looked around. His bald head turned slowly, noticing the small cupboard was open and one of his jars of couscous was out.

«Someone's been eating my *couscous*!» he harrumphed internally.

By now thoroughly upset at the invasion, he went straight to the windowless back room to see how far the abuse had been taken, there finding the greatest shock of all.

«Someone's been sleeping in my bed . . .» he thought as he spied the scrumpled covers, his eyes widening in surprise as they became accustomed to the gloom, «. . . and she's still there!»

That it was a woman was instantly clear from the length of black hair sprayed over the sheet. A young woman, barely more than a girl, though her age was difficult to judge in that her face was filthy in the way of a street urchin, covered in a film of dirt so ingrained and even that it could almost be her natural colouring.

«*Hey!*» he shouted, standing over the bed.

Though loud enough to set the flies buzzing, his cry did not wake her. Amazingly, she continued to lie there, so still that only the quizzical frown upon her brow as she slept convinced him that she clearly was not dead. He was about to shout again when the realization of how exhausted a person would have to be to sleep through such an interruption hit him, stilling his tongue.

For all her cheek, this was one very tired girl lying before him, and he found it hard to maintain his anger in the face of such desperation. Plus it was not difficult to imagine how she might have come to be here. Had he encountered her down in the city, then there could have been a hundred reasons why she might be living on the streets, not all necessarily the fault of others, but up here in the hills there was only one likely explanation.

The war.

He knew full well that the war, as always, had created

126

as much as it had destroyed. Certainly it had destroyed lives by the thousand, broken lines of descent, wiped out inheritances, and made nonsense of generations of patient labour, but that was only the half of it. In a sense, what mattered more now was all the things it had created. Creations such as widows, cripples, madmen, beggars . . . and, of course, orphans. A lot of orphans. They were less visible now than they had been in the first year or so after the fighting had stopped, a period when the countryside had been filled with dazed waifs blowing from place to place with nobody and nothing behind their name, and no plan beyond a vague hope that they might come across something to hang onto, something that would hold them down and bring their drift to an end. He'd seen enough of them in his own months of wandering to know better than most just how common-place they were, but he had been in no condition himself to offer help to anyone even if he'd had the heart for it. They were much fewer nowadays, and he hoped that was because the others had found what they were looking for – a relative of some kind, or at least a friendly face, but he knew that often that would not be the case. More than a few, no doubt, had found nothing more at the end of their stumbling paths than a quiet, worn-out death. Others would have new lives that were little more enviable. A use someone could put their little bodies to.

When a war itself is spent, it leaves behind a generous stockpile of the expendable. And hearts hardened enough to exploit them.

Looking more closely at the girl on the bed, he guessed she might be around twenty years old, which would have placed her late childhood comfortably in the war zone. Fifteen at most when it all ended.

And still, apparently, being blown from place to place. Pushed on by her own hunger, and running from the hunger of others. So, on an instant's reflection, he could not begrudge her a little couscous and the use of his bed.

Saman stepped softly out of the room and sat down upon the stool to wait.

It was early evening by the time she awoke.

Saman had actually dozed off himself, the forward droop of his shoulders as he sat on the stool being brought to a convenient halt by the bulge of his tummy, when he was startled upright by a squeak from the camp bed.

As soon as he opened his eyes she darted from the bed, making a dash for the doorway, but he was surprisingly fast off his feet, bobbing up to block her path. She started one way, then the other, but the lurches of his belly on each occasion squeezed shut the narrow alley between her and the door. Finally, as he stepped forward with his palms towards her in a gesture of peace, she panicked completely and shot back into the bedroom, bouncing off the back wall and disappearing into the corner.

«Please . . .» he called, following her in. «I don't want to—»

She was huddled mouselike in the corner, chin between her knees and hands over her head. Saman stopped in the doorway, palms still outstretched.

«I don't want to hurt you,» he repeated, taking a small step forward.

The girl tightened the ball she had made of herself, and watched him with wary, feral eyes. Seeing that she was far too scared to be approached, Saman took a step back as a gesture of good faith and pointed towards the bed, saying, «It's OK. I don't mind.»

The girl's eyes followed his finger and narrowed as they saw the bed, her lips curling into a defiant sneer.

«What . . . ?» Saman gasped. «Oh no. You've misunderstood me. I don't mean that I want to . . . I mean it's OK if you want to *rest*! I can sleep on the floor!»

He saw that his words were making little headway

on her terrorized mind, and took a step further back, holding up a hand to tell her to remain calm.

«Wait there a second,» he said, «I've got something for you.»

He waddled over to the cupboard, fetched a bowl and two small spoons, then scooped in some of the honey from the Jana comb he'd placed on the table.

«See this?» he smiled, showing it to her from the doorway. «Honey! The best honey in the world!»

Kneeling slowly down, he stretched as far forward as his arms could reach and placed it softly on the floor between them. Then he got up and went back to sit on the stool, far enough away to make it quite safe for her to reach for the honey if she wished.

«Go on!» he urged. «Try it! I'll bet you haven't tasted anything as good as that in . . . well, ever, probably!»

The girl's head rose a little to see better inside the bowl, and a certain sparkle of desire crossed her eyes as she spied the dark, gleaming honey it contained, but her body made no move to come out of its defensive ball.

«OK. You know what I'm going to do?» Saman said, taking hold of the edge of the stool with his fingers. «I'm going to sit here on this stool. This is my stool, and I'm going to stay right on top of it, do you hear? You can stay in the corner there if you want, or sit on the bed, but this is *my* stool!»

He watched her apparent incomprehension with an amused glint in his eyes, then leaned across to take the spoon he'd left in the honeycomb and slipped a scoop of it into his mouth.

«Mmm . . . good honey,» he smiled. «You really should try it. But stay *away* from my stool.»

Something that might have been an attempt to smile, somewhat twisted by lack of practice, flickered across the girl's mouth. Keeping her eyes firmly on him, ready for the first sign of a trick, she reached forward to pull the honey towards her. Her finger ran across the bottom of the bowl and disappeared, dark and dripping, into her mouth.

Her eyebrows rose in surprise at the taste of it.

«Aha!» Saman chuckled. «You see? You *see*? That's the honey from *my* bees! Did you ever taste anything so good? Not too sweet, and just a little bit like you're eating flowers. Isn't that good?»

The girl did not answer, but her hand went back to the bowl, and this time she took hold of the spoon, helping herself to a large scoop of honeycomb. And, for just a second as she tried to cut through it with the blunt edge of the spoon, she allowed herself to take her eyes off Saman . . .

An hour later, Saman's throat was dry with talking. He had sat there, guarding his stool, trying to reassure the girl by explaining who he was as she ate his honey. He'd talked softly, constantly, telling her about himself and his family and the bees and the honey. About how his family died. About how he had wanted to die.

It was a pretty curious form of conversation in that she said nothing in answer to any of his questions, prompting him into yet more personal revelations to fill her side of the discussion, but it seemed to be working. She had been slowly relaxing her body – her ball becoming a squat, then a kneel, and finally a fully-fledged sit upon the floor, legs bent and feet tucked under her thighs as she munched through the tray of honey he had sent sliding her way after the bowl had been wiped clean.

Saman knew that the Jana honey was at least half responsible for the speed of the progress he was making. Its fabled ability to soothe the nerves was evidently at work. The girl was even getting better at smiling.

At times he had hoped she was about to speak, but it had not yet happened. Her mouth would open, and he would stop talking in expectation, but then the points of her lips would curl hesitantly up and her mouth would close again.

«You know, sooner or later you are going to *have* to say something because I can't do all the talking!» Saman suggested. «Come on – won't you at least tell me your name?»

The girl looked quizzically at him and he rolled his eyes, pointing to himself with jungle-explorer clarity.

«Saman,» he enunciated, slapping his chest. «Saman.»

He pointed at her, smiling,

«You?»

The girl winced, and then nodded to show she *had* understood the question. Her hands rose in return, slowly gesturing for him.

First, they touched her chest.

Second, they closed over her ears.

And lastly, before returning to her lap, they closed over her mouth.

«Oh,» Saman said. «Oh . . . I see.»

He nodded to show he had understood, and she smiled as she popped another scoop of honey in her mouth.

«Well,» he sighed, «I suppose I *will* be doing most of the talking then, won't I?»

The End minus 19 days

'. . . has announced that the USS *Kirk* is to move into position off the coast of Errat. Now, how would you respond to critics who accuse the Government of gunboat diplomacy, Mr Secretary of State?'

'That's totally simplistic.'

'But the USS *Kirk is* a very big boat with a large number of guns on board.'

'That's not the point! We are a democratic people faced with a serious threat from a terrorist group being supported by a military dictatorship. We have to make these folks realize that just because Atlantians believe in peace, democracy and human rights, that does not mean we are *weak*. That's what this is all about – we are sending them a message. An appeal for peace.'

'Hand over Saman Muffoody, or else.'

'That's right.'

'. . . or else what?'

'Or else we *will* maintain the peace. Even if that means war.'

Chapter Ten

*In which we meet the Spiegelflugs, an ordinary
Atlantian family that will come to play a crucial role in
the development of our hero's story and, indeed,
beyond it*

'This is ridiculous. No. No way, OK? End of discussion.'
For Ned Spiegelflug Jnr the time had come to be his
own person. He loved his parents dearly, but he was
seventeen years old now and there were certain decisions
about his life that he could no longer let them take on his
behalf. Like this one, right now, over the breakfast table.

He flicked his gaze across to Hermione, picking
silently at her organic fruit salad, and willed her to
close ranks with him in defiance of this latest paternal
edict. Some chance. They hadn't been getting on lately
because she was into this whole Alpha Girl trip at school
and, although two years younger, considered him to
be a social embarrassment. She just glared back as she
pricked a small cube of mango with her fork. Apart from
dropping the odd bitchy comment, that was all the
feedback he got from Hermione these days. She gave
good glare.

He'd caught her practising it in her room a few months
back. She still hadn't forgiven him for that, even though
he had promised not to tell anyone at school, where her

glare was legendary and believed to be a natural phenomenon. If her own brother told people that she did glare workouts at home, the effect would be like people discovering that her breasts were fake. Fake breasts were so out this year. It was for this kind of information that Hermione and her girlfriends were paid a handsome consultancy fee by a market research firm.

'Ned, I know it's not easy . . .' Ned Spiegelflug Snr maintained in the same unyielding tone of sympathy that marked his side of every such conversation, '. . . but surely there are more important issues here than whether or not it's . . . *cool*?'

Ned Jnr let out an exasperated groan, burying his face in his hands. This was a nightmare. He was getting nowhere, his arguments bouncing off his father's shiny bullet of a head without making the slightest impression upon him. What had happened to his dad lately? In the past they had always been able to find a compromise together, but lately he had become totally unreasonable.

'No,' he repeated from behind his palms.

'OK. I'm not asking you. I'm telling you.'

That was it. Ned Jnr's hands slammed down onto the table, his thumb accidentally catching the end of his spoon and flipping it up into the air in a revolutionary uproar of milk and rice crispies as he declared, '*No! Do you get it? N-O! No!*'

He stood up, the chair falling over behind him, and strode out of the kitchen without looking back or apologizing to his mother for the shower of soggy cereals that had just landed on her head.

Slamming his bedroom door, Ned Jnr grabbed the remote from his bed and silenced Ayesha Novak in mid-sentence, then marched straight over to the stereo and pressed the Play button. There was a machine-gun thud of drum and the Huge Hard Gods launched into another screaming dissection of Atlantian society. Their songs, no doubt because of their linguistic violence, were widely denounced in the media as offensive, morally corrupting garbage, but they were actually more sophisticated than people gave them credit for. True, they thought Atlantis sucked, but the perception that they were unpatriotic was quite wrong in that on balance they thought everywhere else in the world probably sucked even more than Atlantis. This was the basic thesis of the album Ned was playing in his room at that moment, the seminal *You Suck*. It was a sentiment that resonated with a fanbase who were caught in the limbo between childhood and their first blow job. Ned, like many people his age, considered the Huge Hard Gods to be total fucking geniuses.

He didn't expect his dad to understand. His dad didn't seem to understand anything any more. His dad, to put it simply, was losing his fucking mind.

Ned felt bad because he knew all this was about love. People imagined, of course, that corporate accountants were about as incapable of passion as most poets probably were of bookkeeping, but they were wrong. Indeed, if love could blind, then his dad needed a fucking Labrador. Everything he'd ever done came down to love for his family – love which, in his eyes, was best expressed through careful management of their financial welfare, through insurance policies, pension schemes, investments, college funds, and a host of other strings woven together to form an unbreakable safety net under life's tightrope. And Ned could see that he had a point. In what way was a love that threw caution to the winds finer than taking one's responsibilities seriously and rigorously studying the options, whether the proposed purchase was a house, or an automobile or a washing machine, actually *reading* the catalogues, comparing prices and deals and payment methods, until you knew *exactly* why you had made the choice you had and could justify it down to the last detail to anyone who broached the subject? So, for instance, every time his mum washed clothes in the Schiffer Galaxy 300, she knew it was costing them at least 50 cents less in electricity and water than any other model of washing machine on the market, which was 50 cents more that would ultimately go towards a holiday, or a graduation car, or a perfect wedding.

And that was love.

But his father was taking on more than he could handle in his determination to protect them all against terrorism. Ned had let it slide when he showed him the survival kit he was going to keep in his office on the fifty-first floor of the UniCom building – a kit that comprised a paraglider backpack with air bag for inflation on landing, a fireproof suit and micro-filtrative gas mask, and, above all, a gun to stop his colleagues from stealing it all off him in the panic – because that had been his own business. But being expected to take his *own* survival pack to school was a different matter.

It was bad enough that everyone called him Skids. For two years now, thanks to a single, dreadful incident in the locker room that it seemed no-one was ever going to let him forget, that had been his name: Skids. Even the kids in Hermione's year called him that: Skids Spiegelflug, the guy with shit marks in his underpants, like this was a daily occurrence. He couldn't walk into the toilets without some wise arse saying, 'Hey, Skids – don't forget to take your pants down!' like he'd been found with an entire steaming packet of the stuff in his clothes.

And now his father wanted him to take a fucking chemical warfare suit to school? Like *that* wasn't going to give them all some good comic material.

His mum understood, but she was torn. And, anyway, she had enough problems with her diarrhoea. It had come on soon after the SECI, and nothing the doctors tried seemed able to stop it. Clearly, given that she worked on the switchboard at Liberty Mansion, fucking *yards* away from the President, there was probably a psychosomatic element to the problem. But she flat out refused to change her job – her President and her country needed her where she was. Obviously she would rather have been working somewhere else, somewhere safer, but Marge Spiegelflug was not a coward and she was not going to allow herself to be scared into letting down her country in the middle of a crisis. That was non-negotiable, no matter how much Dad pushed her. But, on the other hand, she had accepted the survival pack.

As, apparently, Hermione was prepared to do.

Which left Ned isolated. So what was new? he thought as he booted up his computer to play Loser. Those adults who had Ned's best interests at heart – his teachers as well as his parents – had been telling him for some time now that he should spend less time playing Loser, and more time thinking about his future. If not, they implied, the world would decide on his behalf – for already, at the age of seventeen, there were certain career paths that were more or less closed to him. Barring a sudden, radical change of direction, for instance, brain surgery was out, as were all other forms of medicine from the human down to pooch-care. Nor did his chances of ever becoming an astronaut look good.

Ned generally grunted by way of agreement, showing little enthusiasm for the exciting range of choices they laid before him. He was, they concluded, the worst kind of sullen, unappreciative teenager. They were incapable of appreciating, in his opinion, that this entire lack of entrepreneurship stemmed from having given *way* too much thought to the future. Why, he could have answered them, would anyone want to become a brain surgeon when most potential patients were clearly morons? Why should he care about saving the lives of people who were generally selfish, shallow and destructive, or look after the pets they relied upon to fill their emotionally hollow existences? And what on Earth was so heroic about being an astronaut when your only purpose was to launch even more satellites to spy on people and listen in to their telephone conversations? That was just so typical of his country as Ned Spiegelflug Jnr saw it – to have taken space, the Final Frontier, and turned it into the Great Checkpoint.

The better adjusted of his contemporaries were already busy drafting themselves into a CV, looking for the best summer placements and clocking up extra compassion points by being a Pic-Nic Buddy to some innocent little retard who had no idea that their friendliness was just a career move. Ned was not without compassion for retards, although he didn't like the way they tended to drool, but he despised the hypocrisy of people who pretended they were helping others when they were ultimately only interested in helping themselves.

He realized his attitude was not constructive.

And he understood better than the adults around him that his self-destructive behaviour was simply a displaced attempt to attack the society into which he had been born, blah blah blah. Really, they had nothing to teach him about psychology – he had been raised from his earliest childhood to question his every act and analyse his every emotion until it seemed to him that he had no instincts left at all. He had been so suffocated with emotional understanding, so hammered with the message that life was about compromises, that he suspected love itself had been utterly compromised for him as a result, holding no more magic for him now than a mathematical equation for producing human beings.

It was hardly surprising that the most *fun* he had was in killing people. True, they were only jerky little computer-graphic people with pixel-dry blood, but ultimately he considered real humans to be a lot closer to computerized automata than they imagined. *Their* lives were programmed, too, and their idea of reality as virtual as anything else, since their triumphs only existed in the context of the game they were all playing. You reached Level 8 of a game, you were made a vice-president of the company – what was the difference? You got a new car, you got a flying carpet. You charged up your weapon supply, you paid off your charge card. What exactly was reality? The games themselves were part of the game – of course he understood that and was quite aware, as a genuine disaffected teenager, of belonging to a target market of disaffected teenagers. You could not avoid that, no matter how hard you tried. Unless you killed yourself, that is. The best you could do was to know why you made the choices you did, and exercise a certain amount of discernment.

The game Loser was a hit that had come out of nowhere, without the giant marketing machines behind other games, without the research and focus groups and ad campaigns. The company that had created it was small, comprising three young men who had put into it all the passion that they had not been able to put into healthier activities like having girlfriends.

Level 1 of Loser was a light-hearted game called Surf Dude Massacre. It involved no weapons or fighting, but a simple attempt on the part of the hero – a proverbial 97-pound weakling of the kind who supposedly gets sand kicked in his face – to attract the attention of one of the various Blonde Beach Babes tanning themselves on the sand. Periodically, one of the Blonde Beach Babes would sit up and request, 'Say, can one of you boys massage some oil into my back?' Your objective was to be the person who did this, but it was not going to happen so long as there were Surf Dudes in the vicinity.

In this you were helped by the sharks, who would progressively eat the Surf Dudes if you lured them into the water at the right moment. The best way to do this was to pretend to be drowning.

It was all about timing. In a perfectly played game, it was the sixth Blonde Beach Babe whose back you would massage first. If you subsequently managed to massage all the others as well, then you would earn the maximum number of points to take through to the next level: Prom Night Psycho. If you played *that* right, all the star Jocks got killed by either a hate-crazed lesbian PT teacher, a cheerleader they had gang-raped, or the wheelchair-bound former quarter-back of the football team.

He sat down to begin playing, but didn't quite have the heart to hit the Start button. Killing some pixel people, although fun, would not change the fact that the world around him was going mad. It wasn't just his dad. His dad wasn't even an exceptional case, or at least Ned hoped he wasn't. No doubt there were other families where the parents were seriously discussing turning the basement into a fallout shelter.

Like, did he actually think Ned was going to live with them in the basement if someone let off a bomb? No way. They couldn't get through dinner these days without arguing, so months of close confinement would lead to psychopathic incidents, no doubt about it. And what was the point, anyway? The world above would be completely fucked and radioactive, society would have collapsed, and they would spend their whole time shooting mutant marauders. Which, it's true, could be kind of cool, but that was not the way Dad saw it – he imagined the Spiegelflug family emerging unscathed from their Spiegelflug bunker to a world crying out for competent accountants. He probably figured he would one day be remembered as the visionary patriarch of some great Spiegelflug dynasty, the man who appeared in the planet's darkest hour and saved civilization by carrying out a fucking audit.

He just didn't get it.

'You don't get it, do you, Dad?' Ned Jnr began, when his father came upstairs to discuss the survival pack issue.

'Get what, exactly?' Ned Snr frowned. 'Ned – I *understand* why you are embarrassed about—'

'No – that's not what I'm talking about!' Ned sighed in exasperation. 'That's, like, a side issue to . . . how can I put this? What I'm trying to make you understand, Dad, is that you're missing the point here, which is that . . . *objectively speaking* . . . humanity sucks the big one.'

His father's bald scalp rippled up from the eyebrows in surprise. He went to disagree, but stopped himself. Ned saw it – he was being given space to air his opinions.

'Uh-huh,' his dad nodded finally, choosing his words with care. 'When you say "humanity sucks the big one", do you know what you *mean* exactly?'

'I mean that the biological species of *homo sapiens* are creatures that naturally . . .' Ned frowned, searching for a way to break through his father's total denial of reality, '. . . *suck*. You see? They just really, really . . . suck. Except for maybe a few Baoist monks who don't ever move because they might squash a bug or something, and very young children, and a few poets and singers *maybe*, everyone else has stabilized into a condition of comprehensive sucking. Worldwide.'

'That's . . . pretty harsh, Ned.'

'I'm not saying it's their *fault* or anything, because it's congenital.'

His father nodded sympathetically, saying, 'I can see you've given this a lot of thought.'

'Well, it's pretty obvious when you look at what we're doing to the world.'

'So I suck, too?' he asked. 'And your mum? And yourself?'

'I think we suck *less* than most people, maybe, but it would be totally hypocritical to imagine we are somehow exempt from the rule. We're only human. So, from a philosophical point of view, we must suck.'

'Your philosophy being "I am, therefore I suck", if I understand correctly.'

'Pretty much.'

His father nodded, tongue clicking on the roof of his palate as he considered how best to deal with the situation at hand.

'OK, Ned . . .' he announced, '. . . granting you that the world and almost everyone in it sucks, let me propose you a deal. How much would I have to *pay* you to take this survival pack to school?'

The End minus 18 days

'. . . Harouni has vowed, and I quote, that "the Errati people will defend our land with our own blood, and the blood of our sons and daughters, and the blood of all our loved ones down to the very last baby." Now, in light of the General's apparent *intransigence*, Mr Secretary, is there not a danger that this confrontation will turn into a bloodbath?'

'I don't believe so. I think the Errati people are intelligent enough to see this for what it is – the desperate bluster of a man who knows the game is up. They know our quarrel is not with *them* – we've made that very clear all along.'

'But they must be worried that they will get killed?'

'Obviously that danger exists, given the nature of the man we are dealing with. *Obviously*, as in any war, we all accept that some people may get hurt. Even killed. Let's not kid ourselves that war is not violent. It is. But people realize this is something we have to do, so they accept the possibility of casualties. The polls clearly show that.'

'Well, the polls show public support remaining strong for any action involving "between ten and twenty casualties", but dropping away rapidly when asked if they would accept "between thirty and *forty* casualties". How do you respond to that?'

'I don't think a serious government can base its decisions on the response to a hypothetical question like that! In fact, statistically, a clear majority of people say they'd prefer the President *not* to base his decisions on opinion polls.'

'Although that *was* in an opinion poll.'

'True, but I didn't say the President was basing his decisions on it. He makes his own mind up and takes responsibility for his actions. And I'm sure most people respect that about him.'

'By "most people", you mean . . . ?'

'Sixty-three per cent. But higher among women.'

Chapter Eleven

In which the members of the Counter-Terrorism desk at the National Information Commission meet to choose the fifty most dangerous organizations in the world, and find the task poses a serious threat to their plans for the evening

The President wanted a Terrorist Hit List: a clear Top 50 that the public could get a grip on. So far, after six hours of discussion, the meeting at the NIC had only discovered thirty-seven groups who, to greater or lesser extents, could rock their world. And it kept getting harder.

Bob Spotto, the NIC's Director of Counter-Terrorism, rested his elbows on the table, fingers gently massaging his forehead.

'OK,' he sighed, looking around the gathered agents. 'I know this won't go down well with certain members of Congress, but don't we *have* to include the Authentic Republican Army?'

There was a palpable reluctance to respond around the table.

'Let's face it, Tom,' Spotto continued, turning to the doyen of the Counter-Terrorism desk. 'They blow people up. In my book . . . that's terrorism.'

'Yes, they do,' Big Tom answered. 'But are they

terrorists or freedom fighters? There's a long, complex history there. A lot of ethnic support for them over here. On account of the potatoes.'

'We *know* about the potatoes!' Spotto groaned. 'For how long are they going to keep banging on about the damned potatoes? Anyway, I thought the Prime Minister . . . what's he called?'

'Chris Flyte?' Little Tom suggested.

'Yeah, Flyte,' Spotto continued. 'Flyte *apologized* about the potatoes. Isn't it time to move on?'

'Well, I think things *have* moved on since then, sir,' Big Tom reflected. 'Since the elections it seems that the Authentic Republican Army has largely split into two new groups – the Historical Republican Army and . . . um . . . what's the other one, Tom?'

Little Tom looked up from his notes and grunted, 'Ye Olde Republican Army.'

Spotto rolled his eyes.

'Romance is the curse of those people,' he sighed. 'A hundred years from now they'll be doing it out of nostalgia – getting all maudlin after the pub closes and digging Grandpa's balaclava out of the attic for a bit of anniversary knee-capping. On reflection, maybe we shouldn't be taking either group too seriously – it'll only encourage them. So we're still on thirty-seven. Who's got a suggestion?'

For all the billions their budget gave them to play with, the meeting room was cramped and sordid. Returning to the windowless chamber after going for a pee a half-hour back, Spotto had the impression he was getting into a car that had been slept in – the massed breath and body odours of twenty people had quite overwhelmed the recycling powers of the antique air-conditioning system, whose mechanical lungs had been wrecked by passive smoking during the more intense periods of the cold war. Now all it took was some lunchtime onion and a few ripe feet for the atmosphere in there to become intolerable.

Better meeting rooms had been one of his first priorities on taking up the directorship. He reasoned that it was too much to expect people to function at their best in such an oppressive environment. Even back when he was a junior agent he had noticed how detrimental to the actual *intelligence* of any Intelligence-gathering it was to spend too much time in the room – beyond the first hour, the average agent's synaptic connections began to clog. After three hours they were ready to agree to almost any proposition, no matter how vehemently they might have opposed it earlier, so long as it would secure their release from the subtle torture of sitting around this table. Such meeting rooms were responsible for most of the ludicrous decisions reached by committees the world over, and also explained why duller wits usually thrived in the world of bureaucracy: their very dullness afforded them a level of endurance rarely found in sharper-minded colleagues, who were gradually brought down to their mental level as the meeting dragged on. The world would be a very different, and possibly better, place if governments invested in egg timers.

Somehow, however, the money had never been there for him to see his plans through. It all seemed to get swallowed up in cost-cutting studies.

'The International League for the Liberation of Sacred Places,' Mike Boggan suggested rapidly, sliding a folder down the table to his boss. Boggan, as usual, was managing to stay more elegant and clean-cut than the other men in the room. Disturbingly so, like his hair had been sold with his suit. He was inexperienced by the standards of many in the room, but his rise in the Director's esteem had been rapid. Good presentation counted for much in that.

'Don't know them. Sound like a fun bunch of guys.' Spotto scowled, picking up the dossier. 'Are we worried about them? Am *I* worried about them?'

'Not very, no,' Boggan replied coolly. 'They're pretty

bad, though – car bombs, mostly. Definitely legitimate candidates for the list, but, despite the name, not very . . . international.'

'And *we* aren't occupying any of their sacred places? We don't have something tactless on top of one like, I don't know . . . an *air base*, for instance?'

'Absolutely not. It's all to do with the site of this Baoist temple that got knocked down about three hundred years ago, and now has a mosque on it. Really – they're small-time, and very local.'

'They liberated anything yet?'

'Nope . . . well, a few parking spots. But we *do* have evidence of fund-raising activities over here, under the name of the International Foundation for the Restoration of Sacred Places.'

'Aha . . . perfect!' Spotto smiled. 'Small, not very threatening . . . but with a bank account we can freeze. Thank you, Mike. And *Baoist*, too, which is nice. We're not here to engage in tokenism, of course, but we don't yet have a Baoist group. Which is odd – there are billions of poor, oppressed Baoists, so why aren't there more Baoist terrorists?'

'Cultural reasons, probably,' Boggan expounded, puffed from the way his suggestion had gone down so well. 'Because of their belief in karma and reincarnation, they don't rebel against oppression and suffering in quite the same way. Logically, the worse his life is, the more a radical Baoist should think that . . . well . . . it's his own damn fault.'

'Umm . . . excuse me?' Teri Hunt interrupted. 'The International Foundation for the Restoration of Sacred Places is *not* another name for the International League for the Liberation of Sacred Places, Mike! It's the same location, and both are interested in their own ways in the same temple, but these are two *totally* separate organizations. For a start, the League are Baoist, yes, but the *Foundation* is a Wasabi group!'

There was an audible sigh around the table as the collected agents sensed their freedom slipping further away.

'Mike? Enlightenment, please?' Spotto frowned. 'Is it possible that you have underestimated the complexity of this particular . . . planning permission debate?'

'I . . . well, I don't know if I entirely go with Teri on that one, to be honest. I mean, just because the Foundation is apparently *Wasabi* doesn't preclude it from being a fund-raising front for the League. Duping people is the whole *point* of a front, isn't it? You could argue it's the smart move for the League to make – get the Wasabis to *pay* them to blow up the mosque! Maximum karma points, probably.'

Teri stared witheringly at him.

'That's ridiculous, Mike, and you know it.'

'What do you *mean*? It's anything but ridiculous! Excuse me, but how many times have we ourselves armed and financed people who subsequently decided to kill *us*? This is a classic terrorist manoeuvre, Teri!'

'And secondly . . .' she announced, 'they're archaeologists.'

'Who says?'

'*The World Heritage Organization!* If the members of the International Foundation for the Restoration of Sacred Places ever turned to violence to pursue their goals – which I can't seriously imagine happening because archaeologists are *pretty* damned patient people – but just suppposing they did, then the only weapons they'd have to hand would be very small hammers. So – not quite in the exploding car league, Mike, but they could *ruin* the paintwork.'

There was an embarrassed silence.

'Oka-a-ay!' Spotto announced cheerfully. 'Still just . . . *thirteen* more to find, people!'

*　　*　　*

Bob Spotto hated the modern world. He had been trained to combat a single great enemy – a rival empire that matched Atlantis spy for spy and bomb for bomb. He just couldn't get a grip on these enthusiastic amateurs he was up against nowadays. The reports his team produced about each of them – mostly just a compilation of kidnappings, homicides and car bombs covered by the local papers in all of their fucked little nations – passed over his desk in a blur. It always seemed to be exactly the same report, whatever the country in question. Monitoring terrorist groups was the Intelligence equivalent of eating burgers: the identical thing wherever you were in the world – a quarter-pounder of Semtex, regular fries, and triple-thickness mindset. Then they were forever forming new splinter groups with even more grandiose names and insane agendas, but nevertheless just keeping right on with the kidnappings, homicides and car bombs. Because that was the only thing most of them were capable of doing.

They were not, on the whole, wildly intelligent people. If they were, they would have something to lose. Their lives would have meaning beyond The Struggle that had become their sole obsession. And The Struggle, perhaps more to the point, would attract enough supporters for their tight little club to mushroom into a real rebellion. Terrorism, almost by definition, was the domain of losers because when the cause being fought for was a popular one, it could no longer be defined as terrorism, but became guerilla warfare. The difference between the two was simply a question of scale.

This was why it seemed to him that Atlantis, by declaring itself to be at war, had paid the terrorists a compliment they did not deserve.

'The Better World Educational Trust Fund,' offered Big Tom, holding up a file. 'According to our sources, it's a front for either the Vanguard Army or the Sword of God. Or possibly both.'

'Although not the Army of the Vanguard Swords, Tom,' added Little Tom.

'Yeah, I should have made that clear,' agreed Big Tom, nodding at his colleague. 'Thanks, Tom.'

'The Army of the Vanguard Swords being . . . ?' queried Bob Spotto, glancing between Toms.

'. . . a good thing.'

'. . . our kind of fundamentalists.'

Spotto nodded cautiously – wary of such statements, even if he was disinclined to argue with the Unified Front of Toms.

'I see. OK. And *why* exactly are they our kind of fundamentalist, Tom?' he frowned. 'Or Tom?'

'Genuine hard-liners,' explained Big Tom. 'Mad.'

'Whacko. Totally suicidal,' agreed his colleague. 'With strong popular support.'

'Basically, they're like the Amish of the terrorist land-scape. They want a return to a pure, pre-modern society such as existed at the time of the Prophet.'

'And, as such, only use swords. Numerous suicide attacks on government ministers have yet to result in any serious injuries. We feel we should be encouraging them because if all religious fanatics were even *half* as serious about their beliefs as the Vanguard Swords are, then . . . well, we wouldn't have much of a problem.'

'They haven't been . . . discouraged by their results?' Spotto smiled.

'Absolutely not,' replied Big Tom. 'The more members they lose in pointless acts of bravery, the more the common people *idolize* them! In their eyes, these guys are truly *walking the walk*, you know?'

'Right – we were expecting them to basically die out in no time, but their recruitment rate is way outstripping the losses at the other end. Seems like every kid wants to be a Vanguard Sword. And, of course, they still believe

151

that with *enough* swordsmen, they're bound to win one day.'

'So, although psychopathic and fanatical, we're sure they're off the list?' Spotto concluded.

'God, yeah!' Little Tom agreed. 'We should be *giving* them money! They're excellent role models for the violently discontent.'

'Tom? Is that your opinion, too?'

Big Tom sucked in his cheeks, and clucked his tongue three times as he prepared to pronounce on the issue.

'Good quality swords are very expensive items,' he pointed out. 'It is costing them a lot more to fight this way than it would with modern weaponry, and we don't want them to lower their standards for a lack of financing because . . . well, the Vanguard Ground-To-Air Missiles would be pretty bad news.'

It was becoming abundantly clear now that Teri was going to be late home. Perhaps even very late. But she didn't want to slip out of the meeting to call Cameron because she doubted any of the guys would be leaving to phone their *wives*. So it was a question of sexual equality.

Cameron, even though he was someone with a certain track record of being home late, would not be pleased. She'd promised to be home in time to help with his Total Body Scrub. It wasn't her fault, but she was going to end up apologizing for it anyway. She would have minded less if the objective of the meeting was not so pointless – a Top 50, for heaven's sake.

Not that she was surprised. It was the Atlantian way: make a list, quantify the situation, impose order on the anarchy. It changed nothing, and yet it changed everything, because it gave people the illusion of control. And there was nothing that her fellow citizens of the Land of the Free yearned for more than a sense of control. If proof were needed of that, one only had to walk into a coffee shop and try asking for a cup of coffee.

These days there was no such thing as a cup of coffee. *That* you could not have. Instead, presented with a menu like a tax return, you had to choose one of about thirty different *variants* on a cup of coffee. Coffee shops, in Teri's view, weren't really in the business of selling coffee – they were selling people the illusion of being in control of their lives. That was why they could charge so much and get away with it.

In a sense, she supposed, that was exactly what Cameron was planning to do with his Spiritual Stocks: offer people control over the afterlife. And it seemed he had found himself a faith willing to try out his scheme: the Church of the New Covenant – a respectable, but fading sect that was alarmed enough by its diminishing congregations to attempt something radical.

'I thought you wanted to float the group behind the colonic irrigation clinics – the . . . what are they called?'

'The Beyond Communion,' he answered excitedly. 'I am. But I can't use BeComm to launch the whole *concept* of Spiritual Stocks because they're not well known enough. We need an established church. That's why we're starting with NewCov.'

The initial response, he said, was very positive. By no means everyone got what he was talking about, but those who did were very excited. That was all he needed. The launch was set for a few days' time, and all across the country Sunday services in New Covenant churches had included a distribution of leaflets offering the faithful a chance to truly invest in their belief.

Cameron had faith. He believed Spiritual Stocks was going to be the biggest thing to hit the market since the dot-coms, but without their fatal flaw of needing to turn a profit.

* * *

Bob Spotto looked around the table. After nine hours, the Commission's brightest and best were looking a distinctly bargain-basement crew. Even Mike Boggan had gone quiet.

'Come on . . . we're on forty-nine, people!' he encouraged them. 'We must have *one* more organization with an identifiable bank account somewhere in the world.'

He himself was not tired. Or rather, his tiredness had bottomed out several months ago and he had now learned to live with a simple polarity in his life – work and sleep. Paranoia kept him going.

Of course, the entire nation was living in state of constant, twitching paranoia. Not, he realized, that this bothered anyone in government. One could hardly be unaware of how the crisis had allowed them to slip through a multitude of bills, laws and executive orders in recent months, any one of which would have caused an uproar in normal circumstances. Billion-dollar tax rebates for friendly corporations. Oil drilling in wildlife reserves, mining in National Parks. A rescinding of the Freedom of Information Act. Suspension of the right to trial by jury for the millions of full-time residents who were not Atlantian citizens.

It wasn't pretty, but then it wasn't his business, either. There were other people who should have been fighting what was going under the cover of 'war', but it seemed none of them had the nerve. The whole country had gone almost as crazy as these bombed-out hellholes that bred the terrorists in the first place.

Teri knew that Gillian was staring at her long before she turned her way. She'd felt those dark eyes boring into the side of her head, and knew exactly what she was thinking.

She was reluctant to do it. They had looked into the Bee and Comb Union and found very little evidence of terrorist activities. The operation was run on the Atlantian side by a certain Aziz Hamanancy, a man with no known terrorist past, nor even, it seemed, strong religious or political convictions. His credit-card payments over the last six months suggested, moreover, that he was not opposed to the lax morality of the West. Or that, if he was, then he was apparently determined to base his opinion on extensive research. His conversations on the telephone had produced little of interest, barring the odd reference to 'killing the Atlantians' that appeared, when taken in context, to be business metaphors inspired by the book *It Ain't Murder if No-one Calls the Cops*. Unless, of course, the rest of the conversation had been metaphorical, and the apparent metaphors were literal. Either way, the most they could pull him in for at the moment were the usual, all-purpose immigration queries.

Saman Massoudi, the head of the operation in Errat, was more interesting. His wife and children had been killed in the civil war, possibly by the right-wing militia that had brought General Harouni to power. Atlantis had been largely responsible for organizing and financing the General, although he'd since turned against them – the moral of the story being, as always, never to do someone a favour. These days, the NIC was trying to nurture Malek Galaam, the head of the Secret Police, as a possible replacement for the General.

If Massoudi's family *had* been killed by the General's militia, however, he'd at least have a clear basis for holding a grudge against Atlantis. That said, despite the fact that Galaam's police had recently brought him in for questioning, there was no proof that he was a terrorist.

Frankly, the Bee and Comb Union appeared to be in the honey business.

But there remained Ryuchi Takashi's insistence that it was indeed a dangerous organization, with an extremist network spread all over the USA. Teri still hadn't seen his evidence for this, however, because she had yet to receive departmental approval for buying the software they needed to open Ryuchi's file. Taking all of this into account, she was loath to bring the case up in the meeting for fear of ridicule.

But Gillian's gaze did not waver from her until she finally relented and turned to look her way. When, at last, the two women's eyes met, Gillian began to frown questioningly, as if asking why Teri had not brought the Bee and Comb Union up already. Teri shook her head softly. They'd agreed to hold back on talking about it for the moment, and while she was as keen as anyone else to get out of there, she did not see why they should change their position now – except for the fact that Gillian, she knew, had tickets for the theatre tonight.

'The Al-Nur Bee and Comb Union!' Gillian announced suddenly, snatching her head round to face Bob Spotto.

'Now that I . . . *haven't* heard of, I believe,' Spotto answered. 'Do enlighten me.'

Gillian told the whole story, from Takashi's tip to the lean results of their surveillance, only very slightly talking up the evidence. Teri felt sure that no-one would want to add the Union to the list on that basis, and felt vindicated by the pained, doubtful expressions she saw around the table.

'That's not a lot to go on, frankly,' Spotto declared when she'd finished. 'Sounds to me like they're either entirely harmless or . . . very, very good at camouflaging their activities.'

He drummed his fingers on the table, thinking it over.

'On the other hand, I've always heard that Takashi is damn good,' he said.

He carried on drumming his fingers, looking around the other faces in the room, trying to gauge their reactions. Teri could see that they were suddenly starting to hope the end of the meeting was in sight, and letting their judgements be coloured accordingly.

'Of course . . . if they *were* that deep undercover,' he added, 'then this could be the way to flush them out.'

It was a good point, apparently, in that it won over a healthy portion of the table, who were now looking at him with hopeful eyes, nodding encouragingly.

'I don't know . . .' he sighed.

He turned to face Teri.

Everyone in the room turned to face Teri.

'What about you, Teri?' he asked, seeming to give her the final say on whether they could all go home or not. 'Are you with Gillian or not on this one?'

The End minus 16 days

'. . . tomorrow is National *No-Buzz* Day as bee farmers everywhere keep their hives shut to allow emergency forces a bee-free window of opportunity to track down terrorist or rogue hives around the country. Bob Messier, you are Regional Commander for the President's new Bee Task Force, are you confident of a breakthrough?'

'I think we'll have a truer picture of the situation. The problem until now is that we've been inundated by reports of suspect bee sightings, a very high proportion of which have turned out to be inaccurate.'

'How high is "extremely high" exactly?'

'I'm not at liberty to give out that kind of information, but it's . . . high. In a sense we're *lucky* to have this problem, because it shows how tens of thousands of ordinary folks all over the country have been willing to go out there to do their bit for the nation, but the trouble is that a lot of people don't know the difference between a bee and many other species of . . . winged creatures.'

'Such as wasps, you mean?'

'Well, that's an easy mistake. People have been bringing in a lot of *ladybugs* and . . . let's see . . . dragonflies. Especially dragonflies – it's the mating season at the moment and, frankly, it's been getting pretty ugly out there. I don't think next year will be a very *good* year for dragonflies. Or for bats.'

'So, tell us, what can we all *do* to help out on National No-Buzz Day? Are you hoping for a big turnout?'

'*No!* Sorry, I mean . . . no, clearly we appreciate the public's support, but we have the situation in hand, and there *are* some protected species we're getting a little concerned about here, such as the Bald—'

Chapter Twelve

*In which our hero enjoys a peaceful interlude
and we learn something of the history and art of
bee-keeping*

Saman, as promised, had been keeping his end of the
conversation going over the last few days with the girl he
had decided to call Najia because he could not bear for
her to be nameless. Najia seemed appropriate because it
was pretty and was a name for someone who has escaped
from danger – which he was sure was her situation. He
did not like to ask himself what this danger might have
been, but that something terible had happened to her
was clear from the way she shuddered back from the
slightest attempt to touch her, and the way she grew
nervous at the sight of any distant figure upon the
hillside. That was not the result of her handicap –
indeed, if anything, it suggested a possible cause. Saman
had heard of perfectly normal children who lost the
ability to hear and communicate following a shock, and
he could not shake the suspicion that Najia had not
always been this way. There was a knowledge in her eyes
that suggested she *did* know all the words she needed to
communicate her thoughts, but could no longer make
her tongue form them. He had been relieved to see that
she did at least still have a tongue, which had put to rest

the first awful thought that had come into his mind on discovering she was deaf and mute.

He liked to talk to Najia as he tended the hives, even if she could not hear him. He had been talking to her almost constantly for five days now, and even though she never replied, he did not run short of conversation because there were almost four hundred hives dotted about the hills, and each one was worthy of comment. He shared his knowledge with her, telling her everything he knew about bees, telling her about events in the city and the world beyond, answering her imaginary questions and agreeing with her silent comments.

It was probably just as well she couldn't hear him, he sometimes thought, because he had been talking the poor girl's ear off. She *was* around twenty, he had now decided, and, were the world better made, should be hoping to marry a man who loved her, have children of her own, and take charge of a busy home down in the city instead of wandering the hills with a middle-aged chatterbox like him. But none of that would ever be, of course, and he liked to think that his company went some way to filling the void of her stunted life.

«Do you know that people used to think that bees were spontaneously created by rotting flesh, Najia?» he asked as he tied the mule to a tree. The young woman knew exactly what to do now, taking hold of one of the four wooden crates that hung in two pairs over the animal's back. Saman nodded as he took hold of its partner and they lifted simultaneously on the rope handles, walking the two boxes off past the mule's rump and carrying them over to the nearest hives.

«If bees cannot find anywhere better to make their nest, you see, they will do it in a corpse,» Saman announced as they walked, huffing a little as he tried to keep up with Najia's nimble feet. «In olden times, people saw that and they assumed the dead bodies were some-how *generating* bees! Silly, hmm?»

161

In the climax of the afternoon, as summer reached its crescendo, one could almost believe there was a wind blowing from the sun. An airless sirocco blasting with furnal intensity across the empty tracts to crash against the hills above Errat. It was, as the saying had it, hot as a hare's bollocks.

Unlike Najia, Saman wore a headscarf to protect himself from the sun. He hadn't as a younger man, but he'd had more hair in those days. Drops of light streamed over the white cotton as they walked under the trees, the dry grass crackling beneath their feet, and when they dropped the boxes to the ground by the hive, the contents rattled woodenly – but such sounds seemed not to travel far on the heavy afternoon air, slowed as if underwater.

The hive was about chest-high, and comprised two whitewashed wooden boxes – a shorter one resting on top of the taller. At the base of the lower box, there was a small hole through which the bees were coming and going, heads tipping forward like little helicopters as they took flight, and from within there emanated a roar like a waterfall, so deep Saman could almost feel the sound in his belly.

«They're fanning, poor things,» he said, turning to Najia.

She frowned back at him, and he offered her a theatrical explanation – first letting his tongue hang out like a dog, then fluttering his fingers either side of his shoulders. She smiled at his mime, and nodded her comprehension.

«We'll see what we can do about that, shall we?» he proposed, sliding the scarf to his shoulders. Saman never wore any of the protective clothing that less gifted bee-keepers relied on, and it was best not to have his head covered as bees sometimes panicked when they thought themselves trapped between the cotton and his skin. For the same reason, Najia slipped off the faded blue ribbon that was wound about her wrist, bunched her long black

162

hair in her hand and tied it back in a tight ponytail. She was quite calm around the bees, no doubt because she could not hear their roar – and so long as one was not frightened, of course, one was far less likely to be stung.

That was Rule No. 1 of dealing with bees: Just Stay Calm.

So her handicap actually gave her an advantage over other people in this one domain – she was already a better bee-keeper than many people Saman knew who had been doing it all their lives. And she seemed to enjoy it. Indeed, she was so rapidly at home helping him with the hives that he had never even had to ask himself what he was to do with her – it was self-evident that she could, should and would stay here. Saman, unfortunately, could not be here all the time himself, but he had decided to have a word with some of the local goatherds, explaining his decision – there were people up here that he knew he could trust to watch over her and make sure she had everything she needed. And her handicap would not even pose them any particular difficulty as they were a pretty taciturn lot themselves.

He produced a flat, metallic tool from his jacket pocket, slipping one end under the lid of the hive, and grunted as he broke the wax seal the bees had made on the inside. The roaring instantly changed pitch as the trapped air flowed out over his fingers, perfumed and sticky. He lifted off the lid and set it down on the baked weeds, peering over into the darkness inside. A couple of hundred bees instantly took flight and began circling around the hive, paying them no particular heed. Indeed, so long as they made no brusque movements, the insects would not even notice them.

«See?» he said, gesturing for Najia to approach.

As the two of them looked into the hive, hot and honeyed air spraying over their faces, they could see the dark forms of the bees clinging to the combs inside, beating their wings in a unified drive to bring the temperature down.

«Air conditioning and all modern conveniences,» he smiled, tasting the Jana nectar on his tongue as he spoke.

He examined the ten frames on which the bees had built their combs – they were full but for the outer two, and even they were nearing completion. It was time. He knelt down and opened one of the boxes, then started to take out the wooden frames it contained – identical to those hanging in the hive, but empty of honeycomb.

«Amazingly, nobody really understood bees until about two hundred years ago, when a very brilliant man named Lorenzo Langstroth came along. *His* claim to greatness, my dear, was that he invented this,» he announced, holding up one of the frames. «A wooden rectangle. So simple it took goodness knows how many thousand years for someone to think of it.»

He gasped as he stood up, a jab of pain running up his right leg from the knee.

«An Atlantian, you know,» he winced, placing one hand on the hive as he slowly flexed the bad leg. The pain subsided, and his pinched expression melted to a soft smile. «I suppose he'd almost have to be with a name like that, wouldn't he? *Lorenzo Langstroth* – isn't that a wonderful jumble? But then he was a mixed-up fellow all round, Mr Lorenzo, to tell you the truth. He was a very religious man, born on the holiest day of the Western Year, and studied theology because he thought it must be his calling to become a preacher. However, when the day came for him to preach his first sermon, he rose before all the people gathered in the church, opened his mouth to speak . . . and nothing came out! Suddenly, he had no more words on his lips than you, my dear. He became hysterical – *silently* hysterical, that is – and had to be taken away to a madhouse in which, on and off over the years, he would spend fully half his life, poor fellow.»

164

Saman shook his head sorrowfully and took hold of a bee that was walking along the top of a frame, pinching it between two fingers like someone picking a ball of fluff off their clothing. He bent down, and pressed its dart to the side of his knee.

«*Sh-sh-sh* . . . it's all right,» he whispered to the insect, holding it in place. His fingernails reached under the bee's abdomen, wiggling the dart free of his leg without letting the creature rip itself away, and he then placed it unharmed back on the hive.

«One time, when he was coming out of one of these periodic bouts of head troubles, a doctor decided that *bee-keeping* was a healthy, outdoor activity that would help his recovery. Which you know yourself is true,» he smiled, turning back to Najia. «It worked at first, and he found the bees such fascinating creatures that he began writing his great book about them – *The Hive and the Honeybee*. And that book changed the world. Before Mr Lorenzo came along, you see, bee-keepers had no option but to destroy a colony when they took its honey. A true bee master might have managed to save the queen and enough workers to let them rebuild the hive, but most of the time the whole colony was killed. Which, of course, meant that honey was quite a luxury. But now, if there's one thing Atlantians have always been extremely good at, Najia, it is taking a luxury and finding a way to make it cheap and plentiful enough for the common man. They're more socialist than the Socialists, really.»

Saman chuckled, handing her the empty frame, and Najia smiled back. He placed a hand either end of one of the central frames in the hive, and began to pull. It resisted at first, but then – with a soft, sucking sound of tearing wax – began to slide out from its slot in the box. It came covered in bees that Saman delicately brushed off once it was free, some flying off, others dropping dozily back down into the hive. He admired the insects' work – a fat, heavy comb filling the frame to its corners, each perfect hexagon of honey capped with a thin wax seal.

«So thank you, Mr Lorenzo,» he smiled, and leaned down to slot the frame into the crate that had been on the mule's back, putting the lid on to stop the whirring cloud of bees, in which they stood, following the scent of honey in there.

«Lorenzo realized that bees, you see, are very like humans,» he announced from around Najia's knees. «Their attitude to honey is exactly that of men to money – they only need a certain amount to support the nest, but they will make as much of it as they possibly can.»

Najia, not looking at him, perhaps not even aware that he was talking, gently slotted the empty frame she was holding into the space in the hive, giving the drowsy bees time to get out of the way as it slid down the grooves.

«So the genius of Lorenzo Langstroth was that he realized one could build a hive in two parts – a lower part where the queen and her babies lived with all the honey they could ever need, and an upper part in which the workers would store all the excess honey they made, hmm? And separating the two, as you know, a grille through which the queen is too big to fit.»

He took hold of the next frame, and began pulling.

«And that way . . .» he grunted, «. . . the bee-keeper can exploit the colony without laying it waste or even disturbing the ordinary functioning of its society. It's a simple economic system in which everyone benefits – the bees have their hive, safe from predators, and the bee-keeper has his honey.»

The second comb sucked free, and he held it up, once again brushing away the insects crawling over its surface. He placed his nose briefly to the honey and breathed in the heady perfume it exuded.

«Beautifully simple,» he sighed. «And yet, in three thousand years of bee-keeping, all over the world, it wasn't until a half-mad Atlantian came along that anyone saw the solution. All that destruction, all those dead hives . . . all for a lack of imagination. Nothing *modern* about it, really, nothing *technological* – anybody throughout history could have done it, if they'd only looked closely enough at what the bees do, and had an open mind. But for some reason they didn't see it, and so life only tasted sweet to the wealthy. People sneer at Atlantis, and think it has brought nothing but trash to the world, nothing but industrial junk food and fizzy drinks, but they have no idea how profoundly different their life and everyone else's life is compared to two hundred years ago. People hate Atlantians because they are rich and fat and ignorant, but they don't realize how the bitter hardship of their own lives has been softened by the people of that country. Atlantis brought *sweetness* to the world, and we no longer need kill the bees to get it.»

He opened the box, slotting the second comb in alongside the first. As the cover went back over it, he stopped briefly, leaning down with his palms on the wood. It was too hot for working today.

«But if what Aziz says is true, I wonder what old Lorenzo Langstroth would think of his countrymen now – once again killing the hives, but this time from greed rather than necessity. No doubt it would drive him mad.»

He shook his head and cursed softly, sighing, «Mail-order bees.»

Saman lowered himself to a squatting position as he reached for another empty frame. His knee was no longer hurting him so much, the venom already beginning to work its therapeutic magic. He passed Najia an empty frame for her to slide into the hive, smiling.

«But the bees drove the poor fellow out of his mind, you know – soon after he finished writing his book, he had to be taken back to the madhouse. He finished his days so manically obsessed by the creatures that the doctors had to deny him access to any kind of reading matter because he could no longer stand the sight of the letter B!»

He laughed, and she smiled delightfully back down at him, apparently unbothered if she had no idea what the joke might be.

An hour later, Saman was covered in bees.

There were perhaps as many as fifty thousand of them on him, the vast majority clumped on his arm in a bulbous black mass. Enough to kill him a hundred times over if even a fraction of them decided to sting.

As a general rule, it's not a good idea to stick one's hand into the heart of a beehive, as Saman had just done. Bees do not like this. They can be rather short-tempered, depending upon the weather and the political situation in the city state that is their home. Indeed, some of the more antisocial of the five thousand or so strains of bee need very little provocation at all, attacking a person at fifty paces from their hive, simply for being there. If one single bee, at such a moment, stings and marks a person as an enemy with her scent, the entire nation will take up arms against them.

But there are people that bees will not attack, not even when they break open a hive and start messing around with the queen. The sentries will not object to their approach, and the workers will not seem to mind their large fingers reaching into the heart of the hive and pulling out the comb containing the royal daughters. They will fly out and land on the person – sometimes hundreds, or even thousands of them crawling upon their hands and face and body, and yet not one will sting.

Most bee-keepers will take great precautions before opening a hive. They will wear protective clothing from head to toe, sealing off every entry and being careful not to let the netting over their face touch the skin. They will smoke the hive before opening it so that the bees panic and save as much honey as they can by eating it. This the bee-keepers do because a well-stuffed bee is generally too lethargic to attack an invader. But there are people who need do none of these things.

They are called bee masters.

Quite what quality they have that enables them to interfere with the rigid orderliness of the bees' society without fearing attack – taking their honey, substituting one queen for another, dividing or merging entire hives as they wish – remains a mystery. It is not that their methods or gestures are any different from those of another bee-keeper. Nor is it a question of being more experienced. There simply appears to be something about them as people that all of the bees in the hive – perhaps a hundred thousand insects joined in a single, collective mind – recognize as benevolent.

Bee masters, unsurprisingly, are very calm people.

So far as Saman was concerned, there was no mystery to his talent. Indeed, he did not think it a talent at all, at least not on his part. It was the bees who were extra-ordinary, not him. For the bees seemed to understand that he meant them no harm. Perhaps even that he loved them.

He knew most people would find that incomprehensible – how could a human being feel love for something so utterly alien as an insect? Fascination, certainly. Respect. But *love*? The very idea would have something unholy about it for them, their concept of love being inextricably bound up with human qualities like softness and physical warmth, and with human emotions like affection, hope and fear.

In Saman's experience, most people's basic expectation of love was that they should see themselves reflected in it. As with their Gods. Why else look for a God who would love them as they loved themselves? A God who would save them for all eternity, as they were today,

169

and raise that wonderful self to glory. Above all, a God as needy as them, but on a cosmic scale – damning those who did not praise Him to the fires of hell. As though, if you could create a universe and all the life in it, you'd really give a damn what the average mortal in the street thought of you. Or as though you would actually deserve to be praised if you managed to be that powerful and that *petty* at the same time.

That was why, try as he had in the past, he couldn't avoid feeling that religion was illogical. Yet the more illogical a religion was, the more fervently its followers believed in it, as though the depth of their feeling was in inverse proportion to the shallowness of the thing they believed in. And because their beliefs were shallow and obscenely pretentious, it took almost nothing to offend them. So religion, he considered, inevitably led to hatred.

The difference in Saman's love, a real God might be able to note, was that it genuinely was not about himself. Indeed, his love was about everything that was beyond him – all the beauty of a world that was perfect in its indifference to him. His love was for an inhuman world that would continue with the same impassive passion, weaving its webs and building its combs and burrowing its tunnels, whether he were here to see or not. And the love arose from a sense of privilege that he *was* here to see, for a short time, how the world kept itself young.

He was content to call what he saw God, for he had no other word for it. But it was not the God of the books. He paid lip service to that God for his own safety – going to prayer as his society expected, and listening to the holy words, and bowing when everyone else bowed, and not giving a hint of his doubts. For he did not feel that others would understand what he was saying, if he even knew how to say it. For them, those words held everything. But, if he was honest with himself, for all their beauty, what he heard did not match what he *saw*. As much as he'd tried to let the words transport him, they did not reproduce the wonder of watching the bees.

So if they were God's words, Saman was forced to conclude, then apparently not even God could put the beauty into words. And even supposing He could, then what did it say of that God that there were children of His, such as Najia, who were, through no fault of their own, beyond the reach of those words? How Godlike was a God who could not reach equally everywhere? This was a question best kept between himself and the bees, obviously, because some people might be so humble in their devotion that they'd kill him for saying that.

Saman was a practical man. He did not think there was any genuine mystery to the universe. The fundamental question *he* asked himself was not 'How did this all come to exist?' but 'How could it be otherwise?' What was the *alternative* to the universe, after all? What was *nothing*?

He'd tried to imagine a Nothing, and couldn't because the Nothing, paradoxically, became a *Something* in his head. It was a point, or a tract, or an infinity – whichever way he turned it round, there was still a cohesion there. It was still something.

So Zero, he concluded, *implied* One. A Zero was *a* Zero. So it was also One. And that paradox, he suspected, was what powered the universe. Everything reflected it, everything was a manifestation of it, and nothing escaped the equation: at any time some things were and some things were not, and the things that were would eventually cease to be and other things would rise in their place. And nothing could be repeated, but nothing could stop it happening over and over again. And people were no different: they were not, then they were, then were not. Zero and One, a simple binary language that they experienced as Life and Death.

He knew it was a simplistic explanation for a world of

infinite complexity, let alone a universe, but he suspected the explanation *had* to be simple, or else it would not work. And it did work – that was the one thing that was obvious to anyone who cared to look. It had been working for eternity, for so long that the sun itself was just a single spark spinning out from its conflagration.

It was a perfect system that required no maintenance, no outside hand, and that would never have an end just as it had never had a beginning.

So, logically, it was better if there was no God.

Because a God would make it imperfect.

But you could *call* it all God, if you wanted. Call yourself God, in effect. That was fine, so long as you remembered that the universe and that part of each unique thing that is of one with it, the silence in every person's heart, might be intelligent but deaf and mute, and might have some other name that it could not hear, and could not speak.

The End minus 15 days

'. . . of these kinds of weapons be justified against such a small country?'

'Yes, they would be. What these couch-potato pacifists don't seem to *realize* is that Errat has, per capita, the third largest army in the world. This is a highly militarized nation with battle-hardened soldiers who have, in the recent past, fought a long and exceptionally bloody civil war. Add to that the fact that they have the tactical advantage of being on their own terrain, and this is *not* going to be an easy fight, if it comes to that. I don't think we could afford to exclude the use of whatever weapons we have to give our soldiers a fighting chance here.'

'About that terrain – is it really as tough as people are suggesting?'

'Absolutely. Errat has some of the toughest terrain in the world – again, people shouldn't be lulled by the apparent insignificance of the country into thinking a military operation there will be easy. It's dry, it's hot, and it's hilly.'

'But how high *are* the hills, exactly?'

'Any soldier will tell you that it's not about height, it's about *gradient*. Now, if you calculate the total land surface area of Errat, and then divide that by the height differential between the coast and the country's highest peaks, you come up with a more extreme ratio than *any other country in the world*. In that sense, it's actually *because* it's small that it is an exceptionally tough enemy to take on. Atlantis has much higher mountains, obviously, but by the calculation I just explained, ours is basically a *flat* country. So our soldiers would be faced with an *extremely* challenging—'

Chapter Thirteen

In which the situation starts to deteriorate rapidly, beginning with the wrongful arrest of our hero's cousin in Atlantis, an episode that will have serious repercussions on his sex life

Theresa Downe felt good in black. As she crept down the corridor, she wore black combat trousers, and a cropped black combat jacket. Black boots. Black gloves. A black helmet with a black visor. And a black gun. The only element of the ensemble that broke the theme were the three yellow letters over her left breast, repeated gigantically on her back, that identified her as a federal agent.

It had taken her five years of pushing to get assigned to the Bureau's combat division in Corona, but it had been worth the effort. She was a law-enforcement commando now, the best of the best. It was what she had always dreamed of becoming, right back when she was a child, investigating the murder of her Candy dolls.

Nine other agents followed silently behind her, all in identical black uniforms. She reached the apartment in question, and signalled to her colleagues to take up position. One agent hung back, covering the stairs leading up to this floor of the apartment block, another took the stairs leading up to the level above. The rest bunched either side of the door, Rojo and Winston flanking her, sledgehammers at the ready.

She smiled behind her visor as she prepared to listen in through the door, mentally stepping outside her own body to see herself standing there, a warrior leading her troops.

They would see. She did *not* have issues.

'Intelligence assures us that the subject is home, and he is alone,' Hyde had informed them in the back of the van on their way here. 'This does *not* mean that he is not to be handled with extreme caution. We're not dealing with a common criminal here, but a lunatic who *wants* to die a martyr. We don't know what kind of weaponry he may possess, we don't know what his agenda will be when faced with arrest. We want him alive, but he may be determined to die and take as many of us with him as he can, so I want this handled fast and with *maximum force*. For all we know, the entire apartment could be booby-trapped to blow itself to high heaven. Obviously, we cannot allow that to happen. Now, if everybody is clear on the routine, all that remains is establishing who's going to take point. Any volunteers?'

'I'll take point,' Theresa shot back, raising her hand.

There was a silence in the back of the van, the black-suited agents swaying from side to side as they crossed the city. Agent Hyde looked over the benches, gauging the team's reaction. It wasn't easy, because even when the visors were up, the helmets tended to limit facial expression.

'Everybody OK with that?' he asked casually.

He sensed an uneasy shifting in seats. But nobody spoke.

'Good. So nobody has a *problem* with that?'

'Do *you* have a problem with that, sir?' Theresa asked.

'No, I do not, Agent Downe. But I want a . . .

consensus decision by the team. I think that's natural, don't you?'

'Well . . . it kind of sounds like you're suggesting they *should* have a problem with me taking point. Why would that be?'

'I don't know why that would be. Why *would* that be?'

'Because maybe they don't want to be led into combat by a woman.'

Like a spell being broken, the van returned to life, groaning in unison. The magic word had been spoken.

'*What?*' Theresa demanded, turning to face her colleagues.

'Jesus, Downe, can't you take time out?' Agent Rojo sighed behind his dark visor, his voice muffled and distant. 'We don't have time for your issues.'

'What do you mean?'

'I mean you have issues.'

There was a muffled murmur of agreement around the van. It was the considered opinion of most of her colleagues that Agent Theresa Downe had issues. They never went into the question any deeper than that because they weren't inclined to speculate on another person's emotional life. It was enough for them to know that she was the only woman in the team, and women had issues that they, as men, couldn't be expected to understand.

They considered that their behaviour since she'd been assigned to the team had been exemplary in that not one of them had ever made a pass or told a sexist joke in front of her. So the fault lay entirely with Downe herself.

'What do you mean, I've got *issues*?' Theresa snapped. 'What the hell does that *mean*?'

'It means what it means,' Rojo shrugged in his cotton-mouthed voice. 'You know what it means.'

'No, I do not. Did it ever occur to you that maybe the

177

only issue I have is the fact that you all think I have *issues*?'

'You what?' Rojo frowned, lifting his visor. 'Jesus, Downe, this is not group *therapy*! I don't know *what* you're talkin' about. I'm just not sure you should take point until you've dealt with all these fuckin' *issues* of yours, you know?'

'Mind your tongue, Rojo,' Hyde warned. 'OK. Does anyone else think that Downe has issues?'

'*Whoa*! You're putting this to a *vote* now? I don't believe this! You are actually asking them to vote on whether I have *issues*? You can't do that! No fucking way!'

'Hey! What goes for Rojo goes for you too, Downe – I won't have that kind of language here from any of the men *or* . . . the women.'

'The *women*?' Theresa frowned. '*What* women? I'm the only one!'

'I'm aware of that, Downe, but I didn't want to single you out – it makes no difference to me whatsoever that you are the only woman on the team, and frankly, I'm surprised that *you* would want to minoritize yourself like that. We're all together in this. We trust each other with our *lives*. No questions, no exceptions.'

'In which case there's no problem with me – a woman – taking point, then, is there?'

'Did I ever say there was?'

'So *am* I on point, or do I have to conclude that I'm being discriminated against here?'

Hyde took a deep breath, holding back his irritation. He was doing his best to make this work, really he was. Intellectually, he had no problem working with a female agent. But God *damn* the woman had issues.

'OK,' he announced, 'Downe is on point.'

'Thank you.'

'Don't thank me. So far as I'm concerned, it was never an issue.'

*　　*　　*

Theresa lifted the stethoscope from the door.

'He's watching TV,' she whispered to Rojo. 'Sounds like . . . I don't know. Some crap cop show.'

Rojo's dark orb of a head turned slowly her way, and tilted slightly.

'Ready?' she hissed, preparing her gun. 'One . . . two . . . *three*!'

The two hammers swung back in unison, impacting on the door hinges and shattering the wooden frame. The sole of Downe's boot followed through, pushing the door down, and she charged over it into the apartment, shouting '*Federal Agents! Freeeeze!*' at the top of her lungs. The hallway led straight forward, the entrance to the living room six paces down the corridor. The suspect was out of his armchair already, shocked and bewildered by the sudden commotion. '*Freeze, fucker!*' she yelled, levelling her pistol with his eyes.

He was too startled to move, his eyes flicking from one side to the other as the agents flooded into the room behind Theresa and took up positions.

'*Get your hands up!*' she snapped. '*I said get your fucking hands up!*'

His hands rose jerkily, as though his brain was not quite in control of his arms. The room was silent, except for the sound from the TV, on which a character standing in the shadows was explaining that the entire Atlantian government had been infiltrated by extra-terrestrials. Suddenly, a glint entered the suspect's eyes.

'Wow!' he grinned strangely. 'This . . . this is Zero Tolerance, right?'

'*Shut up!*'

'Sorry . . . it's just . . . is the door *included* in—'

'*I said shut UP!*' she snarled, jerking her pistol in his face and taking a step towards him. For the first time amid the commotion, she saw he held a small rectangular object in the palm of his hand. It looked like it was probably a mobile phone or a TV remote, but she couldn't be sure – something in his manner gave the distinct impression that he was excited, as though he knew himself to be secretly master of the situation.

'Drop the device!' she ordered.

'What device?'

'*Drop the fucking device NOW or I shoot!*'

He looked up at his hand, as though only now becoming aware of the object he was holding. He let it go and it dropped to the floor, the batteries spilling out of their compartment.

'Good,' she said, relaxing her grip on the trigger and moving forward to frisk him. This was going well, she allowed herself to think as she dropped to her haunches, running her hand up his leg. 'Now, do you want to do this the easy way . . . or the *hard* way, fucker?'

Aziz Hamanancy could barely find the breath to speak, so exciting was the situation into which he'd been thrust. He couldn't see this woman's face, nor even guess at what kind of a body she had under all that black combat gear, but it didn't matter – this was a completely different kind of erotic experience the agency was offering its clients here, something for true connoisseurs. In a way it was intellectual rather than physical, given that, due to the bulky uniforms the girls all wore, you could almost mistake them for men. Yet the intensity of the Zero Tolerance experience was unlike anything Aziz had come across before – purer, harder, and incredibly realistic. The excitement was already almost too much.

'Umm . . .' he answered, looking down at her with wild, illuminated eyes, '. . . the hard way?'

Theresa froze as her hand reached his groin.

'OK – *he's carrying*!' she yelled over her shoulder.

The team tensed in unison, fingers closing tighter over their triggers. Gingerly, her own hand traced the outline of the object concealed in his pants – it was hard and cylindrical. Possibly a stick of Semtex.

'Is this armed, you sick fuck?' she demanded in an angry whisper. 'Is this going to explode on me?'

'It . . . might do,' Aziz admitted. 'It's on a *pretty* short fuse.'

Theresa paused to consider the situation, the TV co-incidentally providing her with a tense soundtrack as the agents on-screen penetrated into the darkness of the shuttered house with their torches, for some reason not even pausing to try the light switches. A deep, bass instrument was going *duuur-duh . . . duuur-duh* as they crept across the creaking floorboards. It was a huge, widescreen model with a home cinema sound system that resonated around the whole room.

Was he or was he not bluffing about the fuse? Since he could not have been warned that they were going to raid his apartment, what conceivable reason could there be for him to be sitting in front of his TV with an armed explosive in his underpants? Surely no sane terrorist, however ready he might be to sacrifice his own life for his cause, would run the risk of blowing himself up just by reaching for a potato chip. But then he did not have the expression of a particularly sane man – his face was twitching as though he were on the point of sneezing one second and shitting his pants the next.

On the screen, the two agents jumped through an open doorway, guns at the ready, and the music accompanied them with a slight change of rhythm, now going *dur-duh . . . ting! . . . dur-duh . . . ting*! It was making it very hard to think clearly.

The device, she reasoned, could not be rigged to blow if she undid his zipper, because what if he'd needed to pee? There had to be some other kind of trigger.

Meanwhile, the two agents were approaching a closed door, and a somewhat out-of-tune violin had started going *eeeee . . . ee-ee-eeee . . .*

'Will someone shut that fucking TV up, please?' she shouted.

Instantly, a hail of bullets blew the screen into crushed ice and knocked the speakers flying. It lasted a second or two, no longer, and the music stopped. One speaker was left standing, a low farting noise emanating from its punctured woofer.

'Oh my *God*!' the terrorist gasped, gulping heavily. 'This is so *naughty*!'

'*Shut up!*' Theresa snapped, placing her pistol against his testicles.

It was a bluff to get them to back off, she figured. There *had* to be a separate trigger mechanism of some sort, and he was trying to get them to fall back so that he'd have a chance to set the bomb off manually. She was prepared to stake her life on it – though not, frankly, anybody else's.

'OK . . .' she called. 'Everybody out – I'm going to take a closer look.'

If her colleagues had any misgivings about the wisdom of her choice, they respected the fact that she was on point and did as she commanded, slipping back out the living-room door and taking cover behind the wall in the corridor.

Theresa took a deep breath and flipped back her visor for a better view, figuring that if she was wrong about this it would provide her with no protection anyway.

'Don't you *move*, motherfucker . . . or I swear I'll shoot your balls off,' she warned as her free hand went for his zipper, carefully pulling it down. Squinting to look inside, she could see no wiring of any sort. The device, whatever it was, seemed to be contained in his underwear. She reached up for the button to undo his pants, pressing her gun barrel forward against his testicles as a reminder of what she was capable of doing.

'I warn you . . .' he grunted through clenched teeth. 'It's going to blow . . .'

'Is it now?' she whispered, gingerly parting the material and hooking a finger into the elastic of his underpants to peer down inside.

And that was when Aziz couldn't take it any longer.

Most of the agents remained in the apartment after Aziz Hamanancy had been carried out. They were supposed to be searching the premises for evidence of terrorist activities, but had yet to begin. Indeed, the moment Hyde left with the medics, they'd collapsed onto the furniture and begun talking, keeping their voices low enough to not reach Theresa, who had yet to come out of the bathroom.

'I still can't get over it,' Rojo gasped. 'Talk about . . . *fanatical*! I don't get these guys. Fuckin' wacko. Do you guys get these guys?'

'What's to *get*?' Winston answered. 'Fuckin' wacko, like you say. They want to become martyrs, you know? I guess he was just . . . *really* fuckin' excited about his seventy-two virgins.'

'Poor Downe, man.' Rojo shook his head. 'That's . . . not right. We're not paid for that kind of shit.'

'And her a woman, too.'

'Maybe it was better that way,' Rojo whispered, eyeing the bathroom door. 'I mean if that had been *me* . . . the guy was a dead man. I swear to God. A fucking *dead man*!'

'Well, hey, she *did* kind of lose—'

The conversation was cut short by the click of the bathroom door. Theresa appeared in the opening, her face a luminescent pink from vigorous scrubbing. She looked around the room, seeing the discomfort in her colleagues' eyes, and knew exactly what they'd been talking about.

'I'm OK,' she smiled tightly. 'There's no need to look so . . . *embarrassed*, guys. Seriously. No harm done – these things happen, right?'

They nodded softly, but with eyes that seemed to be saying, 'They *do*?'

'OK . . . listen,' she sighed, leaning against the doorframe, 'two things: Firstly, without wanting to hurt your feelings – it's really not such a big deal as guys think it is. I mean, I know you're all very proud of what you can do, but . . . it's just not, OK? This is not a *fire extinguisher* we women have to deal with. Secondly – and I want you all to remember this in future because it seems to me like maybe some of you boys haven't noticed it yet – but secondly, and most importantly, I am one . . . *seriously* sexy lady.'

She placed a hand on her waist and let her hip slide marginally outwards. Her head lowered fractionally, eyes softening, and she dropped her voice an octave.

'Say, Rojo . . .' she rasped, '. . . can I take point?'

The transformation was startling enough that Rojo's eyes widened despite himself. There was a heartbeat's silence as the others watched him, and then the room burst into laughter. A slow smile broke over Rojo's face, gradually conceding defeat.

'Any time, chica . . .' he growled, '. . . any time.'

Theresa pushed herself off the doorway, her body slipping back into its former self, and she strutted over to take a free seat. She grabbed the cigarettes Aziz had left on the coffee table, lit one, and put the pack in her pocket, saying, 'Yeah, yeah . . . you're just scared now that I might shoot *your* balls off, aren't you?'

The End minus 14 days

'. . . to comprehend the level of hatred a terrorist like Somun Mossaby feels towards Atlantis, you have to understand that in his eyes *we* are the Evil Ones, Ayesha.'

'But how *can* they believe that? How do you explain that attitude to the millions of viewers out there who are probably thinking . . . "*Huh?*"?'

'Well, a large part of it is that these people think our society exploits the weak around the world.'

'But, for heaven's sake, can't he see there are plenty of weak people *within* our society? Aren't *they* being exploited too?'

'Well, that's not . . . the point is that we cannot engage in a dialogue with this kind of person because they are not open to *doubt*. If they were, after all, they would not be resorting to violence, would they? Indeed, clearly the *opposite* is happening – because they are convinced they are right, they are becoming more extreme all the time. That's the mark of a true fanatic. Because people like Mossaby are *convinced* that they represent the forces of Good, they are psychologically free to use *any means necessary* to achieve their ends.'

'Even killing innocent civilians?'

'Absolutely. A terrorist believes the death of an innocent is acceptable collateral damage in light of the overall objective. Indeed, this is what differentiates *terrorist* warfare from *legitimate* warfare – it's not about car bombs versus tanks, as most people assume, but about who is an acceptable target.'

'Right. Although . . . *they* would argue that we ourselves have bombed civilians.'

'We don't ever take civilians *themselves* as targets, we are simply attacking the enemy's *infrastructure*. There's no way we can avoid that. But it's totally different. And our cause is just.'

Chapter Fourteen

In which the people of Errat discover, perhaps not without a certain measure of pride in the distinction, that their small country has no fewer than four terrorist groups in the President's Top 50, and our hero discovers that he is one of them

The scrum at the eastern entrance of the bazaar was as intense as Saman had ever seen it, the big red pillars milling the crowd like corn. Of course, he was as proud as anyone else that the bazaar's four gates had recently been declared a World Heritage something-or-other, but that didn't make it any easier for people to do their shopping.

Some years ago, the Revolutionary Government had been planning to knock the gates down. It was a shame, of course, but ultimately sensible given how many people got killed each year coming through them. If something had to be done, then you might as well just do it – and it certainly made more sense than moving the gates outside the city, which is what the so-called intellectuals had urged be done instead. Either they were gates or they were not. Why spend all that money to rebuild them in a place where they would serve no purpose? Fortunately for the world's heritage, however, the Revolutionary Government itself got knocked down by the coup first.

The General had proved more astute about the gates' value to the city, and tackled the problem by having the Western gate, the prettiest one, reserved solely for tourists. The downside of this was that almost the only thing anyone could shop for now on that side of the bazaar was leather bags. Truly, Saman did not understand how any group of people, no matter how rich, could possibly require that much luggage.

Around by what was now effectively the service entrance, Saman clutched a linen-covered tray containing his first comb of Jana honey, which he had placed on a sheet of glass. He surveyed the scene with trepidation, watching the gate grind the breath from the soft little creatures passing through. How was he going to get his precious honey through it in one piece? He'd hoped to arrive when the bazaar was deserted for the afternoon, ropes drawn across the stallholders' wares and the whole populace shut in the cool of the city's interiors. He could have carried the tray safely inside, spiriting it unseen past the white-eyed sheep carcasses and along the silent valleys of beans and spices to his own little shop deep in the labyrinth. That was what he usually did. And he enjoyed the stillness of the bazaar at those moments, the air too fat and lazy to carry noise.

Today was a big day. He'd hinted to the other members of the Union that he was preparing a surprise for them. It was a secret because, in all the years that he'd been working on his Jana bee project, the only people in whom he'd confided were Aziz, out of practical necessity, and his own best friend, Dari, whose stall was next to Saman's. Dari was entirely trustworthy – he made his living reading and writing letters for the illiterate, so discretion was the basis of his profession. His stall was virtually the opposite of Saman's: empty but for a little table and chair, with a stool in front for the client, and a few examples of his calligraphy pinned to the walls. And he himself was a wiry little man, skin almost shrink-wrapped to his body. What Dari and Saman had in common was a certain romantic streak, both devoting much of their energy to thoughts of what could be or might have been if only. Some years back they had installed a tiny door at head height in the wall between their stalls, a kind of chat-flap that could be closed when Dari had a client. Through it, Saman had spent countless hours telling his friend about Jana bees, discussing the day's news and commenting on the people walking past along the alley. Only Dari knew how special today was – that Saman would be bringing in his first sample of Jana honey – and he had sworn not to tell a soul.

Not that anyone outside the Union had the slightest idea what Jana honey was, anyway. In Errat these days, honey was honey, same as in Atlantis. Only Saman refused to accept that.

But again, the two of them had something in common in that way. For despite his claims to the contrary, Saman knew that Dari still dreamed of being recognized for his artistic skills as a calligrapher, although he was realistic enough to accept that the letter-writing would no doubt always be his main source of income. People didn't have money for art these days, or an appreciation of it, and if they bought calligraphy for their walls, it was going to be a print by one of the handful of star practitioners. Making a name for yourself as an un-known was all but impossible unless you had a big poster company behind you.

It was all about marketing now.

By the time Saman was extruded on the inside of the gate, still holding the tray high over his head, he felt himself to be a different man. Taller. Slimmer. Perhaps even wiser, too, for his brush with death. The crush of Errat's bazaar gates, like a crowded subway or a rock concert or a revolution, was a human crucible, capable of stripping the pretension of individuality from people, of control over their lives and the manner and moment of their departure from this world. Your feet were not yours to command, and one trip could see you sucked under and trampled to death. You were a grain of sand in an hourglass.

Once beyond the gate, the crowd breathed out, the white and black paving of the marketplace visible through the blur of legs. Giant cones of light descended from the round holes in the vaults of the bazaar ceiling, a row of giant dunce's hats running along the interior street, thick with the ochre dust that enveloped the whole city by late afternoon. Saman kept his honey aloft as he waddled through the bustle, the swirling speckles of dust winking out before him as the tray cut through the light.

Although the architecture of the bazaar testified to the glory that Errat had once known, the merchandise itself proved how far the nation had fallen. Where once traders had converged from all over the world to buy silver and honey and precious stones in its legendary alleys, it seemed to Saman that these days every other stall was selling pirate CDs, or cheap designer knock-offs, or pop-star bath towels. It was a clearance store housed in a palace – a terrible disappointment to the tourists and a wallow in absolute cultural humiliation for the locals. Hence, no doubt, the lack of protest when the plan to remove the gates had been put forward.

There were those for whom the bazaar symbolized a sickness gripping the nation as a whole, who yearned to cleanse it of soft-porn calendars and lacy scarlet under-wear, and return it – or so they imagined – to some kind of former purity. Quite which moment of the past this would be was unclear to Saman as, historically, moral qualms had never got in the way of a business deal there, whatever the merchandise. And it struck him as less reprehensible to sell lacy underwear than whole women, as they had under the caliphs. But the myth of an

190

uncorrupt, pre-colonial past had now taken such strong hold in some people's minds that he knew there was no fighting it. Indeed, he himself wouldn't object to the moral fanatics removing most of the rubbish from sale, simply because it was so tacky. The problem was that he knew these people would not stop there, given the chance. Their fight against immorality would never be over and one day, inevitably, they would end up whipping people for selling suggestively shaped vegetables.

It was probably because he had allowed his thoughts to drift to such matters that Saman stopped paying attention to what was around him and walked straight into the path of a sheep that was being carried across the alley on someone's shoulder. He collided with its skinlessly grinning head, knocking the bearer to one side. His tray lurched on as he jerked to a halt, and he seized his breath as he felt the sheet of glass slide forward under the linen cloth. He tilted it just in time to stop it slipping out, coming to rest with his body bent over like a man about to dive into water.

«Mind where you're *going*, why don't you?» snapped the sheep, or so it seemed as the man struggled to hoist the beast back onto his shoulder.

Saman peered round the corpse, recognizing the younger of the cousins from whom his brother's family usually bought their meat.

«I'm so sorry!» he said, «I was—»

«Mr *Saman*!» the butcher gasped, recognizing him in turn. «No – it is I who am sorry. I was at fault.»

Saman looked at him in surprise. To his recollection, the man had never addressed him so formally.

«No, truly – it was me.»

«But it was my sheep! I must ask you to accept my complete apology.»

The man, whose name Saman realized he did not know, seemed genuinely mortified by the accident. And clearly it *hadn't* been his fault, or, at worst, no more than half his fault. But there was no arguing with the urgency with which he was laying claim to the blame – to persist in so doing would be rude.

«I . . . well, no harm is done, is it?» he smiled.

«Thank you, Mr Saman,» the man gushed. «You are very kind.»

«It is just as well, mind you.» Saman winked. «If you knew what is underneath this cloth . . .»

«Yes! Yes!» the butcher nodded, «I understand.»

«You *do*?» he frowned.

«No . . . no, I don't!» The man winced. «I didn't mean to suggest—»

«I should think not – it's a secret!» Saman chuckled, unable to hide his excitement.

He realized that several people around them now seemed to be following the exchange, all of them gazing at the tray in question. The butcher's face cracked into a smile that was distinctly curious.

«I understand,» he giggled faintly. «I shall speak to no-one of it, I swear.»

«Come by my shop later and you will see,» Saman suggested. «You can be the first convert to my little revolution!»

«Your . . .» the man gulped. «Yes, Mr Saman. I shall . . . as soon as I can . . . but today we are very busy, you understand?»

«Of course,» Saman smiled. «When you have time. I shall be expecting you!»

As he carried on his way, he felt the butcher's gaze following him, raw sheep on his shoulder. On the edge of his vision, Saman was aware of a little crowd gathering around the man, all of them watching as he ambled along with his tray. It was very curious. He turned the corner into the next alley with relief, finally escaping their regard, and yet, he had not gone more than a few yards before he felt that odd pressure on his back again.

He stopped and glanced over his shoulder, getting the distinct impression as he did so that people were looking away. Taking one hand from the tray, he tentatively felt his bum to see if his trousers had been torn in the crush of the gate, but there seemed to be nothing wrong. Perhaps he was just imagining it. Perhaps no-one was staring at him, really.

And yet, as he walked on, the feeling did not go away. Indeed, it seemed to get more powerful with each successive pool of light through which he passed. There was a noticeable dip in volume behind him, and it seemed as though people coming the *other* way were glancing at him now – or rather, they looked past him down the alley but soon found their gazes being turned towards . . . him. As if they were turning to see what those ahead of them were pointing at. Saman was not given to being fanciful, and he tried to convince himself that this impression he had of being singled out from the crowd was all in his head, but then, as he neared the corner of his own alley in the bazaar, something happened that was undeniably peculiar.

He had seen Rachid, the copper merchant, turn the corner of the alley before Rachid saw him. Their eyes met at about twenty paces, and Saman smiled.

Rachid, however, did not. He stopped dead, staring straight at Saman, then he turned on his heel and quickly disappeared back around the corner. Saman slowed to a halt, frowning. It was irrefutable – the man had seen him . . . and run off. The man had *run off*!

What on earth was going on? The only thing it could possibly be, the only thing that was different about today, was that he was carrying a tray of Jana honey. Now, excited as he was *himself* about this, it hardly justified this kind of reaction. And nobody was supposed to know about it, anyway. Unless Dari had been telling people. But even if that were the case, why would they . . . ?

A sudden thought jolted him. Was it possible that he'd

193

misjudged everyone, and the problems experienced with the bees during the colonial period were *not* forgotten about, as he had assumed? Was *that* what this was all about – had the idea got around in his absence that he was going to unleash a new plague of bees on the city?

He had to talk to Dari.

He strode up to the corner, ready to face the scrutiny of the other merchants and determined to put an end to their ludicrous behaviour without delay. Once they tasted the honey and once they understood that the bees were quite harmless so long as they had their trees, he was sure this whole misunderstanding would be resolved in no time. He turned into his street, and paused to gauge the gravity of the situation. Funnily enough, no-one seemed to be paying him much attention. He walked slowly on, looking from one side to the other, but the merchants appeared not to notice him – calmly going about their trade without looking his way.

Too calmly, it now seemed. They were pretending not to notice him.

Dari was busy with a customer, but since Saman hadn't been there he'd left the chat-flap open.

«. . . and tell Makhti how sorry . . . I am . . .» Dari repeated as he took down the man's letter, «. . . that her daughter . . . stepped on . . . a landmine.»

Saman fitted himself into the stall, pulling the table on which he'd placed his tray back inside, and smiled through the hole at his friend. Dari glanced at him with wide eyes – a look of startled disbelief – and turned back to his client.

«Is that it?» he asked.

«I will pray for her other leg,» the man answered.

«I will . . . pray . . . for her other . . . leg,» Dari scribbled. «OK?»

«And that she gets back the use of her eyes.»

«. . . the use of . . . her eyes,» he repeated, snatching a

furtive look at Saman. «Very good. That's nice. Would you like to mention the nose, too?»

«Umm . . . no, that's not so important,» the man decided.

«So . . . let's see – the drought . . . the sheep . . . your cousin killing his wife . . . thank you for the dates . . . the landmine . . . I think we've covered everything, haven't we? I'll just sign it and send it for you.»

Saman got a teaspoon from the jar beside his chair and, lifting the linen off the tray, dug it into the wax to scoop out a little of the black honey for Dari. As soon as the client had left, he peered through the hatch, grinning.

«Are you ready?»

«What the hell are *you* so happy about?» his friend snapped, pocketing his money.

«Try this,» Saman answered, poking the teaspoon through the hatch.

Dari frowned at the teaspooon, taking it almost as if he were not sure what it was, and turned back to Saman.

«My God, you don't know, do you?»

«I think I do, actually, Dari,» Saman replied. «Have you, by any chance, been talking about my bees to anyone?»

«Have I . . .? Of *course* I haven't been talking about your fucking bees! Have *you* looked at the newspaper today?»

«No . . .»

The newspaper Dari thrust through the gap was so chaotically folded that it appeared to have been read in a high wind.

«*Read!*»

«Read what?»

«*The bloody front page!*»

With great difficulty, Saman located the front page amid the bouquet of paper he'd been offered, extricating it from the rest as any attempt at refolding the newspaper in the tightness of his stall was doomed to failure.

Under the heading Atlantis Targets Local Groups, he began reading about the Atlantian publication of its list of terrorist organizations.

«Oh my God . . .» he heard Dari sigh. «This is excellent, Saman!»

«I don't under—» Saman had begun to answer when he came to the first mention of the Al-Nur Bee and Comb Union. «. . . *What?*»

He snatched the crumpled page taut, speeding on down the column.

«*What?*» he repeated.

«My friend . . . *this* is honey,» Dari congratulated him through the gap.

«It doesn't make any . . . WHAT?»

«Well, exactly – *what?*» Dari answered. «This is what everyone wants to know, Saman! There have been people looking for you all day – police, journalists, the Union, and a few I wouldn't like to ask. *What* is the word on everyone's lips as in *what* have you been doing, my friend?»

«Nothing! I have been doing *nothing*!» he gasped, momentarily putting down the paper. «I don't under-stand – what does this mean?»

«I'd have thought that's pretty clear, isn't it?»

«Why are the Atlantians saying I'm a terrorist?»

«I don't know. Maybe you should ask that cousin of yours.»

«Aziz? You think Aziz is responsible for this?»

«You're asking *me?*» Dari sighed. «What the hell do I know – until two minutes ago, I thought you were probably in prison.»

«In *prison*? Why would . . . people aren't taking this *seriously*, are they?»

«Well, how seriously do you think they should take it?»

«*Obviously* it's a mistake! The whole thing is ridicu-lous! It's a joke!»

Dari looked pityingly through the gap, any doubts he'd had about his friend long since swept aside. The poor man was far too naive to be secretly involved in terrorism.

«Ridiculous or not, Saman,» he muttered, «you can't deny the facts.»

«What facts? There are no *facts* here!»

«Saman . . . the only fact that matters, so far as you or anyone else on that list is concerned, is that it is tantamount to a declaration of war by the United States of Atlantis.»

«A war on *what*?»

«Well . . . on you.»

The End minus 13 days

'. . . wait any longer to own the car of your dreams – it's already *yours* at Shawshank Motors!'

The Angry Teenager is not fooled for one second, but then again that Tokado SUV is one beautiful hunk of machinery.

'*This* is WINN 24/7 – non-stop *World* Information Network News, bringing you *instant* in-depth analysis of the issues, with Ayesha Novak,' God's spokesman reminds him, and he's back with Ayesha – sleek dark hair and a hint of a smile playing over her lips.

He's just old enough to remember how the news used to be delivered by sombre, middle-aged men in serious suits. He can remember a time when his parents thought getting a new car was a big deal. And he knows that Ayesha and the gleaming chrome bumpers on the SUV are one and the same thing, and that she doesn't know the first damn thing about journalism and those bumpers won't help in a crash, but he wouldn't seriously want to go back to that dull, slow world of his childhood even though his head spins with the fairground hysteria of life today. Like movies were better in black and white, but how can you give up colour once it's there?

'Welcome back. A quick Stock Market update – the Bing 100 *continues* its decline, down a further percentage point on last night's closing, but trading on the SpiDer Index remains bullish, with particularly strong performances by FirBap and BeComm. In a minute we'll be looking at last night's fatal shooting of a Dumona surgeon as he was leaving the abortion clinic where he worked – police suspect a Pro-Life activist in the killing. But before that, as promised, we're going to be joining Bill Gundersen, WINN's Special Correspondent, for a report on the growing controversy about the possible *environmental* impact of a conflict. Bill, I believe this is basically all about *trees*, isn't it?'

'That's right, Ayesha – specifically it is to do with the *Jana* trees we've been hearing so much about, given their close symbiotic relationship with the terrorist bees. Now, I don't know if you can see very well on this satellite photo I have here, but this whole hillside is literally *covered* in white dots that could, the millitary say, be beehives. Now, *some* of these are probably decoys because, according to Intelligence reports, the terrorists have been painting *hundreds* of ordinary boxes white in an attempt to protect as much of their bee-strike capacity as possible in preparation for a ground invasion. The problem for the pilots, in the event of a conflict, is going to be clearing *all* of these off the picture before we can expect to see any little soldiers appear on it. I don't know if you can see what I'm talking about here or—'

'No, that's coming across pretty clearly, Bill. It seems like we're talking about an *enormous* amount of work for the pilots, aren't we? I mean, they look like . . . from here they just look like *rocks* or something.'

'Well, some of them probably *are* rocks, Ayesha. Even though this is the highest-resolution photograph currently available, the fact is that you *just can't tell*. So the pilots would have to fly *extremely* low to get a clear lock on their targets, which will leave them wide open to rocket attack – which is why military would prefer to drop *bigger* bombs from *higher up*. Plus – and this is the real problem – there are *trees* clearly visible on this picture. What is *beneath* those trees? We don't know. The pilots don't know. The fact is that *nobody* knows.'

'So they are going to have to take out the trees before they can be sure the terrain is bee-free – and that's pretty tough on the trees.'

'*Exactly*, Ayesha. Now, the military is conferring with various environmental groups on this question because it seems Jana trees are *unique* to this part of the world. What worries environmentalists is that an air campaign could destroy what they say is an *irreplaceable* natural resource. So the moral dilemma facing the military right now is: *bees or trees*? They *have* given their firm assurance that they will do everything in their power to ensure that innocent trees are not destroyed, but that's not good enough for the environmental groups, who are asking to be given time to send their *own* neutral observers into the hills to identify at least a *section* of the terrain that is free of hives and can hence be declared a "no-strike" area to pilots. The military say that is not an option because the terrorists could obviously just move all their hives *into* the no-strike zone as soon as the observers left the scene.'

'So they are in deadlock.'

'Absolutely. But the military is unlikely to give way to what one general privately described as, I quote, "the wacko obsessions of a few vegetarians". I should explain that this comment came after he left a particularly acrimonious meeting with the environmental groups, shouting, "*Don't you people mow your lawns?*" I think that gives you some idea of how heated this—'

Chapter Fifteen

*In which Marge Spiegelflug reappears in her role
as a switchboard operator and, in the course of
her duties, answers a telephone call that will do
wonders for our hero's ranking in the President's
Top 50*

Marge Spiegelflug was a very nice person. So much
so that one of her younger colleagues on the Liberty
Mansion switchboard had once snidely described her as
being 'so, like, *hard-core* nice?' That particular young
woman had since left to pursue a career in amateur
pornography, so it was ironic that Marge, for reasons
few people could now remember, was referred to as
Hard-Core behind her back.

After fifteen years of working the telephones her
enunciation had slurred to the point where she answered
each call with a totally unrecognizable 'Libidimension'.

Fortunately, this was more or less how Saman pronounced it anyway.

'Yes. Hello,' he said carefully. 'This is it's the real
thing Libidimension, baby?'

'Yessir, it is,' Marge answered, immunized by years of
experience with crank callers to the way Saman had
mistakenly addressed her in pop-music vernacular. 'How
may I help you?'

'Yes, I love you so truly to talk about terrorism, please, with someone our bodies together.'

Marge winced briefly as something seemed to snap taut in her abdomen. Terrorism. He'd said 'terrorism'. That was all it took – one word, and her bowels were on fire again.

'Sorry, sir,' she breathed, 'I'm not sure I understand you. Who exactly do you wish to speak to?'

'The man! I . . . *wish* to talk to The Man, please.'

'Which man, sir?'

'I don't know. This is . . . our lips meeting for the very first time, baby. About terrorism for you. About Al-Nur Bee and Comb Union.'

'About a . . . *Nubian* coming in?' Marge frowned, speaking very slowly now. *Was* there a country called Nubia? Could be. It sounded like there should be one, really. She'd never been very comfortable with foreign geography. And besides, if anything important happened somewhere abroad they always showed where it was on the news. 'You have information you wish to pass on about terrorist activities?'

'You bet your booty. I *no* a terrorist, see?'

'You know a terrorist, sir? You mean this . . . Nubian coming in?'

'Yes, I mean no.'

'Sorry, you do . . . or you *don't*?'

'I mean *I* no this terrorist!' Saman snapped. 'From the very bottom of my heart, I *no* . . . kill Atlantians! So this . . . terrorism thing . . . this is a very *bad* mistake for Al-Nur Bee and Comb Union, you know?'

Marge gulped, her heart racing as she digested the information the caller seemed to be passing on. Her butt clenched urgently, she tried to rise above the pain because this was no time for her to worry about her personal problems. There was no waddling off to the rest room possible. She immediately understood that this call could be vital to the security of the nation, so she'd just have to take the pain, for her country's sake.

Her face hardened as she snarled, 'You're damn right he's making a mistake, sir . . .'

The diarrhoea had come back a little over a week ago, on the day they had the Krantzses over for a barbecue. She'd hoped it was just the sausages, but there was no avoiding the truth any longer. The old problem was back again, but now compounded by family troubles as well as her general anxiety about the world being full of bug-eyed maniacs. It had nothing to do with pigs.

Her credit card was maxed out because Ned had forgotten to pay it off. Never, in all their years of married life, had Ned forgotten a thing like that. She worried that he was taking too much on with his determination to protect the family, but he was not open to questioning on the matter. They were an old-fashioned couple at heart, and certain aspects of family affairs were his domain and his alone. Which, up until now, had suited Marge just fine, and so she felt that it was neither morally her right nor in the interest of their marriage to force him into a discussion about it.

If her mother had taught her one useful thing about life it was that you should never, ever humiliate your man. Never, no matter what the rest of the world did to him.

'If your man ever has egg on his face, sweetheart,' had been her way of putting it, 'just smile and make him an omelette.'

It was the first and foremost among the Golden Rules she'd passed on to Marge prior to her daughter's wedding. Her mother was very formal like that – she maintained that half the reason why so many couples divorced these days was that they'd had far too much fun getting married in the first place.

Marge had been kind of depressed by the barbecue. In

earlier years they had been true family occasions – everyone out in the yard, the grown-ups getting comfortably toasted in the lounge chairs, Ned Jnr and Hermione playing with Frankie and Travis. This time, though, it had all seemed to splinter. Once they'd finished eating, Judy and she had spent an inordinate amount of time cleaning up in the kitchen, both pretending it made sense to wait for the dishwasher to finish its cycle rather than admitting that they just didn't want to be outside while Ned showed Tom the rifle he'd bought and they talked civil defence for an hour. As women, they both knew they couldn't really play a full role in the discussion and it would only mean that all four of them got stuck in this incredibly heavy dynamic. By eclipsing themselves, they could reappear once the guys had had a good run at the subject and move the conversation onto something lighter because they'd played no part in it. Only she'd got the squits instead and Judy on her own had been unable to make the men change tack.

To make matters worse, when she got out of the bathroom, there had been the thing with Ned and Frankie – whom they had to call Francesca these days, apparently. She hadn't intended to eavesdrop, but she'd emerged, palm still pressed to her belly, and stopped at the top of the stairs to give the pain time to subside before she went down to join the others. Ned's room was just there, and the door was shut, so it wasn't her fault if she overheard them or caught an unmistakable whiff of tobacco coming through the keyhole.

'They just, you know . . . *totally* freaked?' Frankie was muttering. 'Like, sure – they'd *never* done it doggie-style, had they? I really *believe* you, guys! And Dad was all, like, who is this man and has he plighted his troth unto you, my child? Like all of a sudden he thinks he has to behave like this character out of a novel by some fucking parson's daughter who died of *tuberculosis*? You know, what was *that* about? So I'm, like, I don't even particularly fucking *like* the guy, thank you very much! Which he totally takes the *wrong* way, of course! So I have to resort to arguing that, OK, let me get this straight – the *bad guys* are religious maniacs, and *we're* not, but your daughter should be a virgin even though she's seventeen, and you think I should see a fucking *therapist*? Hell-o? What is wrong with this picture, guys? I really don't know which is worse in a way – at least the terrorists are straight-arrow, down-the-line, fucking *wacko*, right? Whereas we've got this whole, weird . . . *denial* thing going on where on the one hand it's like "Hey, kids, here's this week's video of blondoid teeny-bopper simulating masturbation while singing Give It to Me Now, so *check . . . it . . . OUT!*", and on the other it's like "Excuse me, why can't I find the evolution chapter in my *science* textbook?" you know? On *exactly* what evidence are we so fucking certain that we are the sane ones here, please?'

'Right . . .' she heard Ned drawl.

That was the thing that really got her. Practically every single word that had come out of Frankie's mouth had shocked her, but she was someone else's child. It was Ned's reply that chilled her heart. The way his answer was so completely . . . numb.

That was her child. That was the little boy she'd tucked into bed and made chocolate milkshakes for, whose underpants she'd ironed and whose tiny hand had reached up for hers in the street. All of a sudden alien to her. Disaffected. Weary of a world he had yet to discover, thinking he'd seen it all on TV already. Thinking it had been rendered obsolete by a hundred video games. A worthless world that had lost its novelty but had yet to become an antique.

Part of her wanted to slap him round the face for that single word, shout, 'How *dare* you talk to me like that?' and send him to his room. But he wasn't talking to her, was already in his room, voluntarily, and suddenly he was the one doing the slapping. So mostly she just wanted to take him in her arms and beg him to be a little boy again, promise she'd love him always no matter what and make him chocolate shakes every day if only he would smile and be happy and, above all, not be friends with nasty little girls who did it doggie-style with boys they didn't even like. One hand steadying herself on the banister, the pain seemed to stretch now all the way from her womb up to her throat.

'*Your* dad seems kind of . . . *weird* at the moment,' she heard Frankie suggest.

'You have no idea,' her son droned. 'He's so losing it. It's fucking embarrassing, believe me.'

'I mean . . . *a gun?*' the girl giggled. 'Ned Spiegelflug Senior has a *gun*? Is that a mid-life crisis or what?'

'You got me,' her child laughed. 'I have no idea *what* he thinks he's going to do with that thing. Like what does he imagine – the terrorists are going to be *invading*? He's going to wait until he can see the whites of their eyes?'

Marge listened, wincing for her husband because she knew the laughter was deserved. She did not want to be hearing this. If only they would say something anodyne, it'd be easy to break herself away. But it didn't seem likely and, worse still, she was worried that if she moved now they would hear her and know she'd been right outside his door.

However cautiously she crept down, with every single step of her Mr Whippy legs the stairs would moan under her sprawling suburban butt. Her eyebrows rose in alarm as she heard Frankie ask, 'So what have you got to offer me here? I need something to pick me up.'

'Is this OK?' her son answered.

'Sure. Why not? Blow my brains out.'

'Right. I have to do this at least once a day.'

'Totally with you. It's like taking a dump.'

'Right. Don't you sometimes think it would be so cool to just—'

Marge jolted on the spot as suddenly her son's voice was squashed by three rapid slams of drumbeat, a jack-boot stamping on a bug, and a man began to howl over the clang of electric guitars. Marge seized her chance and skittled down the stairs, thanking God for being spared hearing whatever her child was going to say next.

She stopped at the bottom to regain her composure before joining the others outside, and listened to the racket coming through Ned's door. Marge Spiegelflug knew it was inevitable that she dislike her children's taste in music, of course. She did not expect to understand. But surely Ned could appreciate that this noise was just *horrible*, couldn't he?

The attraction of the screaming aural torture offered by the Huge Hard Gods completely escaped her.

Marge's throat had gone dry. She took a sip from her bottle of imported mineral water, which was all she drank these days. Ned said the terrorists only needed to put a few gallons of arsenic into the reservoir to kill the whole city.

'So,' she gulped, squeezing her buttocks in case the added liquid caused an overflow the other end. You just never knew with the squits. 'Which Atlantians are we talking about here, sir?'

'*Any* Atlantians!' Saman replied. '*All* Atlantians! No problem, yeah? This big mistake – because I *like* Atlantians! You must *believe* me!'

'I do believe you, sir,' she answered cautiously, placing a hand on her aching belly. 'But the terrorists . . . why do you think *they* want to kill Atlantians?'

'Heh? How do *I* know? They are crazy persons! Not me!'

'You mean this . . . er . . . Nubian coming in?'

'*Yes! How many times I have to say this?*'

'Well, there's no need to take that kind of tone, sir.'

Saman did not mean to be rude, but he had the impression of going round in circles. The last two days had been very trying. Once he'd learned about the Union's inexplicable inclusion on the Atlantian list of terrorist groups, it had been instantly clear that he could not go home. Dari had offered to put him up in his house, and the two of them had left the bazaar soon afterwards, spacing their departures by a few minutes so that nobody would see them together. Since then, he'd been holed up at Dari's trying to sort the situation out.

The first thing he'd tried, naturally, had been to phone Aziz. But there was no reply from any of his numbers. This, Dari suggested, could only mean one of two things – either he was on the run himself, or he had been arrested. Either way, it meant that they had no choice but to deal with the problem on their own.

Saman tried to contact the Atlantian consulate in Errat, but discovered that they no longer had one, having withdrawn all diplomatic representation from the country after the Revolutionary Government came to power. Although relations were much friendlier with the general, they had not yet officially recognized his government and so the consulate was still closed. Without any obvious interlocutor he could approach, his limited knowledge of Atlantis had made it seem logical to try phoning the place that everyone knew was the seat of its government: Liberty Mansion.

Getting a number for Liberty Mansion had not been easy, but Dari had eventually found it on the Internet. Neither of them had a computer, even though the Union, at Aziz's instigation, now had a web site. Saman wasn't quite clear what purpose their web site served, but it did exist, which seemed to satisfy Aziz. Dari had helped Saman log onto it once, by going to the city's one

208

Internet Café, and they discovered a page – which was all it was – on which visitors were presented with a picture of a smiling Saman holding a jar of honey, and a link through to the e-mail address Aziz used for work. Saman loathed the picture – his discomfort with the camera was all too clear from that bizarre, lopsided smile. He looked like somebody who was going to do obscene things with that pot of honey.

Calling the number they'd found for Liberty Mansion late at night his own time, Saman had ended up wandering the maze of the building's automated answering system, trying to discover some way of getting through to a human being amidst the interminable options the system offered him 'for his convenience', as the voice said. It had required extraordinary patience, with more dead ends and returns to the point of departure than he could now remember – all of which, he was keenly aware, would be costing his friend a fortune in international charges – but buried deep in a list of sub-options for information about school tours of the Mansion, he had eventually come across a sub-sub-option offering him connection to a live operator.

That was when the system started telling him that 'your call is important to us, and please hold for a short while.' It just kept saying that for almost an hour, over and over between snatches of an orchestral version of the national anthem, and all the while Saman was thinking about just how damned *important* the call was going to turn out to have been when his friend's phone bill came.

Eventually, however, he had found himself speaking to Marge Spiegelflug, whose usual callers, it had to be said, were schoolteachers enquiring about facilities for children with special needs, not foreigners phoning with information on terrorist plans to murder Atlantians.

Not even the crank calls had produced one of those yet, although she had once had a man ring up about bringing a party of clinically diagnosed psychopaths.

'Listen,' the caller commanded. 'This very important thing you must believe me, baby. About the Al-Nur Bee and Comb Union: . . . no bombs, OK?'

'No bombs?'

'No. *Bees!*'

'*Bees?*' Marge frowned. 'I'm not sure I—'

'Yes, bees! Like for honey, you know? But different. This very special Jana bees, very powerful!'

'You mean like . . . *killer* bees?'

Ned said that there were over fifty million rats in the city, and the terrorists probably only had to introduce a single Ebola-carrying rat to infect the entire rodent population and hence spread the plague everywhere. But he hadn't thought of killer bees.

'Well . . .' the caller sighed, '. . . yes, OK, people *say* this, I know. Jana bees very dangerous bees, kill lots of peoples and all that, OK? OK. But they make a special *honey*, too! Only this bees! Very strong honey, like a drug! This is what the Al-Nur Bee and Comb Union bring to Atlantis. This *only*! No bombs, OK?'

'Uh-huh. And then what? What happens when people eat the special honey?'

'They never eat *another* honey again, I think! That's it, you know? Finished!'

'Oh my *God!* Are you *sure?*'

'I think so. Really, yes.'

Marge felt a lurch in her stomach. They were planning to poison the food supply. Ned said they'd probably try that. She had a vision of moms all over the country right this moment, pushing their carts down the supermarket alleys, innocently buying honey for their families, for their children – wanting to give them something wholesome and healthy. The vision switched to a kitchen, the family lying on the floor – eyes staring lifelessly, and swollen tongues hanging out. Half-eaten slices of toast still on their plates.

She saw her own family, Hermione clutching her bared midriff as the poison took hold, perfect white teeth clenched in agony.

No, Hermione ate papaya.

But Ned . . . and Ned . . . they'd had toast.

'Is this honey already here?' she asked urgently, her heart pounding.

'It all ready, yes,' Saman replied. 'Big supply.'

'But has it made it *here*? In Atlantis?'

'Made in Atlantis? No, this is no good. You need special flowers. In Atlantis, Jana bees dangerous – they sting, I think. Maybe kills lots of peoples.'

Marge's breathing was shallow and rapid, her whole midriff a solid block of pain, as if the contents of her bowels were backing up and pressing against her lungs.

'But . . . but . . .' she began to panic. '. . . how can we stop it? What should I do?'

'Tell the President!' Saman answered. 'Al-Nur Bee and Comb Union is *good* for terrorism, yeah? No problem for killing Atlantians! Lot of bees, lot of honey.'

'But . . . I don't know if anyone will *believe* me!'

'They *have* to believe! Very important! Maybe Al-Nur Bee and Comb Union send special *honey* to President? Maybe send some Jana *bees*, you know – like mail-order bees, Atlantian style, because they kill them all, you know?'

Marge was hyperventilating now. It just kept getting worse. The man was describing a truly nightmarish scenario: a two-pronged offensive with poisonous honey in the supermarkets and super killer bees in the postal system. They could send them all over the country – people would open the packages, be stung to death, and the bees would escape into the wild, capable of striking anyone, anywhere. Nobody would be safe.

'OK. OK,' she panted, her belly cramping violently. Any second now – any *second* – it was going to happen. She could hold it in no longer.

'Excuse me . . .' she gasped. 'But can you . . . can you *hold* for a second, sir? I'll be right back. Believe me – your call is *very* important to us, OK?'

She ripped the headset from her ears and staggered to her feet, clutching her abdomen. Hot coals couldn't have made the journey to the rest room more painful.

Back in Errat, Saman began to protest as he heard her give him the by now dreaded assurance that his call was important, but it was too late. She was gone. And he could not wait for another hour at Dari's expense. He cursed softly, and put the phone down.

«So?» his friend asked, passing him his glass of mint tea.

«I think it went very well,» Saman announced.

«So they believed you.»

«Oh yes. No doubt about it.» Saman nodded, sipping his tea with a more relaxed expression than Dari had seen for some time now. «She was in an awfully big hurry to go and tell the President, you know.»

«Good,» Dari sighed. «Well, let's hope that will put an end to this nonsense.»

It was the first time in two days that the pair of them had enjoyed a moment of inner peace, the situation at last seeming to be back in their control. The moment, however, was cruelly short-lived as a heavy, arrogant knock sounded on the door below.

The two men's eyes snapped towards one another, their bodies freezing as they both realized instantly who it must be down on the street.

It was two in the morning. Only the secret police knocked on your door at two in the morning.

The End minus 12 days

'. . . pollen.'

'*Pollen?*'

'Yes. You know, Miss Novak, we have the best and most highly trained Special Forces Units in the world, but people should never forget that, at the end of the day, they are just flesh-and-blood men. Now, just as in the general population, a significant proportion of these men suffer from allergies that mean they are severely handicapped in high-pollen conditions, putting their lives and the lives of their comrades at risk. In a covert operation against a terrorist encampment, a single sneeze can turn what would have been a successful mission into a nightmarish fiasco.'

'Of course. Yes, I can see that. So . . . in that case . . . the trees have to go?'

'Well, Miss Novak – no-one *wants* those trees to go, but we have to make a decision about which is more important: the life of a tree, or the life of a soldier. I'm sure most Atlantians will be pretty clear about where *their* priorities lie on—'

Chapter Sixteen

*In which Teri Hunt, unable to sleep due to her
anxieties about the developing international
crisis, attempts to fondle her husband's penis,
and Aziz, in hospital, searches fruitlessly
for his*

Shortly after she joined Cameron in bed, Teri Hunt's
hand crept over his pelvis and slid down towards his
penis. The two of them were lying on their sides, her
groin spooning his behind. A drowsy moan escaped
Cameron's lips as her fingertips delicately stroked over
his inner thigh, his right leg jerking under the duvet, and
he grunted, *'Tickles . . .'*

Her fingers came to a halt just on the edge of his
tangled little copse of hair, paused for a few seconds,
and then lifted away from his body. Fine. It tickled.
There was nothing more annoying for a man than to be
lying comfortably in bed and have a naked woman start
tickling him in the genital area.

Part of her wished to stay as they were, enjoying the
warmth of his body, but her feelings were hurt and
she rolled over on her back instead. End of story, she
thought, looking up at the ceiling. They needn't have had
sex, for heaven's sake, she'd just wanted to snuggle up
and hold onto his wang for a while. That's all. And if the

214

wang had decided to wake up, well that would have been a different matter. But it tickled, so . . .

She tried closing her eyes, but with no more conviction than if she were taking a jacket that wasn't her colour off a rail and holding it briefly against herself in the mirror. She was closing her eyes for confirmation of the fact that she was not sleepy. How could she be at a time like this, when events were moving so fast and her conviction that a terrible mistake was about to be made seemed to grow by the day? That phone call – everyone was so damned sure that phone call was a serious tip about an imminent terrorist attack. She seemed to be the only one who found herself, with each successive replaying of the tape, growing more and more sure that the reverse was true, that the caller was trying, with his broken command of the language, to say that the Bee and Comb Union was *not* a terrorist group. But try as she did to bring others round to her point of view, they seemed to dismiss it out of hand as Teri Hunt being obtuse for the sake of it. Teri being *difficult*. Teri being a woman . . . why, Mike Boggan had even had the cheek to say she looked *tired*.

'What exactly do you mean by *that*, please?' she'd snapped.

'I mean you look like . . . you need a rest, that's all.'

'No, you don't. Come on – what are you really saying?'

'Teri . . .' Bob Spotto sighed. 'He didn't mean anything at all. Can we get back to the subject, please? We're not here to discuss personal issues.'

With a gun and a means of getting away with it, she could have killed every man in the room at that moment.

She was discussing personal issues?

Of course she was. She was a woman. She, raging with illogicality hormones and a suspected case of PMT, was incapable of judging the issue on its own merits, whereas Mike Boggan was a level-headed male. As was Spotto himself, whose judgement was not in any way impaired

215

by the fact that he was desperately searching for a chance to redeem himself following his failure to avert the SECI. And none of the men there would have let their opinion be swayed by the fact that their boss was so blatantly favouring a certain line of thought. Only women were influenced by personal issues.

So suddenly everyone was acting as though the Bee and Comb Union, far from being a dubious, last-minute addition to their list of target groups, was actually one of their main suspects all along. The facts all fitted: the man Hamanancy had been shot while resisting arrest, the anonymous phone call to Liberty Mansion . . . clearly they had uncovered a terrorist plot in the nick of time.

They were sure of it. In her own case, however, the more the evidence mounted against the Bee and Comb Union, the more her intuition told her not to trust appearances. Like her interview with the terrorist Aziz Hamanancy: on the one hand his admission of involvement in the plot against Atlantis seemed perfectly clear, certainly clear enough for Bob Spotto, but on the other she could not shake the impression that he was innocent . . .

Teri had been sent to interview him in the military hospital outside Corona where he was being treated for the wounds he had received while resisting arrest. The doctors had warned her that he was heavily sedated with painkillers, and drifting in and out of consciousness most of the time, but Teri had figured there would be a positive side to that – his guard would be lowered by the drugs.

He was sleeping like a baby in bed with its parents when she arrived – which is to say flinging limbs out at random, pulling faces, and whimpering. Hamanancy did not, to her eyes, have the look of a terrorist. He was a somewhat overweight, gentle-faced man in his forties – a person who gave every impression of enjoying the good things in life. The very fact that he was apparently a regular client of one of Corona's biggest escort agencies rather argued against his being a religious fanatic, and a search of his apartment following his capture had uncovered no weaponry or terrorist literature of any kind. Yet the arrest report clearly stated that he had behaved in an alarming and threatening manner.

Which, apparently, was why they'd had to shoot his balls off.

He'd seemed to be simmering towards wakefulness as she took a seat beside his bed to watch over him . . .

It had just so happened that, at that moment, Aziz was searching for his penis.

In the confusion of his dream, the doctor's assurance earlier that day that they had 'saved the penis' had come to mean that the bastards were keeping it in a jar somewhere, a jar that he was busy searching for in the surreal hospital of his drugged subconscious.

He had made his way down to a vast basement where he discovered they were keeping amputated body parts of every conceivable kind. It was like a museum of flesh, each room he entered boasting a world-class collection of specimens in glass jars. So far he'd found legs, hearts, livers, intestines, and several rooms devoted to parts of the anatomy that he was unable to identify, but which looked pretty important.

Why were they keeping all these things, he wondered. What had happened to the people to whom they once belonged? He crept through the ranks of shelves, telling himself it was folly to search for his own, not very large member in amongst this junkyard of humanity. Was it some kind of organic Lost and Found, or was this place evidence of something darker underlying Atlantian society? Was it proof of some awful truth about the hidden human cost of these last decades of peace and prosperity, some terrible, cannibalistic secret that the State was covering up?

He sensed he was getting close to his penis when he opened the door into the next gallery, stopping dead in his tracks at the sight that greeted him.

He was in Bums.

It was an entire depot: smooth bums, hairy bums, dimpled bums, tight bums and saggy bums. Pert peaches, fat marrows, cauliflowers, pumpkins and pairs of pears. Impossibly large and shapeless bums, bums like garbage bags sitting out for collection. Each and every pair different.

It was fascinating and somehow very moving, a testament to humanity in all its endless variety. He would never have thought that buttocks could be so eloquent, that they could reveal so much of the lives of those who had once sat on them, somehow evoking their characters and hopes and sadnesses.

He walked slowly down the parade, filled with a kind of melancholy rapture, a sense of tragic revelation. The bums spoke of what was best and worst in humanity. They told him that the world would always be dominated by selfishness, and greed, and arrogance. But the good bums, the courageous and decent bums, would always be there too, holding the line between what was best and wise in human civilization and a descent into anarchic, foul-smelling flatulence.

Hope would always remain, but it would always remain hope.

The bums had spoken.

He reached the far end, where a door led out of the bum gallery into a room that he somehow knew had to contain the penises. Aziz paused with his hand on the door, bracing himself for what he knew might be a traumatic experience.

He was about to learn the Ultimate Truth.

Inside this room there might be thousands of penises of every shape and size. And having seen what lay within, he would finally know *exactly* how he compared to other men. This was knowledge that he would have to live with for the rest of his life. Knowledge, perhaps, that no man was supposed to have.

He closed his eyes and bravely pushed the door.

Hamanancy's eyes had snapped open to stare straight at her, his face drawn as he gasped 'Oh my *God!*' then closed again as suddenly, his head dropping to one side. After taking a few seconds to recover from her shock, Teri had turned on her tape machine and bent forward to ask, 'Aziz . . . do you know where you are?'

His face had twisted in pain, a groan of discomfort escaping his lips.

'All . . . hung . . .' he mumbled in a thickly accented voice, '. . . like horse . . .'

A chill brushed the back of Teri's neck.

'All hung like whores?' she repeated. 'Who, Aziz? Who are you talking about?'

'Atlantians . . .' he gasped, 'all hung like . . . like . . .'

'Like *whores*? Is that what you really want?'

He frowned on the pillow, eyes fluttering open as his head nodded slowly forward. He was still heavily sedated, Teri realized, but it was a good beginning. Hamanancy had already betrayed a murderous hatred of her people, a nation whose citizens he would like to see hung like whores. Apparently she had been wrong to judge him by his gentle face.

Aziz, meanwhile, was struggling to unravel elements of what his slowly waking brain had begun to suspect was a dream from the apparently real woman who seemed to be sitting beside him. He was not in a gallery of giant penises. Of course not. He was . . . where was he? . . . he could remember that he was in a hospital, that he had been shot by government agents, but he couldn't think why. The drugs made him feel as though he had weights tied to his feet that, no matter how hard he strove to clear his mind, kept pulling him down into the dark waters of sleep. He squinted, struggling to pull the woman's face into focus.

'. . . planning to attack Atlantis?' her weak, faraway voice seemed to be saying.

Attack Atlantis? What did she mean, he wondered.

Why would he . . . and then it began to make sense. For no reason, he had been shot and seriously wounded by government agents – and so she was talking about suing for damages. She must be a lawyer. Aziz had heard about these Atlantian lawyers who hung around in hospitals, looking for clients among the patients – they charged you nothing but just took a cut of the damages they secured on your behalf in court. Millions and millions of dollars in damages.

That had to be what this was about. She was telling him that the wrong he'd had done to him was worth money – probably a lot of money. She could make the State pay some colossal sum in reparation. He smiled, thinking how extraordinary it was to live in a country where the Government itself could be forced to pay you a fortune because of the mistakes it made. Where he came from, the Government did what the hell it liked and you could either accept it or choose to get yourself killed for complaining. What a great country this was.

'Yes. Attack Atlantis . . .' he agreed as clearly as he could.

She lowered her face towards his, her words again seeming to break up into a jumble of sounds. Something about bees. How did she know what he did for a living, he wondered, wearily nodding his head on the pillow. Her face seemed to darken as his eyes began to close, and he felt her hand on his shoulder, shaking him.

'*But what is it you want?*' he heard her shout.

Perhaps, he thought as an irresistibly warm feeling came over him, it was up to *him* to decide how much money she was to demand on his behalf. She needed him to tell her what he wanted. But it was so hard to speak.

He made a final, almighty effort to resist the wave of drowsiness coming over him.

'Millions . . .' he answered. 'Make them pay . . .'

'I'm not sleepy,' she sighed, staring at the ceiling.

Beside her, Cameron did not budge. He had his back to her, and so it was difficult to tell if this was a conscious tactic or not. She rolled onto one elbow and leaned her head over his shoulder.

'Are you asleep, darling?' she whispered as loudly as she reasonably could.

There was no answer. He was either truly asleep or determined to be so. When she was about to flop back onto the mattress, however, he grunted 'Ernhh . . . ?' in a discouraging fashion, like a man who walks past a beggar and then, finding he feels bad about it, steps back and drops some coppers in his cup.

'I can't sleep,' she explained, at a pitch that was intended to make him understand that this was not just her problem.

Cameron rolled over, his eyes creaking open, and groaned, 'It's probably your digestive system. Try taking some of my *ficusachea* – it's made from fig leaves.'

'Fig . . . leaves,' she frowned. 'Cameron, are you aware that we actually have *figs* in the house?'

'Yeah, but this is better than the fruit.' He yawned. 'Eating the leaves really sorts out constipation.'

Under the cover of darkness, she rolled her eyeballs.

'So would eating *grass*, I should think, darling.'

'Fine. Be like that. I was just trying to explain that if you can't sleep it's probably because your metabolism is—'

'There is absolutely nothing wrong with my metabolism, sweetheart,' Teri interrupted him. 'Not everything comes down to the state of one's *intestines*, for heaven's sake. This is getting . . . obsessional, OK?'

'Oh, I see. So what's your explanation?'

221

'Anxiety about the *world*?' she sighed. 'I don't know if you've noticed this, but there are things happening at the moment that go way beyond whatever your or my bowel movements might imply.'

'Look, I'm not an idiot,' he snapped. 'I never said it was just *our* bowel movements. But, if you consider humanity as a *whole*, then I don't think you or I are in a position to say whether—'

'Cameron! It's got *nothing* to do with poo!'

'Maybe not,' he answered reasonably. 'I'm not . . . disagreeing with you and you may well be right. But you don't *know* that any more than I do.'

'Oh my *God*!'

Teri Hunt had managed to reach the mid-point of her life without ever feeling truly lonely. If nothing else, she had always felt that there were like-minded people all around her – that she was, for want of a better word, *normal*. But lately she was starting to wonder. It suddenly seemed as though everyone around her had lost their marbles – which, given that she was a reasonable person, was making her doubt her own sanity.

So she felt alone.

For instance, thanks to her report on the interview with Aziz Hamanancy, the Bee and Comb Union had finally hit No. 1 in the Top 50. Yet Teri herself had never been less sure. For some reason she had trouble believing the evidence, and she wondered if it wasn't just the very certainty of everyone else's opinion that was undermining her ability to trust the facts. Because, God knew, these days she was surrounded by people who were sure of themselves – was she the only Atlantian who had been *more* rather than less inclined to doubt she was right ever since this war started? Everyone else seemed not just to be certain that they were right, but above all that they were *righteous*.

Like Cameron. *What* was happening to Cameron?

On the one hand, he had never been better. He was

energetic, and positive, and his professional standing had shot up since he introduced Spiritual Stocks to the world. She should have been proud of him because, right now, church shares were the growth area of the Stock Market. Thanks to Cameron, the Church of the New Covenant had seen itself transformed overnight from a dying strand in Atlantian religion to the standard-bearer of what was now being talked about as a regeneration of the nation's spiritual values. Within two weeks of their launch, shares in NewCov were trading at eight times their introductory price, thus giving the church a market valuation that was several factors greater than the combined worth of all its followers. Furthermore, just as Cameron had predicted, the effect of this on the church's fortunes had been phenomenal – every one of its chapels across the nation had experienced an unprecedented surge in interest, their services being conducted to capacity congregations, seemingly no matter how many extra sittings they added. The capital raised, which the trustees had intended to use for an advertising campaign to halt the church's inexorable decline, was now going into an ambitious programme of expansion, with new chapels envisioned in dozens of cities across the country.

Equally, just as Cameron had predicted, those churches that had loudly condemned the New Covenantists' move as a corruption of the fundamental ethos of religion, had subsequently gone very quiet. Many of the smaller ones had lost little time in announcing their own share issues. Every merchant bank seemed to have found itself at least one client looking to break into what was now being treated as a separate market sector – the Spiritual Derivatives list, or SpiDer Index.

Even an obscure faith such as the Beyond Communion had been able to jump straight from being a rather mysterious sect to enjoying a kind of mainstream respectability. BeComm was a hot share, attractively mixing spirituality with commercial enterprises such as their mushrooming chains of foot parlours and colonic irrigation clinics.

But Cameron was no longer the man Teri had accepted to marry. She was all for health and bodily hygiene, of course, but it was possible to have too much of a good thing. Their bathroom was so stuffed with interior and exterior grooming products these days – all supplied by the Beyond Communion, of course – that she had the impression she was living with some kind of a beautician fundamentalist.

'Why didn't you want me to touch you?' she asked after they had been silent for a couple of minutes.

'What do you mean?' he answered drowsily, having turned away from her again.

'You know what I mean.'

He groaned, rolling over onto his back.

'Look, I'm sorry – I'm just tired, that's all. You know how hard I've been working on the First Baptist launch lately. It's *important*.'

The First Baptist Church claimed to be the third largest faith in the nation. On the basis of its much larger congregation base, FirBap's introductory valuation was set to dwarf anything the SpiDer had yet seen. Most financial analysts viewed this in one of two ways: either FirBap's arrival would bring a much-needed dose of sanity to the highly volatile market, with the current players seeing their valuations revised down to a more reasonable level, or it would quite simply prove too much for the market to swallow and fail to achieve its target valuation, thus putting a stop to the ridiculous hysteria surrounding the SpiDer and turning people's attention back to more concrete forms of investment.

Cameron, unsurprisingly, subscribed to neither of these views. He believed that FirBap's arrival would prove to be the moment when the SpiDer confounded all its detractors and established what he had termed 'the New Spiritual Economy' as a fact of life.

'That's all it is?' she whispered.

'Of course, darling,' he reassured her. 'What else did you think it was?'

'Well, I can't help thinking that sex – and I'm not saying I *wanted* sex, because I didn't – but sex is a messy business, isn't it?'

Her husband said nothing, but she thought she felt him tense slightly beside her.

'Cameron,' she asked, staring vertically at the ceiling, 'is it at all possible that you might have started to feel that I am . . . unclean?'

The End minus 11 days

'. . . going live to WINN correspondent Bill Gundersen with the Atlantian task force on the USS *Kirk* as it makes its way to the Gulf of Errat. Bill – what can you tell us about combat preparations on the USS *Kirk* right now?'

'Thank you, Ayesha, but first of all I should just correctify one detail there – we are actually currently on the USS *McCoy* at this moment in time, which is an aircraft carrier in the same *class* as the *Kirk*, but itself . . . not on course for the Gulf at present. The military are understandably quite *sensitive* about allowing journalists onto the *Kirk* just now, but I think what you see behind me here gives you a pretty good idea of what that *particular* ship must look like as it heads towards the coast of Errat. We're talking about a *very* big ship, with a deck area roughly equivalent to six football pitches, and an overall weight around the four-hundred-thousand-ton mark. To give you an idea of how heavy that really is, an average pickup truck weighs in at a little under a ton, so we're talking about something around a half-*million* pickup trucks all welded together into one *gigantic* mass of floating steel. It's really very impressive indeed. It's . . . it's huge.'

'Well, I can tell you, it certainly looks *enormous* from here, Bill. And so, what kind of activity do you think we would be seeing in progress behind you right now if you were on the deck of the *Kirk*?'

'Yeah, that's an interesting question, Ayesha. I don't know for sure, of course, but my sense is that we would probably be looking at a *lot* of very *intense*, organized activity as the crew members prepared the *Kirk*'s flight of thirty-eight A-19 fighter jets for possible combat. These men are *extremely* well trained at what they do, needless to say, and I think that they would be very, very *focused* on that work right now, which would typically include such essential tasks as fitting the aircraft out with their full complement of laser-guided missiles and . . . *fuelling* them, as well as, I should think, making sure that those cockpit windows were really immaculate and clean before the pilots took off on their missions. We wouldn't be seeing all these guys in welding suits that are in the background here because, of course, that's something you only *really* find when a ship is in dry dock, as the *McCoy* is at—'

Chapter Seventeen

In which our hero, who is now officially the most dangerous man in the world, makes the acquaintance of a person who is only the most dangerous man in Errat, and who should not therefore be more dangerous than him, but certainly is

It was shortly before four in the morning when Saman found himself being wheeled into the single most notorious room in Errat. He knew instantly where he was, although he had never entered it before. The fact of being taken there strapped to a heavy wheelchair had offered him a good hint as to his destination, of course, as had the stone silence of his guards as they led him, hooded and handcuffed, from the car to the echoing interior of the police headquarters. He had remained calm, offering no resistance or argument, but his patient assurances that he was the victim of a misunderstanding and more than happy to answer any questions they had for him met with no response whatsoever.

While inexperienced in such matters, Saman was left in little doubt of where he was being taken – a suspicion confirmed in its full horror the moment the wheelchair was parked and he heard his guards leave the room. With the closing of the door and the fading clatter of their heels down the corridor, he was left in silence. But not alone. He could sense he was not alone, and that eyes were on him. It seemed almost as though he could feel from which direction they probed him, his own gaze moving to meet theirs in the darkness of the hood.

He knew who was there.

And thus he knew how serious was the trouble he was in.

He wanted to speak, and yet dared not open his mouth while fear pressed cold thumbs on his throat. His voice would betray him, he was sure, producing not words but a gargle or a whimper. He had to become calm, as though the danger of this room was no worse than a swarm of bees howling around him. As though the prickling on his arms and neck was just their little feet crawling upon his skin. If a colony of insects could sense that he was no threat to them, then surely it was possible to make another human being understand that. But it was not with words that he would do so, for it was not what he *said* in here that would matter, he knew. A man would say anything in this room, promise anything, confess anything, betray anything. He would do whatever was necessary to get out of here alive and unbroken. So it was not enough for Saman to say he was innocent. He had somehow to *smell* of innocence, just as he smelled of kindness to his bees.

The silence remained unbroken for what felt like five minutes or more, but was probably less. Saman concentrated on his breathing, moving gradually from snatched teaspoons of air, to dessertspoons, and eventually to the point where he was picking up the whole bowl and drinking deep, steady draughts of oxygen. He felt himself calming down, the thumbs easing their grip on his throat and the bees crawling upon his body slowing to a halt.

There was a soft creak of leather just nearby, not two paces from him, and he now heard breathing beside his head as the other person in there bent down to examine him more closely, or perhaps prepare his first sting. His eyes closed tight, imagining an instrument hovering over him now – a blade, or an ember, or an electrode – choosing its spot. Was that how it started – with pain first and questions later? He kept breathing, trying to stop his body from shaking, and to remember that he was innocent.

He felt someone close by his left shoulder, almost touching him, as though their presence there somehow changed the gravity on that side of his body.

«So . . .» a deep voice whispered in his ear, muffled though the hood, «who . . . the fuck . . . are *you*?»

He'd never heard the voice before, but there was something in it, some darkness in the timbre, that left him in no doubt that he was being addressed by Malek Galaam himself, the notorious Beautician. Galaam, they said, always conducted his interrogations at night, when the building was all but empty and the screams would not interrupt his men in their work.

The fur in his ear bristled as though the Beautician's very voice had the power to electrolyse unwanted bodily hair, and Saman's eyes remained tightly shut. But he had to answer.

«Saman Massoudi,» he whispered back, his voice steadier than he'd thought it would be.

«And Saman Massoudi is . . . *what*, exactly?»

«Saman Massoudi is a honey merchant.»

«Saman Massoudi is a *honey merchant*, is he?» the voice continued in that same hushed tone in which the whole conversation was apparently going to be conducted. «Saman Massoudi is not a *terrorist*, then?»

«No. He's not.»

Saman heard a laugh so soft it was barely more than an ordinary breath expelled through a smile.

«They all say that to me, you know.»

«I know. But I'm not.»

«Then you know I could make you say you *are* one.»

«Yes, I do know that.»

He felt something come to rest upon the hood, pressing down on his bald crown. A hand.

«What a lot you seem to know . . .» the voice continued, as the hand balled itself into a fist, «. . . for a simple honey merchant.»

The hood was snatched off his head, and Saman's initial squint, as the light hit his eyes like a bucket of cold water, suddenly froze into an unblinking stare as he found himself looking straight at a pronged spike not two inches from his eyes, the gap between the points quite large enough to fit a nose.

«Honey or terrorism?» the voice snapped.

«Honey!» Saman gasped.

The spike moved closer, his lashes flailing against the points as his eyes narrowed to quivering slits.

«*Honey* . . .» Galaam repeated patiently, «or terrorism? Last . . . chance.»

Malek Adbel Galaam was a reasonable man.

Although he loomed in the popular imagination like some club-wielding ogre – an image he did nothing to discourage as it was helpful in his work – he was in fact a good-looking fellow, with an intelligent face and honest, sensitive eyes. These days people imagined that his nickname, the Beautician, was a sick joke playing upon his reputed propensity for pulling out the fingernails of those foolish enough to come to his attention, but it had actually started as a reference to his own personal grooming habits. For in a country where many men considered dental care to be a womanly concern, Malek Galaam was a courageous exception to the rule. He washed, brushed, flossed and perfumed himself with daily rigour, dressed stylishly, and, on the rare occasions when his wife and he appeared together in public, they formed without doubt the most attractive couple in the whole dictatorship. His wife, Rachida, had an almost miraculously svelte figure for a mother of seven, and

231

Malek's adoration of her and their children was no secret among those who knew him beyond his official capacity as Director of Internal Espionage.

As a family man, he was deeply concerned about the effect his monstrous reputation might have on his offspring, which was why the parents of every child attending their schools had been visited by members of the secret police and informed, in polite but no uncertain terms, that their boss's name was never to be mentioned in the domestic sphere. Thanks to this wise precaution, his sons and daughters had thus far been able to enjoy carefree childhoods, blissfully unaware of how close they were to the most hated and feared man in the whole country.

Rachida knew a little more, not least because his work kept him away from their bed many nights, but even she had never heard any of the ghastly stories that circulated about her husband, some of which were actually true. The Malek she knew was primarily a romantic and humorous man, one that she felt blessed to have fallen in love with because he was almost the only male she had ever met who treated her as a near equal. Their equality was nothing like that of Atlantian television shows, of course, but for that she was thankful as she had trouble imagining how those women could have respect for their husbands, when their supposed sensitivity struck her as weakness. Her husband was strong, and he was her master, and she loved him for that.

As for himself, Malek Galaam had no doubt about what he really was.

He was a reasonable man struggling with an unreasonable world, his heart in the right place even if he was forced to make compromises in his efforts to change society. He was neither a sadist, nor a brute, nor a fanatic, but he did not have the liberty of choosing his methods. The people he was fighting against, while he fully understood the anger they felt towards society and sympathized with their determination to change it, *were* fanatics. If he sometimes lowered himself to the level of hating them – which was a mistake, he knew – it was because a part of him could not help admiring their idealism, however misguided the form it took. They had the courage to rebel against overwhelming force, drawing strength from the belief that their motives were pure. He hated them for that, because he found it easier to understand how they became terrorists than he became a torturer, and so it was only by proving himself stronger than their idealism, by doing such unspeakable things to them that his admiration turned to pity, that he was able to live with himself.

It was a curious paradox. For as long as a suspect held out against his tortures, he could not sleep or face his family because he felt so vile in his core, yet once he succeeded in breaking them, by whatever means necessary, he felt personally vindicated. He could look down on his victim, reassured that he had been right all along, and know that it was their own folly that was responsible for the pitiful condition they were in. They had not listened to reason, and thus had been broken. He did not enjoy breaking them, but in a sense he was being cruel to be kind. He was liberating them from a delusion. And he derived great satisfaction from the fact that not one of them had died with his convictions unbowed. Not one of them had proved stronger than him. In each case, they had lived at least long enough to accept their defeat and know they had willingly betrayed their comrades and cause.

And afterwards, exhausted by the struggle, Malek Galaam was able to sleep again.

He was no fool, and knew very well why the General had entrusted him with this work. Malek had always inspired devotion in his subordinates in his days as an ordinary policeman, and thus was both a valuable ally and a potential threat. By placing him in charge of

Intelligence and counter-terrorism, by obliging him to use these loathsome means to achieve his ends, the General had at once ended any chance Malek had of becoming a popular figure, and bound him utterly to his own destiny. If the General was brought down by the fanatics, then Malek knew full well that he would go down with him.

The General, although suffering from an appalling lack of self-awareness where his poetry was concerned, was not a complete fool. He knew that it was in his favour, and that of his country, to portray himself as a moderate figure, a reformer who was trying to keep the extremes of his own society in check. Malek was well aware that he had been trapped by the General's myth-making, and was now cast as the villain of the tale, the dark alternative that awaited should the General ever fall, but this air of villainy did give him one peculiar advantage. Because other people in the Government feared him more than they feared the General, it was in a sense more important that they be on *his* good side, and once there they found that Malek was not quite the monster they had imagined.

Indeed, the very awfulness of his reputation threw the reality of his essential decency and intelligence into sharper relief. And so while the General had correctly calculated that making Malek Galaam Director of Internal Espionage would neuter him as a potential rival within the general populace, it had only served to make him a more formidable figure in the circles of government. Already it had become too dangerous for the General to consider removing Malek from his current position, unless it was to promote him to Vice-President. Indeed, whether they realized it or not, the people who mattered nowadays saw Malek as the natural successor to their present leader, should he weaken.

This vision, he knew, was shared by certain people within the Atlantian Intelligence community.

«*Honey . . .*» Saman rasped, teeth clenched and eyes shut tight as the spikes stroked his lashes.

He felt the weapon move back, but did not open his eyes for fear that it was a trick. That would be entirely in keeping with the Beautician's reputation – to fool a man into opening his eyes so that he saw the spikes plunge into them. Indeed, it was only when he heard the leather of Galaam's shoes creak as he walked away that he dared hope he'd passed the test. By the time he'd summoned the courage to look, the Director of Internal Espionage was comfortably installed behind his desk, waiting for him to stop wincing.

Galaam's office was somewhat schizophrenic. The desk was situated dead centre of the large room, facing the windows – a very neat desk on which every object was precisely placed: papers stacked as if with a right angle, different-coloured pens lying in a perfectly parallel row, an old telephone whose curling cord was neither stretched nor tangled. An orderly filing cabinet. Disturbingly neat.

Behind the desk the room was in white ceramic and absolutely bare but for a locked steel cupboard. The area in front of the desk, which Galaam looked at and upon which Saman's wheelchair stood, was quite normal and comfortable: there were leather armchairs, a copper coffee table, and a highly crafted mosaic of tiles on the floor. The walls were decorated with paintings: an Oriental watercolour of little men plodding through the snow, heavily laden yokes across their backs; a somewhat gaudy tableau of a mountain stream at which a deer was sipping; and a portrait, familiar to Saman, of a cherubic young white boy with a single, globular tear running down his cheek. He'd always found the crying-boy picture rather disturbing, but it was hugely popular with his fellow countrymen, who considered it a profound statement on the essential misery of the mortal condition. Saman had never been much interested in art, but it seemed masochistic to so dwell upon unhappiness, to find beauty in it as people did. It suggested they had lived so long under vicious dictatorships that they'd developed a taste for suffering.

Were Saman ever to own a portrait, he'd prefer one of those chubby nudes reclining on a settee – although he would not dare to hang such a thing upon his wall, of course.

There was a plastic curtain that could be drawn across the room to separate its two parts. The function of the ceramic half was all too obvious. It was evident that the spikes had been a bluff – Saman was in the wrong half of the room for blood-letting. He wondered, briefly, why Galaam would choose to divide his office in this way rather than simply using an adjacent room for the more unpleasant side of his work, and decided that it could only be because he wanted there to be no pretence about who he was and what he did. He was proud of it, probably.

«So, Mr Honey Merchant,» Galaam continued after allowing Saman time to take in his surroundings, «why are you here?»

«Because . . .» Saman hazarded, «. . . you had me brought here?»

«Well, *obviously* I had you brought here, man!» Galaam scowled. «It was not a literal question! I mean "why" in the larger sense, of course – what winds have blown you, what strange music has led this dance, you know? What the fuck is going on?»

Saman shrugged as best he could with the numerous straps holding him down, and answered, «Well, I *think* . . . and I've been asking myself that same question for the last two days, believe me . . . I don't know with any real precision, but my *theory* is that . . . um . . . there has been a mistake.»

«A mistake.»

«Yes. Some kind of a mistake. That's the conclusion I've come to, at any rate.»

«I see.» Galaam smiled. «Well, that would explain it, wouldn't it?»

«Yes.»

«A mistake.»

«Of some kind,» Saman added.

Galaam stared at the corpulent middle-aged fellow before him, nodding his head slowly. He stopped and narrowed his eyes as if for closer study, as if he had just noticed something odd about the face he was looking at, and then nodded again.

«I suspect you are not a terrorist, Mr Saman,» he sighed. «Which is a blow, because I confess that I was rather excited by the possibility – however far-fetched it seemed – that in you the Atlantians had somehow uncovered the terrorist ringleader who has thus far eluded me. Seeing you in the flesh, unfortunately, I am strongly inclined to accept your explanation that there has been a mistake, as you say, of some kind. You're a great disappointment.»

«I'm sorry.»

Galaam raised his hand for silence.

«*Or* . . .» he continued, «. . . you are the best liar I have ever seen. Which puts me in a very delicate position – do I trust my instinct that you are a completely irrelevant honey merchant with no connection whatsoever to the terrorist underground, or do I pull your fingernails out just to see what happens?»

«I'll scream.»

«Mm-hmm . . . but what else?»

«Well, I'll probably tell you I'm an elusive terrorist ringleader if I think that'll make you stop.»

«Exactly – but if you're such a good liar as I'm suggesting, you'll know how to pitch it so that I think you're just saying that to make me *stop*, won't you?»

«I suppose so . . . but I'm really *not* a good liar, you know.»

«That is the impression I get, yes – but then a really good liar *would* fool me into thinking he was a bad liar, wouldn't he? So what do I do then – pull your teeth? You'll just insist with greater conviction that you're a terrorist ringleader, but I'll be even more convinced that you're lying, and we'll be no further advanced. I confess that I don't know what to do with you.»

He drummed his fingers upon the desk, clicking his tongue in irritation.

«Alternatively, I just dispose of you and be done with it.»

It was said without a hint of irony, as though he were talking about a piece of furniture that he could find no place for. Legend had it that the air force ran regular flights out to sea on Galaam's behalf, disposing of similarly troublesome individuals by dumping them, heavily weighted, into the depths. Alive.

Saman said nothing, sensing that his life depended upon making himself as uninteresting as possible at this very second. Galaam stopped drumming his fingers, and frowned.

«I don't understand you, honey merchant. You do not appear stupid . . .» he mused, «. . . so why are you so calm?»

«I'm not,» Saman assured him softly. «But it doesn't help to panic.»

«True . . . but you don't even seem to be *outraged* about all of this. If you are the victim of a mistake, as you claim, then why aren't you *angry* about it?»

«Well . . . I suppose I am. But the trouble is that I don't know who to be angry *with*.»

«For heaven's sake, man – the people responsible for the *mistake*, of course!»

«But I don't know who they are, and . . . well, I'm sure

they didn't *mean* it, did they? A mistake is a mistake, after all.»

«Don't you *care*?»

«Of course I do – but not half as much as I care about simply clearing up the misunderstanding and getting on with my life.»

«That's really all you care about?» Galaam scowled, the concept seeming quite alien to him. «*Getting on with your life?* Getting back to what – your honey and your little bees? What about your *honour*, for God's sake – does that not count for anything at all to you? The world can screw you from behind and you just accept it? So, if I understand correctly, I could torture you just for the hell of it and you are not even going to *hate* me for it! I could take your pride and manhood from you, reduce you to a whimpering little animal begging for its life, and you will not want to fight back! All you will ask is to be allowed to *get on with your life*! Don't you think that's rather . . . *pathetic*?»

Saman's face fell. He had dared to hope that he was managing to pick his way through the minefield in which he found himself, that Malek Galaam was gradually coming to accept that he was no danger, nor even of any interest to him, and hence not worth detaining. Yet there was suddenly, in that one word 'pathetic', more vehemence and a greater gulf of comprehension than he would have imagined possible. He had tried being honest and good-hearted, and the only reaction it had achieved was disdain. In Galaam's eyes, it made him contemptible.

So be it, he thought.

«No,» he answered softly, rolling his chin to gesture at the room and all its contents – the files, the torture area, Galaam himself – and confessed, «*this* is what I think pathetic.»

«This,» the Director of Internal Espionage repeated, raising his eyebrows. «You mean me.»

«You. The people you are fighting. The things you all

239

are fighting for. And the way you all choose to fight. All of it. *That* I find pathetic. Not my bees.»

Galaam's eyes darkened to slits, his jaw hardening. The fingers, still resting upon the desk where they had been drumming, curled spider-like into a ball. He sat frozen, perfectly still on his web, and regarded the fat little fly before him.

Slowly he began to grin – a sly grin that ate its way across his face and grew into a chuckle. It was a chuckle without warmth, born of a dark humour that seemed to feed on itself, like the crackle of dry twigs catching light upon one another.

«Aren't you worried that I'll kill you just for saying that, honey merchant?» he asked.

«I'm betting that you are intelligent enough to realize that would only prove my point,» Saman answered.

Galaam's fist thumped the tabletop, his laughter finally suggesting a genuine enjoyment of the moment, a love of the absurdity of the conversation.

«Perhaps you're not such a disappointment, after all, honey merchant!» he complimented him.

The police vehicle taking Saman back home on his release from Malek Galaam's office wound its way through the pre-dawn streets of the city. Rocking gently in the back, Saman was suddenly overwhelmed with exhaustion, relief hitting him like a cosh to the skull. Under the hood that had once again been placed over his head, his eyes would not stay open as he slumped on the seat.

The nightmare was over. There was no danger he could face more terrible than finding himself in the room from which he had just been taken, no test to which he might be put more desperate than an interrogation by Malek Galaam. The Director of Internal Espionage had been very civil at the end, apologizing for the inconvenience that had been caused. He even shook

Saman's hand as his underlings came to wheel him out of the office. Then, still clasping it firmly, he'd leaned down to whisper, «And, of course, you *will* tell me if you are contacted by any . . . *unsavoury* characters, won't you? I'll be counting on you, honey merchant.»

Saman had promised to do so, naturally, but he could see no reason why the terrorists would bother with him. They, of all people, knew he was nothing to do with their world. So it was over, and tomorrow he would be free to resume his life.

The two policemen again said nothing, so the car was blissfully quiet beyond the low throb of the engine. He guessed, basing his judgement on the sound of the motor and the dreamily soft suspension, that they were in one of the big old Atlantian cars of the type with bench seats back and front. You saw fewer and fewer of them around these days, but everyone knew that the police still had a small fleet of them for using when they wanted to go incognito – which had made sense back when taxis had all been of this type, but was nowadays no more subtle than having a flashing light on top. Although the curfew was by now over, there were no sounds of life reaching him from the streets along which they passed, but then anybody who saw one of these cars coming their way at this time of the morning would duck out of sight.

He wondered wearily if they would take him home or just dump him on some deserted street in the city centre, pushing him out the door and speeding off before anyone had time to come along. He hoped they would at least spare him a long traipse home after all he'd been through, but no doubt they had a favourite place for dumping suspects on their release from custody: some windowless alley where nobody would see. The journey already seemed to have taken too long for him to have much hope of finding himself on his own street.

The car coasted to a halt, and he sat up as he heard

one of the policemen get out. He stiffened as the door beside him opened and a hand grabbed him by either shoulder, half-leading, half-dragging him out of the vehicle.

«Kneel,» the man commanded once he stood on the street, pressing down on his shoulders.

Saman obeyed, landing heavily on his knees and letting the man push his head down into a praying position.

«Stay down,» he ordered, whipping the hood off and jumping back into the car.

Saman did exactly as he had been told, so relieved to be finally out of their clutches that he waited until their vehicle had sped off down the street and could be heard no more before even opening his eyes to see where he had been taken.

The first thing he saw as he raised his head was a pair of feet in front of him. He stopped in surprise, eyes flicking to either side. Two more pairs of feet flanked the first.

This, he suspected, was not good.

The End minus 8 days

'. . . admission that diplomacy has run its course and left the Government with no choice but to conclude that General Harouni is determined *not* to allow a peaceful settlement of this dispute. Obviously the question everyone is asking themselves here, Bill, is "What next?"'

'Well, the USS *Kirk* is now *in* position on the Errati coast, Ayesha, and—'

'Sorry, Bill – I should have reminded viewers that you *are* on board that ship yourself, aren't you?'

'Yes, absolutely. As I explained earlier, the military have granted WINN 24/7 journalists *exclusive* access to on-board preparations, meaning we will be the *only* channel reporting direct *from* the front line should the President decide to go in there to capture Suman Mussadie.'

'Do we have clear information about *where* Mussaby is at the present time?'

'Yes, according to Intelligence reports, there are two possibilities – he may be hiding in the Errati capital or, alternatively, outside it in the hills that make up the rest of the country. Those are the two scenarios that strategists are planning around right now.'

'So they think he *is* still located in Errat?'

'Yes, they do, although they are not excluding other possibilities.'

'OK, Bill, we'll be coming back to you for regular updates

from the USS *Kirk*. Meanwhile, returning to a story that has touched a lot of people back here in Atlantis, a happy ending for the children of the Warren P. Giddings Infant School who, as many of you will remember, were heart-broken when told their production of *The Magic Honeypot* had been cancelled on the grounds of good taste. It now transpires that the five-year-olds *themselves* have saved the day by suggesting to their teacher that they could remove the yellow from their costumes and pretend to be *flies* rather than bees! Now renamed *The Magic Doo-Doo*, the production will go ahead with a slightly revised story-line whereby the flies discover a giant—'

Chapter Eighteen

In which Teri Hunt resolves to do everything she can to put a stop to the insanity she sees taking hold all around her, and plans for war are made between the fourth and fourteenth greens

'Morning, Mrs Hunt,' the elderly guard smiled as Teri stepped into the body scanner. 'Working weekends again?'

'You know what they say, Moses,' she sighed. 'No rest for the wicked.'

He glanced briefly at the screen before him, and nodded to her.

'That's fine – go right on in, Mrs Hunt.'

'Thank you,' she answered, moving forward to press her NIC badge against the security barrier. 'And please – call me Teri.'

'Yes, ma'am.'

Will I keep my name as Hunt? she wondered as her thighs pushed through the turnstile. I don't want to go back to being Teri Smith, so why should I? I've earned that name. I can call myself Teri Hunt, married or single. That's who I am now.

She checked her watch. Five to ten. She would go straight to Spotto's office for the meeting – she had nothing to pick up from her desk, anyway, because there was no evidence to back up her argument. This was about her gut instinct.

Gut instinct – a turn of phrase, she reflected, suggesting people had always suspected the ultimate truth lay somewhere around their colon.

'Cameron . . .' she'd frowned on her return home the previous evening, '. . . what's with the new look?'

'My suit, you mean?' her husband had answered brightly. 'Do you like it?'

'It's very . . . *white*.'

'That's right – and, do you know, they're harder to find than you'd *think*.'

'I can imagine.' She nodded. 'And the shoes, too. Did you . . . um . . . go to a store for magicians, maybe?'

'It's bespoke. I had the guy run up four of them.'

'Four? So this is . . . clearly this is a style you are comfortable with.'

'It's how I feel.'

'You mean you feel like . . . *God*?'

Apparently these days they were calling her husband the Prophet of Profit. Following the astoundingly successful flotation of the First Baptist Church, the SpiDer Index had overtaken technology stocks in terms of overall value – a state of affairs that was completely ridiculous, and thus only increased the hysteria surrounding it. Everyone wanted to buy themselves a piece of heaven, and the lone brokers who still spoke out against the boom, who insisted that it was insane and bravely refused to invest their clients' money in it, were becoming harder to hear with each passing day. Mainly because they were rapidly losing their jobs.

'God is in all of us, Teri,' Cameron explained softly. 'If you would only cleanse yourself of all the impurities in your—'

'*Cameron!*' she snapped. 'This has got to stop! I preferred it when you were pigging out in the *medicine*

246

cabinet – at least I *understood* you then! Do you have any idea how mad you are now?'

Her husband smiled, his expression one of pity for the confused soul before him.

'So that's it, is it?' he asked softly. 'I'm just . . . *mad*?'

'You need help. This purification trip of yours . . . this whole spiritual shares market you're running – it's . . . it's *bonkers*, Cameron.'

He chuckled indulgently, answering, 'There's a little over three trillion dollars of money out there betting you are wrong on that, darling – ordinary people's money.'

'Just because millions of people believe in something does not prevent it from being bonkers!' she declared. 'Churches don't *make* anything! This cannot carry on for ever, don't you see? All that money is being invested in a fucking *mirage*!'

'So you think faith is a mirage nowadays, do you?'

'No, but . . .'

'You still don't get it, do you?' he laughed, eyes sparkling. 'Let me explain: these investments are an expression of faith in God, Teri – and God is infinite. If God is infinite, then faith in Him must be infinite. If *faith* is infinite, then the value of the SpiDer . . . do you see where we're going here?'

'Towards a *crash*?' she answered. 'I'm no economist, Cameron, but even I can see that money only makes sense as a symbol of the material things in life! If you apply it to something *infinite* then, sooner or later, the symbol ceases to mean anything – it will just become paper again!'

He shook his head sadly.

'You only think that because you don't have faith. I don't know if one day *all* money will flow to and from the SpiDer, Teri, but I do know that we are in the process of creating a new world of spiritual capitalism. By putting our faith – and our *money* – in God's trust, we may *at last* be on our way to creating God's kingdom on Earth.'

Teri's jaw dropped as her husband's words sank in. She looked at him in his white suit, arms spread wide in joyous contemplation of this new age where the material and the spiritual would become one.

She'd staggered across to the couch and slumped into it, her legs losing their strength. In different circumstances, she had suddenly realized, the man she was married to would be prepared to kill in the name of his faith.

'Oh my God . . .' she gasped, because at that moment she knew her marriage was over.

Teri reached Bob Spotto's office, taking off her coat before entering. Rebecca, his personal assistant, looked up as the door opened.

'Hi, is he in?' Teri asked.

She barely broke her stride, so desperate was she to see her boss. If one good thing could be said to have come out of last night's argument, it was that she had decided once and for all to do whatever was in her power to stop the insanity running wild through society. She was resolute. Someone had to put the brakes on the Errat situation before it was too late.

'Stop!' Rebecca called after her, smiling apologetically. 'He told me to say he was sorry and ask if you'd mind waiting an hour or so, Teri.'

'But we have a ten o'clock meeting,' she objected, her face falling.

'Yuh. He's with the President.'

Bob Spotto stood with the security team a few paces behind President Hedges and Mitchell Madison, his Defence Secretary, hands behind his back, waiting for an opportunity to speak. The moment called for silence, for inner contemplation. Not a thing stirred. The President looked straight ahead, across grass like a Green Beret's haircut, his face solemn. Actually, he wore that oddly pained frown of his that always made Spotto think of a man pushing with all his might upon the toilet. The very birds seemed to hold their breath.

At last, he moved. His arms swung down in unison, sweeping the club through the little white ball. It seemed to dematerialize on contact only to reappear, a few seconds later, as it bounced and trickled to a halt on the fifth green. It was a masterful stroke – that of a man who had taken the time to perfect his game, even if he wasn't a naturally talented player. A lot of time, in other words. The Secret Service man beside Spotto tilted his head to whisper into his lapel: 'Go.'

Suddenly, there was movement all over the place, the branches of the trees shaking as if a gust of wind had run up the fairway in the ball's slipstream. Spotto could see figures darting through the shadows, twigs snapping under their feet as they dashed ahead to take up new positions around the presidential golf ball. He couldn't judge exactly how many men there were out there – maybe twenty or so actually on the move, but no doubt there were others already stationed ahead of them all along the course. The ruckus lasted about half a minute before stopping almost as abruptly as it had begun, the men's silhouettes melting back into the shadows and silence.

The other Secret Service agent stepped forward to take the President's club, his impenetrable expression giving no hint of whether he felt pride at being so close to the nation's leader, or frustration at the thought that after goodness knows how many years of training and proving himself in the field, he was expected to be a caddy.

President Hedges turned to Spotto, constipated frown still in place, and said, '*Bees?*'

'Yes, sir.' Spotto nodded. 'Some kind of new strain they've been developing.'

'You ain't serious, are you, Bobby?'

'Very serious, Mr President. The phone call was the clearest lead we've had yet on a planned attack.'

The President nodded slowly, letting his big, presidential imagination picture the scenario. He turned to Mitchell Madison, wincing with concentration.

'You know what I'm thinking, Maddy? I'm thinking that bees . . . they must be pretty darned hard to shoot.'

'Impossible, sir,' the Defence Secretary agreed. 'Even our best snipers couldn't take out a bee.'

'And you can't bomb them *either*!'

'Not unless they settle, sir. If they're on the wing . . . well, we don't really have the weaponry to deal with that scenario.'

'You can *nuke* them,' President Hedges pointed out. 'No matter how small a thing is, in the final resort you can *always* nuke it.'

'Well, as you say, sir – in the final resort. Clearly we wouldn't anticipate that as a first option.'

The President seemed not to be paying attention any longer, gazing instead down the fairway in search of his Defence Secretary's ball.

'A *little* nuke, I mean,' he reassured him with a frown. Suddenly his face broke into a smile as he spotted a white dot in the distance. '*That's* where it went! Oh boy, you're gonna have trouble catching me now, Mr Madison!'

While Spotto and the two Secret Service caddies stayed a respectful distance behind the President, the Defence Secretary kept pace with him, relighting his cigar as they walked.

'Seriously, Maddy, what do you think?' President Hedges muttered. 'Sounds pretty far out to me. Terrorists using *bees* . . .'

'Well, I didn't want to say anything while we were

in earshot,' the Defence Secretary answered softly, lips pouting as he sucked the big stick back into life between snatches of information, 'but this *is* something we've been working on ourselves. It's called zoological warfare. Killer bees, cable-chewing roaches . . . there's huge potential. Radio-controlled lobster bombs . . . amazing stuff. Cheap. Zero risk. Tough little soldiers if you can train them right.'

The President turned to him, eyebrows cranking up.

'You mean the terrorists stole the idea from *us*?'

The cigar now smouldering nicely, the Secretary let it hang by his side as they walked, seeming to forget about it.

'The *idea*, maybe. Not the technology. We don't have it yet,' he confided. 'It's all on paper for the moment. Stuff the GM guys figure they ought to be able to do with an adequate budget: spy flies with miniature cameras, exploding hedgehogs, germ-warfare bugs, bunker bugs . . . you name it. It could revolutionize the whole way we fight wars. The great thing about bugs is that they can go anywhere – you can drop a whole goddamned army in a single missile. So say we've got some son of a bitch holed up in a bunker – we don't have to bother trying to bust it open, we just send a couple of million little critters crawling down the ventilation shafts and wait for him to come running out the front door, tearing his clothes off and dancing about like a man possessed.'

'I *hate* bugs.' President Hedges shivered. 'Why does *anything* need more than four legs? It ain't reasonable.'

'Well, believe you me, ordinary bugs are *nothing* compared to some of these tropical insects our guys are working on. It's a real treasure trove of no-mistake, *nasty* little critters down there, I swear. Without redeeming qualities of any kind whatsoever. Makes you wonder what the Lord had in mind sometimes.'

'Who can say, Maddy, who can say? Did He have zooillogical warfare in mind all those aeons of years ago? Was He giving us the means to defeat our enemies? We are but actors in His drama, guest stars of a single week's episode . . .'

'Well, either way, sir – we cannot let fanatics get their hands on that kind of technology, let alone unleash it on us. If the NIC believe terrorists are developing bug weapons, we have to destroy that capacity before it's too late.'

'Damn right. And I don't see how even our so-called allies could whine about us squashing a few *bugs*, do you?'

By the fourteenth green, the two men and Bob Spotto had hammered out a basic strategy to deal with the situation. A swift response, they all agreed, was the only solution – spring was here, meaning the meteorological conditions would soon be perfect for a bee-based attack on the Atlantian homeland. Presuming the Errati government did not itself hand over the terrorists and completely destroy their bug warfare capacity, granting Atlantian observers unrestricted access to oversee the process – demands that Bob Spotto believed would almost certainly be refused by the General – then a military reaction was both justified and necessary. Errat, according to the Defence Secretary, posed no great challenge either in physical or military terms – it was a small country with poor natural defences and an ill-equipped, conscript army. Using a combination of air strikes and elite ground forces, it should be possible not only to destroy any terrorist bases, but also to liberate the country from its current dictatorial regime. Removing the General, they could install the pro-Atlantian Malek Galaam at the head of a provisional government that would organize democratic elections at the appropriate time. With their own mid-term elections due in the summer, furthermore, a short and muscular military campaign at this stage would no doubt help boost candidates of the President's party.

'How much time do you need to organize this, Maddy?' the President asked, kneeling down to check the line on his putt.

'Well, let's see now . . .' the Defence Secretary answered. 'We have the USS *Kirk* stationed in the Gulf *anyway*, so most of the actual equipment is already on site. An Alpha Force contingent can be got on board in a matter of days, which just leaves the matter of identifying our targets on the ground and, of course, preparing public opinion back here. If we brief friendly journalists about the threat straight away, making it clear that we're facing an imminent attack here and need to retaliate before the enemy has a chance to strike first, then the country should be ready for it by the time everything else is in place. I think that's everything, so . . . a *fortnight*, say?'

President Hedges did not react, his attention taken up with the matter of gently tapping his ball towards the hole. It rolled straight and true, disappearing over the edge into the darkness with a soft plonk.

'Cool . . .' he announced.

As it was unclear whether this was a comment on his stroke or the plans for impending war, neither of the other two men spoke.

'So what's the agenda here?' the President mused aloud, leaning down to retrieve his ball. 'Tomorrow is Sunday. People are watching sports, so we hold back our media briefing for Monday morning – a transcript of that phone call would be good, by the way, Bobby. TV leads with it Monday evening, the press on Tuesday morning. I follow up with a calm but firm address to the nation on Wednesday, making it clear that the ball is in the General's court and we will not allow ourselves to be threatened or negotiate with terrorists. He calls for negotiations . . . *four* days from now. The next day I say "I said no negotiations," which means . . .'

He stopped to count off the days on his fingers.

'. . . by Friday night there's nothing left to be said and I can get out of town for the weekend, right?'

He looked cheerfully at the two men.

'I can't see any reason why that shouldn't be possible,' the Defence Secretary smiled. 'We'll make it Objective Friday Night.'

'Except . . .' Spotto began, wincing slightly as they turned his way, smiles disappearing from their faces, 'there is the *rest* of the world, sir.'

'Yes,' the President frowned, 'what about it?'

'We have to expect our allies and other countries to *respond*,' Spotto explained, sensing he was horribly alone, 'and . . . and . . .'

'And what?'

'Well . . . they may not keep to the agenda. Objective Friday night, I mean.'

The President looked bemused, turning to his Defence Secretary for guidance. Mitchell Madison blew out his cheeks in disgust, answering, 'Hell, Bob, if they can't even be bothered to say their piece with a whole *week* to do it in, then they can damn well wait till the following Monday. We're dealing with a *national emergency* here! We can't let a bunch of international . . . *foreigners* dictate the pace!'

'Relax, Bobby . . .' President Hedges smiled, tapping him on the shoulder, '. . . it's not like what they say is going to change anything, right? We don't need them, after all. So, you know . . . *que será será*! Anyway, that's what we have ambassadors for, isn't it?'

'But don't we at least want *one* ally going in with us? Just for appearances' sake?'

The President and his Defence Secretary looked questioningly at one another.

'I guess it can't do any harm for me to phone . . . um . . . you know, the pansy,' President Hedges suggested.

'The *pansy*?' Spotto frowned. 'Who's the pansy?'

'Prime Minister Flyte?' Madison answered, ignoring him. 'Sure, why not?'

'Chris *Flyte*? A *pansy*?' Spotto continued. 'Are you sure about that? I haven't heard anything that would lead me to think he was—'

The two men turned to look pityingly at him.

'Well, I mean . . . he's married!' Spotto protested. 'He's just had another kid!'

They smiled sympathetically, as if dealing with a child.

'And . . . and . . .' Spotto floundered, '. . . hey, nobody could have been more *robust* in their support for us over Kalashnistan, right? Hell, if anything he was in more of a hurry to send in his troops than we were, and it wasn't even his own country under *attack*, for God's sake!'

'Yeah, Bobby – it's called "being in the closet"?' the President drawled. 'Like you say, the man slaps his balls on the table at the drop of a hat. So . . . hey, I could be wrong, but it seems to *me* he may be wrestling with some underlying doubts about his own masculinity, don't you think?'

Spotto's mouth hung open as he thought it over. It was true that there was *something* about the guy that had always bothered him. A certain . . . neatness.

'As a matter of fact, Mr President,' Madison said, 'I believe they call it "being in the *cupboard*" over there.'

'You wanted to see me because you have *doubts*?' Spotto gasped.

'Yes, sir, I do,' Teri answered, standing stiffly in front of his desk back at the NIC. 'I have profound doubts.'

He stared at her, fingers drumming furiously on the desk as he tried to control the urge to shout very loudly.

'Well, I'm afraid it's a little late in the day to be experiencing *doubts*, Teri,' he began, keeping his voice unnaturally soft. 'You see, I have just briefed the President *himself* on the situation, and I'm not about to go back to him now saying that my principal expert on the issue has suddenly decided to . . .'

Spotto clenched his jaw, biting off the sentence. He'd been tempted to continue with something along the lines of 'exercise her prerogative to *change her mind*!' but that could be construed as creating a hostile working environment, which was dangerous. So instead, he took a deep breath and said, '. . . to revise her position in a fashion contrary to that which a reasonable person might initially have understood to be that which she considered definitive.'

This, of course, meant something entirely different.

'I realize that it's not . . . not . . .'

'Professional?' Spotto offered. 'No, it's not professional, Teri.'

'I wouldn't go as far as to say—'

'Does it make me look like an *idiot*?' he asked.

'I suppose it does, in a way, yes.'

'Well, then it's not *professional*, is it?'

'I suppose not,' she admitted.

'And what usually *happens* to people who are employed in a profession – any profession at all, Teri – but who are not professional about it?'

'They . . . lose their jobs?'

'They get *fired*! Yes!' he exclaimed. 'But I absolutely do *not* want to fire you, Teri, so for your own sake I want you to consider exactly how *sure* you are about these doubts you have now developed and whether you might not, having developed doubts once, develop doubts *again* – doubts, that is, about your doubts. Do you follow me? For instance, what *proof* do you have that the Bee and Comb Union is, as you now seem to think, *not* a terrorist organization?'

'Well . . . none. It's more a case of having a strong hunch.'

'OK. It's a hunch – that's fine, we all get them. Several of us in the NIC had a hunch that the rumours we'd been

256

hearing of an imminent attack on the Stock Exchange were not serious, for instance. We were wrong. So are you prepared to bet the lives of thousands of your fellow citizens on *your* hunch?'

When she heard it put like that, Teri did indeed begin to doubt her doubts. But then, as a question, it was not unlike the old catch of asking a man whether he had stopped beating his wife. She could see that. But, nevertheless, was it not the lesser of two possible mistakes for her, as an Atlantian, to be responsible for the deaths of innocent Erratis, rather than those of her fellow countrymen? Sure, a life was a life either way, but if she turned out to be wrong in one way, would it not be easier for her to live with *that* mistake than if she turned out to be wrong in the other?

Teri closed her eyes for an instant, trying to find the courage to resist the temptation of a lesser evil.

'Can I . . .' she frowned, '. . . put it another way?'

Spotto shrugged, seeming to relax in the face of the evident difficulty she had in answering his last question.

'If there *is* another way of looking at it, Teri, I would love to hear it.'

'It's a more general question, OK?' she began, leaning forward in her chair and eyeing him keenly.

'Uh-*huh* . . .' Spotto answered cautiously. 'I trust you don't mean, by any chance, that you want to talk about . . . the Big Picture?'

'Yes. Absolutely.' She nodded enthusiastically. 'The Big Picture! As a peaceful society, is *violence* really the best way to achieve our ends?'

'Oh God . . .'

'But *is* it?'

'Teri. Every society has the right to *defend* itself, doesn't it? That is the first duty of the State towards its citizens, for heaven's sake! Self-defence is *not* aggression!'

'But *are* we defending ourselves if, by our actions, we

only engender further aggression against ourselves?' she exclaimed passionately. 'Right now, in the absolute worst-case reading of the situation, we are faced with a minuscule number of individuals who have a genuinely *murderous* hatred of our country. In every million people out there in the world who resent or even hate Atlantis, there is probably *one* fanatic who would think himself justified in killing an innocent stranger simply because the stranger was born here. These fanatics are needles in haystacks and, because it's so hard to find them, our strategy is to set light to the damn hay! But in so doing, surely, are we not morally bringing ourselves down to their level? By allowing ourselves to be provoked into mass destruction, are we not in the process of becoming the very monster they accuse us of being? And once we've become that monster, won't many *ordinary* people out there, quite rightly, see us as the aggressors who must be fought? What exactly are we saying to them, after all, if not "We have no problem with you *personally*, guy, but we're going to bomb your family anyway?" Where is the moral high ground in *that*, for God's sake? How can we claim to be the injured party if, twenty years from now, the problem has grown exponentially as a result of what we do today? Do you know what I'm saying?'

'No. Do *you* know what you're saying, Teri?' Spotto sighed. 'What, we should just let them attack us and do *nothing*?'

'No . . .' she winced, '. . . and . . . maybe . . . *yes*.'

The Director's head jerked back in bafflement.

'I mean . . .' Teri hurried to explain, 'obviously we do everything in our power to thwart terrorist plots, but beyond that perhaps we *would* do better to accept a small proportion of casualties on our side in the short term while concentrating all our energies on winning the *moral* war here. If we show that we are doing all in our power to *avoid* exploiting what everyone knows to be our overwhelming military strength, then we isolate the terrorists in people's eyes the whole world over and identify them as the true evil-doers. Gradually, they find their own people turning against them more and more until they are forced, by the weight of opinion in their *own* countries, to renounce their course of action.'

'Yes, I know. It's called the battle for hearts and minds, Teri. And it's a *nice* idea, but . . . well, I can't think of a single instance in history of a society defending itself that way, can you?'

'What about the cold war?'

'Totally different. Our two sides were evenly matched in terms of military power, so neither of us dared start a war.'

'So . . . because the terrorists are infinitely *less* powerful than us, it's all right to fight?'

'No,' Spotto groaned, rolling his eyes. 'But it *is* . . . an option.'

'In other words, advanced as we claim to be, the only time we will refrain from war when we feel threatened is if we think there is a genuine danger of losing!' Teri scoffed, raising two fingers of either hand in the peace sign. 'Like . . . Give Fear a Chance, Man.'

Her superior was not amused.

Not that she was, either.

'Look,' she continued in a softer vein. 'I *know* what I'm suggesting has never been attempted, but if we – the wealthiest, most powerful and secure society the world has ever seen – is not in a position to even *consider* attempting a moral way out of this situation . . . then no-one ever will be, will they? We might as well admit that peace on Earth is just a fairy tale. A sweet dream that we ought to disabuse our children of around the same time as they start questioning the logistics of Santa.'

Spotto did not immediately reply. He was a man who enjoyed being able to consider himself a realist, and yet he had enough imagination to like to think, like everyone else, that in some distant future humanity could possibly . . . get less stupid.

'I do know one thing,' he answered finally. 'It is *impossible* for an elected leader to say to his citizens that, in the interest of creating a better world, he is prepared to sacrifice even one of their lives rather than use every means at his disposal to defend them.'

'But we agree to that sacrifice every time we go to war, don't we?' Teri countered. 'A soldier's life is no less valuable, is it? So why weigh it differently? The sacrifice is still there – we've simply made a profession out of it. We've *paid* him for it. And, in this instance, it is not as though that guarantees us protection from terrorist attacks on civilians in the meantime, does it? Arguably, we are actually *increasing* the level of sacrifice. And that is only counting our side – which brings me back to my original doubts about whether Errat should be a target at all.'

'And I come back to *my* original position, Teri, which is – what, exactly, do you want me to do at this stage? Do you want me to go back to the President of United States of Atlantis and tell him to call off a military operation that is *already* under way, simply because of your hunch?'

'What do you . . . ?' she gasped in horror. 'How can it be?'

'The USS *Kirk* is in position . . . *right now* . . . in the Gulf near the coast of Errat, Teri,' he informed her sternly. 'We're talking about a multi-*billion*-dollar aircraft carrier here. This has already gone way beyond you and me chewing over the options, and . . . the *fallout* if we insist on changing our position is going to come crashing right back down on our heads.'

He paused to let her take that prospect in.

'However, I want to do the right thing as much as you. I sincerely do. And, more importantly, I value your judgement, Teri. If you are *certain* that you want to change your position at this late stage, I will back you. I will defend you . . . to the bitter end.'

It was a stirring speech, but its underlying meaning was not lost on her.

He would place responsibility for the entire episode squarely on her shoulders.

'So what it's going to be, Teri?' he asked her sympathetically. 'Your call. What am I supposed to tell the President? And the Defence Secretary, and the Joint Chiefs of Staff, and, well, everyone else, I suppose.'

'I . . . I don't know . . .' she stammered. 'I *know* it's not quite as black and white as everyone seems to think, but I can't say for sure what . . .'

'We can't *have* grey here, Teri. When we're talking about a major military operation, there is *seriously* little room for nuance. So what are you going to say?'

Was it even possible, Teri asked herself, for her to put this process into reverse? With the momentum that already existed behind it, could it be turned around like that gargantuan machine cutting its way through the waters of the Gulf towards Errat could be? On the word of an obscure researcher at the NIC?

Was that possible?

Or would she simply be throwing away her career for nothing? She would do it. She would accept the blame for the situation if she thought there was a chance of it helping.

A career did not bleed.

The strength of Teri's moral fibre was such that, even faced with the forces marshalled against her by her superior, it took her a long time to reach a decision.

'I say . . .' she answered, softly, as though hoping to form the words without the aid of her own breath, '. . . we maintain our current position.'

The End minus 5 days

'. . . amid growing expectation of imminent air strikes, WINN's Bill Gundersen has an exclusive, *live* report from the heart of the action on the deck of USS *Kirk*, currently in position off the coast of Errat. Bill – as the only journalist on board, could you tell the Atlantian people exactly *what* is happening on the *Kirk* right now?'

The screen splits to show Bill Gundersen, sporting a khaki jacket with an amazing number of pockets, against the backdrop of a grey steel wall.

'Well, no, Ayesha – I'm not at liberty to say *exactly* what is happening here, and indeed I'm not actually on the *deck* of the USS *Kirk* at the moment in that the military have asked us to keep clear of the deck area while the men make what may well be the final preparations to the aircraft before the pilots take off on their missions, if indeed they do. They have, however, very kindly allowed us complete access to what is arguably the heart of the ship – which is to say the kitchen, or *galley* section where the cooks are engaged in what I can only describe as *intense* food preparation for this morning's breakfast. Standing with me now, I have Midshipman Benjamin Berkoff, who probably knows more than anyone here about what the pilots will be eating on this potentially dramatic morning. Benjamin, what can you tell us about breakfast today on board?'

'Umm . . . we are preparing a full range of classic bodily sustenances for zero seven hundred hours, including cereals, toast, eggs, bacon, and bananas, with a choice of orange or grapefruit juice, tea and coffee.'

'Now, although I realize you cannot reveal too much, is that the kind of breakfast you might serve to men who were about to leave on combat missions?'

'Absolutely it is, yes. These are all high-energy food substances with a gradual calorific release that would be ideal for sustaining an individual who was going into action, at least until and, if need be, well beyond lunch. Especially bananas.'

'Do the pilots tend to eat a lot of bananas before going into combat?'

'Yeah, they eat an *incredible* number of bananas – it's a very good source of energy and, above all, relatively easy for the body to *digest*, which can be vital when you consider the G-forces these individuals have to withstand on take-off and the peak physical performance they have to deliver when at the controls of an aircraft.'

'And, presumably, ease of digestion is a serious issue when they are executing complex, often *dramatic* aerial manoeuvres?'

'Absolutely it is. On a mission, the guys usually find bananas are a far better choice of sustenance than, say, *cereals*. But there are some who prefer plain toast.'

'So would I be right in saying that we can get some kind of idea of what may be going to happen today by gauging the *quantity* of bananas that are consumed this morning?'

'Well, it's usually a pretty good indicator, yeah.'

'And have you prepared *more* bananas today than on a typical morning?'

'I'm afraid that I'm not at liberty to reveal the relative quantities of specific foodstuffs being provided at this particular time.'

'But there *are* bananas this morning?'

'Yes, I can confirm that bananas *will* be available.'

'Well, without revealing too much, I can say that if I were General Harouni I would be pretty worried right now, looking at the awesome *mound* of yellow that we can—'

Chapter Nineteen

*In which our helpless hero finds himself in the hands of
terrorist murderers and loses some of the weight he has
been carrying these last years*

«Are you the leader?» the man with the gun asked him.

It was so far the only thing he had said. But he'd
said it several times already. The first time had been out
on the street where Saman had been dumped by the
police car, finding himself looking up at three balaclava-
wearing men.

«I'm sorry – I'm not sure I understand you,» Saman
had answered nervously, trying to figure out what was
going on.

The man had motioned to his two companions, who
had taken Saman by the arms, helping him to his feet
and leading him into the house outside which they were
standing. The interior was messy and comfortless, clearly
not a home, and Saman had been shown to a white
plastic chair of the kind they had on café terraces and
which tended to go bendy on hot days. The three men
had taken up positions around him and the question had
been repeated.

«Are you the leader?»

«That . . . that depends,» Saman had suggested, trying
not to panic. «The leader of *what*?»

«Are you the leader?»

This appeared to be something of a conversation-stopper.

Furiously analysing his situation, Saman rapidly saw two possibilities. On the one hand, it appeared he was in the hands of a terrorist cell – either of the Sword of Destiny, or the Vanguard League. The question in this case was whether they suspected him of being *their* leader, or the leader of the rival group. On the other hand, however, it was also possible that this was a bluff of Malek Galaam's, and that these men were policemen in disguise, trying to trick him into admitting his involvement in terrorism. Whatever the truth of the situation, the safest response was simply to tell the truth.

«I am the *leader* . . .» he softly answered, «of the Bee and Comb Union. Trust me, I'm just a simple bee-keeper.»

The man nodded, a wry smile showing in the gap of his balaclava.

«Ah . . . but are *we* your bees?»

«*What!* No! You are not my bees.»

The man's shoulders slumped, and he looked down at the floor, sighing. His hand reached up to the top of his head, taking hold of the balaclava and pulling it off.

«We are not worthy?» he asked, head still bowed.

«Well, that's really not your fault because . . . you're human *beings*!» Saman replied.

«And so we are weak, is that it? You cannot place your trust in us?»

«Not to make *honey*!»

The man nodded sadly, clearly shattered by the answer he had received.

«I understand,» he said, looking up.

«I'm not sure you . . .» Saman began, his voice trailing off as he regarded the man's face.

It was unmistakable. Saman had encountered this man before. He had aged since then, but this was him. He was the soldier who had murdered Saman's family and then told him that if he was a real man he would kill himself. He had said that if he ever saw Saman again, he would kill him. Yet this same man was standing before him now, looking at him without even a glimmer of recognition.

And no doubt he still held love of the common people to be his cause.

«What . . . what's wrong?» the man asked, nervously eyeing the fury in Saman's expression.

«You have no idea who I am,» Saman breathed. «You have no *idea* what you have done to me, do you?»

«I . . . you mean . . .» he frowned. «No . . . what did I do?»

«You should not have shown me your face.»

The man's eyes widened in horror, and he scrambled to pull the balaclava back over his head.

«I'm sorry!» he gasped, «I wasn't thinking! It was the disappointment, you understand . . . I didn't . . . I mean *you* didn't . . .»

He turned in panic to his two companions, who moved imperceptibly back from him.

«*I've seen your face!*» Saman snarled. «I know who you are!»

«What . . . what are you going to do to me?»

Saman's eyebrows lifted in an expression of surprise that might, were one to be under the impression that he was the mastermind behind an entire terrorist network, have looked like fury at finding his intentions further questioned by a bungling underling. The truth, however, was that until this moment Saman had not stopped to ask himself that very question – his response had been entirely spontaneous, a natural reaction to coming face to face with the man who had destroyed his life. It was, he now realized, a very good question.

What *was* he going to do? Logically, there was nothing he could do. He was, just as he had been that last time,

267

unarmed and entirely at the mercy of these three men. So the real question ought to have been what did *they* intend to do, but that was not even under consideration here because they thought he was their shadowy leader. They *wanted* to believe that, with the same overriding belief that allowed them to kill innocent people and sacrifice themselves for their cause. The power, he suddenly understood, lay in his hands.

A great calm came over him.

These men *were* bees, and he was a bee master. It was just possible that he could reach his hand into the hive, and not be stung.

«Why did you have me brought here?» he asked.

Where once, years before, this man had looked at Saman with a face of stone, unmoved by the blood he had just spilled, he now seemed to have lost control over certain muscles in his cheeks, the skin twitching spasmodically as he met Saman's gaze. And his eyes now flickered alight with fear of this man he did not recognize, where once they had been so cold in their superiority.

«I thought . . .» he stammered, «I wanted . . . when I heard you had been . . . I had to find out if it was really you . . . to *know* who I was following . . .»

«You had to *know* if I was him?» Saman repeated. «So you lack faith in your leader.»

«*No!* I have *always* been loyal!»

«True faith requires no proof.»

«It was a *mistake*, I know! But it . . . it's *understandable*, isn't it? After all these years . . . please, my loyalty is only to the cause. I would *die* for the cause!»

Saman looked at the crumbling creature before him, and almost allowed himself to give in to pity. This man's whole life was meaningless without his cherished 'cause'. Was it not sad that this was the love of his life, manifesting itself through violence and hatred, and that were this cause to which he had so utterly tied himself to disappear, there would remain nothing but a shell of a human being? He seemed almost too pathetic a creature for Saman to tarnish the memory of his family by taking vengeance upon him. But then he opened his mouth again.

«Please . . .» he begged, «. . . believe me.»

The pity kindling in Saman's heart was instantly snuffed out.

How many times had he said just that? Had he not begged to be believed when this man held a gun to his children?

«Prove it,» he growled.

The man's face froze, his mouth hanging open. His companions stood stiff as ice either side of him, barely daring to breathe. Only Saman, at that moment, was not scared. Because it suddenly did not matter one iota to him if he *himself* got out of here alive or not – he was once again the man standing over the bodies of his loved ones, his own life a thing of no value to him. And that made his will the absolute force in this room. He *was* the leader.

«Go on . . .» Saman urged him gently from the chair. «Prove to me you would die for the cause.»

The pistol by the man's side shook in his hand, the hand that had been so steady and calm as it took aim at a woman and her children.

«Now?» he asked, his knotted throat struggling to speak. «Not . . . as a martyr?»

«You *will* be a martyr. Do you think you have to kill *others* to be a martyr? A martyr is merely someone who gives their life to a cause . . . I am telling you to do it now.»

The man looked imploringly at his two companions, seeing horror in their eyes but no support, seeing doubt in him reflected. In the twisted logic of the moment, they were asking themselves if this man *they* had followed, who had ordered their brothers to sacrifice themselves, was himself capable of sacrifice. And that, perhaps more than anything else, was intolerable to him.

The gun shivered upwards.

Saman sat quite still and relaxed in the chair as the weapon rose to point his way, its intention briefly ambiguous, and then carried on towards the man's own temple. The terrorist's gaze snapped defiantly from one companion to the other, and then he closed his eyes, his finger tightening on the trigger.

The seconds boomed past: *one . . . two . . . three . . .*

His left eye squinted open, giving Saman one last chance to call a halt. But Saman merely raised an eyebrow by way of reply.

Six . . . seven . . . eight . . .

«I can't!» the terrorist shouted, the gun back down to his side. He dropped to his knees and implored Saman, «Tell me to give my life in any other way and I will – but not *this*!'

A great weight lifted from Saman's shoulders – a physical unburdening so real that he found himself rising to his feet like a ball bobbing to the surface. He looked at the huddled sobbing wreckage at his feet, and calmly told him, «If you were a real man, you would kill yourself.»

Then he looked at the two others, and said, «I leave it to you to decide what is to be done with him. I never want to see him again.»

And then he stepped over the man who had murdered his family, and walked out the door to the street.

The End minus 4 days

'. . . respond to those of our democratic allies who basically seem to consider us the aggressors here, Mr Defence Secretary?'

'I'm not aware of anyone having suggested that, Miss Novak.'

'Well, not in as many *words*, perhaps, but they have clearly stated that Atlantis should seek the approval of the international community before embarking on such action which . . . if you think about it . . . they wouldn't do if they *did* approve, would they?'

'No country is obliged to seek approval from the Security Council in matters of its own *self-defence*, Miss Novak! Let's not confuse the issue here – our commitment to world peace and human rights is without doubt, as I think our democratic allies would be the first to grant, and we have a responsibility not just to ourselves, but to every other decent, law-abiding nation here. That is why in a situation like this we cannot, in good conscience, allow ourselves to be forced into a policy of *appeasement* that will, as the history of our democratic allies has proved, only lead the entire world towards catastrophe.'

'Right. That's self-evident. So . . . trying to look at it from their point of view . . . I suppose what they might be saying is "What exactly is the Security Council *for*?"'

'That's a good question, and let me be quite clear that

we, as members of the international community, are as committed to answering that as anyone else. But it is certainly not there to protect dictators and terrorists, as some people appear to believe, and even if that were to be the case then I would respectfully remind everyone, our democratic allies included, that it's a pretty good thing for them that there wasn't such a thing as a Security Council back when – to put it bluntly – they needed us to save *their*—'

Chapter Twenty

In which we take Sunday tea in the company of Prime Minister Chris Flyte and his wife, and learn how it is that a previously peace-loving man has come to start behaving like some blood-splattered warrior king

'"Grandmother dies on operating table as nurse 'pops down to local chemist' for surgical thread,"' the Prime Minister's wife declaimed, peering over her newspaper. 'Have you seen this?'

'I have heard, yes,' her husband replied, sipping his tea. 'It's terrible.'

'It's a *scandal* is what it is!' she snapped. 'It's one thing not having enough dialysis machines, but not enough *thread*, for God's sake? It's a disgrace! They say here that young interns have taken to bringing *fishing reels* to work in case they run out!'

'That's an apocryphal story.'

'So much for your promise to put the Health Service back on its feet,' she sighed. 'It's all very well for you to sit there, sipping your tea. People are dying!'

'What do you want me to do, darling? Yes, I am drinking a cup of tea – but I have no medical experience, so I don't think I'd be more useful in a hospital right now.'

'Anyway,' she sniffed, turning back to her paper, 'tea's carcinogenic.'

'I thought it was an antioxidant,' he frowned.

'Mmm? That too.'

As always, the tea was perfectly made, reflected the Prime Minister as he replaced his cup on the silver tray. So there were perks to the job.

His wife could not say that their lot was entirely sordid compared to the Heads of State in other countries, even if it was outrageous that they had to live in a small courtesy flat while his foreign counterparts generally got the use of a palace. And were better paid. And their wives got clothing allowances. And they didn't have to learn how to curtsey to an overbred relic of the feudal era whose palace in the capital, ugly as it was by Continental standards, at least ought to be lived in by the person who really ran the country. And his family, of course. And so on until no amount of opinion polls and electoral landslides were sufficient to convince him that he was not a failure.

It was all true, but the tea was really very good. No doubt prepared with all that hoopla of warming the pot beforehand and standing on one leg. The PM had always been a tea-bag man himself. Out of laziness, to be sure, but partly as a political statement. It was absurd, but people noticed a thing like a box of shop-floor tea bags next to the kettle in your constituency office. Made you human in their eyes. One of them. Not that he'd been back to the constituency since the election.

No doubt the box was still there, awaiting his return.

The tea helped him get through days like this. He'd expected the job to be hard, naturally. The problems he had inherited when his party returned to power after a long sojourn in the wilderness ran deep through society. Despite a surface sheen of dynamism and localized pockets of prosperity, the nation as a whole was like

274

some grand old country house that had been transformed into luxury apartments by cowboy developers. In each of its metaphorical rooms, behind the cheap paint and the polystyrene mouldings, lurked structural horrors from a surveyor's worst nightmare. In places, the nation's timbers were like sponge.

People accused him of having no answer. But there *was* no answer. Under sodium pentathol, any intelligent Prime Minister of the last fifty years would have admitted the same thing – the problems of the nation were so overwhelming that no government could take them on in a serious fashion. Any such attempt to change things for the better would be political suicide. And then the other party would take all the credit when things improved.

So it couldn't be done, or at least not by a democratic government with a five-year lifespan. The successful politician's life is back to front – while Chris Flyte had a secret passion for the blue-rinse dame of serious government, he was stuck in a loveless marriage to the big-breasted slapper of tabloid popularity. He snatched the occasional tryst with his mistress in a debate on some minor issue like extending pub opening hours, but then the gaudy tramp he'd married would reassert her hold over him when Bonjy the Plucky Piglet had to be saved from becoming pork chops. The trouble was that the whole idea of a five-year tenure in office came from the days when politicians weren't really responsible for a great deal – an era before national education, health and transport. Back then, anything that a government was likely to do, such as wage a war, could be seen through to its conclusion before an election came round. They did not have to undertake seriously long-term projects because five years, in those days of infant mortality and sea battles, *was* a pretty long time. You could conquer a continent in five years.

For a modern PM such as himself, the only realistic

objective was to keep one's job for as long as possible. Fortunately, this was made easier for him by the fact that the Opposition had gone completely barmy and seemed to be doing everything in their power to stay out of power. He still wasn't sure why – was it some post-traumatic collapse brought about by having been given the responsibility for these insoluble problems for too long, or had they just eaten too much beef? Whatever the reason, they had eschewed the electoral middle ground by offering the public a series of leaders who were increasingly radical in their baldness.

Bugger the manifesto or the track record – the focus groups proved that he could get his mandate renewed on the sole basis of a follicle count.

'Oh my *God*!' she spat. 'It says here that "one in five teachers failed a basic history test, some not being able to name a single king in the nation's history."'

'Uh-huh?' he nodded, brow folded in concentration as he tried to decipher the Treasury report on his lap.

'That is *twenty per cent*!' she pointed out.

'But presumably they are not *history* teachers,' he sighed, giving up on the 'underlying fiscal broadband quotient'. The Chancellor made him read these things just to prove he was more intelligent, the bastard. It was probably just a fancy way of saying 'money'. 'Anyway, I thought you were against teaching children a triumphalist, phallocentric version of their history.'

'I am – but the *teachers* should still know it!'

'How are teachers going to know it if nobody teaches it?'

She narrowed her gaze, fixing him like a dartboard.

'Being facetious isn't going to hide the fact that the educational system is a *joke*!'

'Darling, I am doing everything in my power to improve it. And, according to the latest statistics, there's good reason to think that it *is* moving towards improvement!'

'Oh come off it – you know statistics can be made to say anything.'

He didn't say it. He could have said it, but he didn't.

'You're right,' he nodded. 'But look at it the other way and an eighty per cent pass rate is really quite impressive.'

'Mmm.' She frowned. 'If I didn't love you, I'd say that was political spin.'

Spin. God, how he hated that term. As a means of accusation, it was almost like witch-dipping. Why could only a politician ever spin a fact, after all? As though journalism wasn't *based* on spinning the truth every day. As though a priest did not spin, or a therapist, or an astrophysicist. As though spin wasn't a principal ingredient of social interaction between people all over the world. As though anybody could ever raise a child, or fall in love, or write a poem, or paint a picture, without *spin*.

People accused him of being obsessed with presentation, but what else *was there*? Did they not understand that he would love to be able to do something, but if he really did what was necessary they would crucify him come the first electoral opportunity, and long before he actually achieved anything? Some of them did know that, of course. The bastards in the media first and foremost.

And they called *him* cynical. Accused *him* of twisting the facts. The fact, as they well knew, was not that the Health Service was crap, although it was, but that when it wasn't crap, it was *far* too good. It kept tens of thousands of absolutely pointless people ticking over who were either clapped out beyond repair or in some state of stable vegetation. These people, as a result, were guzzling the entire budget and parking up all the beds, which meant that younger, fitter and more productive people unavoidably ran the risk of bleeding to death on a trolley in a broom cupboard while the nurses waited for someone to wheeze their last. And every year, as medicine improved, there were more and more old bangers clogging up the market. What was needed, frankly, was a cull. It was a job for the Countryside Alliance, not more sodding *doctors*, for God's sake.

But he'd known that before he came into power, so he had no right to complain now – although the criticism irked in that he'd never claimed to have a solution to any of the nation's problems up his sleeve. Indeed, he liked to think that he had retained his integrity better than most Prime Ministers – he hadn't lied, he'd simply smiled and said 'Trust me'.

Well, nobody could accuse him of breaking that trust, because he'd never said *what* they should trust him about, and they had never insisted on being told. That was their fault, not his. He'd known exactly what he wasn't saying.

He had surfed to power on a great wave of enthusiasm for getting rid of the other lot. In the run-up to that historic landslide, poll after poll conducted by his party's advisers had shown that the only thing that could possibly endanger his certain victory was an unnecessary discussion of what he intended to do once in government. His sole firm commitment in policy terms, therefore, had been to replace all those people presently in positions of government with people from his own party.

At the time, this had struck the electorate as an astoundingly good policy.

Clearly, it was always going to be downhill from then on, but he'd nevertheless been surprised to find that the hardest days were not those when he was being attacked by the media or the Commons or little old ladies. The hardest part was the Sundays. The days when it all went quiet and he was left alone with his wife and family.

Her taste for palaces aside, she had always been more idealistic than him, even though she was the more intelligent of the two. She had never been at ease playing the political wife, only putting up with it in so far as she did because she thought he might be able to achieve great things. She genuinely believed that.

Sundays, therefore, were the days when he paid for his failure to change society. On Sundays every aspect of the nation's gradual decline since the loss of its empire somehow, in some extraordinary way that he could never quite put his finger on, became inextricably mixed up with a question mark hanging over his masculinity.

It was very odd, especially in a feminist, but there was a vague sense in everything she said that all of society's problems could be overcome by a man with sufficiently high testosterone levels – except, naturally, the root problem of men themselves. She never said as much, but the suggestion was nonetheless there that a real man should be able to go out into the world and wave his penis around like some magic wand, curing the ills of pensioners, single mothers and inner-city crime. And then chop it off when he got home.

It was, not to put too fine a point on it, driving him round the fucking bend.

That was why it had been an unexpected relief when the Barkins had flared up all over again. It was hard to say which of the various ethnic groups had been at fault because the origins of the quarrels between the Zerks, Croanks, Barmenians and others were buried so far back in history that they were half-mythological. Now *there* was a long-term project, if ever there was one – not that anyone understood what the plan was in the Barkins, least of all the people who lived there.

It was a little embarrassing for the rest of the con-tinent, the way they carried on – everyone else seemed to have got this urge to kill their neighbour out of their system in the last World War, barring the shorter-haired breeds of football fan, but down there they'd apparently been hating each other for so many centuries now that it had become genetic. It was odd because they were perfectly intelligent, cultured people most of the time, but once every generation or so this hereditary madness would grip the whole region, and the man who'd invited his neighbour round for a barbecue one week was quite capable of feeding him to his dog the next.

But at least no-one could accuse them of being inconsistent in the Barkins.

They had always been that way.

The PM had been almost as surprised as everyone else when he decided to send the troops in to put a stop to the massacres. But by God it had felt good. Years of feeling that his balls were being weighed on an almost daily basis done away with in a single unexpected move. That had shut her up. All his pent-up frustration had burst forth, revealing itself in a hitherto unseen talent for playing the fire-eyed war leader.

'How was . . . *work* today?' she'd ask cautiously when they were alone in the evening.

'Bombed Svjetlost,' he'd grunt, flopping back into an armchair as if brought down by the sheer force of his testicular mass.

'Svjetlost . . . ?' she'd frown, striving to keep up with the complexities of Barkin geopolitics. 'Is that Zerk or—'

'It's flat,' he'd answer. 'Hey, you know what? I want beer.'

'*Beer?* But you don't—'

'Cold. In the bottle. Please.'

It had been good while it lasted. Sundays had been the day then. The day of worship. Prostration before the Warrior God. Strangely, the media hadn't seemed to notice how the timing of her subsequent, middle-aged pregnancy had tied in with the start of the Barkins War. She'd even wanted to call the boy Victor, but he'd suggested they choose something a little less obvious.

It was too good to last, of course. Victor, as he was not called, and victory had come all too quickly, it

280

seemed, and with it a slow seeping away of his potency. Real Warrior Gods just do not change nappies.

No-one should have been surprised, then, that when President Hedges declared his War on Terrorism, the Prime Minister was the first foreign leader to announce, with no equivocation whatsoever, that he was right behind him.

Positively groin-to-posterior, some said.

Not for him the weaselish caution of other leaders, who supported the President's war in principle while refusing to commit their forces to a fight against an unknown enemy in an as yet undetermined location. From Day One the PM had his metaphorical gunbelt on, promising the public a difficult and bloody, but unavoidable struggle somewhere. Possibly in several places. And for a long time. A fight that would take determination and patience, and in which victory might never be clear. Indeed, a new century having just begun, there was a temptation to suggest right now this was to be its theme, and they should waste no time in getting started.

Certainly, he didn't. His infant child was not even given time for a last poo before the PM was out the door, bouncing from one world leader to another like a diplomatic volleyball, so energetic in his attempts to build an international coalition behind the Atlantian proposal that he had to be reined in before he started bringing in countries that President Hedges had kind of planned on bombing.

Back home, people's initial enthusiasm started to wobble once it became apparent where the first battlefield would be. Many were those who predicted that the military campaign in Kalashnistan, a country so violent and anarchic that it made the Barkins look like a civil war theme park, was bound to end in disaster. How, they argued, could the West hope to achieve anything in this place whose people and terrain had defeated all previous armies? A place without strategic points to base any stategy around. A place so desolate and worthless that there was nothing there worth bombing.

And yet, just as in the Barkins, they were proved wrong.

There is *always* something worth bombing.

Then there were those who argued that the war would be counterproductive because by killing a terrorist you only breed *more* terrorists. These people, of course, were partly right, but were basing their logic on a huge misunderstanding of what was being proposed: yes, there is a danger in killing a terrorist that he will become a martyr and an inspiration to others, but not if you kill *lots* of them. This was not a strategy that the PM could explain in public, but the whole objective of this war was to flood the terrorist market with martyrs and hence bring about a collapse in the perceived value of martyrdom.

Finally, and most ludicrously of all, there were some who were not against the war in principle, but who felt it was unfair to fight it in *Kalashnistan*, of all places. The logic here seemed to be that the people of Kalashnistan had suffered enough already by virtue of *being* Kalash, and shouldn't have somebody else's war imposed on them when they had enough wars of their own already. Meaning, presumably, that these people felt the Allied order of priority should be to start by bombing terrorists who were hiding out in tranquil middle-class suburbs.

In the event, of course, the Kalash had joined in with the fighting more enthusiastically than anyone, *making* it their war. And he knew for a fact that some of them had been pleasantly surprised to find how rich their country still was in places that were considered worth destroying. Furthermore, the more moderate and forward-thinking Kalash realized that being bombed was ultimately a good thing because when it was over the West would assuage its guilt by helping them rebuild their shattered country, probably to a higher standard than was presently the case. So blowing everything up was a highly constructive thing to do and represented their best hope of one day passing a better land on to their children, which was what everyone finally wanted. Their children would inherit a nation with all the comforts that they themselves had lost through decades of warfare – a land with roads, and electricity stations, and water plants, and hospitals, and all the other things that were worth fighting for. Which, in all probability, their children would.

There was a gentle tap on the door of the living room, and it opened just enough for Ruddock to poke his head inside.

'May I clear the tea away now?' he asked in that perfectly pitched tone of his. A tone that was both unintrusive and yet managed to suggest that he was deeply interested in this question.

'Yes, I think so, James,' the Prime Minister smiled. 'Thank you.'

'No problem, Chris,' he winked, stepping into the room.

One of the first changes the Prime Minister had made on taking office was to insist that everyone around him address each other by their first name. This had proved impossible for certain members of the staff, in particular the man who had been head butler to the previous two leaders of the nation. He'd chosen to take early retirement, which was something of a relief because he frankly wouldn't have fitted in with the image Flyte wanted to give of his country. He was like a character from the TV adaptation of some classic novel. He fitted in perfectly with the whole Gothic mustiness of the place, with its glowering portraits of figures from the nation's past, looking pompously over their mantelpiece moustaches – but all that had been cleared away, too, naturally. The walls were now covered in works by young contemporary artists, showcasing the creativity and vibrancy of the nation. They never failed to attract the interest of visiting dignitaries, who were generally still stuck on the idea that paintings – while they could be abstract – should nevertheless involve paint. Which some of them did, of course, even if people inevitably tended to fixate on works such as Gavin Vaughn's *Observing Quarks According to the Uncertainty Principle (Dog Poo I Trod in)*, Mark Townsend's *Post-it Note*, or Sarah Clarke's *Goddess Behold, I Menstruate. Oh Fuck, Fuck, I'm out of Tampax.* Tiffany Wates, for instance, was a painter in a more classical sense, although she didn't use brushes, producing her extraordinarily visceral tableaux by drinking various acrylics and then throwing up on the canvas. Such paintings weren't to everyone's taste, he realized – not even to his own – but that wasn't the point.

James Ruddock was far more in keeping with this fresh approach than his predecessor would have been. He was black, for a start, although that was irrelevant. Indeed, the fact that his colour was neither here nor there was the very point Flyte had wished to make. More important was that he represented the entrepreneurial, complex-free spirit of the younger generation – domestic service was neither a vocation for him, nor a source of shame, but part of a clearly planned career path. A spell as butler to the Prime Minister would enable him to command a lavish salary in the future, freelancing for visiting foreign industrialists and dignitaries.

'The richest one per cent of the country . . .' the PM's wife read out as Ruddock put the cups back on the tray, 'now earn more than the lower eighty-five per cent combined.'

'Yes.'

An alarm bell was ringing in his head. This was not the moment for this conversation. He knew his wife – she was capable, motivated entirely by her pronounced sense of social injustice, of saying something that was going to be deeply insulting to someone who was employed as, say, a butler. Flyte stared at her with wide eyes, trying to draw her attention to the fact that they weren't alone.

'Well?' she asked.

'Well . . .' he muttered, willing Ruddock to get on with it, '. . . yes.'

'That's it? That's all you have to say, as a so-called socialist? You don't think there's anything wrong with a country where one in three young people are now employed in menial service industries, then?'

He felt the blood rushing to his cheeks. Menial. She'd said menial.

'Well, we have a very *dynamic* service sector, darling,' he answered hoarsely. 'I think it's one of the *strengths* of our—'

'It's *exploitation*, pure and simple!' she gasped. 'How can you sit there and tell me that it's *dynamic* for people to be—'

'Thank you, James!' he smiled as Ruddock carried the tray out of the room.

'No problem, Chris,' the butler winked, pulling the door shut behind him.

'Darling!' he began as it clicked shut, 'could we not have these discussions in *private*? That was a hideously inappropriate moment to—'

'What?' She frowned. 'We can talk in front of the *butler*, for heaven's sake! Who cares what James thinks about—'

The door opened again, and Ruddock's head poked back in.

'Sorry to interrupt,' he smiled, glancing at the PM's wife. 'Apparently the President is on the phone, Chris.'

'The President?'

'Of Atlantis,' he explained. 'Would you like the call put through here, or—'

'Yuh,' Flyte announced, standing up. 'Yuh. I'll take it in my office. Excuse me, darling.'

His wife took a deep breath, sighing as she picked up the newspaper again.

'It's impossible to have a conversation here,' she muttered.

'Chris,' the President drawled a minute later, 'I really apologize for disturbing you on the day of the Lord, but we have a situation here.'

'A situation?' Flyte repeated. 'What kind of a situation?'

'The bad kind.'

'Good,' Flyte instinctively answered. 'Sorry . . . I mean . . . gosh. How awful.'

'I need to know if we can count on your friendship in a military kind of way if this turns out—'

'Of course,' the Prime Minister interrupted, sitting down at his desk with a smile of relief. 'So . . . who are we talking about?'

The End minus 3 days

'. . . with only days, or maybe even *hours* left to go before possible military action, we ask "What of the ordinary people of Errat, many of whom have no involvement in terrorism? Who are they, and how are they preparing for imminent air strikes?" On site in the heart of the Errati capital for World Information Network News, Clarissa Wong has been taking the pulse on the street. We present an In-Depth Special Report.'

Clarissa Wong appears, her head wrapped in what might be a Mantovani silk scarf that matches her khaki casual combat jacket, standing in front of the Western gate of the bazaar.

'I am standing in front of the main entrance to the central bazaar – the magnificent, ornate gate that is a protected World Heritage site and testament to better days, when Errat was a rich and powerful nation, its merchants trading with people from all over the world. Today, it is still the commercial heart of the city. But whereas normally, at this time of the morning, you would expect that heart to be pumping 120 bpm, the scene here is more reminiscent of cardiac arrest. The only people here now are the beggars and street urchins with nowhere else to go, but even for them the pickings are slim in a city that has battened down its hatches as storm clouds gather on the horizon. Inside, the craftsmen vending their traditional leather goods sit

287

glumly, waiting for the customers who for centuries have prized the bags and jackets for which Errat was famous. This is a city where life has ground to a halt, where people are staying home with their loved ones, gathered around the television – or, in many cases in this poor, simple country, the radio – and waiting. Waiting for news that they know will, at best, only offer them a doctored answer to the questions that they are asking themselves – what is going to happen, why is it happening, and what is going to happen next? Most people here are not terrorists – they are mothers and fathers, or sons and daughters. Their goal is not to kill but simply to live, to put food on the family table, and eat it. But that is an objective that is already, in the shadow of war, becoming hard to fulfil . . .'

Change of scene to the interior of the market. The camera pans along an empty alleyway, the cones of light dropping vertically down from the ceiling. The food stalls are unmanned, the meat and fruit covered by cotton sheets.

'This morning, when we came here for the first time, this part of the market was bustling with life – a huge crowd of people hurrying to buy food while they still could because already, at midday, the vendors have shut up shop and retreated to the safety of their houses. The only person we see here is a lone security guard, staying on to protect the produce from looters who could take advantage of the tense international situation to ransack the shops. At first he did not want to let us in to shoot this film, saying that the market was closed. When I asked him for how long it would remain closed, he just shrugged and said, "It depends on the heat" – the heat, he no doubt meant, that is cruising a few miles offshore from his beloved city. At times like this, however, money talks, and he let us in to film for a handful of *takals* – little more than a dollar in real terms, but a welcome windfall to a man who knows his children may soon be starving. He thanked us and said, with a pained expression, "It would be better to come back when things cool off" – like many people here, he was philosophical about war, knowing that one day life in his country would return to normal, and wanting us to see it *then*, when all this was over. We promised we would and penetrated into the stifling atmosphere of the bazaar, thinking that it was almost as though the place itself was reflecting the intense, pressure-cooker-like tension that has gripped the whole—'

Chapter Twenty-one

In which General Harouni makes the fatal, but quite understandable decision not to bow to the outrageous demands of a foreign superpower, and our hero resists the demand that he get out of bed

Malek Galaam, like anybody else, did not get to see the General, or even set foot inside the Presidential palace, without an escort of Patriot Guards. Being the second most powerful man in the nation, he was entitled to a squad of twelve Guards accompanying him through the building this morning – six in front and six behind – a measure that was presented as a symbol of status, of course, rather than as a sign of how little the General trusted his chief of internal security. Galaam, on the other hand, could at least be relied upon not to sacrifice his *own* life in an attempt to assassinate the General – so there was no need to search him for explosives or remove the pistol from his belt.

As befitted the military elite of the nation, the Patriot Guards were immaculately turned out, heels clicking in robotic unison on the marble floor. Their devotion to their job was evident in the pride with which they bore their black and gold uniforms, designed by the General himself and individually tailored for each Guard, and the weaponry which, contrary to the somewhat antique guns issued to ordinary soldiers, was the best that the Atlantian arms industry could offer foreigners. And naturally there were other perks to joining the Patriot Guards – most notably the fact that their families were housed in a luxury, guarded compound on the coast. Not that the guards of that compound were Guards.

The General was a firm believer in checks and balances.

Unusually, the nation's leader was dressed this morning in a white laboratory coat. He was standing behind a table on which there was a bewildering array of flasks and spiralling glass pipes along which bubbled brightly coloured chemicals. As Galaam entered the room, he was holding a test tube up to the light and examining the mysterious liquid within.

A photographer was nervously shooting off pictures as another squad of Patriot Guards watched. The camera began to whirr as the film automatically rewound itself.

«I . . . I have to change the film . . .» the photographer announced, reaching cautiously down towards his bag. «Is that OK?»

«No, I'm bored of this,» the General sighed, lowering his arm. «Surely you've taken enough pictures already?»

«Well, I just wanted to be sure, your excellency . . .»

«Enough, I said,» he snapped, tossing the test tube onto the table. «You will come back tomorrow to photograph me playing the piano. Go away now.»

The photographer barely had time to close his camera bag before the Guards began leading him out of the room. The discarded test tube rolled off the table and broke on the floor as the General walked away from the laboratory equipment.

«Good morning, your excellency,» Galaam nodded, trying not to smile at the man's pretension.

«*Is it?*» The General snapped, striding towards his

desk. «Do you mind telling me what the fuck is going on?»

«You would be referring to . . . Atlantis.»

«Of course I am! What is that idiot President of theirs talking about? It seems I have until the end of the week to hand over this . . . this . . .»

«Saman Massoudi.»

«Yes, that one, or "suffer the consequences". Who the hell is this man?»

Galaam glanced across at his military escort, the discomfort of his expression making it clear that what he had to say was for the General's ears only. The General looked up as he lit his cigarette and said, «Guards! Fingers and anthem!»

The soldiers snapped to attention, their hands rising ceremonially to ear level as if to deliver a double salute, but instead they inserted their index fingers in their ears and began to sing 'We Are Errat', the new national anthem based on one of the General's own poems.

«We are Errat . . .» they boomed. «We are your children . . . We fought your enemies . . . And we killed them . . .»

As the song continued, Galaam approached the General's desk and leaned across it with his palms on the leather surface to be heard over the soldiers' chanting.

«It's a mistake!» he half-shouted. «The man is a complete nobody! I have personally interrogated him and can promise you without any doubt whatsoever that he is no more a terrorist leader than . . . than . . . I am *myself*! Saman Massoudi is just a simple honey merchant, your excellency!»

«Well then – if he's a nobody, let's hand him over to them and be done with it!»

Galaam nodded, his eyes creasing into a wince, and answered, «Of course, I will do whatever you order, your excellency, but I wonder if that is the best response.

The man is of no importance, but he is *innocent*, after all. He is a loyal citizen, and should we allow the Atlantians to bully us into sacrificing every poor bastard their Intelligence services, who are clearly incompetent in the extreme, have decided is a terrorist? They haven't even produced any evidence to support their accusation – their President just calls a press conference, accuses a citizen of ours of preparing some ludicrous . . . *bee* attack, and then threatens us with war if we don't hand him over! What kind of a way to behave is *that*? Would he even *consider* giving up one of his own people when faced with a similar demand? Of course not! And aren't *Atlantians* the ones who are always lecturing the rest of us about the rule of law and respect for human rights, for heaven's sake?»

The General drew deep on his cigarette as he considered the point, blowing out the smoke in a series of short puffs. The voices of the singing Guards, meanwhile, swelled up to proclaim:

«We'll hang the traitors . . . And cleanse your cities . . . We'll stone every woman . . . Who shows her titties . . .»

Galaam could see the General was wrestling with his inclination not to provoke the wrath of the world's military superpower, and needed further convincing.

«I am just worried, your excellency,» he confessed, «about the consequences of your being made to look . . . *womanish* in the eyes of the people . . .»

«You cannot stay in bed *for ever*, little brother!» Farrukh was shouting through Saman's door at that precise moment. «You can't just flee *reality*!»

Saman cursed softly and cupped his hands over his ears. Farrukh, as always, was so sure of what he thought: if one stayed in bed, one was fleeing reality. Saman could not be bothered to explain to his brother that he realized practical difficulties were *bound* to arise with his present course of action, but that it was the best plan he had come up with so far. It was certainly not ideal in that, apart from anything else, he was already getting rather hungry, but it was currently better than the alternatives.

God only knew what awaited him outside the calm of this bedroom, what further insanity he would have to endure. Because the whole world was mad. He understood that now. For years he had been protecting himself with this lie that madness, however terrible its consequences had been for him personally, was not the norm. That by and large people were reasonable creatures who, in exceptional circumstances, could behave as maniacs. As if the deed and the doer could be judged separately, making time and place carry the bulk of the guilt. But he saw now what nonsense that was. Indeed, what madness it was of his own.

Circumstances might explain, but excused nothing. In anyone's behaviour. Ever. Because it supposed that people had no choice, whereas the truth was that, in each case, an individual was either prepared to do a certain thing or they were not – so there was nothing temporary about it, and nothing enforced – and the world was doomed to relive its nightmares over and over again for as long as people refused to recognize that about themselves. For as long as they denied what they were.

Lunatics.

People were capable of wonderful things – wisdom, love, and understanding. Ultimately, though, they were no better than their worst moments, their truest moments, when all the constraints they had willingly agreed to put upon their behaviour at other times proved insufficient to stop them diving into the abyss. No law, no moral code, no Commandment, nothing, just them in their universe.

The reasons for their behaviour were immaterial, because people would always find a reason. A cause. An enemy. A hope. Something to which they could surrender their fragile sanity, pretending they served it rather than the other way round, because even a howling psychopath requires a logic for his actions, requires a belief that he is a dog, or that a dog is telling him to do it. A dog, or a god, whatever . . . it made no difference because it was just them all along, *wanting* to do this, and choosing to deny they had a choice.

And that, Saman suspected, was a possible definition of madness.

A person who thinks he has no choice.

Saman, however, believed he had a choice at all moments, everywhere, and thus he believed in his absolute, inescapable responsibility for everything he did. This, by his reckoning, was what qualified him as sane.

And that was why, no matter how ridiculous his behaviour might seem to Farrukh, he was not really fleeing *reality* by choosing to stay in bed.

«Saman!» Farrukh screamed. «The fucking President of the fucking United States of Atlantis has said he's going to *war* if you don't give yourself up! Staying in bed is *not* a viable option!»

Saman did not answer. Did his brother not understand that if things had really got to this point of insanity, then staying in bed was probably the only sane option *left* to him? It couldn't last for ever, he knew that, but why hurry to end it?

He was calm. He was in charge.

Malek Galaam stayed silent as the General's palms slammed onto the desk.

«It is unacceptable!» the dictator seethed. «The people of Errat are not cattle who can be herded by some Atlantian *cowboy*!»

Had the Atlantians been just a little bit subtler in their approach to the situation, making their demands known through diplomatic channels rather than grandstanding in front of the world's media, then Galaam would never have been able to manipulate the General like this. But now he was convinced that he had no choice. To comply would constitute a personal humiliation. He was getting more irate by the second, his own words fanning the flames of his outrage.

It had been even easier than Galaam had anticipated to lead him into the trap.

«Right to the end . . . We will fight them . . .» the Guards were roaring for the second time, carrying on as long as they were not given the signal to stop. «If we have no arms . . . Then we will bite them . . .»

«It is an insult to our manhood,» Galaam pointed out.

«Exactly!» the General squawked, bug-eyed with anger. «But they will find that we are not *women*! We are not scared to fight for our honour!»

«Although it is important the world understand that we are not the *aggressors* here, either. We should make it clear that we are prepared to negotiate in the spirit of peace.»

«Yes!» The General shouted. «Yes! I shall call a press conference and we will show the world that Errat is a *peace-loving* nation! I will call upon the Atlantian President to *negotiate*!»

Galaam smiled.

Everything was working out rather well.

«This is very bad, Saman, very bad indeed,» Farrukh announced, showing him that morning's newspaper. «What have you *done*?»

The paper featured a photograph of Saman himself – the one from the web site that Aziz had insisted on creating, in which he was shown holding up a pot of honey and grinning strangely. Only it had now been cropped to cut out the honey, leaving it to the viewer's imagination to decide what it was that he held in his hand that had him cackling like a madman.

«You know perfectly well that I've done nothing,

brother,» Saman replied. «I am innocent of all these charges and I expect your complete suppport.»

Farrukh's eyebrows rose in surprise, unused to being addressed in such a firm tone by his younger brother. Indeed, ever since he had reappeared from his room, something seemed to be different about Saman. He was holding himself with unaccustomed dignity, as though he had reached some momentous decision while hiding in his bed.

«Why is your smile all . . . twisted?» Farrukh frowned. «You look like you're holding a *bomb* in your hand!»

«I don't like having my picture taken, that's all,» Saman answered, pulling on his jacket and heading to the door.

«How can you be so *calm*? The Atlantians are threatening to go to *war* over this!»

«That's not my fault.»

«Think about *other* people for once, can't you?» Farrukh shouted. «How do you think this affects *me*? Do you think I am going to be able to hang onto my contracts with Atlantis when my own *brother* is their Public Enemy Number One?»

«I will make it clear that you are nothing to do with this.»

«What good is that going to do? You can't even convince them that you're nothing to do with it *yourself*! Do you think that's going to mean they spare my factory when the bombing starts?»

«Why should they bomb your factory, for heaven's sake, brother?»

«Because it's right next to the baby-food factory!» Farrukh screamed. «Don't you know they *always* bomb the fucking baby-food factory?»

Saman looked pityingly at him.

«I am truly sorry that this situation is causing you such distress, Farrukh,» he declared calmly. «I will do everything in my power to ensure that you are not drawn into it.»

«How can I not be drawn into it? You live in my *house*!»

«Not any more,» Saman said. «As from today, I intend to remain in the hills with my beehives, where my presence will not represent a danger to anyone else. I will be quite alone, brother. Goodbye.»

He leaned forward to kiss his brother on the cheeks, and grasped the handle of the door that would lead him out onto the street. He was pleased that he was managing to remain calm and deal with this in a mature fashion. He had a plan.

Unfortunately, in arriving at his decision whilst secluded in his bedroom, he had not taken into consideration the sight that awaited him as he opened the door.

A crowd was waiting silently. A big crowd.

In all his life, Saman had never heard such a terrifying sound as the roar of adoration that went up as they spied their hero . . .

Who quickly shut the door again.

The End minus 2 days

'. . . was Bill Gundersen reporting live from the USS *Kirk* on how the *bilge pumps* could save countless lives in the event of a hypothetical torpedo attack by an Errati submarine. More from Bill later, as well as a panel discussion with our team of experts here in the studio on the issue raised by that report, namely "The Dangers of an Errati Counter-attack: Do They Have any Submarines?" Coming up next, however, we continue our series of special features on how ordinary Atlantian families are coping with the crisis and preparing themselves, if need be, for a summer of terror and death. Benson Gloag reports.'

Cut to Benson Gloag walking down a leafy suburban avenue, microphone in hand. Here we go, the Angry Teenager thinks. *Now* there's going to be some fucking news.

'This is the quiet, middle-class neighbourhood of Spotsboro, just half an hour's train ride from the heart of the capital. In many ways, it is a place like so many others – the kind of place where *families* live, where their children go to school, and people live right next door to their neighbours. Walking down this peaceful avenue, it is very hard to believe that tranquil Spotsboro could ever be the target of some terrorist atrocity, and yet that is the unthinkable possibility that the modest people behind these doors have had to come to terms with in recent months. There is fear in Spotsboro and, if you look closely, the shadow of genocide has fallen over these sun-dappled front lawns . . .'

He stops walking, and the camera turns to picture the front yard of a house where workmen are busy replacing all the windows of the building.

'Ned and Marge Spiegelflug are an average couple,' Gloag's voice-over continues as the camera pans towards the front porch. 'They are not wealthy, both working full-time to support themselves and their two teenage children. Ned is currently unemployed, another victim of the multi-billion-dollar fraud that brought UniCom crashing down last month. Although under no suspicion of wrongdoing himself, the fact that he worked in the accountancy department of the company means that he has been having difficulty finding new employment. He and Marge had been putting money aside over the years to pay the college fees for Ned Jnr and Hermione, and perhaps a retirement home for themselves in the sun, but the terrorist situation has changed all that . . .'

'It's called positive pressurization . . .' Ned Spiegelflug explains, waving his arms around to take in his whole property. 'Basically, the air pressure inside the house is slightly greater than that outside, meaning that it's almost totally proof against chemical or biological attack.'

He looks tired, but driven – burning eyes sunk deep in their sockets. Marge smiles stiffly, and holds her husband's arm in a show of conjugal solidarity. It's not clear if she shares his enthusiasm or is rigid with horror that the whole nation now knows he is losing his mind.

'But . . . it doesn't come cheap,' Ned continues. 'Replacing the windows has taken up whatever money we had left and more, but the family realizes that—'

'The bank repossessed my car last week,' Marge adds with a small laugh.

'We'll get it back, sweetheart, I promise,' Ned assures

her softly. 'Just as soon as I get a new job. So anyway, like I was saying . . . it *has* been difficult for everyone recently, and we've all had to make sacrifices, but I believe that the family is probably *closer* as a result – we discuss things, we argue, we shout at one another in a way that we never did before all of this started. That's all been very positive. And, for me *personally*, this has been the most amazing period of my whole life – I've discovered a-a-a . . . *passionate* side to myself and the love I have for my family that I wasn't really aware of before. It's been kind of like a liberation to realize that . . . I will do whatever it takes! You know what I'm saying? I think every man asks himself that – if the worst came to the worst, would he have what it takes to protect his loved ones? And . . . well, I know people think I'm a little crazy *now*, but if they won't if . . . well, let's hope it never happens, right?'

Cut to interior of house. Ned and Marge are sitting on a couch, either side of Hermione, each with an arm around her. Her blonde hair is moussed into a finely judged tangle, and her flat belly is visible under a cropped pink top. She smiles towards the camera with her head subtly dipped, face slightly to one side, perfectly judging her most flattering angle.

'Hermione,' Benson says, 'do *you* think your father has gone crazy?'

'Sure!' she laughs. 'Dad has just . . . *lost it*! But in a *good way*! He doesn't care any more about, you know, stupid stuff like how I dress and who I go out with so long as I'm, like, responsible about the *dangers*? He's become a lot cooler about me staying out late, going on dates, or being a virgin and stuff so long as I take my survival bag. So-o-o . . . I'd say we've reached a compromise that suits everyone.'

'What's in your . . . *survival bag*, if you don't mind me asking, Hermione?'

'Oh, you know . . . stuff.' She shrugs charmingly. 'There's, like . . . a gas mask, short-wave transmission radio, medicines in case of biochemical *attack*, a light-weight anti-toxin suit . . . that kind of stuff, you know? It all fits into a small shoulder bag, so it's *really* no sweat.'

'Don't your *friends* think that's a fairly strange collection of things for you to have in your bag?'

'No – they think it's really *great*!' she laughs. 'They've just got mobile phones and make-up and stuff – my bag is *way* cooler! They *all* want one! And when *guys* see it they're, like, "Whoa! Kick-ass babe at twelve o'clock!" you know what I'm saying? I *love* my bag!'

The camera mounts the stairs, pausing before a door at the top.

'But not *everyone* in the Spiegelflug household is so sure about recent developments in the family,' Gloag narrates. 'At first, it looked as though Ned *Junior* would be unavailable for comment when we visited, shouting from his closed bedroom that he did not want to speak to the media. Eventually, however, he opened the door to talk to us.'

The bedroom door opens a crack to reveal Ned Junior's face, the rest of the room staying out of view. He remains unsmiling as the microphone approaches him, his eyes twitching warily to and from the camera. They roll as he listens to an unheard question.

'Yes, my father is *insane*, OK?' he snaps. 'This whole *country* is insane. Of course, there's no point in me *commenting* on that when people like you are at the *heart* of the problem, is there? You're not going to *listen* to me. You're probably not even going to show this on TV! This war is just a—'

The camera keeps filming as he talks, but his voice fades out. *I knew it!* the Angry Teenager thinks, furious even though he'd been expecting this. They censored it all!

'Ironically,' Gloag's narration returns, 'given his supposed reluctance to talk to the media, Ned Junior turned out to have an *awful* lot to say about what he thought was wrong with his country. He reminded me somewhat of my own teenage son back when it seemed we could find no common ground together in life – a difficult period for both of us, but one familiar to generations of parents the world over. He did not know it, but Ned was really showing just how much his father's son he really *was* – here was the same passion, the same determination, but directed towards a normal, and no doubt *healthy* desire to rebel. Listening to his quasi-apocalyptic point of view, one might have thought ours was a country on the verge of complete social and moral collapse, and yet I knew, seeing the father reproduced in the boy, that here was actually proof of the strength and *endurance* of that country's ideals, and so, in that sense, that the future was in safe hands. It is a country where families can disagree, where the arguments are never won or lost, but where people like the Spiegelflugs, a family no different to so many others, are passionately engaged in the effort to make it better, stronger and *safer* for the ones they love. This has been Benson Gloag in Spotsboro, reporting from the front line . . . perhaps not of the terrorist *nightmare*, but of the Atlantian—'

The sound cuts out as the Angry Teenager hits the mute button.

'*Oh wake up!*' he snaps.

But the TV carries on as if in a dream – Ayesha Novak's soft lips moving, yet making no sound . . .

Chapter Twenty-two

In which the last barrier to the war comes down as a special task force meets to discuss what to call it

'Bees,' Geena Mason, the President's spokesperson, announced, writing the word up in capital letters on the flip board. 'Any first thoughts?'

There were fifteen people around the table in Room 202 of Liberty Mansion that night, an even split between military and civilians, discounting Geena because she was the Chair – a term she found ridiculous because, in her experience of similar brainstorming sessions, the Chair was the one person who almost never sat down. A more correct term would have been the Marker Pen.

There was a moment's silence, the military and civilian factions of the meeting waiting to see if the other would make the first suggestion.

There was going to be a war. And the war needed a name.

'Buzzing,' Elaine Fisher suggested eventually. 'Bees buzz.'

Geena gave her a look of thinly disguised condescension.

'OK. Let's start simple . . .' she commented, lifting her felt-tip to the paper. 'Bees *buzz*!'

It was no secret that the two women did not get along.

The problem was mainly a territorial issue – Geena spoke for the President, but Elaine, as his speechwriter, was the one who put words into his mouth. She was the author of three poetic, somewhat depressing novels about down-trodden women that had been well received in those sections of the press that considered anything written from the aspect of a victim to be of literary importance. Indeed, she had made it onto the shortlists of two awards now, although she had not yet managed to win anything. She did not like to say so, but felt certain that she had fallen victim both times to the fact that she was white and middle-class.

That said, her main claim to fame was that she had come up with the phrase 'I'm a Doer, not a Sayer' during the election campaign.

What Geena objected to in Elaine was the fact that she was not genuinely committed to the President's political agenda – indeed, her personal beliefs were almost diametrically opposed to his. There were few things that Geena despised more in this world than a bleeding-heart liberal who was nevertheless prepared to suppress her convictions if the pay was right.

'*Bombs* buzz!' pointed out a young man from the Press Office. 'Maybe we can make some kind of connection between—'

He was cut off in mid-flow by a hard palm slapping the table.

The military contingent had decided to make its move.

'Bombs do *not* buzz!' grunted Colonel Du Pane. 'You have no idea what you're talking about, do you, son? Bombs *scream!*'

'But I thought—'

'You thought *nothing*, son,' Du Pane interrupted. 'Bombs haven't buzzed in over *fifty* years! They scream. It psychologically unbalances the target.'

'Before he's blown up?' the young press officer smiled. 'Isn't that a little like overkill?'

'Oh . . . you want to give them time to *run*, do you?' the colonel laughed. 'Give them a sporting chance, is that it? This is *war*, son! Anyway, bees don't *buzz*, either – they *sting*! They're venomous! That's all we care about here – this isn't the title of a goddamned *pop-up book* we're looking for . . .'

'OK . . . fair point,' Geena nodded, writing up STING and VENOM. 'So . . . the objective of this operation is to *drain* that poison. How can we get that across?'

'*Operation Suck Venom!*' someone called out.

There was a momentary silence, soon broken by Geena. 'That's gross. Can we have something a little less graphic, please?'

'*Operation Smoke Out!*'

'Not bad . . .' Geena mused. 'Might not sit well with the tobacco companies, but let's write it up. What other ways do we have of dealing with bees? How do we *kill* bees? Elaine? A bee is in your home . . . what do you do?'

'Well . . .' the novelist hesitated. 'What I *do* is I wait until it has settled on a flat surface, then I . . . trap it in a cup, slip a piece of card underneath, and let it out the window.'

Geena contemplated her for an instant, a look of pity on her face.

'I bet you do,' she smiled.

'Yes, I do.' Elaine struck back. 'I suppose you just *squash* them, right?'

'*Operation Bug Squash!*' someone shouted.

'No,' Geena answered her nemesis. 'I get my husband to do it. Bees freak me out.'

'Well, there we go . . .' Elaine smiled. 'Operation Geena's Husband!'

The rest of the table did not join in with her laughter, which was short-lived.

'Operation *Fly-Swatter!*' Colonel Du Pane suggested, eyes dark slits.

'Ah! *Aha!*' Geena nodded. 'I like the *swatting* aspect! It's a little . . . brutal, perhaps even a touch arrogant, but it's better than *squashing*. It just needs tempering with a sense of . . . humility, of the burden of duty. Justice.'

'Operation *Righteous* Fly-Swatter!' the colonel smiled, warming to his vision.

'They're bees,' Elaine sighed.

'How about *Noble* Fly-Swatter?' Geena frowned, scribbling furiously with her marker pen now. 'We have to be wary of seeming to impose our sense of morality. Think of foreign sensibilities.'

'They're *bees*.'

Geena turned to look at Elaine, who was obviously determined not to go with the flow here.

'They're not flies,' Elaine explained. 'It sounds like we can't even tell one insect from another.'

'You may not be aware of this, being so busy with your cups and cardboard, Elaine . . .' Geena smiled coldly. 'But there's no such thing as a *bee*-swatter!'

'I just think we're on the wrong track altogether,' the novelist continued, disregarding the comment and turning to look down the table. 'Surely we need to get away from the language of . . . *flattening* . . . and concentrate on the positive aspects of what we're trying to achieve. We are the Good Guys, remember. We are doing this as a service to the *world*! We're not saying that yet. Don't we want to give the world a *positive* message here?'

'OK.' Geena nodded. 'So what is the positive message we have for the world in conducting this campaign, Elaine?'

'Well, bees should be about flowers and *honey*, shouldn't they? They're our friends! They pollinate the plants! *We* shouldn't be demonizing the bees, it's the terrorists who are doing that by messing around with *Nature*! I think we should be presenting this war as being about protecting the simple, wholesome pleasures of life for all people. Honey is a whole *symbol* of goodness – it's up there with milk and bread and apples! I'm saying this is like Operation Restore *Breakfast*!'

'Operation . . . Restore . . . Breakfast . . .' Geena repeated, her hand poised over the paper. 'Now . . . do you want me to write that up, Elaine?'

'OK, that's ridiculous – but don't you see my *point*? God, what do *you* give your kids for breakfast, Geena?'

'Pop-Tarts.'

The two women locked gazes. Their mutual loathing was becoming increasingly embarrassing to everyone in the room.

'Why am I not surprised by that?' Elaine grinned, dismissing her rival as she addressed the others in the room. 'Come on – don't any of you here get what I'm saying?'

There was an uncomfortable silence, nobody wanting to be drawn into the conflict betwen the two women. When support finally came for Elaine's viewpoint, it came from an unexpected source.

'Yes, I believe I do.' Colonel Du Pane nodded. 'I may not agree with you on many things, Miss Fisher – but I believe you are right. This *is* about protecting a whole way of life. These bees are a direct attack on that way of life. That's what Massoudi wants to destroy – the simple pleasures of the Atlantian summer. We're talking about a man who wants to make us afraid of letting our kids play in the yard. He wants to turn our patios and swimming pools into his battlefield and punish innocent teenage girls for the crime of wanting to be tanned! I never heard anything so *warped* in my life! Speaking for myself, as a family man rather than a soldier, this is Operation Protect Barbecue.'

'I copy that, sir,' one of the more junior officers agreed. 'It's Protect Barbecue . . . it's also, for me personally, Protect *Volleyball*!'

Suddenly, to Elaine's surprise, the entire military

contingent seemed to be lining up behind her point of view. There were grunts of agreement around the table, and people who had as yet not spoken were suddenly moved to voice their own concerns.

'Protect Hiking and Camping!'

'Operation Defend Beaches!'

Geena, who had been at first too shocked by the way the tide had rapidly turned in Elaine's favour to react, was by now furiously scribbling suggestions.

'Hell, let's face it – this is Operation Defend *Bikini*, guys!' one young officer spoke up to a roar of approval.

Elaine wrote something down on her pad, and let a smile of contentment spread over her face. She had it. Victory was hers.

She let the soldiers consolidate their position behind her concept, waited for a lull in the chorus of suggestions about everything from drive-ins to picnics and then leaned forward to say, 'Gentlemen, can I just make a suggestion that I believe might cover all your concerns? Why don't we choose the codename . . . *Operation Protect Summer*?'

Geena was only halfway through writing it down when she stopped.

Obviously.

There was no further discussion necessary. It said it all – they were fighting on the side of Nature itself. They were protecting *God*, not to put too fine a point on it. She turned to Elaine, graciously inaugurating a round of applause for her rival.

'Good. Thank you, Miss Fisher,' Colonel Du Pane grunted. 'Now maybe we can get on with the real work of *annihilating* these bastards.'

The End minus 1 day

'Ladies and gentlemen, the President of the United States of Atlantis . . .'

A hushed silence falls over the room as President Hedges strides across the platform to take his position behind the lectern bearing the seal of his office – a symbol of a diving eagle, olive branch clutched in one foot, thunderbolt in the other, surrounded by an inscription in Latin whose meaning, according to a recent survey, is unknown to ninety-eight per cent of the nation. The Angry Teenager is in the other two per cent. After the President come Prime Minister Chris Flyte and Defence Secretary Mitchell Madison, who take up position behind and to the left of him.

His hands grip the edges of the lectern and he frowns – perhaps out of emotional pain, or perhaps in an effort to read a teleprompter.

'My fellow Atlantians, and people of other nations,' he begins. 'As I have often said – I am a Doer, not a Sayer. That said, let it *not* be said that a full and genuine opportunity has not been given these last weeks for *words* to do what must now be done by deeds. Let it *not* be said that, faced with a threat to our national security that *cannot* be ignored, this administration has not tried with all its might to resolve the present crisis in a peaceful, diplomatic manner. *Reason*, however, has failed to win the day. The military government of Errat – I believe against the wishes of its people, who have *not* been given a say in this matter – has chosen to ignore our repeated demands to hand over the terrorist leader Suman Moossodi, so placing our two nations on a course where conflict has become unavoidable. We will *not* avoid that conflict. I have this evening given the order to launch Operation Protect Summer in an effort to bring this conflict to a swift and just conclusion so that the citizens of our great, peace-loving nation may assert their God-given right to live their lives without fear of attack. I cannot say how long the operation will last, or what the cost will be in terms of the lives of our own brave sons, but I *can* promise you that we will *not rest* until the individual in question is captured, either alive or dead, until the terrorist army he has amassed in the hills of Errat is destroyed, and the dictatorship that has chosen to protect him is permanently and entirely dismantled.'

He turns his head to face a grimly nodding Chris Flyte, saying in an aside, 'In this just struggle, we are joined by our allies – most notably the great nation of . . . of people whose Prime Minister is with me here today and whose soldiers will be going into battle alongside our own. Thank you, Mr Prime Minister, on behalf of the Atlantian people to all the people of *your* country. We will not forget.'

He turns back to face the camera, the frown deepening.

'Our quarrel is not with the Erratian people. Whatever they may have been told by those who seek to abuse their trust, this quarrel is not about their great culture or their spiritual beliefs, for which we have the *deepest* respect. We *know* the Erratian people are a peaceful people, and we do not wish to cause them *any* unnecessary suffering, although – as in any conflict – innocent lives *may* be lost. We urge them to join us in overthrowing the tyrants who have brought their great nation into disrepute and to accept the hand of friendship that we offer them now by launching our fighter planes against an enemy of *all* peace-loving people everywhere. Let us make this conflict as short and painless as possible for all of us who stand for *peace*. God bless you all, and God bless Atlantis, and . . . and God bless God. Thank you.'

Chapter Twenty-three

In which our doomed hero, adopting the most noble course of action that he can come up with under the circumstances, takes to the hills to await his fate alone, and fails

«Look . . . for the last time . . .» Saman shouted, standing on a rock to address the crowd that had been following him doggedly up the hillside, «. . . will you all . . . *please* . . . go home!»

The crowd shuffled to a halt some fifty yards further down the track. There were about three hundred of them – overwhelmingly male, and for the most part dressed in ordinary clothes. His eye, however, was inevitably caught by the few dozen military and police uniforms mixed in with the rest. At first he'd assumed they had been sent to observe him – perhaps even to kill him, if necessary – but he was starting to doubt that. Surely they would be in disguise if that were the case? Furthermore, given that they were *not*, surely they ought to be acting as coherent units if they were on a mission from their superiors? Instead, however, they were mingled in with the rest of the crowd in an entirely haphazard way, and the others seemed to accept their presence as completely natural.

The truth, Saman was beginning to accept, was that

these men had deserted to follow him into the hills. *He* was their leader now.

This was not working out in the least bit as he had hoped. His plan, which he had decided was the only decent and honourable thing to do, had been to remove himself from the city and remain with his bees up in the hills. That way, he reasoned, no-one else need get hurt because of him – he would house Najia with a friendly goatherd until it was all over, on the understanding that, if something *were* to happen to him, he wished her to have the care and profit of the hives. Then he would simply wait in the hills – not hiding, by any means, as clearly by now his movements could hardly go unnoticed – and if the Atlantians truly intended to invade, then their bombs would not fall on innocent people.

During his long sojourn in bed, he had considered giving himself up to the police, but decided there was no point. Malek Galaam's men already knew perfectly well where he was, so they could have taken him in any time they wanted. But they hadn't. So either they had no idea *what* to do about him, in which case it wasn't fair to force the problem on them, or it somehow suited their purposes to let him remain free. What that purpose was he could not imagine – clearly, from everything Farrukh had told him, his continued freedom was about to cause the world's military superpower to wage war on his tiny homeland, so it was hard to believe there was any constructive alternative to just handing him over to the Atlantians.

He was certain he was doing the right thing, yet it had not been an easy decision to take, as every fibre of his being urged him to remain locked in the house and just hope the whole nightmare would go away of its own accord. But he had tried inaction in the past, and it had cost his family their lives – Saman was not prepared to make that mistake twice. If the Atlantians, or anyone else, wanted to come for him, then it would be in the place of his choosing. A place where no innocent people would be killed.

What he had not anticipated, on the other hand, was this crowd following him up the hill. They had kept a respectful distance throughout the entire walk, and they talked in hushed voices as if not wishing to draw attention to themselves, but this deep respect apparently did not oblige anyone to *obey* him when he told them to leave. It was madness – surely they realized that they were turning themselves into sitting targets if anyone came after him? As for the members of the military and police he could see with them, they risked court martial and execution just for *being there*, regardless of what happened next.

«I want to be alone!» he shouted, seeing no sign of a break in their ranks. «I don't *want* you here! Go *away*.»

Few of them actually looked at him when he spoke, as though they thought themselves unworthy. But those who did seemed to stare back with canine stupidity, like strays that he had made the mistake of feeding and now could not shake off his tail no matter how he shouted at them. Or maybe they just thought he was testing their loyalty.

«*Please!*» he implored them at the top of his voice «*Fuck off!*»

Saman turned round to carry on up the hill, hoping that his wishes were by now abundantly clear. He'd taken no more than a dozen steps up the dirt path when he heard the by now familiar wash of their scuffling feet, and he could not resist looking back to see which way they were going. They froze on their way up the path, like children in a game of grandmother's footsteps.

«*Fuck off!*» he shouted. «That is an *order*!»

He stomped on up the path, not bothering to look back this time when he heard the scuffling start up again.

*   *   *

315

Saman's followers were apparently not sure what to do once he reached his hives. As long as he had been travelling along the path, their role had been clear – they were *followers*, after all. But now he had sat down. Their confused demeanour suggested there was some disagreement over whether they too should sit down or whether that would be disrespectful.

Unbelievable, Saman thought to himself. Complete cretins.

He got to his feet and marched towards them. This caused a certain amount of panic in the ranks – those closer by began to back away as he approached, some tripping over those behind, which gave rise to a brief chorus of shouts and accusations, but they fell silent again when he caught up with them.

«Why are you here?» he demanded of the man nearest to him, who was looking nervously around in the hope of finding someone he could slip behind. «Yes, *you*! Why are you here?»

«We . . . we've come to follow you,» the man answered, struggling to keep his eyes level with Saman's.

«Oka-a-ay . . .» Saman sighed. «Well, you've followed me. *Now* can you go away?»

«Umm . . .» the man gulped, horrified at being put on the spot. «How . . . far?»

«The whole way. Home far.»

«But . . .» the man winced, seeming genuinely confused, «. . . *this* is our home now. Wherever you are. We have sworn to protect you at all costs.»

«Well, you see – I don't think that's a very good idea,» Saman explained. «I do appreciate the thought, but if you stay *here* . . . you may very well get killed.»

«Uh-huh.» The man nodded enthusiastically, as though they were suddenly speaking the same language. «We know.»

«OK . . . put it *this* way, then: you might get *me* killed,» Saman emphasized.

«*No!* We are here to *protect* you!»

«Well, it's just – I don't think it's going to be particularly helpful for me to have anything that may look like an *army* around me, you see. I'm really *much* better off on my own!»

«With all due respect, sir . . .» the man frowned, «. . . you can't *possibly* take on the Atlantians single-handed! It's *madness*!»

«But I have no intention of taking on the Atlantians, don't you see?» Saman groaned. «I'm not going to be fighting *anybody*! It's going to be very *boring* for you here!»

«Not . . . if we die.»

«Yes, clearly that part would not be dull for you . . .» he muttered. «But, until then, there's no *food* for you all here! All I have is honey.»

«We shall survive.»

«Until you die.»

«Until we die. Of course,» the man agreed with satisfaction.

It was hopeless. There was nothing Saman could say that would penetrate their fanatical death wish. He raised his arms in a final attempt to drive some sense into their skulls.

«Listen!» he shouted to the gathering. «You've got this all wrong! I do not even *believe* in God!»

There was a shocked collective intake of breath, followed by a murmur of confusion. The man to whom Saman had been talking turned to confer with his companions in a brief but heated discussion. Eventually, he too raised his arms to address the crowd.

«See? See how *great* God's love *is*?» he bellowed. «See the great test he offers us? I ask you, brothers and sisters – what better way to prove our faith than martyring ourselves for one who does not even *believe*?»

There was a momentary pause as the gathered fanatics worked through the logic of the situation, and then, as

317

the penny collectively seemed to drop, the peace of Saman's honey farm was shattered as a huge roar of approval resounded across the hillside.

He turned away in despair, looking out to sea.

In the distance he could see the black dots of a flight of geese heading their way in perfect arrow formation, migrating across their world. And, as he watched, he felt a familiar tug in his heart, and all the rage that had boiled in him an instant before began to abate. At every moment there was beauty, and the world never stopped making sense to most of its inhabitants. Maybe not to him or other people, but to those for whom there were no nations, no languages, no history . . . and no cause but that of life.

A world that was not earth, but water.

He sighed as the roar of the crowd began to fade until only a stubborn pack at the back could be heard still distantly bellowing their approval, unaware that the others had stopped, and apparently determined to keep on howling enthusiastically despite probably not having been able to hear what was said in the first place.

They went on and on, mindless and monotonous.

And then he realized.

That was not the roar of human voices.

And those weren't geese.

THE END . . .

Epilogue

The sun rose in chaos, accompanied by the chatter and squawk of a thousand birds insisting on their rights, the whip and wash of the trees, the beating of the water upon the shore, and even the occasional thunk of large fruits falling to the sand, but the sun rose in peace.

There was peace in the first shot of blue into the black stillness of the cosmos; there was peace in the snuffing of a billion stars; peace as the horizon broke into view, and the clouds puffed alight to smoulder in saffron and paprika fires. The unimaginable inferno spread a gentle reach upon its world, pelting it with colour and chasing the night into pockets of shadow where it would huddle for another whole day, powerless to stop everything from growing still more abundant and chaotic than the day before. Somewhere else, inevitably, the colour and chaos was seeping from the world, and at this same moment flowers were closing their petals and birds falling silent as the soft-spoken predators stepped out with the regathering shadows, but here, for now, it was hard to imagine that place.

Here was an island. Here was a single hill thrusting out from endless sea – its perfect cone already so absurdly green, so cascading with life upon life that it seemed as though the alighting of one more bird or the budding of one more leaf might sink it back into the waters. Or at least it seemed that way from out to sea. But from the sea, for that matter, the pair of figures sitting upon the shore looked like lovers watching the dawn – not because of anything in the way they were sitting, although they sat close to one another, but because why else would two people sit upon a beach to see the sunrise if they were not in love?

Ordinary people were in no hurry for the day to start. If anything, they watched the sun set in magnificent anger, red boiling down to black, and imagined dawn was the same thing in reverse.

But these were not lovers. On closer view, they were two men, both somewhat overweight, though not as much as they had been. They were sitting on the edge of the forest, where the trees gave way to low, creeping weeds, and as the sunlight touched the beach, it was clear that they were no longer looking out to sea but staring intently at the little flowers before them.

After a few minutes of this silent observation, one turned to the other and said, «I've finally figured out what we're doing here, cousin.»

His companion, a balding, corpulent man with a kind face, broke his concentration upon the flowers to look at him questioningly.

«It's simple,» the first man announced. «I think we're dead.»

The Errat War had been over for almost a year now, and the country was settling down under the leadership of its new President, Malek Galaam, a moderate reformer who had promised to hold elections 'when the time was right' and who was lavishly praised by President Hedges as 'a man we can do business with'.

The war had ended in victory for Atlantis, although nobody in government used that term. They referred to it as a *success* because the word 'victory' would imply it had, indeed, *been* a war rather than an operation of

320

a defensive nature with the specific objective of neutralizing the terrorist threat by establishing military domination of the terrain, which was something quite different. Operation Protect Summer, therefore, was just 'a successful operation' rather like the removal of a polyp, and one would hardly expect the doctors and nurses to parade around a hospital every time they whupped some polyp butt.

But everyone else called it the Errat War. Except for the Erratis who, rather grandly, called it the Atlantian War. Some even went so far as to maintain that the Atlantian War had ended in victory for their homeland, at least on a moral level, in that they had faced an overwhelmingly powerful aggressor and were still – even against those odds – mostly alive. Even the General was alive, hiding out somewhere in the hills with the rump of his Patriot Guard and a ragtag following of ex-terrorists who had warmed to him when he became the target of a genuine superpower. Most of his Guards had died in the heroic defence of the presidential palace, which they had managed to hold for a full three weeks after the General's departure, taking potshots at the Atlantian planes from amid the growing pile of rubble. They hadn't managed to bring any of the planes down, of course, but they had put up a sufficiently convincing show of resistance to dissuade the enemy from sending in their ground troops, who only invaded once the Guards ran out of ammunition, at which point they declared the exercise to have been 'a textbook success'.

Since nobody has ever read the Atlantian textbook on war, it is unclear what does not count as a success.

The bombing campaign was surgical, of course, although not carried out by practitioners one would want to go to for, say, a nose job. Indeed, there had been a considerable number of 'incidents' which, under Atlantian legal jurisdiction, would certainly have given rise to some fairly major out-of-court settlements in medical malpractice suits. The baby-food factory, in particular, was later found to have been manufacturing baby food. Rather than chemical weapons. As usual.

But one day, no doubt, the military planners would turn out to be right about that one. Logic dictated that there *must* be some place in the world whose people were stupid enough to mix the production of infant foodstuffs or medicines with manufacturing deadly toxins. There just had to be. Whether *bombing* a nerve-gas depot would be a clever idea is an entirely different question, however.

More contentious, in any case, was the assertion that their missiles had erroneously hit the new hospital because it was 'very shiny'. This smacked of a cover-up.

The important thing was that the official death toll had been well within the boundaries of what the Atlantian public was prepared to accept, and that was *including* friendly-fire incidents and helicopter crashes. On the Errati side, of course, no official figures were available.

And, even if General Harouni had somehow escaped, at least Saman Massoudi was widely suspected to be dead.

«*Ow!*» Aziz shouted, rubbing his thigh. «What the *hell* did you do that for?»

«To prove that you're not *dead*, of course!» Saman laughed. «Honestly, Aziz – I didn't think that you believed in that nonsense.»

«I don't mean that we're in *heaven*, you bloody psychopath! I mean that I think we are *officially* no longer alive! It's the only explanation that makes any sense.»

Saman frowned as he considered the theory which, like all his cousin's theories, seemed somewhat far-fetched. But it did explain a thing or two. It had been many months, after all, since he had last been interrogated.

Indeed, he could not recollect the last time that *any* of the prisoners on the remote island of Tobad had been interrogated.

«You're saying . . . you think we are *never* going to be tried?» he asked.

«They can't put us on trial because they haven't got a case. They know they would lose, even in a military tribunal.»

«So why don't they just let us go?»

«Because that would be admitting we'd done nothing wrong. And if we've done nothing wrong, then they *have* done something wrong because hundreds of people are dead.»

«Thousands,» Saman corrected him.

«Maybe. Who knows.»

«Aziz – you weren't there,» Saman insisted. «It was not *hundreds*, believe me.»

Saman had worked it out. There had been several hundred Patriot Guards in the palace alone. Then there had been the hospital, the baby-food factory, the military bases, the power stations, the airport, the railway depots, the telephone building, the TV station, the water-treatment plants and every identifiable government building around the country. All of these places must have been filled with people because, even though there was a war on, they were still vital elements of the nation's infrastructure that had to be kept working. Which was precisely why they were bombed. And that was not counting the unknown number of missiles that went astray, landing at random throughout the city.

And, of course, there had been his own 'army'. Lunatics though they had been, he owed them his life. As that first wave of jets came in, their spokesmen had humbly requested the honour of being allowed to cover him while he sought shelter amid the rocks. How they intended to do this, armed only with rifles and pistols, had not been clear until he watched the stand they made

323

from a safe distance. Their strategy, it turned out, was simply to provide the fighter pilots with more obvious targets – splitting into groups that scattered across the hill in every direction except that in which Saman had taken flight, drawing the fury of wave after wave of planes on his behalf. He had scrambled up the slopes towards his hut, sometimes being knocked off his feet as jets passed yards over his head, eventually reaching the calm of his shelter, where he found Najia sleeping, deaf to the bombs.

They had watched from on high as the Jana groves turned black – bodies and branches spinning through the smoke, swarm after swarm of bees taking to the air as their hives were blown apart, the angry howl of insect wings joining those of the metal machines as everything in sight became war: bees fighting men, and men fighting machines, and machines fighting Nature, until finally there was nothing left to sting and nothing left to burn, and the fighters circled aimlessly over the scorched earth before giving up and returning to their metallic hive.

And the bees, lacking a better option, began making new nests in the bodies of the dead terrorists. Later, when the helicopters landed and disgorged a small army of soldiers in camouflaged bee-keeper uniforms, they saw the insects flying in and out of the terrorists' open mouths and backed away in sheer horror, concluding that the secret relationship between these madmen and their awful bees held something even more perverse and unholy than anyone had dared imagine.

The only living person they found was Saman, who was searching through the still-smoking pyre for serviceable bits of beehive. Quite calm, he placed his hands upon his bald head, and walked towards their nervously raised guns, announcing as he drew near, 'I think you were looking for me.'

And so had begun the journey that had brought him to the island of Tobad, a little-used military base far

324

out to sea that was subject neither to Atlantian nor international law, never having been important enough to figure on any treaty. As such, it was an ideal location for a terrorist internment camp. In particular, as Aziz had correctly surmised, it was for the internment of those who fell into the troublesome category of captives against whom the Government had insufficient evidence to build a case. Although Tobad was a young island, Nature had already rushed to fill it with all that the cycle of life required. Freshwater streams chuckled down from its single, cloud-topped peak through forests that were entirely devoid of predatory beasts and insects. Migrating birds and the random wash of tides had brought a large variety of edible plants and fruits, and the surrounding coral reef was so abundant with fish that it took only a morning's practice for anyone to become adept in the art of spearing lunch. Escape was impossible and the detainees could be kept there indefinitely and at minimal cost, requiring only basic supervision and medical attention.

«But . . .» Saman frowned, «. . . if the story is that we are dead, or were never even in custody, then what is to stop them deciding it's simplest just to be done with it and kill us all?»

Aziz's eyes snapped round to gawp at him in disbelief.

«*Cousin!*» he rebuked him. «They don't *do* things that way in Atlantis!»

The months since the war's end had not been happy ones for the good people of the country where they didn't do things that way.

First of all, it appeared that the war itself had been in vain, in that Jana bees *had* made it to Atlantis. Officially, of course, this amply justified the considerable destruction that Operation Protect Summer had wreaked upon the small country from which the bees originated, although certain lovers of conspiracy theories maintained that it was not the *terrorists* who had brought the insects to the mainland, but the Atlantian government itself. Their supposed evidence for this wild supposition rested on the fact that the first recorded cases of Jana bee attacks were all within a small perimeter of the location where Defence Secretary Mitchell Madison's plane had crashed in the woods as he was returning from a whistle-stop tour of the peacekeeping forces in Errat. Why Madison would be stupid enough to bring the bees home *himself* was not clear, but there were one or two aspects of the crash that did seem peculiar. Firstly, given that there was no sign of mechanical failure, nobody could explain why the pilot had lost control. And secondly, the rescue party that arrived on the scene found one more body than was accounted for by the flight log – who this person was remained unknown, but some said that it was the body of an Errati terrorist in which the bees had made a nest. Possibly even the body of Saman Massoudi himself.

Thus far, the massive campaign of insecticide-spraying had failed to stop the bees being reported over an ever-widening perimeter, and the calls for more radical measures – such as the wholesale burning of the forest in question – had been successfully blocked by environmentalists who pointed out that it was home to a unique species of woodlouse.

Concern over this problem, however, had largely disappeared from the media in the light of the more pressing matter of the economy. It was now clear that the slow-down was going to be far more traumatic than initially suggested, and many of the larger companies had already started tactically restructuring, usually by moving all or part of their labour capacity abroad and citing the high cost of domestic workers as the reason why, if the Atlantian economy was to remain competitive, they could no longer employ Atlantians.

While no one factor could be blamed for the downturn, the watershed between readjustment and deep recession, in most people's minds, was undoubtedly the collapse of the SpiDer Index. This began with what financial analysts insisted was an isolated incident – the mass suicide of members of the Beyond Communion, who believed they had reached a point of such ultimate purity that they could now attain a higher plane. Naturally, this seriously hit BeComm's share price, but the panic soon spread right across the Index. BeComm, after all, had been one of the SpiDer's's top-performing shares and not a single one of its investor reports had given any prior warning of an underlying lack of sanity within the organization. With the subsequent refusal of other religious groups to open themselves to independent psychiatric auditing, the loss of confidence in the market soon developed into a full-blown crash, wiping out trillions of dollars of ordinary people's investments.

Quite where the money disappears *to* in such situations was something that most of these unfortunate, ordinary people were quite unable to understand. If they no longer had their money and nobody *else* had their money then where exactly had their money gone?

Some, on the other hand, argued that the answer was quite obvious.

God had it.

«*There!*» Saman hissed excitedly, pointing to a spot a few yards away.

Aziz stared at the patch of flowers his cousin was indicating, at first seeing nothing. After a few seconds, however, a tiny movement amid the petals caught his attention and his eyebrows rose in pleasant surprise as a small bee hovered up from the flower and floated across to its neighbour.

«Well, I'll be damned . . .» he whispered. «How the hell did bees make it all the way out here?»

«God knows,» Saman answered, grinning like a child.

«I thought you didn't believe in that nonsense,» his cousin muttered.

«Hmm? Oh . . . I don't,» came the hushed reply. «But sometimes it's pretty tempting, isn't it?»

They sat still, gazing at the bee going about its business as though this was the most fascinating sight that life could offer them.

«So what do we do now?» Aziz asked.

«We wait. When she's finished, she'll head back towards the hive.»

«And then we . . . chase her.»

«Yup.»

Aziz looked down at his cousin's corpulent body, and across at his own, and commented, «I don't think we can keep up with a bee.»

«Of course not,» Saman answered. «But we follow her until she loses us, and then we wait again. She'll tell the others about the flowers, they will come, and when one heads back over us, we chase her again. And so on.»

«Until we find the hive.»

«Until we find the hive. Simple. People have been doing it for centuries.»

Aziz nodded, his cousin's excitement beginning to rub off on him. This was going to be fun.

«So we find the hive, and then . . . ?»

«That's the tricky part. I have to get a queen for our hive. *Hopefully*, we won't have to cut the tree down, but . . . well, we'll cross that bridge when we come to it.»

«And then we have honey?»

«And *then* we have honey.»

«How *much* honey?»

«Well . . . as much as we *want*! There's no *limit*, Aziz – we just keep taking young queens from one hive and putting them in another until we have all the hives we need.»

«Uh-huh . . . and that's all there is to it? That's bee-keeping?»

Saman glanced across at his cousin, and patted him gently on the shoulder.

«*That*, my friend, is bee-keeping.»

Aziz, still drawn to a good business opportunity even if he was imprisoned on a tropical island, worked the scenario through in his head. He surveyed it from all the angles, looked for the loopholes, and eventually reached an informed conclusion.

«That's . . . very cool,» he announced.

«Isn't it just?» Saman agreed.

They grinned at one another, two little boys about to set off on an adventure, and then Saman said, «So you really think that we're here for ever, do you?»

«Trust me. I'd bet my life on it.»

Saman narrowed his gaze, probing further.

«Would you bet *my* life on it?» he asked.

Aziz hesitated as he considered the question, a deep frown upon his face. His lips pursed as he held back the words in his mouth.

«No,» he laughed at last. «But not because I'm wrong.»

«In that case . . .» Saman decided, turning back to keep an eye on the bee, «. . . *I* think I want to get married.»

*　　*　　*

No.

She was not there and, even if she had been, the love Saman bore for Najia had always been closer to that which he'd had for his children than for his wife. He had left her, safely hidden in the hills, before descending to offer himself for capture, making her understand that she would have to look after the bees on her own now. She had smiled her crooked smile at him, nodding her comprehension. And then she had suddenly opened her arms to take his rotund body in an embrace, squeezing him with a strength that took him by surprise. He felt her shuddering breath in his ear, and felt a kiss upon his cheek, and then she had stepped back again, having no more to say.

And so Najia remained in the hills of Errat, repairing the beehives, and living off their healing honey and the gifts of milk and food brought to her by the taciturn goat-men into whose care Saman had entrusted her. It was not the safest of places for a young woman on her own, least of all in the chaos that once again broke out after the war, but it was safer than anything she could bear to remember. And she was not entirely without defence.

The proof of that had come on the day when three men in the tattered uniforms of Patriot Guards had wandered into the remains of the Jana orchard as she worked on one of the new beehives. They came from behind her, signalling silently to one another as they approached in a slowly widening fan until they had her caught in a snare.

«Well, well, well . . .» the middle soldier announced, eyeing her rump. «If this isn't a sight for sore eyes! What are we going to do with a half-dressed slut like this, boys?»

He frowned when the young woman before him failed to drop whatever it was she was working upon and wheel round in shock. Extraordinarily, she seemed to be paying him no heed whatsoever. And he did not like that.

«Hey!» he shouted. «Look at me! I'm talking to you, *whore*!»

Even this did not bring a response from her. He grabbed hold of her left arm, pulling it roughly.

«Rule No. 1, bitch: when a man speaks, you *obey*!»

Despite the tug on her arm, Najia turned calmly to face the soldier. She looked at him, one eyebrow rising as she took in his sad, ragged uniform. And then she removed her right hand from the hive, slowly raising it to reveal an arm that was black and fat with crawling bees.

She smiled, holding it towards his face.

The soldier staggered back in horror, his partners doing likewise as she waved the arm once around her head, sending up a swirling smoke of insects. The men cursed, turning and breaking into a panicked sprint down the hillside as the bees bore down after them.

Najia laughed as she watched their stumbling, howling retreat, shouting after them at the top of her voice, «How about a *new* Rule No. 1, boys? RULE . . . NO . . . ONE!»

As for Saman, no-one could have been more surprised than he to find love again. Especially with a terrorist.

Leila was a full fifteen years younger than himself, yet there was a wisdom to her – born of a bitterly hard life in her war-torn homeland – that made her every bit his equal in maturity. Their romance had not been a sudden thing, coming about only once the gentle rhythm of life on the island had been given time enough to wear down her angry shell and let the kind, humorous girl she should have been venture out into the open. Saman, for reasons she could not explain, had always been a soothing companion, a man with whom she felt safe. That initial sympathy had slowly deepened, and deepened further, until they realized that, without ever having imagined they would or could do so, they had fallen irrevocably in love with one another.

And then they kissed.

It had been some time before Aziz realized what was going on under his nose, preoccupied as he was with organizing life in the prison colony. He was very good at this. Saman had come to admire his cousin since their arrival on Tobad. That same enthusiasm which he had found grating when Aziz had applied it to his endless business schemes and his worship of all things Atlantian, had turned out to be a far greater quality than Saman had ever appreciated. The man apparently bore no anger, despite what had happened to him, and he was a guiding light in the prison colony's gradual evolution towards a society – getting people to work together and build things, resolving disputes and always looking to the bright side of their situation.

He himself had formed a happy relationship with a woman whose former appetite for violence was amply satisfied in the privacy of their hut. The structure's thin walls meant, however, that this privacy was only visual, and the jungle creatures would be regularly stunned into silence by the extraordinary yelps of the strange animal living on the forest's edge.

And although at first some of the other prisoners had trouble accepting Aziz's tastes, his many undeniable qualities as a leader of men had eventually obliged them to concede that a man's manliness perhaps did not depend upon his ability to dominate women.

«*Here we go!*» Saman shouted, jumping to his feet with surprising agility and setting off after the nectar-laden bee.

Although late off the mark, Aziz soon drew alongside his weightier cousin as they charged along the seashore, following the dipping, swerving dot ahead of them.

«*Come on!*» he yelled, pulling ahead. «*She's going to lose us!*»

«*Well, I might be faster if you two hadn't kept me up half the night!*» Saman answered, turning as the bee turned inland.

«*Sorry!*» Aziz laughed breathlessly over his shoulder. «*Couldn't help it!*»

«*It's fine . . . by me,*» Saman puffed, keeping his eye on the bee as she headed into the jungle. «*Leila says that if . . . we're not crazy, then . . . we're crazy!*»

The End plus 30 days

'. . . not whether you can *afford* life assurance, but whether you can afford *not* to have it. Standard Mutual . . . because tomorrow might just be too late.'

'*This* is WINN 24/7 – non-stop *World* Information Network News, making sense of events, with Ayesha Novak.'

'Welcome back. Returning to this morning's top story, a horrific shooting at a high school prom claims eight lives – Bill Gundersen reports from the shocked community of Spotsboro.'

'Thank you, Ayesha. The police here have asked us to respect the need for students and their families to be given a "grieving period" in which to come to terms with the terrible events of last night, so we haven't been able to talk to any *witnesses* to the shooting as yet, but we do know that the shooter was a lone student named Ned Spiegelflug, aged seventeen. Spiegelflug appears to have planned the attack carefully, arriving at the prom with his father's gun concealed under his coat. What could have motivated this otherwise unremarkable student to carry out this *inexplicable* act remains unclear, but people here are already pointing out the chilling similarity between last night's massacre and the scenario contained in a popular *computer* game named Loser, of which Spiegelflug is known to have been a fan. Numerous churches and political figures have called for immediate action to be taken against these graphic and often gratuitously *violent* games which, they say, are to blame for creating a generation of—'

LET THERE BE LITE
by Rupert Morgan

'Rupert Morgan's satire of modern life is brilliant. He is like Ben Elton at his wittiest but minus the worthiness: although he makes salient points about our time, taking swipes at democracy, big business, justice and celebrity – you don't feel as if they are being rammed down your throat. His writing is fast and his characterization superb . . . Definitely one to watch'
Express

What kind of person gets elected President of the world's most powerful nation? And, more to the point, what's he had to do to get there? What makes a software squillionaire tick? After all, once you're so rich you can do any damn thing you want then what, exactly, do you do?

How does a burnt-out hack scraping the sordid bottom of gutter journalism's barrel live with himself? And, while we're about it, are there any heroic bank managers? What would a restaurant run by Hell's Angels be like? Can you really buy someone else's nose? And what would the Old Testament say if you were to reduce it to just one sentence?

Questions, questions. Isn't life just full of them? For the answers, you need look no further than this, Rupert Morgan's laceratingly funny first novel (and by the way, why is there a rather saucy-looking chicken on the cover?) . . .

'At its best when taking pot-shots at a wide variety of modern ills – fast food, tabloid media, downsizing, soap-opera politics . . . One of Morgan's nicer inventions is a computer program that boils down complex texts to their essentials. Its treatment of the Old Testament renders it down to: "Because I say so, that's why"'
Independent

A Bantam paperback
0 553 81284 X

SOMETHING SACRED
by Rupert Morgan

'A scathing tale about the power of the media . . . It's clever, stylish and potent stuff'
Mirror

Nick Carraway was once a journalist and a damn good one, too. So how come he's about to take one of the longest journeys any man can make – from prison cell to court room to stand trial for murder? As the fateful first day of the trial begins, so Nick reflects on how he came to be accused of killing another human being, and remembers those who played their part: Jordan Baker, a poor, persecuted transvestite; Frank Bosch, the crooked cop Nick thought he had in his pocket; Kevin O'Neil, his editor at the *Daily Post*; and McQueen, the *Post*'s proprietor and chairman of the far-reaching conglomerate InfoCorps. But above all Nick is haunted by the memory of Jamey Gatz, the beautiful, mysterious heroine of a subway shooting. He so desperately believed she would be his big break, and hers would be the story that would make his name, his fortune, and change his life. And how right he was, for life would never be the same again . . .

Confirming its author as a maverick young writer of supreme talent and invention, *Something Sacred* is at once a searing satire on the media and a beautifully written and affecting story of love, betrayal and – maybe, just maybe – redemption.

A Bantam paperback
0 553 81361 7